The Best American
Mystery and Suspense 2021

The Best American Mystery and Suspense™ 2021

Edited and with an Introduction
by **Alafair Burke**

Steph Cha, Series Editor

MARINER BOOKS
An Imprint of HarperCollins*Publishers*
BOSTON   NEW YORK

marinerbooks.com

ISSN 2768-1920 (print) ISSN 2768-1939 (e-book)
ISBN 978-0-358-52569-1 (print) ISBN 978-0-358-52590-5 (e-book)
ISBN 978-0-358-57848-2 (audio)

Printed in the United States of America
     1 2021
     4500834717

Contents

Foreword

WHEN *The Best American Mystery Stories* series began in 1997, I was eleven years old and an eager consumer of the criminal and the macabre. I'm glad I spent my childhood without the Internet for many reasons, but one of them is that I didn't have access to Wikipedia's list of serial killers by number of victims. Instead, I savored whatever I could get from my closed universe of resources: reading materials chosen by elementary school teachers and my easily scandalized Korean immigrant mother. I treasured my mass-market collection of Edgar Allan Poe stories, and over twenty years later, I remember "The Lottery" by Shirley Jackson and "The Landlady" by Roald Dahl—a creepy story about a boardinghouse owner who makes taxidermy of her handsome male guests—better than I do whole months of my childhood. My sixth-grade teacher, who read us the Edgar-winning murder story by our favorite children's author in class, explained that the taste of bitter almonds in the narrator's tea came from cyanide. I later subjected this teacher to my first (and considerably less subtle) attempt at prose fiction, the opening of a story about blood-spattered walls. It was really more of a mood piece than a story, without the benefits of a plot or even any characters I can recall, but I did delight in the details.

Over the past twenty-four years, I've learned just about everything I know about crime fiction, storytelling, and the relationship between our twisted imaginations and the terrifying, beautiful, unpredictable real world. I've glutted myself on mysteries and thrillers and written four crime novels and a handful of short stories of my own. I've reviewed books, served on judging panels, edited the noir section of the *Los Angeles Review of Books*, and worked with friends and students on crafting their stories, taking every opportunity to promote and champion this glorious, versatile, dynamic genre. And almost that entire time—every single year since the Backstreet Boys' US debut and the film adaptation of *L.A. Confidential*, up until mid-2020—my predecessor Otto Penzler presided as the first and only series editor for *The Best American Mystery Stories*. He worked with some of the greatest and most famous names in crime fiction, who offered their time and expertise as guest editors: Robert B. Parker, Sue Grafton, Ed McBain, Donald E. Westlake, Lawrence Block, James Ellroy, Michael Connelly, Nelson DeMille, Joyce Carol Oates, Scott Turow, Carl Hiaasen, George Pelecanos, Jeffery Deaver, Lee Child, Harlan Coben, Robert Crais, Lisa Scottoline, Laura Lippman, James Patterson, Elizabeth George, John Sandford, Louise Penny, Jonathan Lethem, and C. J. Box. The resulting anthologies showcased the talents of hundreds of wonderful writers—I'm sure many of you have favorites you first encountered through this series.

I am proud to introduce myself as the second series editor of this illustrious anthology, which, in the spirit of new beginnings, will now be known as *The Best American Mystery and Suspense*. The intention is the same—to share the best American short crime fiction published in the previous calendar year. The execution, of course, will be different, for the very simple reason that I am a different editor. We know the world's fastest runner, the world's richest man, but when it comes to art, there is never an objective best. Every reader, from your mother to the head of your favorite publishing house, looks for quality according to their own taste, and taste inevitably folds in life experience and personal bias in addition to aesthetic preference—an endlessly wide-ranging variable in itself, even if we pretend that others do not exist. You might see more stories by women and writers of color (both categories I happen to belong to) in this series going forward, but not because of some secret agenda to sacrifice quality for diversity. I gravitate toward some stories over others because I have opinions, a worldview, and a pulse.

When it comes to mystery and suspense, I tend to like stories that use crime—acts of transgression and violence that both occur under and create extreme circumstances—to highlight character as well as social and, yes, political realities. I understand that some people prefer to keep their reading segregated from politics, but storytelling is inherently political, even when fiction is methodically scrubbed of real-world context. Crime reveals the cracks in our characters, our relationships, our communities, our countries, and it is this quality that drew me to the genre in the first place. Of course, I also read for entertainment, and I enjoy juicy plots and pulsing thrills and rich, interesting writing. The stories in this book were chosen for a multitude of reasons—the bottom line is that they moved and excited me, and I'm pleased to be able to share them.

The year 2020—I don't have to tell *you*—was unusual and traumatic. COVID-19, a cold, faceless killer, took over 300,000 lives in the United States alone, and many of us spent most of the year in social isolation (I am still in lockdown as of this writing, and the death toll has passed 500,000). The pandemic came with widespread job loss and depression, and in its midst, we witnessed the fatal consequences of structural racism in the deaths of Ahmaud Arbery, Breonna Taylor, and George Floyd, Black Americans killed by white vigilantes and police officers. We closed the year with a contested election and a lame-duck president resisting a peaceful transfer of power, sowing the seeds for a violent attack on the Capitol. The year of Everything Going On Right Now, 2020 was full of desperation and injustice and crime, and if mystery writers are paying attention (and I know we are) it should have a transformative effect on the genre. All this tragedy and terror, all this pathos and *story*—we are already processing this crude ore so we can understand our new world, and we will do what we do and turn it into words.

While Everything Going On went on, our crime writers got to work and produced an outstanding array of stories. As this was my first year editing for *Best American,* I can't say how the 2020 harvest compares to others, but I was deeply impressed with the level of artistry on display. I reviewed countless short stories—I don't have a tally, but if you had an eligible story in a mystery publication or anthology last year, I can almost guarantee you that it got some level of consideration (the exceptions, this year and going forward, were stories by me, my guest editor, and our direct family members). It was a challenge selecting fifty to share with my guest editor, let alone the twenty we chose for the final anthology.

When Nicole Angeloro at HMH approached me about this

position, I had very little idea of where to find all these stories. I knew that my predecessor and his assistant reviewed thousands every year, and I was intimidated, not only because I gave birth during a pandemic and wasn't sure when I'd find the time, but because I just didn't know where to look. I am grateful to Nicole for getting me started by giving me a list of sources and hooking me up with publications like *Mystery Tribune, Ellery Queen Mystery Magazine,* and *Alfred Hitchcock Mystery Magazine.* I also knew to seek out Akashic's excellent noir series. This initial batch kept me occupied until September, when I was announced as series editor and started soliciting submissions. I started receiving stories, journals, and anthologies from both writers and editors, and used individual submissions to seek out more journals and anthologies. I also combed through lists of short story collections and literary journals without a particular genre focus, contacting editors to submit stories that might fall under the broad crime/mystery/thriller/suspense umbrella. I reviewed every individual story submitted by an author or editor (I say "reviewed" because I didn't read every single one from beginning to end, but I did at least skim most of them) as well as many stories I sought out on my own. Reading the traditional legacy sources, I began to understand why this series has tilted so heavily male and white. Anthologies and newer publications, many of them online, seem to feature a more diverse set of voices, and interestingly, I found a wealth of superb crime stories by women in mainstream literary journals.

As I read, I shared my favorite stories with this year's guest editor, the brilliant, multitalented thriller luminary Alafair Burke. She's the internationally best-selling author of the Samantha Kincaid and Ellie Hatcher series, as well as several stand-alone novels, including the recent powerhouse domestic-suspense trifecta of *The Ex, The Wife,* and *The Better Sister*—three of the most compelling page-turners I've read in the past several years. Alafair is also an accomplished attorney and a professor of law at Hofstra University, where she teaches criminal law and procedure. I have a legal background too, and let me tell you, that is a monstrously impressive day job. I feel lucky that she agreed to work with me on this first anthology—it was an incredible honor and a lot of fun too.

There are so many things we've missed over the past year, but one of them, for me anyway, is the casual pleasure of reading something great and talking about it with other book people. This was once a constant in my life that I look forward to getting back, and it was nice to talk stories with Alafair, who is a friend and a reader and writer I deeply admire. We both loved many more stories than we could fit into this single volume, and they gave us a lot to discuss. After several enthusiastic conversations, in which we extolled the merits of dozens of stories, Alafair selected the twenty you find printed here. You will also find a list of thirty honorable mentions at the back of the book. These stories are all worth tracking down, and any combination of them would have made a fine *Best American* anthology.

As I wrap up this first volume, I look forward to getting started on *The Best American Mystery and Suspense 2022*. I have a better idea of where to find stories now, but I still worry about missing out on a hidden masterpiece, so please—authors and editors, send me your eligible work. To qualify, stories must be originally written in English (or translated by the original authors) by writers born or permanently residing in America. They need to be independent stories (not excerpts) published in the calendar year 2021 in American publications, either print or online. I have a strong preference for web submissions, which you can send in any reasonable format to bestamericanmysterysuspense@gmail.com. If you would like to send print materials, you can email me for a mailing address. Because I got a late start on my reading for this anthology, I decided not to set a hard submissions deadline and continued to read new stories through the beginning of February. Going forward, though, I request that all submissions be made by December 31, and when possible, several months earlier. I promise to look at every story sent to me before that deadline. Afterward, you rely on the personal generosity of the mother of a toddler.

Thank you for reading and writing and keeping this genre we love alive and vibrant and thriving.

STEPH CHA

Introduction

AT THE 2019 Academy Awards, *Green Book* snagged the Oscar for best picture, beating out seven other nominees, including *Black Panther, Bohemian Rhapsody, A Star Is Born,* and my own favorite that year, *BlacKkKlansman.* Spike Lee was not the only person visibly outraged by the decision. At the viewing party in my friend's living room, the few celebratory *yesss!!es* were drowned out by groans and jeers. Voices were raised. The two most ardent *Green Book* haters demanded to know how anyone could possibly think the movie was *best.*

What does it mean to be *best?* By what objective criteria do we quantify the merit of art? For the sake of living-room-party harmony, we all finally agreed to disagree, chalking up our differences to personal preference.

It was difficult — painful even — to narrow this year's *Best American Mystery and Suspense* to only twenty stories. Crime writers, forgive the pun, are killing it right now creatively, and I encourage you to seek out the other excellent stories given honorable mention. I truly believe that in a different year, any one of them could have made the short list.

So why exactly am I confident that these twenty stories should be named *best?*

To help answer the question, I researched (okay, googled) what makes a good story. I found these eight rules from Kurt Vonnegut's *Bagombo Snuff Box: Uncollected Short Fiction* (1999), which seemed as good a source as any.

1. Use the time of a total stranger in such a way that he or she will not feel the time was wasted.

This one's easy. Not a single story here will waste a moment of your time. Each author proves that a talented writer does not need a lot of pages to tell a big story. In Nikki Dolson's "Neighbors," you will be able to picture every house and every family, lot by lot. Alison Gaylin's "Where I Belong" expertly packs into one short story a twisty plot worthy of a full novel. In "Let Her Be," Lisa Unger leads the reader through the sights and smells of the East Village as masterfully as through the nooks and crannies of a troubled mind. In her beautifully written story, "The Killer," Delia C. Pitts captures her series characters Sabrina Ross and SJ Rook so well that you'll be eager to follow them anywhere.

2. Give the reader at least one character he or she can root for.

Where do I begin? Perhaps with the young boy in Eliot Schrefer's "Wings Beating," who effortlessly crafts a confident zinger in the face of hateful bullying. Or a single mother in Aya de León's "Frederick Douglass Elementary," who has a plan to get her son into a "good school" while struggling with her definition of what makes a school "good." Christopher Bollen's "SWAJ" made me feel like I was back in high school, but with a new best friend. I can't promise you'll approve of every character in this collection. Some of them even do very bad things, but that brings us to . . .

3. Every character should want something, even if it is only a glass of water.

Oh, how the "wants" in these stories will break your heart. In Gabino Iglesias's skillfully written "Everything Is Going to Be Okay," it's a desire for a loved one to receive basic health care. In Ravi Howard's searing "The Good Thief," all a man wants—as a final meal before his execution—is a specific type of cake from his childhood. Faye Snowden's devastating story is about a woman who simply wants to vote. In "90 Miles," Alex Segura flawlessly conveys the depth of a man's desire to give his family a brighter future. In Joanna Pearson's haunting story, "Mr. Forble," a mother wants nothing more than to believe that her son might be a normal child. Kristen Lepionka's "Infinity Sky" spins a twisty thriller of a story from an aging pop star's desire to see the view from a hotel penthouse. The authors in this collection explore with empathy and compassion the tragedies that can result when a person's wants, needs, and desires lead to desperation.

4. Every sentence must do one of two things—reveal character or advance the action.

So many of these stories demonstrate the axiom that character and plot work best hand in hand. In "Return to India," Jenny Bhatt uses the structure of witness statements to build a tightly woven mystery, while effortlessly balancing a broad cast of diverse characters and voices as they collectively narrate the painful series of facts leading to a crime of violence.

In Laura Lippman's deliciously cagey "Slow Burner," the characterization *is* the action, as we watch the disintegration of a marriage in real time as a wife is forced to see her beloved husband for what he really is.

Gar Anthony Haywood's "With Footnotes and References" introduces us to two college students who feel absolutely real. Through Megan's eyes, Parnell "appeared from every other angle to be industrious and self-sufficient, if wildly unscrupulous." Through Parnell's eyes, "Megan was smart and streetwise, and people like her never stayed in one place too long." I'll let you decide for yourself which one proves to be the wilier in this fiercely clever story.

5. Start as close to the end as possible.

Another rule satisfied. From the beginning of "Mala Suerte" by E. Gabriel Flores: "When you are a murderer on the run, accompanied by an accessory after the fact, you might as well discuss what brought you to this sorry pass." Bad luck indeed.

The first sentence of Charis Jones's "Green-Eyed Monster": "You think I killed my wife because I was jealous?" I guarantee you that the pages that follow will make your skin hot and send your pulse racing.

6. Be a sadist. No matter how sweet and innocent your leading charac-

ters, make awful things happen to them—in order that the reader may see what they are made of.

I wouldn't call any of the talented authors in this collection "sadists," of course, but, oh boy, do they put their characters through some things. In "Land of Promise" by Brian Silverman, a moment of bravery earns a local hero a key to the city, but the ceremonies, accolades, and limousines do not tell the messy truth he suffers with in silence.

In some ways, Preston Lang's story is one of the most *fun* reads of the bunch, taking us to a joint called Fat Lad where a disgruntled customer demands that "'some Kennedy Center shit better happen for my coupons,'" and the manager replies with "'Hey, Mario Kart. Don't talk to my staff that way.'" Even the title—"Potato Sandwich Days"—puts a smile on my face. But then Lang lets other things happen to his character, and you won't forget the results any time soon.

> 7. Give your readers as much information as possible as soon as possible. To hell with suspense. Readers should have such complete understanding of what is going on, where and why, that they could finish the story themselves, should cockroaches eat the last few pages.

To hell with suspense? With all due respect, that's a real quick no from me. The title of this collection is *The Best American Mystery and SUSPENSE.* We love suspense. But the key to good suspense, in my humble opinion, is to give the reader all of the information they would need to finish the story themselves, and yet somehow prevent them from actually doing so. The ending should feel completely surprising and yet utterly inevitable. I won't spoil the many satisfying twists contained in these pages, but trust me—there are some doozies.

And now here is one final rule from Mr. Vonnegut: Write to please just one person.

> 8. If you open a window and make love to the world, so to speak, your story will get pneumonia.

I reviewed the notes I jotted down as I reveled in the fifty amazing stories that Steph Cha forwarded to me for consideration. Not as eloquent as the Vonnegut rules, but they were intended to record my immediate response to the words on the page: *Really good. So good. OMG! Really good. Excellent. Really well written. Beautiful. So damn good. Holy shit. So good.* Put another way, maybe — despite all of the other supposed rules for determining the merit of a short story — these were the ones that most made me feel like the author was writing just for me.

Will every reader agree that these are the twenty best American mystery and suspense stories of the year? Probably not. In prior years, with other editors, perhaps it would be an entirely different collection. Perhaps like the fierce debate among my friends about the 2019 Oscars, *best* simply boils down to one person's gut feeling. Their preference. Their taste.

These are the twenty stories that I most wanted to share with fellow mystery and suspense fans. I hope you enjoy them as much as I did. Thank you, Steph Cha, for introducing me to work I may never have found on my own, and to all the authors for giving me hours of enjoyment. Congratulations.

ALAFAIR BURKE

JENNY BHATT

Return to India

FROM *Each of Us Killers*

Kristin Loomis
Engineering Director, Prime Prototyping Services

YES, OFFICER, I was the first one they called. Joe, the owner of
the Silver Crown, gets a lot of business from our company. Can I
just say . . . I have never identified a dead body before. Dan was
lying there, flat on his back, with that bloodstained tablecloth over
him. There was an open wound under his left eye from where the
edge of the barstool must have hit him. His right eye was staring at
the ceiling. They said there had been two bullets — in the chest and
the stomach. I'm sorry, give me a moment.

What was he like? I guess you could call Dan a quiet sort of person. I mean, I only knew him for a few years. I moved here fall of
2012. We were coworkers before I took over from our boss, Jerry
Lester. Jerry retired about ten months ago. They'd worked together
nearly twenty years — Jerry could give you the real scoop. I mean,
if there is any.

No, yeah, we had a good working relationship. Even after I became his boss, sure. It's always tough, right, when you've competed
for the same promotion? Jerry had all but promised him this job.
Of course, it wasn't up to Jerry. The folks at Corporate weigh in on
Director-level and above positions.

Friday? I mean, it was the usual. We had a project update meeting first thing with Brad and his team. Brad Stanton is our Sales
Head — the big athletic guy at the end of the hallway. Brad had
sent several urgent emails — all caps subject lines, lots of exclama-

tion marks—overnight about our key automotive client, Sanderson. Brad likes to make a statement. At the meeting, Dan agreed to work the weekend to finish the 3D drawings for the main body prototypes. We had to ship them by the end of the coming week.

The urgency? Hmm. True, it was a bit sudden. Officially, per the signed-off project plan, all the prototypes were due at the end of the month to Sanderson. But, as Brad had explained, they needed the main body sooner because their own customer had moved dates on them.

Dan was not happy about the weekend work. I could read his body language. I promised him right there in the meeting that he could take a couple extra days off after the end of the month. See, in Jerry's day, we always had one or two interns in our department. Since I took over, they slashed my annual budget so I can't give my project engineers extra help for these crunches. Dan was a good team player, though. Always got the job done.

After the meeting, I didn't see him until lunch hour. I had gone out to pick up a salad but stayed sitting in my car with the radio on. I was having a bit of a bad day. Personal stuff. Nothing concerning him. It was snowing pretty hard. Beautiful when you looked up and watched it floating down like soft cotton—before it turned into thick piles of gray slush on the ground.

His car pulled up next to mine and he knocked on the passenger window and mouthed, "Okay?" I was all red-nosed and puffy-eyed. I didn't know what to say, so I opened the door. We sat together, not talking. He had, hmm, a calming presence, you could say.

A bit of classical music came on. Not my thing but we listened as my windshield and windows got completely blanketed. It was stuffy in my Beetle, I remember, and there was a strong odor coming off him. I was used to it—all that strong Indian food.

The music ended and he reached over to turn the volume down. He cleared his throat a couple times—he did that a lot—and told me it was called *Miserere Mei, Deus,* Latin for "Have mercy on me, O God." That he first heard it in *Chariots of Fire* and liked it better than the theme music—especially when the sopranos soared, going up at least a half-octave each time. He said how he enjoyed cranking it up for the full effect. Then he told me how it was sung originally: in the seventeenth-century Sistine Chapel by two polyphonic choirs of nine people. The service was called Tenebrae, Latin for "shadows" or "darkness." It began at dusk and, during the ritual, candles were put out one by one. All but the last. The finale was sung in near-darkness with a single, flickering candle lighting up those ancient frescoed walls and painted ceilings.

Looking back, that was such a lovely thing for him to share. I was seeing it all like a movie as he described it. Certainly, it took my mind off my trouble. We had it playing during his—the cremation service.

What I feel awful about, though, is how I couldn't stop thinking about his alcohol breath as he talked. I mean, it was the middle of a workday. So I asked, "Dan, have you been drinking?"

It was definitely alcohol, yes. You've never seen a person move so fast, I tell you. I mean, he all but jumped out and ran into the office. I suppose it was scary—being found out by the boss.

No, I did not see him again after that. Conference calls and meetings all afternoon. So that was the last thing I said to him. Can you imagine?

Hmm. There is one other thing I should show you. I came back to the office late Friday night after—after all the formalities. Didn't feel like going home. And I found this on my dry-erase board. Here, I took a photo of it. See that big heart drawing? That's usually Brad's doing. Whenever I or someone on my team does something good for Brad or his team, he leaves a red heart on my board with little x marks and his initials, BS, at the bottom. Now see how the red outline is all colored in with black? And that big black x over the initials? That wasn't Brad. And these lines to the side—that's definitely Dan's writing: "You can do better. We can do better."

I don't know what he meant, truly. There was also a handwritten resignation letter on my desk that gave no clues either. It simply said he needed to return to India immediately for an indefinite period of time. I assumed it was some family emergency. Though he never talked about his family much at all. Here's a copy. Please keep this letter thing to yourself. I—we—Corporate—thought it best not to make it public.

Vanessa, our receptionist, tracked down Dan's ex-wife, Nirali, in California. I've talked with her and told her the company will take care of all the arrangements. She came for the service. She tried reaching Dan's family in India but they did not respond. How odd, given he'd said he was going back.

Sure, please don't hesitate to reach out if you need more information. Whatever you need. So terrible what happened. All of us are still in shock. Thanks for your time, officer.

Vanessa Vandemark
Receptionist, Prime Prototyping Services

Sorry for the delay, Officer Unwin—did I get that right? I'm good with names. It's my job. Been managing that front desk since the company started. Just a babe in the woods then.

Ooh, you're a cute one, if you don't mind my saying. Don't worry. I've got three boys at home about your age. I'm not flirting. Unless you want me to. Jus-sst joking, officer. Look at me. I'm like an old, faded, out-of-shape cushion. You have nothing to worry about.

Yes, so-oo sad what happened to our Mr. Patel. Dan, we called him. But his real name was Dhanesh, you know. Only Jerry Lester called him that. And his wife—ex—when she called.

Friday? No unusual calls or visitors for Dan that I can recall. It was a wicked stormy day—winter's last big hurrah. Co-old! Who'd want to be out in that weather. Not at all as nice as today. You've brought the warm weather with you. Anyhoo, Dan rarely got any calls or visitors. The design engineers don't usually, you know. Customers go through the sales reps. And suppliers go through the buyers.

Can't say I knew him too well, really. I chatted with him briefly whenever he stopped by the kitchen for coffee—it's to the right of the reception area. Sundays are my baking day so, on Mondays, he'd be the first here to see what I had brought in. He lo-oved my chocolate nut brownies. For his twenty-year anniversary recently, I brought an entire pan of them just for him, you know. His face lit up like a firecracker.

He never had much to say for himself. I would often tease him about how he needed a good woman to take care of him. He was so rumpled and worn—like he'd been dragged through a hedge backward. Hadn't always been like that, you know. For a long time, he was always rather well turned out in his ironed button-downs and khakis. That was before his wife left in—let me see—2007? Goodness, has it been ten years already?

I never understood why he never found himself another woman.

He wasn't bad-looking. Thick black hair, lush cocoa skin, plum-colored lips, and those dazzling teeth. Such a somber expression, though.

Yes, I met her—Nirali—once, at our 2000 New Year's Eve party. They had just married over Christmas. Very articulate. I remember her explaining to me how they hadn't gone in for that arranged marriage thing their people do. Met through a professor they both knew. She got a job in the university's IT department. Pretty, petite thing with long black curls. Strong jaw. You can always tell about people from their chins and jaws, I say.

I invited them to my church for New Year's Day service, you know, but I guess they had their own religion. We never saw them together at other office events after that one. Don't know why. He came to the last Halloween do but that was it.

No-ow, I do remember something about Friday afternoon. Just came back to me. Charlie Withers, the shop supervisor, was making photocopies in the print room. That's to the left of the reception area. I was teasing old Charlie—he and I go way back—about his son Joshua and how all the young women at church are crazy about him. Joshua's in Afghanistan. We're all so proud of him.

Dan came to get fresh coffee just as Charlie was telling me there were rumors about serious US action in Syria. I began to argue how our president had promised he would not do that.

And Dan jumped in with how things change easily in Trumpistan. That word—"Trumpistan"—really does not sit well with me, you know.

Then Charlie said how, with all these Muslim countries, we're fighting a tar baby. How neither the United States nor the rest of the Western world has the stomach for what it takes to win a war. How we won the Civil War and WWII with a scorched earth policy. That's just Charlie, you know. He always says that kind of stuff to anyone who'll listen.

We-ell. You should have seen Dan's face. As if Charlie was about to bomb his house or something. Dan gave Charlie the up-down look and said something about innocent people being brutally killed and the need for a measured response.

Charlie doubled down, saying how, ultimately, fewer innocents will suffer or die because the conflict will end sooner.

Then Dan went all sarcastic, saying, sure, like Hiroshima and Nagasaki and Vietnam.

And Charlie came right back with how that was all tragic yet necessary or the conflicts never would have stopped.

Dan just twisted his mouth in that funny way he had and raised his coffee cup, offering three cheers to carnage and hell.

What did I say? I changed the subject, of course. We Pennsylvania Dutch are pacifists. Did you know we weren't really Dutch? Our ancestors were Deutsch, originally from Germany. Many people don't know that.

So I asked them about their weekend plans. Charlie was looking forward to skiing. Dan just walked away. Odd duck.

No, he had never talked about war or any such thing before. Not in front of me. Wait—I remember something else. I'm going way back now to 9/11. In those days, I kept a little portable black-and-white TV under my desk. When the towers were hit, I put it up on the desk and several people gathered around to watch the news. It was the only time I had seen him really upset, you know. Of course, we were all upset—more than upset.

His relationships with his coworkers? I never heard much there. I'm sure he wasn't thrilled about Kristin getting promoted over him. She's all smart and professional but he had been here much longer. And, from what I understand, he's better than her at all the technical stuff. Jerry Lester certainly thought so. But, you know, they have all these diversity metrics nowadays at Corporate. They had to promote a woman to Director level, I suppose.

Come to think of it, probably wasn't easy for Dan to start taking orders from a woman, given the part of the world he's from. And someone younger than him too. What do you think? Yes, it's hard to say. Of course, I stay out of all office politics. More than my job's worth. Believe me, honey, if I started connecting the dots between all that I see and hear, a lot of people here would have a lot to worry about. Like, Mr. God's Gift Stanton with all his fun and games, if you catch my drift.

We-ell. I don't know what else to tell you other than I'm so sorry for what happened. No one could have guessed it about Dan in a million years. You think you've known someone for a long time. Maybe he never really took to us. Never really became one of us. Why? Why, I don't know. Nowt as queer as folk, I guess.

Can I get you a coffee or something? No? We like our visitors to be comfortable. Just let me know if you need anything at all, will you? I'll be right there by the main door at my desk.

Brad Stanton
Business Development & Sales Director,
Prime Prototyping Services

Look, I hardly knew the guy. I'm sorry for what happened but, point is, bad things happen to good people, right?

First time I had a proper talk with Dan, he came to see me about wanting to ride shotgun with some of my sales guys on customer calls. He'd been told by HR and his old boss, Lester, that he needed sales experience to get promoted. He wanted Lester's job, that's no secret. He didn't make any fuss when they gave it to Kristin but he must have been disappointed after having worked for Lester all those years. Know what I'm saying?

Sure, I wanted to help. But, look, I can't put rookies in front of customers. And Dan was, well, Dan needed to loosen up a bit first. I invited him to join our bowling nights and our golf league. Not his thing, it seems.

Look, point is, he wasn't sales material or Director material. He didn't have that—that energy or the game face needed for tough negotiations and calls. Great guy for blocking and tackling but I couldn't see him carrying the ball, if you know what I'm saying.

Friday? Yeah. What a day. Crazy snowstorm. Most of us work out of the office on Fridays instead of being on the road. Catch up on paperwork, calls, meetings. So, yeah, it was nearly a full house here. We had an early project update meeting. I gave it to them straight. We had to comply with Sanderson's new deadline or say buh-bye to more business. They're feeling the squeeze too from their customers. Shit always rolls downhill, know what I'm saying?

Kristin was cool with it. I'd know if she wasn't. Kristin, look, she's a bright, sharp kid. I sorta took her under my wing when she went after the Director position. I know enough of the right folks at Corporate and put in a good word, know what I'm saying?

Dan? He was fine about it too. He was crazy about Kristin. Couldn't say no to her. Know what I'm saying?

How? Ha. Buddy, I don't miss much around here. He was always following her around with those cow eyes. Not saying much when she was around. Like a schoolboy with a crush on the teacher.

Shouldn't joke about the dead but here's a quick, funny story. Last year, we had our office Halloween party at the Silver Crown.

That's like our local, being just across the road. Then again, not a lot of options around here in rural West Michigan, know what I'm saying? We're stuck in the middle of endless fields and narrow country roads.

Dan showed up real late and he was not in costume like the rest of us. He'd stopped at Harding's around the corner and picked up a couple packs of those house-number stickers—the ones people put on mailboxes? Stuck them all over his shirt and pants. I asked what he was supposed to be. He said, "You can count on me." Clever, huh? I grabbed a marker from the bar menu board and scribbled some numbers on his face too. Just for a laugh. How was I to know it was a permanent marker?

He rushed to the bathroom to wash it off. Kristin went after him with her hairspray because, of course, soap and water wouldn't do it. A few minutes later, I saw them together outside the ladies' room. Him sitting there, head tilted up. Her in that cute Supergirl outfit, holding and wiping his face gently. I went up and asked what he thought of Kristin's outfit. Mind you, he'd had a fair bit to drink by then. He mumbled something about her china-blue eyes and yellow, seaweed-fine hair. I kid you not. Kristin blushed redder than her cape, know what I'm saying?

Sure, back to Friday. After the meeting, I went over to thank Dan again and invite him to join us for a Red Wings and Blackhawks game in a couple weeks—Sanderson lets us use their suite at The Joe sometimes. He was looking at this woman's Facebook page. I joked about whether he was stalking his girlfriend. Turns out, it was his ex-wife. I said, "I thought you Hindu men knew how to keep your women in line. Keep them veiled up and all." That did not go down too well, know what I'm saying? Didn't see him after that.

What are you smiling for? Hey, if you ever need pointers on how to keep 'em on a tight leash and still panting for you, I'm your man.

Look, I've told you all I can. No, not everything. Don't like to throw coworkers under the bus. But I guess you know everything else, so might as well share this.

Dan had been getting sloppy with his work in the past year or so. When I took this job on, old Lester talked Dan up big-time, like he was some rock star. My guys began telling me a different story. How his drawings sent to customers for sign-off were frequently returned for rework—dimensional errors, typos, missing parts. I told Kristin. She discussed it with him in his last performance review. She was playing it by the book, though, know what I'm saying? She had to give him a verbal, then a written warning, and so on. She didn't tell you? Bless her, she's still protecting his reputation.

Why was it happening? I have no idea, man. Who knows what was going on inside? Maybe he was distracted by personal stuff, still hankering for his ex-wife, stalking her on Facebook and whatnot.

Talk to Charlie, man. They were drinking buddies. Charlie will know. All I know is that, when I started here, Dan was the guy who talked the least in any room. And he never joined us for office events—except last Halloween, that is. Other than that, he came to work every day, did his job, and stayed over to work weekends when asked.

Here, let me walk you to Charlie's office. Glad to be of help.

Charlie Withers
Shop Supervisor, Prime Prototyping Services

Hello, officer. So you want to talk about Dan? Or rather, you want to know what I know about Dan. Correct?

I've been here since this place was opened. Jerry Lester and I almost started together. He retired a year—no, correction, ten months—ago and I retire next year. We've seen a lot of things happen in this place; a lot of people come and go. But what happened with Dan . . . a real tragedy. Jerry cried at the cremation last Saturday—no, it was Sunday, my bad.

Dan worked on a lot of different projects as a lead design engineer and I worked closely with him before my boys out here in the shop made the prototypes and shipped them.

He'd interned for Jerry while at the university. After graduating, he took a year to backpack around Europe for a few months, then hitchhike across the United States for a few months. Jerry and I both told him he was crazy. His family was all back in India—who knows how they must have worried.

But that was the wildest thing I ever knew him to do. After he started working full-time here, he was straight as a pin. Nineteen ninety-eight, that was. No, wait, 1997.

Drinking buddies? Yeah, sure, we drank together some. Especially after my own boy, Joshua, was shipped off overseas. My wife, Angie, passed away a few years ago and, well, after Dan's divorce, he was at loose ends too, I think.

Yeah, I met Dan's wife once before. At the work New Year's Eve party. Never saw her after that till the cremation service. After their divorce, she'd moved to—where was it?—California, I think. Nope, he never discussed her and I didn't ask. Seven years of wedded life. A lot to unravel, I reckon. I think it was seven, you'd best check.

Anyway, we'd find ourselves together at the Silver Crown without having planned it. It got to be a regular thing on Friday nights. I didn't go on other nights. Don't know if he did. Wasn't my place to ask. And he wasn't much of a talker. He liked his whiskey, liked taking time over it. Knew a lot about wine too. He had this wine club membership where they ship you bottles from all over the world each month. Or was it each week?

Yeah, for a small guy, he put away a good bit. Better alcohol tolerance than me. Funny thing is, he told me he grew up in a dry state in India. Don't recall the name. Bit of a tongue-twister. He only started drinking when he moved to the United States, I think. I wouldn't say he was an alcoholic or anything. But he was what Joshua would call "hardcore."

Sloppy, did you say? I wouldn't call his work that. Sure, when there was a lot of pressure and tight deadlines, he made mistakes. After Jerry, we stopped taking on interns. The design engineers have to do all the drawing, detailing, and finishing too. I'll bet Brad used the word "sloppy," right? He's the one creating most of the stress and pressure with his tall promises to our customers.

Sure, Friday. It's hard to remember. I guess we'd met at the bar as usual. Place was not too busy due to the bad weather. I got there a few minutes earlier than him and ordered our drinks. Dan's usual single-malt Scotch on the rocks. I'm a beer man myself. Scotch, for me, is only for weddings and funerals. We sat for a couple of hours. He wasn't happy about having to work the weekend. You look confused? He told me this clearly—how, since Brad had come on board, he had worked more weekends than he cared for. He knocked those glasses back that evening. I was worried I would have to carry him home.

No, that didn't happen often. His apartment was nearby and, if he'd had a bit much to drink, he would leave his car in the parking lot and walk home. If the weather wasn't too foul. The last time I drove him was because we had a blizzard. Must have been—let me think—shortly after New Year's. That time, instead of leaving him by the entrance, I walked him in. First time I'd seen his place from the inside. It was bare except for a mattress and a TV in the living room and, from what I could see, a mattress in the bedroom.

I had teased him about it the next week, asking if he had been robbed. He'd said he never got around to furnishing the place because he'd intended it to be a transitional stop after the divorce while he looked for something better. I'd been surprised because the divorce had been so long ago. It sickened my heart to see him living with all the emptiness. Vanessa said it meant he hadn't moved on. Who knows?

She told you about the little back-and-forth on Syria that Friday afternoon? Pay no mind to that. Dan got into this mood sometimes. He knew where I stood, and I knew where he stood. Didn't stop us from being—what did you call us?—drinking buddies.

That Friday night, I left at my usual time and he stayed on. Who knew it would be the last time I would see him? When Angie, my wife, passed away, the last thing I'd said to her was something about the dog's worm pills. What were my last words to Dan? I think all I said was "Be careful out there." One of our jokes. From *Hill Street Blues*? You're too young for that, I know.

What a thing to say, huh, in light of what happened? It shook me when I found out. It shook us all. Most of us who work here are lifers. He was here for twenty years. You see someone five days a week, spend so much time with them—more than some get to spend with their own family members. Right? I think, for him, living alone like that, we must have been all the family he had. Poor bastard.

Return to India? I think he was lonely but he never mentioned that to me. He liked West Michigan well enough, I guess. Maybe, just not the life he had here. Maybe, like that apartment, this was just his transitional place till he found something better. Maybe, all this wasn't his idea of the American Dream. Who knows? I'm just the old white guy here. The "forgotten America," as the politicians say. Our American Dreams don't go beyond putting food on the table and a reasonably comfortable retirement.

The question I keep asking myself is this: did we fail Dan or did Dan fail us?

You'll have to excuse me, officer. They're paging me for a meeting. Can I walk you out?

Nirali Rainier
CIO, PlanNow Services Inc.

Officer, I don't know how much help I can be. Dhanesh and I divorced ten years ago. We have had almost no contact since then, other than to deal with some financial matters. I live in California, as you know, and have not been back to Michigan till now. My husband, Amos Rainier—we married a year after my divorce from Dhanesh—and I have our own business and an eight-year-old boy, Niam.

Yes, we met in Michigan in 1999. I was on a six-month university exchange program from India. Dhanesh had already graduated by then but one of the professors, Emily Tippett, knew both of us and introduced us via email. Oh, we hit it off right away, you might say. Our first date began at the Indian grocery store—well, it was a backroom in a gas station near the university—to pick up some items for a home-cooked meal. The nearest decent Indian restaurant was a three-hour drive away in Chicago.

He proposed just before my six months were up. We went to India to get married but his family in Ahmedabad were—well, they didn't like him marrying a non-Gujarati. I'm Maharashtrian. Lower caste and different culture. They did not come to the wedding. We're not religious people so we had a small court affair. My family and friends were there and Dhanesh had a couple of friends from his college days too.

No, I never met his family or heard from them the entire time we were married. Dhanesh's older sister was the most upset with him and had a lot of influence over their parents. It had hurt him pretty bad to be cut out of their lives like that. Yet he often said how he was proud of not being guilted into an arranged marriage with someone who checked off all their boxes even if she didn't check off his.

Impulsive? I wouldn't have described him as that. The only time

I had known him to make any major decision without taking his time was—let me think—oh, it was on a trip we took to Mackinac Island for our five-year anniversary. It was one of those green-and-gold Junes that only happen in the Midwest. We drove up and stayed at the Grand Hotel. He had booked the *Somewhere in Time* suite because I loved the movie. The lilacs were in full, breathtaking bloom. We lazed on that open, endless porch in enormous white deck chairs and stared in stunned silence at the lake's shimmering immensity. Oh, and those fancy high teas every afternoon!

One afternoon, there was an antique book fair at the hotel. Casually browsing, we stumbled onto a tooled leather, eighteenth-century edition of the English translation of an ancient Sanskrit play. Kalidasa's *Shakuntala* translated by William Jones. Just like that, Dhanesh bought it for a few thousand dollars. We sat up all night reading out loud to each other. What prompted him, I've never quite understood. It was probably the only thing he held on to after the divorce.

Why?

Is there ever a single or simple explanation for why relationships end? I don't know. I take full responsibility for the end of our marriage. Oh, I guess I needed something more than the IT job at the university. Before we had met, Dhanesh had been living here, what, five or six years. Prime was sponsoring his—*our*—green cards. Also, though we had both agreed at first, I was slowly changing my mind about not having children.

And I could not shut India so completely out of my life. Oh, it's not fair to say he shut it out. We watched and sang along to Hindi movies, we cooked Indian meals, we celebrated Diwali. But he refused to go back even for a visit. Right. Because of his family. So I traveled back alone to visit mine, making excuses for his absence each time.

Fit in? Oh, it seemed to me he had assimilated well enough for someone not born and raised in the United States. But, well, we first-generation immigrants try so hard to fit into our new culture while holding on to the old one. We become too foreign for home and too foreign for here, never enough for both. I stole that last line from a poet.

Sure, I met some of his coworkers at an office party right after we had gotten married. Nice people with that famous Midwestern politeness and their well-regulated churchgoing, family-loving, out-doorsy lives. Dhanesh and I had very little in common with them. Some of them had never traveled out of the state, let alone to an-other country. Almost all of them had worked at Prime since it had opened its doors.

After 9/11, we—I had a bit of bother in our neighborhood. Every time I left for work, someone on our street called the cops on me for driving too fast. Oh, I don't think I was. But, after I got tick-eted three times and had to pay hefty fines, we thought something was going on. It was a quiet cul-de-sac and we weren't—I guess we weren't very neighborly people. We kept to ourselves. I tried to convince Dhanesh to move to a larger city. I had friends working in Silicon Valley and doing so much better than us. He wanted to wait till the green card was done. Well, with 9/11, that whole process slowed down considerably too.

Eventually, in 2006, I began applying for consulting jobs in the Bay Area. I planned to tell him and talk him into moving if and when there was a firm offer. Happened sooner than I thought. A consulting firm with headquarters in Chicago called me in. I did a couple of day trips for interviews and had an offer in hand. Well, not in my hand, exactly. They emailed it and, as luck would have it, Dhanesh saw it pop up on my laptop.

That was the beginning of the end, as they say. I came out of the shower and saw him reading the message. Didn't even have to ask what had happened. He—we—well, we argued for nearly a week, both emotionally exhausted in the end. Oh, he had all this stuff that needed to get out. I guess I did too. We both agreed it was best to separate.

Why did he not want to go? It seemed to me, at the time, he hadn't figured out exactly what he wanted in life. Who does have it all figured out, really? If someone tells you they've figured out exactly what they want to do with their entire life, they are either lying—to you and themselves—or they haven't thought about it enough.

He took care of everything. I simply packed a bag and moved to California to start my new job. He sold the house, shipped ev-erything to me, did it all. So many times, I wondered if I had done the right thing. Then I met Amos and knew I was going to be okay. I just didn't know if Dhanesh was going to be okay. Emily Tippett, our mutual connection, stayed in touch with us separately through

Christmas cards and such. But, well, life goes on. I got busy with our startup, raising our son, making a life.

Drinking? Oh, Dhanesh liked his Scotch. I don't think he had any sort of drinking problem during our marriage. I can't speak for what might have happened after I left. Why? You don't think?

Can I say one more thing, officer? Dhanesh was not a violent man. I don't know what happened that night and I appreciate you are piecing everything together. But he — the man I was married to — he was not a depressive loner as some news reports have said. I don't have anything more to tell you. It's been ten years.

Yes, please let me know when you can. Thank you.

Walter Dejong
Retired Machinist

Officer, I already told the other policeman everythin'. This is gettin' to be a nuisance now. I'm sorry what happened to that man. I really am. May God keep his soul in peace. But there is nothin' new to report.

I understand. You're doin' your job. Who's payin' for your job though, huh? Us taxpayers. And then y'all come and harass us decent citizens like this?

My Irene, she says I oughta be more polite with y'all. Be more patient. What for, I ask her.

Fine. Sit down over there and I'll tell the whole story all over again if I must. You better write it all down good and proper so another one of you guys don't show up next week botherin' us.

Joe, who runs the Silver Crown, is my wife's cousin. Friday mornin', Irene hands me my toolbox and my coat sayin', go help Joe with 'em cabinets 'cause you promised him a month ago. I say, woman, I ain't goin' out in this evil weather and you can't make me. She says, we'll see about that, and pushes me out the door. Got the truck already runnin' and everythin'.

You work hard all your life and then you're made to take early retirement so they can shut the factory down and send all 'em jobs to China. Then your wife turns into Hitler overnight, orderin' you to do this job and that job every other day. A man has no peace till he's in his grave.

So I come over to the place with that wind nearly nippin' my nose and ears off and Joe's eyes are on stalks. He says, why, Walt, what dragged you out so early? I say, let's get on with it, Joe, I ain't got all day.

So he shows me the back kitchen where he's ripped out all the old cabinets and got all this readymade stuff waitin' to be fitted. You know the cheap stuff that's not even real wood? He wants to slum it in his own establishment, who am I to tell him otherwise?

I start workin' around 9 a.m., I reckon. Take a break at noon. It's hard work and my eyesight ain't what it used to be. You'd expect he'd come out back to help when things was slow in the front and his staff could take care of all. Hell, no.

For my pains, I get cold meat sandwiches and beer. I send the boy back with both and say, surely you can do somethin' better in this weather to keep a man goin'. He sends me chicken pot pie and a half-bottle of cheap vodka. A man who can't even pay for quality cabinets or get a professional carpenter to put 'em up for him ain't goin' to show proper gratitude.

What? Yes, yes, I'm gettin' to that. So I work straight through till evenin'. When I'm all done, I go to the bar and say to Joe, you'd better stand me drinks for the rest of the night for all the work I done for you. Or you can pay me for a honest day's work and I'll take my custom elsewhere, ta very much.

He tells his barman my drinks are on the house. And dinner too, I add. I ain't goin' out in that foul weather till 'em plows have cleared 'em roads up a bit.

Anyways, so there I am, sittin' and mindin' my own business. Eatin' my steak and chips and drinkin' my bourbon. Not botherin' no one. Then this guy knocks into me from the back. Nearly makes me spill my drink.

When I turn around, it's this darkie fella I never seen before. Well, this is not my regular bar anyhow. I tell him to mind where he's goin' and can't he see a grown man before his eyes?

He mumbles somethin' in a thick accent and I have no clue what he says or if he understood what I said.

So I say, where you from? He has trouble focusin' on me and gives me this sort of dumb look. So I say, don'cha speak no English?

He just stands there, lookin' at me with his empty glass tap-tappin' on the counter.

Now, my day, as you can understand, had been rough. I'd had it with rude, mean people. And I didn't care for the look in his eye. So I put a hand on his arm and I say, I asked a decent question. Where's your manners? Don't they teach no manners where you come from?

And he moves toward me. Like, his body just comes at me.

Whoa there, buddy, I say, no need to attack me.

And I reach for my handgun. Per the law, I have Joe's permission to open carry in his establishment, the other officer will have told you. I was only plannin' to scare him off of me.

Git outta here, I say, git away, you drunk bastard. Go back to yer country.

And that's it. He grabs my gun with both hands, tryin' to get it from me. I fall off the stool. We both fall onto the floor. People start screamin'. But I don't let go. My grip is still strong—for an old man. He don't let go neither. We're wrestlin' like two octopuses, arms and legs all tangled up.

How'd it go off? I guess one of us racked the slide with all that pushin' and pullin'. But the thumbprint on the trigger—hoo, boy —you know they got his. They have it clean and clear.

Why was I carryin' that day? What kinda question is that? It's a free country, ain't it? I abide by Michigan's open carry law, mister. I exercise my Second Amendment rights 'cause a right unexercised is a right lost and 'cause I want to protect myself and my family. That there gun saved my life that night, officer. I'm an old man. Lookit me. Could I have survived a younger man attackin' me like that? No. If I had not been able to reach for that gun quickly, I would not be standin' here talkin' to you today. No sir. It was that foreign man's foolishness to grab onto another man's gun like that.

Excuse me? You oughta check my records before even askin' somethin' like that, officer. I never, in my seventy-plus years, been on the wrong side of the law for anythin'. And, maybe, you oughta check that troubled man's records too and see what you find. I wouldn't be surprised, the look he had on him that night, if he did not have some kind of history. All 'em Middle Eastern men are always killin' each other at the slightest thing.

Say what? Yah, I heard he's from India. Same part of the world, ain't it? They're all the same anyhow. Comin' here, takin' our jobs, as our president says. They come out of nowhere, anywhere, and they show no respect to patriots like me. My family been here for generations—laid down lives for our great country. I says to Irene the other day, I says, Irene, if they try to make me out to be the bad guy here, I'll take it all the way to the Supreme Court.

Some of 'em papers makin' me out to be some kinda mean racist. What do they know? I never said a bad word to no colored man or woman. This fella just—there's too much crime nowadays. You hear about the Waffle House got robbed the other week by a gang of Blacks? They carved up the old owner's face and left him bleedin' and dyin'. He shoulda had a gun to protect himself.

What happened to—to Mr. Patel—it eats away at me. Ask my Irene, I haven't slept a full night since that Friday. I never meant no trouble. Things got out of hand too quickly. I had to protect myself, see?

They all said not to go to the funeral but I went. His wife, she was cryin' and yellin' at me. I went to say somethin' but the words choked my throat and set my insides on fire. I'll tell you now: this America of ours—it's not the country me and my kind grew up in. It's not the America these new people come to find neither. And, seems to me, this unknown country no longer cares for what either of us got to offer. The handful of folks who've figured out what they want, well, they grab it from the rest of us without askin'. What has happened to America, can anyone tell me?

SWAJ

FROM *The Brooklyn Rail*

DEAD OF SUMMER. I was lucky to get this job. Delivering sandwiches for Loeffler's Deli isn't exactly what I had in mind for myself after high school, but we are living in unprecedented times.

Before the disaster, I'd been waiting tables up at the Gilded Clipper. I actually liked the uniform, the red bowtie with a matching cummerbund and the little brass swordfish pin with a fake ruby eye that we wore proudly on our shirts. I know it was just a costume, part of the upscale-dining experience. Still, putting it on for the night, feeling the sharp corners of the bowtie on my chin as I listed the chef's specials to a table gathered around a reclaimed ship's wheel, made me feel important, ordained. For the past two summers, I'd languished in the herd of busboys at the Gilded C—but loyalty apparently counts for nothing at that restaurant because after the third shark attack, I was among the handful let go.

"Michael, your father runs the only pharmacy in Amity," the manager, Don, with his liquid brown eyes and rust-orange mustache, told me. "I'm sure he can hire you for the summer. Even if the whole economy tanks, people will always need their medications. These other guys don't have options." To think I once had a crush on Don. To think I wasted an entire afternoon driving to a dress shop in Quogue just to see whether Angela, the girlfriend he always talks about, actually existed.

Don was wrong about my father. He would never give me a job at his pharmacy. He disapproved of nepotism as staunchly as he believed that young men should pay their own way through college. I waited two days to give Dad the bad news. I figured he'd blow up and threaten to kick me out of the basement. But for a man with so few surprises in him, he managed to pull one out as I stood in the living room, blaming my dismissal on the lack of hungry tourists. He simply folded up his copy of the *Leader,* set it gently on his lap, and said, "You better find something else quick." I nodded obediently. Then he added, staring at the floor, "Take whatever job you can, before they get any scarcer, just as long as it isn't selling belts."

I tried to keep my face from going red and the air from getting stuck in my throat. But I caught the sharp point of his reference. Last August, when I was seventeen, I sneaked away on a Saturday morning and took a ferry over to Fire Island to explore a scene I'd only heard muttered about derisively by the Amity fishermen. Weatherwise, it was the wrong afternoon for such a visit, a lacquered gray sky quickly turning to rain, but it proved ripe for my purposes. On the boardwalk, I met a thirty-six-year-old accessories designer from Manhattan named Terry Bartholomew and we spent the most redeeming twenty minutes of my life in the damp garage of his shared oceanside house rental.

Terry smoked a joint afterward, rolling it from a massive bundle of grass he kept in a brown lunch bag. I didn't partake, only watched him, already half in love. I couldn't give him my phone number, but he scribbled his down, and I waited until the following Tuesday to call him. It was, to put it mildly, a disappointment. Terry's manly, hairy beauty dissipated into a prissy, untuned voice, complaining about the bitchy merchandise buyers at the department stores who refused to stock his extra-wide snakeskin belts with diamanté buckles. I listened to Terry with Amity ears, unaroused, embarrassed, scared I sounded like him, and never called him again. My father must have listened too, eavesdropping from another phone in the house. I don't know how much he heard. We never discussed it, not a word, but he began to drop little incendiary objections about belts— *ridiculous accessories for vain women and girlish men who can't keep their pants up.* It was a stance that must have seemed utterly bizarre to my mother and little sister, but it couldn't have been clearer to me. The Gilded Clipper's red-silk cummerbund, I was relieved to discover, didn't count as a belt.

I went looking for work. At that point no one had actually seen the shark, and yet it was all anyone in town could talk about: the monstrous Great White prowling the coves of Amity, waiting to eat your children, your grandparents, you, and, more important than any of those potential victims, the tourists with gobs of money who drove out from the city to dip a toe in the ocean. We make a big show of looking down on the invaders from the city—all they do is eat, eat, eat, and then beach themselves in the sand until they can eat more—but Amity is a lonely town without the summer influx. In winter there are barely a thousand people, and unlike some of the more picturesque East End villages—Southampton, or Sag Harbor, or Amagansett—Amity doesn't possess the rustic charm of clapboard architecture or cobblestone side streets bathed in weedy wildflowers. Amity is like an ugly face made pretty by a suntan; once the color fades, it's all pockmarks, stray hairs, and holes. Amityites will tell you we need the money, and that's the honest truth. But we also need the tourists themselves. We crave their crassness and insatiable appetites, because we Amityites are a people in contrast. More than anything else, we define ourselves as *not them*. But now, with the tourists too scared of the shark to venture to our shores, we're stuck alone with each other.

I was having zero luck with the job search. And once Sheriff Martin Brody officially closed the beaches, even more of us were out of work. I applied to park cars at the yacht club. I applied at the Yellow Napkin to scoop ice cream onto sugar cones. I volunteered to fold towels at Maxx Muscle for less than minimum wage, partly because I figured it would be a treat to cruise the clientele. I asked my only friend who wasn't from high school, Daisy Wicker, if she could get me a job at the Bibelot, but she said no one, not even *our kind,* was buying antiques right now. I love Daisy. She's four years older than I am, with long brown hair drizzled with split ends, and full pink lips that tend toward brooding. She's forever being dumped by an older woman who lives way up in Mattituck. But what I like best is her bluntness: "Don't they need someone at Maxx Muscle to measure all their shrinking penises?" "I already tried them," I told her. "They're cutting their hours in half." My last stop was Eddie's Relief, the gas station that once prided itself on being the only stop for fuel between the highway and the Hamptons. I should have known my chances were zilch. Eddie was reading a copy of the *Leader* with the headline "Two Killed by Monster Shark off Amity Beach. Number of Victims of Killer Fish Rises to Three."

Eddie had a tic of wiping his nose with the underside of his wrist even when his hands weren't covered in grease. When I asked him if he needed any help pumping gas, he wiped his nose, peered over at me for a good minute, and told me if I really wanted to help him, I'd call the sheriff's office and file a complaint against Brody for ruining everyone's livelihoods by keeping the beaches shut and the tourists at bay. "Better yet," he grumbled. "Kill the idiot! That'd be your first assignment, day one. I already rang up the mayor with my thoughts. You want to see real carnage? You want to watch a bloodier death than shark bites? Let this nonsense of closing beaches and scaring everyone play out for one more week. Then you'll get a front-row seat on the bloodletting. 'Cluding mine!"

I felt bad for Sheriff Brody. It was true, though. The beaches were deserted, like stretches of vacant football fields off season, and yet we were still trying to peddle Amity summer merchandise in the empty bleachers. The few high-school friends I kept in contact with were busing over to Montauk or East Hampton to find work where the shark seemed disinclined to venture. I was thinking of doing the same. I even considered calling Terry Bartholomew to ask for help, hoping he might connect me to his pot dealer so I could try selling small quantities to the locals. But it had been nearly a year since our tryst, and I wasn't so delusional to presume my bumbling acts in that Fire Island garage had earned a spot in Terry's sexual trophy case. There must be dance floors full of boys like me in Manhattan. I was walking down Water Street, feeling sorry for myself, when plump Rose Loeffler stepped out of her deli, carrying a giant wedge of provolone. The wedge nearly slipped from her fingers, and I rescued it before it bounced on the sidewalk.

"Thank you, Michael," she said, her cherubic face tightening into a smile. "How are you?"

"Unemployed," I replied.

She nodded like it was the chorus of a song she'd been listening to all summer. "Isn't there a constitutional right about citizens being free to congregate wherever they want to, shark or no shark?"

"I think Brody's just trying to"—*Keep us safe* was the intended terminus of that sentence, left unspoken because I was reading Rose's face for the desired response; I sensed she wanted a different answer—"show what a big man he is by taking on this fish on his own."

She nodded approvingly. "I hope Ben Gardner is the shark's last lunch, so we can go on serving our own!" Rose cringed at her own tactless joke. But I was too taken aback by the name to cringe along with her. Ben Gardner was a beloved town fisherman. His wife was a regular at Amity Pharmacy and once tried to teach me the clarinet.

"Ben? He was eaten too? Oh my God!" It dawned on me that one reason the townsfolk were desperate to open the beaches might be to offer the shark a larger menu, so that the only items weren't the locals. Couldn't the city people be offered up instead?

"Ben's missing," Rose said pointedly, "from his boat, which had giant teeth marks in it. You do the math. And from what I hear, Brody sent him out on some cockamamie fish-hunting expedition, chumming to draw the shark close. Don't we have a military for these kinds of situations?" Her smile didn't ebb, but she glanced at me with the cold gaze of calculation, weighing invisible pros and cons. "You know, when the news came in about Ben, my delivery boy up and quit. He was terrified. This was not his kind of beach town, he said. I told him, your deliveries never cross dangerous bodies of water, unless you count the drunks outside the Randy Bear. He wouldn't listen. And now we need a delivery boy for the lunch rush. Doesn't pay much, but . . . You got a bike, Michael?"

So began my career in sandwich delivery. There may not be vacationers on the streets, the stores might be papering up their windows right and left with FINAL LIQUIDATION and EVERYTHING MUST GO, the *Leader* might be declaring the town coffers all but empty, but Amity still has a healthy appetite. The locals ate the run of the Loeffler's lunchtime "between the slices" chalkboard specials. Liverwurst with pickles on wheat. Roast beef and Swiss on sourdough. Paul's "ain't-it-spicy" Chinese chicken salad on rye. The special sandwich Rose dreamed up, a "Shark Beach BLT" with an actual bite carved out of one side, fashioned from a repurposed cookie cutter, was the rare misstep in the otherwise savvy understanding of customer stomachs. And it was up to me and my navy-blue Huffy bike, which had been my Christmas present in the eighth grade, to deliver them. Tips were rare. Two dimes, a quarter. Once a crisp dollar from the psychologist who was treating poor Mrs. Kintner over her grief for her eaten son. Delivering for Loeffler's Deli was not going to pay for college, but at least it kept me employed and out of the house when my father banged on the basement door.

Occasionally, an order would come in that would send me to one of the beaches that was officially off-limits. As I pedaled toward

Russet Cove, a semi-private U of sand popular among the teenagers, I dreaded the last name scribbled in Rose's wiry handwriting on the ticket: Ferlinghetti.

I steered my bike and the ration of seven sandwiches toward the dunes. Shirtless Ted Ferlinghetti and four of his friends were tossing a Frisbee on the otherwise empty beach. As much as I hated Ted, I pined to see a flash of his black armpit hair every time he snagged a high throw above his head. Two girls I didn't know with long straight hair wearing rope bikini tops sat on a blanket nearby, sipping on beers. Amity High was a tiny place, a drain filter of a school that collected the poorest kids who couldn't afford private or test into the more advanced regional school with its AP classes over in Westhampton. Ted Ferlinghetti could have been a bully, but to his credit, he elected to elide easy categories. Still there was a lingering charge of violence in him that simultaneously turned me on and kept me perpetually on my guard.

Ted dropped the Frisbee as I hopped off my bike, and he strutted over to collect the bag of sandwiches. "Michael!" he yelled from close range and gave an obnoxious snort as if to test whether his friends thought my delivering sandwiches was funny. His muscled body was silver from the shine of tanning oil in the sun. He had curly dark hair and his top front teeth were chipped. "Nice summer job, man! Or is it permanent?"

I smiled and handed him the bag. I knew that Ted was cursed to remain in Amity for the rest of his life, and however mean he was, that was too severe a punishment; plus, I had ravaged his body in hundreds of obscene ways, surprising even myself with my creativity, during the math class we had together. Those fantasies were so real to me, I almost felt like I had permission to reach out and stroke his oily chest.

Ted distributed the sandwiches, lobbing them to his friends, and when the bag was empty, he crumpled it. "Wait, no napkins?"

"Sorry about that," I said.

"It makes it harder to give you a tip." He offered a menacing smile. "Tell you what." He pulled a folded five-dollar bill from the pocket of his tight brown corduroy shorts. "Five bucks. It's all yours. All you need to do is go for a quick swim."

"Huh?"

"Right out there." He nodded toward the ocean, a flat horizon of copper blue without a single wave or dorsal fin fracturing its surface. "Just thirty feet out and back. Five minutes. Five dollars."

In theory, I was as terrified of the shark as anyone else in Amity, with one slight, and now I realize, significant caveat: I was never going to swim in the ocean. Had the Great White not materialized, I still wouldn't have clocked a single afternoon splashing around in the town's popular swimming spots. It's not that I'm embarrassed about my body in a swimsuit—or not only that. I find all the required interactions of a day at the beach—the forced jocularity and hysterical relaxation—exhausting. I was never in any actual danger of being eaten by the shark.

"Ted," I whispered. "We're not allowed to swim."

"No cops around," he said, and winked at me. I suspected that Ted knew about me, knew what I wanted, and was willing to use it to get me into the water. "Come on, Michael. You scared? Three minutes. Just up to your neck. Don't be a pussy."

The two girls glanced over their shoulders. Their eyes slid over me and they went back to talking to each other. They wouldn't be sprinting in to rescue me or even gather up my severed body parts.

"No," I mumbled softly. "It's not safe."

"Not safe?" he squealed. "That thing's probably long gone by now. The Atlantic's a big ocean. How about I'll go in with you! We'll run in together. Holding hands! And you still get the five bucks. Come on, don't be a—"

I looked out at the sea again, the flat silky blue, and for the first time, I sensed the shark out there, right under the surface, waiting for me, as if its purpose, all along, had simply been my extermination. "Pussy, pussy, pussy. Hairy pussy."

I climbed on my bike, backed it out from the sand, and without another word to Ted, pedaled toward town. Along the way, as snippets of the coast appeared at cliff turns and from between the pricey clapboard mansions, I had the unshakable feeling the shark was following me.

Then I fell in love. He was standing on the sidewalk, out in front of the Abelard Arms Inn, on a sweltering Wednesday afternoon, his face starry with perspiration. He was tall, just over six feet, more narrow than lean, and he was dressed in the typical rich-summer-person uniform of khaki pants and a bright-white short-sleeve cotton shirt with a small green alligator sewn on the chest. He had the crisp aura of privilege, oblivious to the fact that he was blocking a pedestrian path as he searched through a bag for what turned out to be a file of photographs. He glanced up at me as I neared him, and I admired his face, long and thin, with light-blue eyes and a surprising deep crosshatch of lines at their corners for someone who couldn't have been older than thirty. His thick hair, brushed back but still unkempt, was blond from the sun, and it struck me that he had the head of a lion, not the lazy established males, but the hungry unproven loners who possess a skittish grace. Our eyes met, and for a reason I would only discover later, when we were naked in his hotel room, we both smiled with a kind of mischievous greed—slightly caged with eyes shifting around at passersby to make sure no one else noticed.

"Hi," I said, shocked at my own bravery. "You look lost." He didn't look lost. I assume I did.

"No," he said, keeping his smile. "I'm staying right here at the Abelard. I noticed your delivery bag and wondered where I could pick up a sandwich."

"I can get you one!" I promised. "What do you want?" He laughed, shifted his bag on his shoulder, and ordered a turkey on pumpernickel.

"You sure it's not a problem," he said, not in the tone of a question, more out of customary politeness.

"I can get it to you in, *ohh,* five minutes." Four if I ran to the deli and back instead of riding my bike.

"Bring it up to room 207. I'm Matt, by the way. Matt Hooper. I'm here to save your town from that shark. Not that you asked."

I can't remember whether he explained what he did for a living before or after we had sex on his hotel-room bed. He did eat the sandwich first, and we must have made small talk then, but I was so petrified, my blood rushing through my ears, I couldn't say what subject we discussed. I remember afterward lying with my head on his chest, drowsy from our exertions and from the Abelard's gale-like air conditioning, while Matt explained the field of ichthyology. He was an expert on fish and traveled around the world, as far away as Australia, to observe sharks and dolphins in their native habitats. He had gone to Yale and had spent summers as a kid out on Southampton, with his older brother, David. It was clear that he came from wealth. I could tell that by the pony leather bags piled by the TV stand, dangling with more brass tackle on them than a fisherman's vest. Matt lived on Cape Cod, near the Oceanographic Institute in Woods Hole, in a little shack all alone in Hyannis Port. He'd been invited to Amity by the editor of the *Leader*, with the mayor's blessing, to explain the shark's predatory behavior and also, perhaps, to rid us of it.

"You really think you could kill it," I asked, lifting my head. I'd left a tiny puddle of saliva on his chest, right by his brown nipple, and quickly wiped it with my hand.

"Maybe," he said. "But I'm really here to observe it. To see it with my own eyes! God, the thing sounds like a once-in-a-lifetime beauty. Like a kind of god."

I thought of the fat gray shadow menacing the waters, darting from dock to cove, following me on my deliveries through Amity, biding its time until I'd make the careless mistake of entering the water.

"Observe it how?"

"From a boat," he said. "Or as close as I can get."

"But?" I widened my eyes in fright.

"But what?" he said, grinning, a flirt of the life-and-death variety. It got him off to make people worry for his safety, I could see that about him.

"It could eat you," I said.

He pushed me off, located his underwear on the extra-long ol-ive-green shag, and brought them up to his hands in the grip of his toes.

"Michael," he said, and studied me for a second to make sure he'd gotten my name right. "It was fun. You're a wonderful kid. But this is just a crazy little fling, okay?"

I nodded. "It's not like you live here," I added, to downgrade the possible repercussions for his own comfort.

He confessed to me, as he got dressed, that he slept with both women (I liked that he didn't call them girls) and boys (I liked that he didn't call them men). He was open, fluid, curious, freaky, but also not nailed down, not "nail-downable." Did I understand?

"Absolutely," I said. "I'm like that too. I'm just having fun." Yet it scared me all of a sudden, as I lay there naked, that he could leave town at any hour, that he'd be gone in his green Pinto with the shark decal on the window. Maybe Ted was right. Maybe the shark had already moved on to another town with a better buffet of humans. Or maybe the shark would prove easy to kill and would be slaughtered by this evening and there'd be no further reason for Matt to hang around. For the first time, I felt in league with the beast and prayed that it would flourish in these waters, at least for a few more days.

"You look pale," Matt said. He snapped his fingers, crossed the room, and dug through his suitcase. He pulled out a small scarlet drawstring pouch and shook out a charm, shaped like a fossil, its top capped in silver.

I was reluctantly getting dressed, trying to hide a mustard stain on my T-shirt, but I could see there were several more of these charms inside the pouch. "From Macao," Matt said as he presented it to me. I caressed its smooth, sharp edges with my thumb. "A tiger-shark tooth. It's meant to protect you from getting bitten. You wear that, and you won't be scared anymore." He laughed, looking a little embarrassed about the gift, and gathered up his file of shark-bite photographs. "All right, get out of here. I've got a meeting with your sheriff in half an hour. He's a real asshole, isn't he?"

I lingered at the door, nervous, pushing the tip of the shark tooth into the padding of my thumb. "Can I come back?" I asked.

He smiled. "As long as you bring a sandwich."

I returned each afternoon at the end of the lunch rush, a standing date between Matt and me, bringing along his turkey on pumpernickel. Loeffler's allotted me one free sandwich for my shift, and I donated it to Matt, so that he could scarf it down, leaving only the long, tan legs of the crusts on the wrapper, before we spent fifteen minutes rolling around on the creaky Abelard double bed. I'd used some twine from my father's knickknack drawer to hang the shark tooth around my neck. Matt yanked lightly on the pendant as he lay next to me. "See, you're safe," he whispered, and then pretended to take a huge bite out of my arm, before gently, lovingly, guiding my head between his thighs. I had already learned with Terry on Fire Island what a rare blessing it is to actually get to do what you fantasize about—but it is a living, breathing heaven to be able to do it twice, and then three times on consecutive weekdays. I was, without question, in love with Matt, deeply, irrevocably, devotedly. I wanted to ask him about the best community colleges around Hyannis Port. I wanted to invite him to meet for a beer at the Randy Bear, where we could play slow songs on the jukebox and listen while our elbows touched on the mahogany bar. Instead,

I made small forays into his progress on the shark hunt. I was relieved to hear that despite spotting a long, ominous gray shadow off the coast, they'd been unable to close in for a kill.

"What will you do once you catch it?" I asked.

Matt winced. "I'm afraid there's no catching it. Way too big. It's like a semi-truck going ninety miles per hour the wrong way down the highway with giant lawn-mower blades for a front grille. Don't tell your sheriff, but I plan to photograph it before we kill it."

"What will happen after you kill it?" I asked lightly. "I mean, you'll still need to stay in town in case it has brothers and sisters. There could be more than one shark attacking us, right? There's no telling how many are out there."

Matt looked at me, catching the worrisome hope in my voice. "Nah," he bellowed. "There's only one feeding on your neighbors. Sharks aren't like dolphins. They don't hunt in packs. We'll get this bad boy and then I'll hightail it back to the Institute." He climbed off the mattress and I quickly leaned over the side of the bed to retrieve the gift that I'd put in my pocket for him. It was an exchange for the shark tooth, and I pictured Matt wearing it on the helm of a boat, keeping him safe. Matt disappeared into the bathroom and reemerged with his pants on.

"I meant to ask you," he said. "What do you know about the sheriff's wife, Ellen?"

"Mrs. Brody? She's nice enough." I noticed that he was listening attentively to my answer, and a spike of jealousy jabbed into my brain. "And pretty, I guess, for an older lady." I liked Ellen Brody and I was ransacking my head for anything else degrading that I could say about her.

"My older brother, David, dated her when they were kids. Did I tell you about David? He's—"

I was sick of hearing about his older brother, David, or anyone else who took up space outside of this hotel room. I stood and moved toward him, my heart twisting, my teeth gritted, and handed him the pin. He glanced down at the brass swordfish as if it had just emitted a tiny electroshock.

"For the shark's tooth," I said, grabbing the pendant at my neck and holding it out as if it were a crucifix. "Something to keep you safe too. From me."

"You shouldn't have." He stared up at me with a tilted head before giving the pin a closer appraisal, even squeezing it in his fingers to test the metal. I thought it looked more expensive when it wasn't pinned to the chest of a waiter. "*Xiphias gladius*," he said. "My gosh. I hope that isn't a real ruby in its eye?" He sounded concerned, like I might have raided the pin from my mother's jewelry box.

"I don't know if it's real or not. It might be. I found it at an old antique store that my friend runs. It's supposed to bring you luck. Maybe it will get you your shark photos."

He breathed through his nose and touched my cheek with his warm, calloused palm. "You're a very special young man," he said softly. "I appreciate it. A good way of remembering you."

Every morning proved a high-wire walk of hoping. Coming down to the breakfast table, I feared news splashed across the *Leader*'s front page that the shark had been captured or killed; I prayed that it had been spotted, that it had bitten off a foot or even a forearm, to keep the fear alive, but I never wished that anyone had actually died—just enough of that person eaten so there would be a reason for Matt to stay.

When my father told me that he had to give Janice, a gray-haired angel who had worked at the pharmacy for fifteen years, her notice, I decided it was only fair that the people of Amity sacrificed for my happiness. "Even after they slashed all the broker fees," my father grumbled, "there's been no takers for house rentals for July or August. Two stores shuttered on Main Street, not to reopen anytime soon." He slammed the coffeepot into its cradle so hard that I checked to make sure it hadn't cracked. "That mother-effing shark is murdering us. Orders are down at the pharmacy thirty percent."

"They have a very capable fish expert here from Woods Hole," I informed him. "They'll get it soon." But I begged every saint I could think of to watch over the shark and protect it from us.

The lunch rush ended fifteen minutes early, thanks to the halted construction on the town's new waterfront gazebo. I ordered my usual turkey on pumpernickel and hurried over to the Abelard. I noticed that Matt's green Pinto wasn't parked in its usual spot across the street, and when I sailed by the front desk of the hotel, Mr. Portnick whistled. "Hey, slow down, Michael. Your customer is out today." I turned to face him, the alcove dark and dingy and only his circular glasses holding light.

"Where is he?" I demanded.

Mr. Portnick pinched the skin at his Adam's apple. "I presume he's out trying to save our town! If you want to leave the sandwich with me, I'll make sure he gets it when he comes in."

Heartbroken, I biked around Amity, hunting for the frog-green Pinto. I didn't spot it anywhere, not at the police station or in front of the mayor's office or by the docks where the fishermen were mending their nets with grandmotherly concentration.

"Did something happen?" I asked them. "Did they catch the shark?"

The eldest fisherman erupted into croupy giggling. "When they git 'em, you'll haar a cheer all o'er town. Then you'll knaw."

I arrived home late that afternoon, checking to make certain that my father was out. Then I proceeded to dial the Abelard every fifteen minutes asking for Mr. Hooper, for a Matthew Hooper from the Oceanographic Institute, for room 207 please, disguising my voice each time. The fourth time I called, asking for that marine-life expert who went to Yale, Mr. Portnick hissed into the receiver, "For God's sake, Michael, stop calling! He isn't in!"

There was nothing I could do, except to meet up with Daisy at the Randy Bear. She was the only person I could trust in Amity, and as we sat, swiveling on our barstools—both of us fidgety by nature —I confessed all the delicious, sordid details of my love affair with Matt Hooper.

Daisy nearly spit out her bourbon at the news. "You've got to be kidding!" she shrieked at a very low level so that the bartender wouldn't overhear us. "I met Matt two nights ago at the Brodys' house. They had a little dinner party, and I got the weirdest feeling they were trying to set me up with him. Obviously, that wasn't going to happen."

Brody. The name soured in my ears. Ellen Brody. Why was she haunting my romance? "I can't stand that woman!" I sneered. "Matt mentioned her too. Apparently, she used to date his older brother."

"She's got bravado," Daisy said. "I'll give that to her. She was flirting up a storm with Matt, right in front of her husband. Like, you know, touching his wrist, talking close to his ear. I felt sorry for her a little bit."

I shook my head in fury, and Daisy, realizing I was getting worked up, patted my hand. "Cool your jets, Ke-mo sah-bee. No one, not even someone as cocky as your charming Matt Hooper, struts into town and sleeps with the sheriff's wife. Trust me."

She was probably right. And yet for the next two days, when I appeared as usual with a turkey on pumpernickel at the Abelard, I was told by Mr. Portnick that Matt was out, Matt was, in fact, so far out, he was a mile out at sea past Montauk Point and wouldn't be home until very, very late. I was desperate to ask whether Mr. Hooper came back at night alone or if he ever had company, but I couldn't figure out how to broach the subject without endangering myself and left the inn on the verge of tears, dumping the sandwich in the trash can.

The next day's *Leader* splashed details of a near attack. The beaches had been opened due to pressure from the Chamber of Commerce. And within a few hours, a boy swimming off High Beach had almost been cut in two by the ferocious shark. Brody and Hooper had saved him just in time. It seemed so unfair, this poor starving animal working slyly and assiduously to creep up on an unsuspecting morsel, only for his prey to be whisked to safety before he could close his mouth around it and savor his prize. But in another second, I realized my insanity, and was glad for the boy's survival, and for Matt that he'd gotten his eyes on the creature. That would keep him in Amity for a few more days.

"It's a little early for sandwiches," Mr. Portnick said when I arrived at eight in the morning at the Abelard.

"I know," I murmured, before offering up a cover story. "But I had an idea where the shark might be. I want to tell Matt. I know they've been out looking for it on that fisherman Quint's schooner."

"Oh, you know where it's been lurking, do you?" Mr. Portnick said sarcastically, leaning over his desk. "Do tell."

"It's private," I said. "I'm only telling Matt."

Mr. Portnick sighed and reached for the phone.

"Sorry to bother you so early, Mr. Hooper. Michael's here *again* for you." I heard Matt's hearty, crackling voice on the line, and Mr. Portnick blinked twice and let out another sigh. He hung up and shuffled some brochures around on his desk. "Go right up. I suppose you remember the room number?"

I climbed the stairs, uncertain of my plan. I hadn't thought about anything beyond getting past the front desk. My hands were sweaty, my pulse racing, but there was nothing else to do but knock on the door. Matt swept it open, and a wash of sunlight filled the room. I had never seen it without the blinds drawn. I glanced at

the bed, terrified to find somebody—Ellen Brody or a young man
—sprawled across it. But the bed was made, the starchy peach comforter already tucked militantly in at the corners. That left only
Matt to behold, dressed in the same outfit he wore when I first saw
him, except for his bare sunburnt feet. He had an amused smile
on his face, a tight twist of the lips, and he issued a faint grunt,
expressing either bafflement or frustration. I didn't wait for him to
ask me in. I stepped into the room, and it took all my strength not
to lunge for him, to pull him onto the bed and hold him until he
stopped resisting and went limp in my arms.

"I was just about to leave," he said, putting his hands on his hips.
"It's a big day. Quint, Brody, and I know where the shark is."

He wasn't wearing the swordfish pin. I wanted to remind him
that it would bring him luck, but my mouth was dry and I was having trouble moving my tongue.

"So today's your last day, maybe?" I managed.

"Maybe," he said. "Look, I really have to get the equipment in
the—"

"I meant to ask you, before you left," I said, stumbling over my
words. I wanted to tell him that I could be packed and ready to
leave with him by noon. But I turned into a coward and let the sentence take a different path. "I'm really interested in oceanography.
In itchiography."

"Ichthyology," he corrected.

"Yeah, that. I want to do what you do. Study fish. Help them. I
want to save the fish." Matt nodded thoughtfully at the news, as if
he understood the calling.

"Gosh, Michael, why didn't you tell me earlier?" He laughed and
rocked on his heels. I could sense his relief, and he grew comfortable in front of me, like it had been between us the first time we
met. "I think that's terrific! I'd be happy to give you some pointers.
When I get back to Woods Hole, I can mail you some books to read.
We can talk about this another time, and—"

I didn't want him to leave the room, not yet. I stalled for time.
"Are there any internships up at the Oceanographic Institute? Or
classes? Maybe I could come and study up there. I don't want the
fish to die. It's not right how we invade their waters and extermi-
nate them whenever we feel that they get out of control. We should
save them at any cost."

"I know exactly what you mean," he said genially. "And sure, I can give you some contacts. I'm really glad to hear of this interest, Michael. Really." He clapped my arm and spun around to pick up a steel box that contained an underwater camera. He sprung toward the door, and I quickly blocked it, my shaky fingers reaching for his belt buckle. He stepped back.

"No," he said sternly. "There's no time for that anymore."

"What about later today?" My voice came out as a whine. "When you're off the boat."

"Michael, please. We had a nice encounter with each other. But let's put that aside. I need to concentrate on the shark."

I could feel my face burning. I tried to fight off the rejection, biting the insides of my cheeks, nodding affably, even giving a little idiotic laugh. Instead of his belt buckle, I reached for the steel case in his grip. "At least let me help. I can carry your equipment down. Assisting is the only way I'll learn."

"Sure," he said warmly. "I'd appreciate that."

As we walked along the hotel corridor, lacking anything of substance to say to each other, I repeated my newfound interest in ichthyology. I asked him a question about gills and respiration, but I didn't hear a word of his convoluted answer. All that came into my mind were the four soulless hours of sandwich delivery ahead of me with no visit to the Abelard ever again. I'd left his room for the last time.

On the street, the green Pinto was nowhere in sight. Instead we marched toward a blue pickup truck with the stenciled insignia of the Woods Hole Oceanographic Institute decorating the door. On the truck bed loomed a large aluminum cage made of thin bars glittering in Amity's aquatic morning light. I squinted at Matt. "What is that?"

Matt grinned at his own daring, relishing my distress. He hopped onto the truck bed and I couldn't resist staring as the waistband of his pants dipped to showcase a peek of his ass. That too I would likely never see again. He stood by the cage, the way a fisherman might pose next to a huge catch on the dock for a picture, and rattled one of its bars. "I spent all morning assembling it," he said proudly. "We're going to lower it off the side of Quint's boat, with yours truly inside, and I'm going to take pictures of the shark before we kill it. No one's ever photographed a fish that big before."

"You're going to be *in the water* like bait while it swims around—"

Matt enjoyed my horror, and laughed in satisfaction.

I hoisted the steel box onto the truck bed. Matt stretched his arms and scanned the shops around the hotel, the majority of them shuttered in the worst tourist slump in Amity history.

"Hey, do you know where I could get a quick egg sandwich to go?" he asked.

Loeffler's Deli would be open by now. I told him I could run and get him one. "Are you sure it's not a problem?" he asked. He knew what my answer would be. I loved fetching him sandwiches; it seemed that feeding him was the one last gift I had to offer.

I waited outside the deli for Rose to fry up Matt's egg and for Paul to slather the butter on the bread. Next to the deli was the hardware store, and through its front window I saw Ellen Brody at the counter having a pair of keys copied. She was pretty, with her hair waving over her ears and a pair of red-tinted sunglasses perched on the top of her head. She wore a white silk blouse and a loose linen skirt. When she exited the store, a shaft of light blinded her and she struggled to pull the sunglasses over her eyes. The harsh sunlight also revealed a winking silver chain that ran between her breasts, and I saw the shark tooth dangling from it, a pendant exactly like mine, to protect her from being bitten.

"Michael!" she cried, as if I had purposely materialized in order to scare her. She put her hand over her heart. "I didn't see you. How is your family?"

"Okay," I mumbled. I tried to work up a smile for her, but I couldn't part with one for my competition. Or maybe she wasn't my only competitor. How many others were there scattered around Amity, wearing their own tiger-shark tooth and believing they were safe?

"Tell your father," she said, "that I'll be in to pick up those prescriptions for Martin." Then she departed along the sidewalk, clicking her brand-new keys together.

I hurried the sandwich back to the truck. Matt was crouched on the bed, testing the cage bars, screwing them tighter. Inside the cage, he had already placed diving equipment and air tanks.

"Here you go!" I said. He grabbed the sandwich, unpeeled the wrapper, and took an enormous bite out of it.

"So that cage is all that's going to keep you safe from the shark?" I asked, staring up as he chewed, my head at the level of his sneakers.

He swallowed the egg and bread down. "No! I'm not that stupid!

That shark is a maniac! A twenty-foot White! I'm also going to be armed with a very special underwater gun. I borrowed it from the Institute. You load it with a twelve-gauge shotgun shell, and when I'm done taking pictures, and that monster swims in real close, *bang!*"

Matt clapped his hands together, wiping off the sandwich crumbs. "Speaking of, I left the gun up in the room." He peered down at me with his beautiful light-blue eyes. "Well, fish assistant, can I trust you to climb up here and make sure all of these bars are nice and tight, while I go get it?" I nodded eagerly and pulled myself up onto the truck bed. Matt patted my shoulder. "Just give each of them an extra hard twist to the right—*righty tighty*. I'll be right back."

I went to work turning the bars as Matt jogged across the road. He reappeared a few minutes later, with a long black case that might have held a saxophone.

I jumped from the truck, and he let me hug him. Our chests pressed together for the duration of one breath. Then I let go, backing up, and he laughed awkwardly as he locked the tailgate.

"Your town's going to be a whole lot safer the next time you see me," he said.

I waved from the sidewalk as he drove away, holding back my conscience. I had only made the fight a little fairer. Matt had his special underwater gun and I had loosened four bars of the aluminum cage, twisting them left instead of right. How hard can a shark really strike a cage? It would be Matt versus the fish, and, as the truck disappeared down Water Street, I had no idea which one would win. Even then, I half-believed in happy endings. Matt and the shark might never find each other in the ocean. Instead, the Great White might cough up every single one of its victims before swimming off, and the town could go on pretending that summer was a harmless season.

NIKKI DOLSON

Neighbors

FROM *Vautrin*

HALFWAY INTO A bottle of wine, I checked my email. All of it
junk mail from crib companies, baby magazines, online dating
sites, etc. Emails I had signed up for over the years, for one reason
or another, but I just couldn't bring myself to unsubscribe from.
Who knew when I might want to update my dating profile or pe-
ruse the baby websites at some later date, in some rebuilt life? Then
I opened the email with my name in the subject line, expecting
nothing more than a phishing attempt or a link to porn, one of
the ways my ex-husband could still track in and out of my life, but
it was neither.

I'm sorry this happened. You deserve so much better. —A

That "A" made me think of Anika. Was this her apologizing after
three years? Maybe she needed some closure. I deleted it. I had
moved on.

Of course, I thought about her for days after. My life now con-
sisted of a small, two-bedroom apartment, work at a midsized engineering company a hallway away from my ex-husband, polite conversations about our daughter and her needs, and wine. Lots and
lots of wine. I hadn't quite made the leap to happy divorcée. Most
nights, after putting my daughter to bed, I drank and surfed the
Internet looking for something. Maybe I'd been looking for Anika
all along.

My life had been contained in the bubble of the neighborhood.
A three-bedroom house on a nice-sized lot, nestled midblock on a

lovely street. I had a good husband. I had good neighbors. We had a good life. Then they showed up. Anika and Adam had been the talk of the neighborhood since that March day when they drove down our streets in their BMWs. He drove the SUV and she was in the sports car. They were a childless couple on a block with children behind nearly every door. The Montessori school was a mere two blocks away from our neighborhood. Our kids would walk in pairs, little backpacks bouncing, that day's parent chaperones in front and behind, keeping them together. Each morning Adam and Anika would wave from their driveway and watch the procession of our littles pass like a parade.

I remember Anika clearly and how much I had wanted to be like her. The sweep of her long braids against her bare shoulders while we stood in backyards holding sweating glasses of iced tea. Her laugh was loud and unselfconscious. She didn't care what any of us thought about her. We'd see her husband drift by her and touch an elbow or draw a fingertip up her bicep. He'd whisper in her ear and her smile would appear. Most of us were in the early years of marriage with small children so we all watched them and took notes. They reminded us how a couple in love should look.

Within a week of their move in someone gave them the password to our neighborhood online board and soon Anika was there, sharing recipes and offering to bake cupcakes for school bake sales. We learned early on that Anika and Adam couldn't have children of their own but participating in our events, cheering our children on, made them feel good, she told us. We liked how invested they were in our kids' welfare. That they cared enough to be involved. She came to soccer and peewee football games, and on the truly hot nights, she made us cold, neon-colored drinks like the casinos made for the tourists, heavy on the alcohol. Collectively, we decided to involve Anika like she was any other parent. She was in our group texts. She offered up costume-making hacks for upcoming St. Patrick's/Easter/Earth Day plays. She became our personal B. Smith. She even took over the book club I ran. Her house was bigger, and under her rule, our group expanded to include more parents from the school. Somehow, she understood them better than I did. Once when I suggested a short story collection to mix things up, she countered with a new romance novel. "*Outlander* but with Black people," she said. It was a hit and for once everyone read that month's book.

Anika sold and managed real estate in the valley and Adam developed and invested in properties. Las Vegas was coming back, they said. It was 2015 and everything was getting better. Some of the neighbors invested with Adam and made money. A string of car washes across the city netted the Chos and O'Briens 20 percent profit over their initial investment. Others went in bigger and helped buy large swaths of undeveloped land on the edges of new subdivisions.

One night after a choir performance at the local library, while Thomas and the other parents wrangled the kids into their coats, Anika took me aside. "I wanted to let you in on a small thing Adam and I are thinking about doing. There's a developer looking to open a few laundromats. One or two definitely near the college, a few more near some apartments. You wouldn't need to invest much, and the return could be fifteen percent over investment."

Could be. That was always a sticking point. No guarantees. It felt so risky. I told her no and she patted me on the shoulder and nodded like she understood. Later Adam bumped into Thomas and me at the grocery store. He helped load two turkeys into my cart and gently, oh so gently, broached the subject of the laundromats. Thomas listened and asked questions. I could see the gears turning and the yes coming. I shut it down. Said no, thank you, and told Adam to come by that weekend for game night. I ushered Thomas away. The next year our daughter, Willa, would be in first grade and we'd agreed to have one more baby to complete our family. But I was thirty-six years old and it wasn't going to be easy this time. We had money set aside for IVF. We couldn't afford to invest and lose the money or at minimum, have it tied up in a land deal for two years or more while the right project was found for the land. Then to go through city approvals and construction and finally selling off what was built, if a buyer could be found. Getting pregnant and gestation were all we wanted to worry about. I should've worried about more.

The second email came a week later with a link to a video. The short message read:

She betrayed me too. —A

She. This wasn't Anika. It was Adam. Adam who disappeared and ruined us all.

I touched the link. Another window opened and the video began. There was a reporter in a parking lot, suited and armed with a black microphone. A white woman earnestly explained why she didn't inoculate her twins and how she was convinced they'd be fine. She was keeping them home for now. The caption beneath them read "Measles outbreak in exclusive enclave."

Another white woman appeared pushing a cart behind the reporter and interviewee. They must be in a grocery store parking lot. A Black woman, with braids just past her shoulder, pushed a cart across the screen too. I leaned in close. She was in a sleeveless shirt, khaki pants, and sandals. Her face was in profile, but I couldn't make it out. Off-screen someone yelled and the Black woman turned. It was Anika, still beautiful and still all smiles. Our Rose Red.

The first adult Halloween party of the season, the first fall party Adam and Anika attended, was thrown in the middle of the school-costume-party scrambles and extra-goodie-bag-creating parties where all the parents huddled in rotating dining rooms assembling twenty-five bags a classroom. I went to the party as Black Barbie, '80s edition. Purple leotard, a crop top that hung off one shoulder with Barbie written in jagged lightning script across the front, pink tights and neon-blue leg warmers for me, and Thomas was a *Less Than Zero*, Robert Downey Jr.–esque Ken doll in a short-sleeve button-down shirt, skinny tie, and pleated khakis, with the sides of his hair slicked back.

We had nothing on Anika and Adam though. Adam wore chain mail and a chest piece with leather leggings and a broad sword on his hip. Anika wore a red full-skirted princess gown. She stood at the entrance to the room, tall and expectant, as if waiting to be seen, waiting for the applause. She floated to the drinks table where I stood. Kat Cho looked her up and down and said, "I don't get it," and went back to crunching on her baby carrot and double-dipping into the ranch.

"I'm Snow White's sister," Anika said.

Kat just shook her head. Leo Madison came swinging into the room and said, "She had a sister? I don't remember that from the movie."

Anika laughed. Smiling and good natured as always. I said, "You're Rose Red."

Anika turned her beatific smile on me. "Yes!"

Leo said, "The fairest of them all, right, Adam? Tommy?" Adam only nodded his head. He was very focused on making drinks.

"Different fairy tale," Thomas said.

We were all in awe of her beauty that night. The way her skin seemed to glow under the lights. It was only later that I realized how Thomas had looked at her. They'd been sleeping together for months by that point and I hadn't known. I pulled at my crop top, declined the wine Leo offered me, and blocked Kat's next attempt to double-dip with my own carrot.

I tried to sleep but the wind blew the branches of a tree against my bedroom windows. The night Thomas and I ended was much the same. The wind smacking the Chos' overgrown oleander bushes into the wood fence that separated our backyards. Anika called. I couldn't understand her through her heaving sobs. I told her I would come over, but she said no. She sniffled and told me Adam had left her. He'd taken their money and was gone. She didn't know what she would do. I was speechless. All this time I thought they were happy like Thomas and I were happy. I told her I would call the next day.

Thomas came home and I had to wait until after he'd crept in to see his sleeping daughter to tell him. I pulled out beers and handed him one. Then in my very best inside voice, I told him about Anika and Adam. I caught the sound of giddiness in my voice and I tried to quash it. The revelation that they weren't perfect electrified me. I talked about them while I paced, drinking and wondering about the ramifications of their marriage ending. Who would bring cupcakes to next week's kindergarten holiday parties? Did Thomas think we should try to find Adam? Did he know where Adam went? Thomas said nothing. He sat with his elbows on his knees, fingers picking at the label on his beer.

"She said he took all the money they had?"

"Yep. Cleaned out their checking accounts." I sat down on the couch and put my feet up on the coffee table. I took a big swallow of beer.

"And the investments?"

"Oh my God," I said, dread finally creeping over me. Our neighbors. Our friends' money. "He wouldn't have. Would he? I'm so glad we didn't go in for that. With the new baby coming."

He cut me off. "You're pregnant?" He sounded panicky instead of happy at the idea. Six months of needles and nothing yet, but I was confident.

"No, but I will be, and we'll need our savings. I doubt I'll want to go back to work right away. Thomas, what's wrong?"

"You're always so busy with the neighbors, with Willa, with work," he said. "I made up excuses to leave the house, to stay out late, and you never questioned me. Did you even notice I was gone?" I thought of all those summer barbecues where we drank too many beers and bottles of wine. Where we lingered too long and mingled too close with other people's spouses. Our kids asleep or watching TV in a neighbor's living room. At some point, I'd lost him and hadn't realized it.

He talked on and my body went numb. Thomas felt guilty about Adam, so he'd given him fifteen thousand dollars of our savings to invest. Anika convinced him it was a good deal. He crouched down in front of me and touched my knee. I looked at his hand on my leggings. How much I loved his touch, but I couldn't feel him now.

"I don't love her," he said. He loved me and Willa and our family.

As he spoke, I kept thinking, we were happy, weren't we? I pulled the knitted blanket off the back of the couch and left him in our living room. I slept on the back seat of my minivan that night, huddled on the bench seat, crying into the stuffed stegosaurus Willa liked to hold when we went on errands.

The next day we found out just how badly Adam had ruined us. Nearly every parent in our online group had given Adam money. We were so easy.

Anika swore she didn't know about the fake land deeds. She didn't know where Adam had gone. Eventually, she moved into a hotel away from us and our gossip. For the next year, we watched each other slowly slip away from our neighborhood. Tears were shed. Houses were sold. Support groups formed and were dismantled within days due to infighting. The police talked to us all. The FBI talked to us. We gave them pictures of Adam, the paperwork full of empty promises, and all our gossip. We pointed fingers at one another. Everyone started driving their children to school. Birthday parties were held at grandparents' homes with only family in attendance. The sidelines at our kids' games were no longer safe spaces. We were not neighbors anymore. We were strangers. Playdates were forever broken.

*

To distract from the eerie quiet of a childless night and the memories of a lost life, I emailed A.

Who is this?

Minutes later, A answered like they'd been waiting all night. Like they'd been waiting for weeks. *You know who this is. What took you so long to respond?*

Where are you, Adam? Belize? Switzerland?

Funny. A Black man in Switzerland won't stand out much.

What do you want?

Nothing. I'm sorry it was you she chose to mess with.

Me? What about our neighbors? We trusted you.

I don't care about them. You were nice but she liked messing with you. That's why she slept with Thomas.

I don't understand.

She thought you had it easy. She had to fight for what she wanted. You got it handed to you.

I didn't want to believe him. Maybe Anika and I weren't best friends, but we had been friendly. It was easier for me to believe it was just Thomas being weak because he was unhappy and not Anika being cruel. I wrote to him, *You said she betrayed you. How?*

She got the police involved too soon. I was barely out of town. I had to hide the money. I got out with barely anything. She has it all.

Why tell me?

I'm going to be caught soon. But they can't touch her. Maybe you can give her hell for me. For us both.

Adam was using me, I was sure, but maybe I could find Anika and make her tell me the why behind it all. I played the video Adam sent again. The clip was over a year old. The news station was Portland based. I did a search for her name. Nothing.

I pulled down an old picture of her from my cloud storage and uploaded it to Google image search. She was Lila Martin now. She ran a small bookstore that was featured in a small business newsletter. Her clients mostly came from a nearby retirement home. She looked the same. All smiles.

The plane ride from Las Vegas to Portland, Oregon, was over two hours long. I drank bourbon on the plane and dozed, dreaming of Anika in my own backyard, our feet dangling in the pool. The night sky exploding with red, white, and blue fireworks. Our spouses inside watching baseball highlights. A mishmash of summer parties that resolved into one particular evening with her.

"How did you get here?" Anika had asked.

"The house? We bought when they were still building this neighborhood."

"No. I mean this life."

"I don't understand."

"The house and the kid." She waved her hand around her head. "This is some very 1950s movie life you've got going on out here."

"You live here too. This is your life."

She laughed. "No. I don't fit here. I don't know how to pretend like you do."

"I'm not pretending."

"I might've made myself fit too if it would've helped me."

"Anika, you fit in here. You're involved in everything here. Everyone comes to you when they have questions or when they need advice."

She patted my leg. "You know, you talk proper even when you're with me and no one else can hear you. You don't switch. You don't have a switch. You make yourself beige for them. You want to be this suburban doll. An average Jane when you could be *more*. You don't have to fit in, but you press your hair straight. With your white husband and your little girl who will always be able to pass."

"Excuse me? I have a good life. A life that looks a lot like yours."

Anika took a long drink from her tumbler of rum and Coke. "Don't get mad now." She laughed and set her glass down between us. Anika slipped into the water fully clothed. Under she went and then she rose up in the middle of the pool, her braids fanned out around her head, a halo of inky blackness stark against the softly lit turquoise pool. I'd been so angry and confused that night. Now I woke up determined as the plane descended.

I rented a car at the airport and put the address of her bookstore in the GPS. I barely saw the town. Traffic was light. There was fog. There were trees. Then there was her bookstore, small and unassuming, on the bottom floor of a white stucco two-story building. The bookstore's door faced out to the intersection.

A bell rang as I entered the space. I half expected her to be standing behind the counter, but no one was. The bookstore was small. The books weren't split into genres but simply arranged alphabetically. Nonfiction and fiction, poetry, and academic texts all shelved together. It seemed lazy and wonderful at the same time.

"Can I help you find something?" a familiar voice said. I turned to see Anika. She was putting books on a shelf behind me. Her mouth fell open and her eyes widened.

"No, I've found what I was looking for." We both started moving down the aisle toward the register. She went behind it. On the counter was a collection of Anne Sexton poems and an Angela Clarke short story collection. I shoved them at her. "These."

"That'll be $38.73."

"Excellent. I'm sure you can afford to cover me." I put the books into my purse.

She frowned then shook her head. "What are you doing here?" she asked.

"You lied. You scammed us."

"Let's not do this here." She came out from behind the counter and helped an older white lady bring her selection of paperbacks to the counter. Regency romances, from the covers. "Mrs. Mavern. How are you?"

I stepped back while they chatted. The door's bell clanged again and a tall man in his twenties walked in. He had tattoos up the arm that held the strap of the backpack he wore. His face was wide and pale and there was an indentation that started above his left eyebrow and disappeared near his hairline. "Hi, Miss Mavern. Miss Martin." His voice was a slow and measured baritone.

"Kevin, help Mrs. Mavern to her car please and do you remember that trunk I have in storage?" He nodded. "Good. Will you bring it for me? Just leave it inside the door. I'm going to lock up early today."

He said okay and Miss Mavern put her hand in the crook of his elbow and the two walked out of the store. Anika turned the sign in the window to CLOSED.

"He must be a help," I said.

"He is. He's the old owner's son. Car accident damaged him." Anika touched her forehead. "But he knows this bookstore better than I do. Keeping him working here is the best decision I made after buying this place."

"Portland prices must have eaten quite a bit of your nest egg."

She rolled her eyes at me and locked the door. "Come on. Let's talk upstairs."

Anika led me up a slim staircase that connected the back of the bookstore to the upper floors. A window at the top of the landing was high to get above the building next door and showed the city laid out under a pale-blue sky.

"Here's my place," Anika said. She opened a door and stopped just inside the doorway to remove her sneakers. The walls were painted a vibrant blue and the floor was white tile. "My mother was a maid. Did you know that?"

"How could I know? All you told us were lies."

"She taught me how to clean. Oh, how I hated it. Do you want tea?" Anika continued, walking deeper into the apartment, her voice growing fainter. Between the living room and the kitchen was a long wood dining table with six chairs.

"Sure," I called. She had pictures on the wall. There was a picture of Adam in khaki shorts and plain white T-shirt standing with one hand on the hood of a car, a desert spreading out behind him.

"That was on our honeymoon. We went to Death Valley." She was behind me. I backed away from her. She glanced down at my feet.

"Yep, my mama was a maid. She taught me to clean floors like this. The secret is a paste made of baking soda and water and bleach. Also you need a stiff fiber brush to really grind the paste in. Tile cracks. The glaze will crack and dirt will get caught and make white turn gray. Shoes carry that dirt." She pointed at my shoes. "Please take your shoes off."

"I'd rather not. I won't be staying long."

"You won't be staying at all if you don't take those shoes off, Val. Unless you want to leave. You can. Right now."

I shook my head.

She turned away when the kettle started to whistle. "Do you want sugar in your tea?"

"Yes, please." I pulled out a chair and sat at the dining room table to unzip my boots. A minute later, Anika was back with jade-green porcelain cups and matching teapot and sugar bowl laid out on a rattan tray. She set it between us on the table and sat across from me. She poured for me and I added sugar cubes. We sipped tea and looked each other over.

"Why did you choose us?"

Her eyebrows raised. "What do you mean?"

"You stole from us."

"Oh, Val. That was Adam. I am so sorry though. I wish I had known." She reached across the table to pat my hand.

"Funny. He says you have the money."

The hand withdrew. "You've been talking to him? What do you want? Money? I don't have much but I can probably get you what you lost."

"I want answers. Why us?" My hands shook. I clasped my cup and drank the rest of my tea.

Anika sighed. "What is the point of this? I tell you and you'll go away?"

"Yes."

"Oh, please. How much money did Thomas give Adam?"

"Fifteen thousand."

"Let me see how much I have." She walked back to the kitchen and opened cabinets and drawers like she was hunting for something. I stood and looked over a bookshelf in the corner. She had one lone cookbook, a compendium of Black Hollywood actors, and one shelf had nothing but books on land development and investments. She wasn't done. This little paradise of a life she was hiding in was temporary. She was waiting for something. I turned my head just as she stepped behind me. I didn't see her hand coming the other direction until it was clasped over my nose and mouth. Her other arm looped around my neck and pulled me backwards. My socked feet slipped on the tile floor. I couldn't get any leverage. She took me down to the floor.

"Hush now. Just breathe."

I opened my eyes. My head hurt and Anika was rolling me over, plastic crinkled under me. "Anika, please."

"You're back. I thought you were out. You know, there were five houses we looked at. Neighborhoods we could move into just like yours. Affluent and ripe. But the house in your neighborhood was available first. I liked your block because of the Chos, that Serbian couple, the Dimtrus, and because of you, actually. We could blend in better on your block and you welcomed us."

"What did I do to you? You stole from us. Thomas. You ruined everything." My tongue felt thick in my mouth. My fingers twitched.

"Oh, poor baby. You know, Adam wanted to stop and stay in that neighborhood. You people gentrified him." She shook her head, amazed. "Anyway, I didn't hate you. I thought we could be friends, but the longer I watched you, the more disgusted I became. So, I screwed your husband and stole your money. I could've done worse."

"We were friends."

She waved my words away. "Really?" She settled down next to me and looked me in the eyes. "When I told you he left me, weren't you a little thrilled? How long did you wait before you called the neighbors to tell them?"

I tried to shake my head but couldn't. She was right. I couldn't wait to tell Thomas that night.

"We could never be friends, Valerie."

I heard metal clink. She lifted her hand to show me the saw. "This is my new start and I won't let anyone steal from me like I stole from you."

E. GABRIEL FLORES

Mala Suerte

FROM *Ellery Queen Mystery Magazine*

AS THEY DROVE away from the Glass Man's house, Carmelita asked the question that had haunted her all her life:

"Do you think bad luck is passed down in families? Is there really such a thing as a family curse?"

When you are a murderer on the run, accompanied by an accessory after the fact, you might as well discuss what brought you to this sorry pass. Better than worrying about what might happen next, bad luck–wise. The dead body in the trunk—a pale form loosely wrapped in an old green sleeping bag like an enormous California roll—could serve as Bad Luck Exhibit A. Did *mala suerte* lurk in a person's DNA like a genetic disease, dormant until life circumstances triggered a flare-up?

"No, that's a ridiculous notion. Bad luck doesn't run in families. How could it?" her companion responded. "There's no such thing as the evil eye or hexes or family curses. You make your own luck. I'm living proof of that."

It was said in such a matter-of-fact way, it brooked no argument.

But as a child, Carmelita had heard the stories that purported to explain the origins of bad luck, *la mala suerte*. A girl—why does it always have to be a girl?—pops open a mysterious box and all the ill fortune flies out into the world. Why do bad things happen to good people? Well, see, it was the fault of that stupid little girl.

Until you realize that the story leaves out the most important bits, like (1) Where did all that bad luck come from to begin with? and (2) If you made a box strong enough to hold all the misfortune in the world, would you leave it lying around where any nosy kid with a penknife could get to it? Wouldn't you weld it shut and leave it at the bottom of the ocean?

"Yeah, Pandora. Right." The passenger smirked in the darkness. "Nowadays that's a music service on the Internet. Times change."

The other so-called explanation says there was this lady—yeah, again, a female—who ate the wrong piece of fruit. And what happened? Pain and suffering for everyone, all because a woman got hungry. How did this story ever catch on? As silly as the one about a girl opening the box. Some dude gathered up all the bad luck in the universe, and instead of blowing it to smithereens like any sane person would, *put it in a goddamn fruit?*

"Oh, Eve and the apple, now that's a classic. My people loved that one. Heap all the blame and guilt on some woman's head. Typical."

Then, with a laugh, "They named a feminine hygiene product after *her.*"

Carmelita looked out the driver's-side window of the car, watching the garish lights of fast-food places sliding by. Talking about eating fruit made her hungry.

"Do you think it's safe to stop for something to eat?"

"No," her partner in crime said. "I don't think that's a good idea. Not yet. Not until we are well out of the city."

They kept driving.

Wherever it came from in the first place, Carmelita thought, she knew that her family had terrible luck. Her father, Glenmore, he had called it bad juju. He told her about how it hit his father, Grandaddy Bartholomew, back in Jamaica.

Handsome and charming, Grandaddy Barth used to be the biggest numbers runner in Montego Bay. Selling numbers was a very lucrative—and very illegal—underground occupation in those days. Grandaddy hired folk from the slums to sell numbers to their neighbors all week. He then pulled the winning numbers every Friday night and delivered the cash prizes in person Saturday morning. Grandaddy Barth also sold lucky-number dream books, magic candles, good-fortune charms, and blessed water to help his customers pick the right numbers. Customers who won had inevitably used one of his dream books or charms—or so Grandaddy said.

On the back of this simple enterprise Grandaddy Barth built a fairy-tale existence—he wore fine clothes, bought a house on the beach, drove a fancy car. He went to the fanciest parties, hobnobbed with reggae stars and politicians. He had lots of lady friends and made many babies. Good fortune poured over him like a waterfall on the Martha Brae River.

Carmelita's companion liked that story. "Your grandaddy was smart. Running a gambling joint is just about the easiest way to make money. As long as you know what you're doing."

Then suddenly, overnight, Grandaddy Barth's luck had turned sour: The country decided to implement a national lottery. The illicit numbers business simply dried up and disappeared, like a water drop on a hot skillet.

Grandaddy Barth never recovered his mojo once the numbers game went legit. He lost the house, the car, the fancy friends. He ended up waiting on tourists—British, Germans, and Americans —in a resort hotel, humiliating himself for tips. It was a terrible comedown, but better than sewing clothes in a noisy, dirty factory or breaking his back in the hot sun on a coffee farm.

Carmelita's father, Glenmore, remembered his daddy as a disappointed, bitter man, with a string of angry women (including Glenmore's own mama) badgering him for his tip money to buy diapers, baby formula, school shoes. Carmelita had learned from her Daddy Glenmore that legit work never pays, not really. If you have to depend on a straight job to make your living, well, that is bad luck for sure.

The passenger beside Carmelita agreed. "Your daddy was right. I read somewhere that you can survive on a normal job, but only if absolutely everything goes your way for, like, twenty years straight. You work for the world's greatest boss, marry the perfect person, buy into the right neighborhood at the right time, never get sick, don't get screwed in a divorce, don't get laid off, don't get hit by lightning, don't get sued, don't speed and get pulled over by the cops when you have a dead person in your trunk . . ."

"Yeah, I guess I better slow down," Carmelita said. "I was going twenty over the speed limit."

On Carmelita's mother's side, bad luck ran like water out of a busted drainpipe. Her Mama Beatriz said it started with their ancestors back in Mexico. Quetza, a Toltec noblewoman, was given in marriage to Huatemoc, an Aztec man from a powerful family. Quetza bore Huatemoc many children, and then, it appears, the Aztec in-laws were done with her.

When the youngest male child was about a year old and deemed strong enough to survive, the proud father, Huatemoc, appeared on top of the pyramid of the sun for the spring festival wearing the flayed skin of his wife, Quetza, as a cloak.

You can't scrape the hide off a Toltec noblewoman and walk away, so there was a war over that, but still. It doesn't get much worse than being killed and made into a windbreaker.

"Is that a true story?" Carmelita's companion asked.

"True as anything," Carmelita replied, squinting at the road.

More years of bad luck went by, until one of Quetza's descendants, a mestiza slave, disappeared with a chest of gold coins and her two children by the landowner. The rich man was found dead in one of his outbuildings, a large kitchen knife in his stomach. The wily woman had disguised herself in the clothes of her own mistress and had bribed a ship's captain with gold to take her and the children away from Spanish colonial Mexico to start a new life in Spanish colonial Cuba.

"Now that's what I'm talking about, Carmelita. There was a woman who took charge. She made her own luck."

They kept driving and talking, talking and driving.

After several generations, Mama Beatriz's family had left their humble origins behind and were firmly ensconced in the upper echelons of Cuban sugar-plantation society. Life was good, for a while. And then the bad luck reared its head again like a horror-movie monster.

Not-yet-Mama Beatriz was eight years old when her family flew from Havana to the United States to spend some sugar dollars on a lavish month-long vacation. First, a week of shopping in Miami, shipping their purchases from the finest stores back home to Cuba. Next, a week of sightseeing in New York City, visiting the Statue of Liberty and the Empire State Building. Then across the vast continent by rail, to end their holiday in a newly opened amusement park, Disneyland.

The family never got to see the Magic Kingdom. Shortly after arriving at the train station in Los Angeles, they discovered that the US-backed Batista government had been overthrown by Castro and his Communist rebels. Relatives and friends still in Cuba were being arrested and jailed. Little Beatriz and her family were targeted by the new regime as enemies of the state. All their property—homes, businesses, land, automobiles—appropriated by the government. Their bank accounts, frozen; their assets, liquidated.

The family took the Greyhound bus from California back to Miami. With English skills limited to dimly remembered private-school lessons, and the need to earn a basic living, the formerly wealthy Cuban exiles found themselves cleaning hotel rooms and washing dishes in restaurant kitchens.

Beatriz eventually met Glenmore, a handsome immigrant from Jamaica. The couple had two children and supported them by selling merchandise of questionable origins. Carmelita and her brother, Daniel, grew up in a freewheeling environment of scrappy survivors living on the fringes of middle-class normality, bouncing between Miami's various Caribbean immigrant communities.

Daddy Glenmore took his children along on his frequent trips to secret hidey-holes in the swamplands northwest of the city to park stolen merchandise until things cooled off, returning to retrieve the items when he later wanted to sell them.

That is where Carmelita and her companion were now heading — to one of these secret swamp hideaways. With a dead body in the trunk . . .

One day Daddy Glenmore left, lured back to Jamaica by a highly lucrative new scam based on the country's national lottery. For a while, he sent money to help Beatriz out, but when he got a new woman and had more kids, the money stopped. Carmelita stayed out of trouble, but her brother, Daniel, became wild and ran with a gang. He got lots of tattoos, used drugs, was in and out of jail.

Daniel became sick and was diagnosed with AIDS. He said he got it from an infected needle in prison, but Carmelita knew different. While visiting him in the public hospital, she had seen the name BERTRAN tattooed inside a heart on her brother's chest. At Daniel's funeral, she saw the boyfriend, sitting in a far corner at the back of the church, crying by himself. Shortly thereafter, Mama Beatriz also died, of grief, so everyone said.

"Things like that happen to lots of people. Nothing to do with a curse. Your family wasn't singled out."

"Maybe not. But how do you explain why my mother's life was just one long suck? My brother's too. Everything went wrong."

After her mother died, Carmelita was alone in the world. Social services placed her in a group home where she and a boy named Silvio became an item. She earned her GED certificate and got a series of low-paid, mindless, uninspiring jobs. One day, while putting in more applications at the local mall, Carmelita joined a crowd watching a man in a kiosk demonstrating glassblowing. It was fascinating, how he could control the molten glass with a blowtorch and treat it like a liquid, swirling it quickly, magically, into colorful shapes—swans, hearts, stars, and flowers. He was middle-aged, ponytailed, and bearded, dressed like a leftover hippie in patched jeans and a leather vest.

After his demonstration, the crowd pushed forward to buy his "hand-blown glass gifts and ornaments," mostly smaller versions of the swans and so forth that he had made. Carmelita watched silently as the man wrapped up the delicate glass objects and rang up the purchases. She estimated that he had entranced the crowd for fifteen minutes or so with his glassblowing and had then taken in several hundred dollars in about three-quarters of an hour. There was definitely potential here. When the crowd had dispersed, Carmelita remained behind.

The Glass Man put up a sign that promised, in puffy psychedelic lettering, NEXT DEMONSTRATION IN 30 MINUTES. He noticed Carmelita standing alone watching him, her arms folded across her chest.

"What do you want, miss? A pretty glass swan?" he asked.

Carmelita raised a skeptical eyebrow and pointed at the tiny swans swimming around little glass flowers on shaped mirrors.

"I want to know when you have time to make all those little versions of the big ones."

"C'mere." The Glass Man beckoned her over. "I can tell you have the heart of a scammer, because I am one myself."

He reached under the counter and pulled out a cardboard box. It was full of white tissue paper. He set it on the counter.

"Look in there." She did. Nestled in the paper were dozens of tiny glass swans.

Carmelita picked up one carefully and turned it over.

"See the label stuck on the bottom? I get this shit for pennies apiece from Asia. In the two months before Christmas I make about half my year's straight income."

"What do you do to earn your crooked income?"

"Bongs and pipes, *chica*. Custom dope-smoking paraphernalia. That's what I make most of my money on." He laughed and winked. Carmelita smiled back.

She leaned on the counter and pointed at the cardboard box. "You could move a lot more of this penny shit from Asia if someone else started doing the selling while you were still doing your demonstration."

"Someone else meaning a sharp young lady such as yourself?"

"Yes."

"You have papers to work? Not that I care, since I would pay you in cash. But I am supposed to ask."

"I can work legally. I'm good with numbers. And I have my high-school equivalency."

"You're hired. Start tomorrow. Be here at nine to help me set up. The mall stores open at ten."

And so it began, the business partnership between the young Jamaican-Cuban and the old hippie. In the kiosk they looked like a magician and his attractive female assistant. The Glass Man moved a lot more merchandise with Carmelita ringing up the purchases while he did the glassblowing.

Carmelita treated the ornaments like exotic treasures, wrapping the delicate glass pieces in tissue and placing them in small boxes with care as if they were from the Ming dynasty. "After all," she remarked to him after a thousand-dollar day during the holiday season, "this is as close to a rare Chinese artifact as these folks are ever going to get."

Time passed and soon they had accumulated enough money to open a permanent gift shop in the mall. Now they sold year-round, while the Glass Man kept doing his glassblowing demos in a kiosk in front of the store. Carmelita helped to expand the business on-line and took care of the books, keeping two sets. One set was for the gift shop and the other for the paraphernalia business. She and her boyfriend, Silvio, moved out of the group home and into an apartment not far from the Glass Man's house.

Carmelita suggested selling weed along with the glass parapher-nalia. The Glass Man readily agreed. She didn't smoke, but Silvio did and used his contacts to secure a regular supply of the drug. The Glass Man gave Carmelita a set of keys to his place so she could deliver the marijuana whenever Silvio brought it home. Now they were running three businesses, each bringing in several thousand dollars a month.

But then the bad luck raised its head, this time in the form of a woman.

Asmarte Rose had driven down from New York and was living in her RV on the edge of the mall parking lot. She was thin, pale, frizzy-haired, and in her forties. She wore gauzy, drapey clothes and lots of jewelry. When she talked—and she seemed to talk nonstop —her voice was artificially soft, her innocent brown eyes wide and credulous. Carmelita had once seen an old movie with the actress Marilyn Monroe in it. Asmarte talked like that, in a breathy whisper, childish and seductive at the same time.

Within a week, Asmarte was parking her RV in the Glass Man's driveway and a month after that she had moved in with him. Carmelita was irritated with the woman from the first. "Why the hell can't she speak up and talk like an adult?" she thought to herself.

Her behavior was obviously an act, a silly and contrived phony persona, but the Glass Man seemed to buy it.

Where Carmelita was hardheaded and believed in nothing —except in, perhaps, *mala suerte*—Asmarte professed to believe in absolutely everything: she carried on about yoga, astral projection, kabbalah, tantric sex, acupuncture, goddess energy, natural foods, hypnosis, alien abductions, feng shui, alternate universes, Sasquatch.

She said that she was a "free spirit" just like the Glass Man. Her business card said "Wellness Therapist." Of course, she endorsed the medical use of marijuana. Of course.

One day, out of the blue, the Glass Man announced to Carmelita that Asmarte was going to run part of their enterprise. Not everything, he said, just the marijuana end of the business, which was currently having a setback. Carmelita had found out what she had suspected from secretive texts and phone calls—that her boyfriend, Silvio, had a longtime baby mama. After an ultimatum from Carmelita, he had left to move in with the woman and their two-year-old child. Good riddance, but no more weed from him.

It was just a matter of time until Carmelita secured a new supplier. She saw no reason to turn the trade over to some ditsy flower child who had rolled in from New York. It was the first disagreement she and the Glass Man had ever had. The money had been split two ways and was now going to be divided into three. Carmelita knew that it would not end there. She determined that this woman, bringer of bad luck, had to go.

Asmarte had taken to making a grayish-brown yeasty substance in a bowl and leaving it in the Glass Man's fridge. Every evening she would drain off some of the nasty-looking liquid into a glass to drink and add more water to the bowl. She called it kombucha, claiming that it was healthy. Carmelita had tasted it once and could not swallow more than a sip of the vile-smelling, sour-tasting fluid. It tasted of dirt and decay, like drinking a grave.

A plan began to form. Carmelita knew what days each month the mall exterminators came. The next time they sprayed for roaches and put down poison to kill vermin, she followed them and quietly obtained a quantity of the rat poison. She tested it on some rats that had made a nest in the alley behind her building and found that it was indeed lethal—the rats died within minutes of eating the tainted food she set out. Choosing a time when she knew the Glass Man was going to be gone overnight visiting friends, she let herself into the kitchen and added the substance to Asmarte's kombucha bowl.

After Asmarte drank her usual big glass of the stuff that evening, she would be dead. Carmelita only had to drag the body out to the woman's RV under cover of darkness, drive to her Daddy Glenmore's secret swamp hideaway, and abandon the body there. Asmarte would become one of Miami's many missing persons, and the business would go on as before.

Late that night, Carmelita returned to the Glass Man's house to find, as she had expected, a dead body lying stretched out on the kitchen floor. But it was not Asmarte. It was the Glass Man. The half-full kombucha bowl sat on the counter beside a glass with a bit of the stuff still in the bottom. The Glass Man had apparently come home early and had drunk Asmarte's poisoned kombucha.

Her mind in a whirl, she heard someone come into the house. Carmelita looked up in panic, her hand flying to her throat. It was Asmarte. Next would come police, neighbors, jail. Carmelita should have known that it would go all wrong. It was the family curse.

Asmarte stood in silence for several moments, looking up at the stricken Carmelita and down at the Glass Man's body on the floor. Then she spoke. "Is he dead?" she asked. Carmelita stammered that it was an accident, that something was wrong with the kombucha, that—

The other woman made a calming gesture. "What's done is done," she said. Her voice was pitched low, with a hard, flat inflection, totally unlike the irritating whisper she had affected as long as Carmelita had known her.

Carmelita stared at the other woman. Asmarte said, "You thought it would be me, didn't you? I've had him drinking this stuff for a few weeks now. How could you have known?" She smirked. "I told him it would help with his virility." She shrugged. "It didn't."

Carmelita swallowed, her heart beating in her throat. Was her luck going to hold or give out? "Why aren't you calling the police?" she asked.

"Because I go with the flow. The flow just turned away from this guy"—she pointed at the man on the floor—"and is aimed in your direction. A two-way split is way better than three ways, isn't it, sweetcakes? By the way, what were you going to do with my body?"

"I—I was planning to take it north to a hidden swamp place I know about," Carmelita said reluctantly. It was weird to talk about getting rid of Asmarte's body with her standing right there. "I was going to . . . dump it out there."

"Uh-hmm. Since I only weigh a scrawny hundred and forty-five, you figured you could wrestle my carcass out of here by yourself." Asmarte was frowning absently, tapping her fingers on the table, like she was trying to decide whether they should order barbeque or Thai.

Her face cleared; she had made up her mind. "Okay. We will go on with your plan. He weighs about two seventy-five, so it will take the both of us to handle him. It's dark enough now. I'll get his keys and you can pull his car around back."

The two women unzipped an old sleeping bag, rolled the Glass Man up in it, and carried him down the back stairs. Once he was safely locked in the trunk, they returned to clean the kitchen, thoroughly scrubbing the floor and flushing the remaining poisoned kombucha down the john. They each threw a change of clothes and a spare pair of shoes in a backpack, put the kombucha bowl and glass into a plastic trash bag in the back seat, and took off for the swamplands, a three-hour drive away.

As she drove, Carmelita told Asmarte about Quetza and her grandfather Bartholomew. About her father Glenmore leaving them, and about her brother Daniel dying. About Mama Beatriz, who never got to see Disneyland. All the family stories of *mala suerte* and misfortune. Carmelita left out the part about how much she had disliked Asmarte Rose when they first met. That was probably self-evident; after all, she had tried to poison the woman.

Asmarte told Carmelita that bad luck was bullshit. "You make your own luck in this world," she said. "Life is ninety percent chance and ten percent genetics. And that ten percent genetics? That's chance too. Nobody gets to choose the hand they get dealt at birth. But everyone gets to play that hand out.

"Look at me. My real name? Rosie Lorraine Shulman. That's where I got the Rose part. I saw the word Asmarte on an old perfume bottle in a thrift shop and I thought, that's me: As Smart as anyone else. My ancestors came from crappy stinking villages in the rich cabbage and turnip lands of Eastern Europe. Every few years some bastard's army would tromp through and kill everyone who couldn't run away fast enough. The borders changed hands so many times, people didn't know what the hell their religion or nationality would be the next month. You don't get much worse luck than being born into that. Only difference between your people and mine is that my slave ancestors froze while they starved."

"So what did they do to make their own luck?"

"Bought themselves some forged papers with different names so the Nazis or the Cossacks or who the hell ever couldn't find them, got on a boat, and started making bank as soon as they got to New York."

"Folks would want them deported, they try that today."

"Damn straight. What had following rules ever done for them but get them stepped on by the people who made up the rules? My people did whatever they had to do to survive and taught their kids to do the same. They couldn't afford to believe in good or bad luck.

"So here we are, you and me, kiddo. We are making our own luck. With a dead man in the trunk. Can you believe this mess?" Asmarte laughed.

Carmelita laughed too, the absurdity of their situation vying with the lingering shock to create a feeling of near hysteria. "You may be right, Asmarte," she said. "This may just turn out to be my lucky day."

An hour more of driving passed. The travelers decided it was safe to get some food, gas up, and stretch their legs. Carmelita was bemused at how glibly the professed health nut Asmarte ordered meals from the fast-food menu by number. When candy bars, snack cakes, and bags of chips from the gas-station convenience store appeared in the car, Carmelita had to comment. "Isn't this stuff bad for you?"

"What?" Asmarte responded. "You expected fresh-squeezed juice and organic produce from a 7-Eleven?"

Then it was back on the road and more driving, toward the fringes of the Everglades.

They planned their future on the road.

"No reason for us to spend twenty-to-life in prison for wanting to make a living, right? So here's what we gotta do. First, we get to your daddy's swamp and leave this poor guy there; he's dead and nothing will change that. Second, we go back to Miami and go on with the business as usual. After a few weeks we report him missing."

Carmelita was getting into the spirit of the thing. She added, "Third, we get rid of all those stupid glass trinkets—shit wasn't selling anyway, and the store was starting to look more like what it really is, a dusty front for hippies selling weed."

"I like how you think, Carmelita. Fourth, we rebrand the shop to carry new-agey merchandise instead, keeping the weed business going strong on the side. We live simply, save our money, pay our taxes, donate to the animal shelter, volunteer at the food bank, and keep our noses clean."

"And fifth," Carmelita said, "when we have enough scratch to retire, we pack up and buy a bed-and-breakfast hotel in a nice warm place like Mexico or Jamaica."

"Exactly. I always knew you were the brains of the operation. We'll be sitting pretty until they legalize weed in this state. Gotta plan ahead so we don't get caught with our pants down like your grandaddy when they legalized the lottery. I figure we have about ten years max before Amazon is home-delivering cannabis cookies by drone."

In one of the alternate universes—that Asmarte Rose did not really believe in—the two women reached the hidden swampland and dragged the sleeping-bag-wrapped body from the trunk. With the car's headlights creating a circle of visibility, the conspirators carried the body out to the edge of a pond and waded into the slimy dark water waist-deep, pushing it out as far as they dared go. They climbed onto the pond's muddy edge and watched the sleeping bag, a pair of sandaled white feet sticking out one end, slowly sink into the murky depths.

Back at the car, the women changed into the dry clothes they had brought with them, bagging up the sodden, smelly ones and discarding them in another pond nearby. They hid the bag with the poisoned kombucha materials in yet another swampy pool. Then they drove back to Miami, where they took long, hot showers.

They never spoke of that awful night again, and managed, just as they had outlined on that fateful night, to successfully convert their front business from low-end gifts to upscale new-age products: hemp yoga mats from Nepal, books on connecting with past lives, probiotic vegan energy bars, scented oils to combat the stresses of modern life, antiaging herbal teas that flushed out wrinkle-producing toxins.

Within a decade, cannabis legalization finally dried up their weed business, as Asmarte had predicted. The partners had amassed several hundred thousand dollars in each of many offshore accounts. They sold the new-age shop at cost to three earnest polyamorous tech zillionaires, and bought a B and B in the Yucatán on the Caribbean coastline.

In that universe, you can find Carmelita and Asmarte Rose living the good life, drinking piña coladas with cute college boys from the Midwest, enjoying late seafood suppers on the beach with handsome retired Brazilian soccer stars, and arranging day trips to the Mayan ruins for wealthy European tourists.

However, we are in this universe. The one where, about two hours out of Miami, with Asmarte now behind the wheel, the right front tire blew. The car swerved and limped onto the shoulder of the road. A state-trooper patrol car pulled up behind them within minutes, the rotating roof light illuminating the night.

The female trooper got out first and approached the driver's side. Carmelita and Asmarte sat stone-faced and sweating in the sudden closeness of the car, contemplating their all-too-brief future as free citizens.

The officer asked for license and registration. Lorraine Shulman from New York and Miami pulled her ID from her wallet while Carmelita rummaged in the glove compartment and found the Glass Man's car registration. The other trooper got out of the patrol vehicle and stood on the passenger side while his partner inspected the documents.

"The car is registered to a Jack Albinini. A friend's car?" she asked.

"Yes, Officer. Just borrowing it for the evening."

"Well, we don't see any reason to let this flat tire hold you ladies up. If you would pop your trunk latch, Ms. Shulman, my partner and I can help you change your tire and then you can be on your way. Lucky for you both that we were passing by, huh?" She leaned down and smiled at the women in the car.

In an alternate universe . . . but no, not this time. The trooper lady was going to open the trunk and let all the bad luck out into the world, thought Carmelita. Then the two women in the dead Glass Man's car would indeed be on their way—to prison. For murder.

Quetza, Beatriz, Bartholomew, Daniel. Carmelita. The Glass Man, the very unfortunate Jack Albinini. Now Lorraine Shulman, aka Asmarte Rose. Yes, bad luck was inherited. It was also contagious.

ALISON GAYLIN

Where I Belong

FROM *Coast to Coast Noir*

SOME CARS, YOU stay away from: Full-sized vans with sliding doors. Town cars with tinted windows. Anything you can't see into thoroughly. I was told this by Larry, an old junkie I met on the FDR a few days after I ran away from home. There's a reason, he told me, why they don't want you to see inside.

Larry could have been anywhere from fifty to one hundred years old and he smelled like ass, but I did trust him on the car thing. "I've hit up probably five thousand drivers so I know what I'm talking about," he told me. "I've been on the street for ten years."

Ten years. I mean, come on. Ten years ago, I was eight.

Anyway, a traffic jam is a captive audience, and the FDR (aka Fuck Dis Road) is a nonstop traffic jam. So, for a couple of days there, Larry and I had a pretty good thing going. We'd split up, knock on windows, and show them our signs: NEED FOOD. WILL WORK FOR $$. JESUS LOVES YOU. The soft-hearted types would throw cash at Larry because he looked so pathetic, and I'd get the scared ones because I'm a big dude—six foot three, two hundred thirty pounds. At the end of the day, we'd pool our earnings, split everything fifty-fifty, and go our separate ways. It was working until Larry decided to go his separate way and never come back, taking all the money with him, along with my duffel bag and iPhone. That was a week ago. Fucking junkie.

It's a hot day. That type of New York summer heat when the air feels solid and weepy and when you take a deep breath, it's almost like drowning. I'm moving down the center of the FDR with my old sign in my hand, but at this point I think I'm probably both scary and pathetic, so I'm not getting any takers. Everything stinks of exhaust fumes and the car windshields shimmer at me. I'm pretty sure I'm going to die soon.

I don't know how long I've been out here, but it's long enough to start thinking that it was a stupid idea to run away, that I should go back home to Staten Island and apologize to my mom and stepdad for making them nervous, because they have to be nervous, right? I've been gone for so long. And if they've tried calling, they've gotten crazy-ass junkie Larry, or whoever he sold my iPhone to, probably telling them I died or something. If I were to go home now, they'd think I was a ghost.

I picture myself banging on the front door and them opening it. My mom hugging me and crying and jumbling her words together, the way moms on TV do when their missing kids come home unharmed. "ThankGodyou'reback—wherewereyou—weweresoworried—isitreallyyou—it'samiracle . . ." But then I remember. It was my mom who kicked me out of the house, not the other way around. I think about all the shitty names she called me, how she told me to never come back and she hopes I drop dead, and I let go of my sign and fall to my knees, right in the middle of the FDR. You don't belong in this home. You don't belong here. I'm sobbing like a girl now, my stomach churning, the pavement hot on my hands and arms, then my lips, then my forehead. Horns blare. I taste blood in my mouth.

This is it. This is how I'm going to go. Facedown on the FDR, crushed under the wheels of some pissed-off Tesla driver. And no one is going to miss me. No one at all.

"Hey." It's a woman's voice. My mom's voice.

But when I push myself up from the macadam to look at her, I can see even through tears and bright sun that she's not my mom. I can also see that she's driving a white, full-sized van with sliding doors.

"Get in," she says. Or "Get him." I'm not sure which. The van's door slides open and some big guy spills out of it and yanks me up to my knees and shoves me in.

Any other time, I would have yelled and kicked and thrown punches. But not now. I just let him do it. There are seats inside the van and I collapse onto one, the air conditioning washing over me. I figure he's going to slug me or shoot me in the head or worse, but I'm too tired to fight back or even care. What he does, though, is this: He pulls the seat belt over me and buckles me in, as though I were a little kid. Then he slips into the front passenger's seat. I close my eyes, fuzzy images of long-ago road trips with my parents, my real parents. My dad singing along with corny country songs on the radio. My mom laughing. The leather seat hugs me.

"Are you all right?" The woman says it like she knows it's a stupid question.

"Yes, ma'am."

"Are you sure? Do you need to see a doctor?"

"No, ma'am."

The man says, "We're driving home, but we live far from here. The Hudson Valley."

I'm not sure how I'm supposed to answer. "Oh?"

He turns around in his seat and looks at me. He has a shaved head that seems as though it was carved out of granite. His fist sits on the chair, the size of a catcher's mitt. He's old—forty at least—but there's no question he could beat the crap out of me.

"Would you like to stay with us?" he says. "We live upstate. Just outside of Woodstock."

There are times in your life when you're forced to weigh options. Either one feels doable, and the best choice keeps shifting back and forth to the point where you feel like you can't trust your own instincts and you wind up paralyzed.

But when your skin is raw and peeling and your stomach is sucking in on itself and your throat feels as though someone rubbed it with sandpaper, options aren't a thing—especially when you're in a moving vehicle, strapped to a chair. "Sure," I tell the man.

There's a small cooler between the two front seats. He flips open the top, hands me a cold bottle of water. He smiles, and it's like a fissure in the earth. "Bet you're thirsty," he says.

I drink three bottles of water, then pass out for most of the ride. When I wake up, it's dark, and my ears are clicking. We're driving up a mountain, a twisting road shrouded with trees. The front windows of the van are rolled down and the air is warm and alive with crickets. It's like nothing I've ever seen or felt, but it brings back memories: summer camp, toasting marshmallows, having a home to miss. It isn't 'til I'm fully awake that I notice that the man and woman are whispering furiously to each other.

"I don't know," the woman says. "I just don't know."

I clear my throat.

The man says, "You awake, son?"

"Yes, sir."

"Well then. Welcome to our home."

The woman huffs out a sigh.

We're pulling up a driveway now, so steep it's almost perpendicular to the road below. She parks the van, gets out, slams the door without saying anything. I watch her through the windshield. She is tall and slim and wears a tight skirt, and as she heads for the door, she doesn't turn around. Not even once. All these hours, and I still don't fully know what her face looks like.

As I unlock my seat belt, the man gets out of the van and opens my door from the outside. "Is she mad?" I ask him.

He shakes his head. "No, Kurt."

I blink at him. "You know my name?"

"Yep."

"How?"

"The video."

"Video?"

He just looks at me.

"Oh . . . I . . . There's a video?"

"Viral."

"Oh . . . Oh God."

"We're not big Internet people, though. We saw it on the local news."

"Look. Look. I can explain . . ."

"No explanations necessary, man." He smiles again, teeth gleaming. "I get it. I get angry too."

The house is built into the side of the mountain—all glass and sleek lines like a rich person's house from some nineties movie. By the time the man and I are inside, she's already in the bedroom, the door slammed behind her. He leans in close, speaks in a whisper. "My wife didn't recognize you 'til you were sleeping. She wanted to throw you out of the car, but I wouldn't let her."

It's like I've been dropped into deep water, and I have to start treading. "I . . . I didn't mean to hurt him. I swear."

He puts a finger to his lips. "Like I said. I get it."

"No sir, no. With all due respect I don't think . . ."

He hands me his phone. The video's rolling. Two guys yelling at each other on a square patch of lawn, the taller one slugging the other in the head, then knocking him to the grass and kicking him —a much older man, his hands covering his face . . . Monster, I want to say. Because even though I know it happened, it's hard for me to believe that the tall guy was me, just two or three weeks ago. The older guy was my stepfather.

"What made you so angry, son?"

"I . . . I don't know."

"I think you do." The man takes the phone back. Claps me on the shoulder. I almost fall to the ground. "Videos like that. They only tell one side of the story."

I try and think back on it, but I come up with nothing. Everything's such a blur since she kicked me out. The nights under the overpass by the side of the FDR, Larry shooting up beside me. The hot sun and the cheap beers and bags of fast-food scraps, slipped through the windows of cars. Like a dream you never wake up from, the kind caterpillars must have when they're in the chrysalis, their body parts rearranging. Here in his sleek living room, the big, bald man looks older, kinder. He feels like a second chance, and so I can't lie to him. "I'm sorry," I say. "I really don't remember."

He nods. "Okay. Well . . . help yourself to whatever you can find in the kitchen," he says. "The guest room's over there to your left. It's got a bathroom, with clean towels in it. Take a shower. Catch a few hours of sleep."

"Thank you."

"I gotta get you out of here in the morning though, okay? I promised my wife."

"Yes, sir." I look around the living room—there's a big comfy couch and a glass-topped coffee table with photographs all over it. The bald guy and the woman wearing leis on white sand. Another of her blowing out candles, the man beaming next to her. Still another of the two of them, toasting each other with champagne. She has blond highlights, high cheekbones, the type of smooth, shiny skin that only rich women have. She's probably my mom's age, and

I have to say, she doesn't look younger than her; just better taken care of. "I'm sorry if I made her upset," I tell the man.

He shrugs it off. "Women."

"Yeah."

"Listen though, can I offer you one bit of advice?"

I look at him.

"You're practically unrecognizable with that beard." He says it with a smile. "I wouldn't shave it off if I were you."

The guest room is all white—walls, bedding, dresser, draperies —all of it spotless, the way my house never was. There's a white terry-cloth robe hanging on a hook in the guest bathroom. After I shower, I put it on and get under the white comforter. It feels like I'm in the middle of a cloud, or in heaven.

As I drift off, my mind clears for a few seconds and I remember three weeks ago—the fight on the front lawn, my stepfather's bloody face, the neighbors screaming, my mother calling the police and shielding him. Coughing blood. His teeth on the lawn. My mother's voice: "That's right, run, you little piece of shit. Get out of here and never come back. If I see you again, I'll have you arrested. You don't belong in this home. You belong in jail."

I remember running until my lungs ached, 'til the muscles in my legs felt like broken rubber bands, my fists clenched so tight, it was as though they'd never come undone.

I want to believe I had a reason. I want to believe I was justified in what I did to him—a man forty years older than me and fifty pounds lighter. I want to say I snapped after months of cruelty and verbal and physical abuse. But it wouldn't be true.

The truth is, I have a bad temper. I beat the crap out of my stepfather because he cut off my allowance. "You're eighteen. You have to get a job," he had said. "Money doesn't come easy. You need to learn that."

The truth is, I'm an asshole. It's the last thought I have before falling asleep.

"Okay, Kurt, up and at 'em," says the bald man, whose name I still haven't learned. He's standing over the bed, light pouring in through the white draperies and haloing all around him. "Gotta get you outta here before the wife gets up."

I rub sleep out of my eyes. My clothes are neatly folded at the foot of the bed, a stack of twenty-dollar bills resting on top of them.

"Washed your clothes," the man says.

I sit up in bed. My throat tightens. I have to swallow hard to keep from crying. I don't deserve this. I don't deserve any of this.

"I wish I could pay you back."

He smiles in such a way, it's hard to tell what he's thinking. "Get yourself changed, buddy."

He leaves the room. I dress quickly, count the money out. It's a hundred bucks—less than I'd hoped. I pocket it, hoping Woodstock isn't as expensive as NYC.

We drive down the mountain in silence. The clock in his car reads 6 a.m., and the sky is still pink from the sunrise. He makes a few turns, until we're on a narrow street with a few restaurants, some art galleries, and hippy-type gift stores, the windows packed with tie dye and bongs. Everything is clean and colorful and, except for a Cumberland Farms, everything's closed. "We're here," he says, pulling into the Cumby's.

I gaze up and down the street. I see a health food store. A bank. "Where's the rest of the town?"

He smiles. "This is it, pal," he says. "Greater metropolitan Woodstock. Home of peace and love." He says goodbye, and I get out of the van. Take in the clean morning air, the chirping birds. My new home, I think. It doesn't make me very happy.

At Cumberland Farms, I buy a breakfast sandwich, a couple bags of Funyuns, a big bottle of water, four ready-made sandwiches, and some gum. I try to buy a six-pack, but the frizzy-haired woman behind the counter cards me and I remember I have no ID—fake or otherwise—thanks to Larry. I figure I look older with the beard, though, so I give it a shot. "I left my driver's license at home," I tell her. "I'm twenty-four, I swear."

"Uh huh."

"Come on. It's just beer."

"You gotta be twenty-one," she says. "See the sign?" She gestures with her head at a sign behind her: YOU MUST BE 21 TO BUY ALCOHOL.

I feel anger bubbling up inside me. "That sucks."

"I don't write the laws."

"I know, but . . ."

"No ID, no beer. That's how we roll."

I hate Woodstock. I hate it more than the underpass next to the FDR. Hate it more than my mother or my stepfather or Larry, who at least bought me beers. "Fine." I say it between clenched teeth. I want to break everything in the place. Instead, I buy a JUUL starter pack and some extra pods. My bill is close to eighty bucks.

"Fucking great," I whisper.

She glares at me as I dole out the cash. "You look familiar," she says.

I aim my eyes at the floor. "We've never met."

"No, but you're . . . I've seen you somewhere. Recently."

"I've never been in this town before," I say. "Can I just buy my stuff, please?"

"Wait a minute . . . Aren't you . . ."

"No."

"You're Kurt Campbell. From Staten Island."

"I don't know who that is."

"Don't bullshit me, Kurt Campbell. I have a photographic memory."

"I swear I'm not . . ."

"You're even wearing the same clothes. Jesus. The same clothes as in the video. Oh my God. It's you."

"Can I have my change, please?"

"You're sick, you know that? What you did to that man. Your own stepfather. There's something wrong with you."

"I'm not him," I say. "I'm not Kurt . . ."

"What are you even doing here?"

"I . . . I . . ."

"You should be in jail. There's a warrant out on you. I'm calling the police."

"No, please."

She picks up her phone, and I get out of there fast, running down the silent street, sweat pouring down my back. Last night, I emptied that couple's refrigerator before I took a shower and went to bed, and I'm regretting it now—the leftover spaghetti and the pint of Ben and Jerry's and the entire box of Hot Pockets. It's slowing me down now, all that food. I've got a stitch in my side.

I see a police car ambling up the road about three blocks away, and I pivot up a side street, past a real estate office and a clothing place and an art gallery with a flower on the sign, and I keep it up, this wheezing, painful run, up a sloping hill and through some open gates and onto a field.

I run until I can't run anymore, and I'm bent over, grasping my knees, struggling for air. Finally, once I've caught my breath, I look around. I'm in a cemetery. Perfect.

I sit down on the damp grass, thinking about that bitch in Cumby's, how I'd run out of there without taking my food or my money or even the damn JUUL. I want to cry again, but I won't. I'm never going to cry again. I lean up against a headstone and stare up at the sky.

Back when my real dad was alive and my mom still loved me, she used to take me to church every Sunday. I'd fuss about the starched collar she made me wear, the stupid clip-on tie and the uncomfortable shoes. But deep down, I liked it. The smell of the candles and the priest's soothing voice and my mom's hand on my shoulder —it all made me feel . . . This is going to sound weird, but it made me feel safe. Listened to. Understood. I used to pray there too. I didn't just pretend. "God always answers your prayers," Mom used to say. "It just may not be the answer you expect."

A cemetery may not be a church, but it's as good a place to pray as any. So, I close my eyes and I pray for something, anything, anybody, to get me out of this town. "Please," I whisper, again and again, "take me to where I belong."

It has to be an hour later, maybe even two, when the bald guy shows up at the cemetery gates. He's behind the wheel of the white van, and when he calls out to me, I get up and jog over to him, thinking about prayers and unexpected answers.

"What?"

"You heard me."

"You want me to—"

"Kill me."

The bald guy and I are sitting in his van. It's started to rain— one of those crazy summer downpours, big drops splashing on the windshield, gusts of wind bending the trees. The perfect backdrop for this conversation, which had started with, "Remember back at the house, when you said you wish you could pay me back?" and ended with what he just said. Kill me. Is everybody in this town freakin' nuts?

"Why would you want me to kill you?"

He draws a deep breath, then lets it out slowly. "I'm dying, Kurt."

"What?"

"Pancreatic cancer. I haven't told the wife because she'll want me to get treatment, but the doc says I'm far gone. It'll be a waste of time. And you know what? I don't like pain."

"How long have you known about it?"

"Weeks. I knew it when I picked you up. It's part of the reason why I did."

"What?"

"Look. If I kill myself, the wife won't get my insurance. You break into the house, shoot me, she gets the money, I get off this earth. It's win-win."

"Not exactly."

"What do you mean?"

"Well . . . what do I get?"

"How does ten grand sound?"

I stare at him. "You're serious."

"As a funeral. Pardon the pun."

"I don't know . . . what if I get arrested?"

"You won't. I've got it all worked out, starting with the ten grand."

I turn to him. "Really?"

"I pick you up in the van, drop you in the woods behind my house. You wait there, 'til it starts getting dark, and you hear the wife's car, driving away. She's got her book club tonight."

"Okay."

"Okay. So, you go through the screened-in porch at the back of the house. The door will be open. Unlocked. There's a big basket out there with a cover on it. It's where we keep firewood, but if you look inside, you'll find a leather wallet with ten thousand dollars in it. Count it if you want, but I promise it'll all be there, along with a loaded gun."

"Then what do I do."

"You go into the living room. You wait behind the couch 'til you hear my car pull up. I'll come in through the front door. You shoot me. I die. It's that easy."

"But . . ."

"I guarantee you'll get out of there before anybody calls the cops. I'll leave the key in the van and you can just take it. Drive up to Canada or wherever you want to go."

The rain starts to let up, the wind dying down, the sun peeking through the clouds. I turn to him. "One question."

"Yeah?"

"How do you know I won't just take the money and run?"

He shrugs. "There's only one way out of there, and that's down the mountain. You try that, I'll have you arrested before you get to the bottom."

"Oh. Uh. Okay."

"But I'll tell you what else, I know you won't do that. I know it because I know you, Kurt. I know you have integrity."

"I've never killed anybody before. I don't know if I can."

"I know you can do it." The man says it like a coach, or a dad. "It's why I picked you up, Kurt. It's why I took you here."

The storm is over now, everything bright and clean, and I know there's a rainbow somewhere too, that Bible sign of hope. "I know you can do it," he says again, and I want to do it for him, more than anything. I want to help him with his problem of being alive. "When I come through that door," he says, "just imagine I'm someone you hate."

I turn to look at him, and we both smile.

"Imagine I'm your stepdad, coming back for more."

An hour later, he picks me up in the van, and leaves me in the woods behind the house with a bag of food — turkey sandwich, ice-cold Snapple, a bag of those gourmet chips. I eat what I can, which isn't very much, then I stay there waiting. It feels like hours.

Finally, I hear her heels clicking on the driveway, her car leaving. Ready, set . . .

The door to the back porch swings open. I lift the lid off the basket, and there's the wallet and the gun, just like he said. The wallet is packed with bills I don't bother counting before I slip it into my pants pocket. The gun is heavy, but it fits my hands well. My fingers wrapped around the grip, I feel like a movie hit man. James Bond, even. Back in the van, he'd told me the safety would be released, so I make sure to handle it very carefully, just like he said, as I slip into the living room. It's pitch-black in here, and with my free hand, I feel around for the couch and slip behind it, the gun cradled in my hands like some fragile living thing.

More time passes. With the dark and the quiet, I almost fall asleep. I tell myself it's not going to happen, that this is all some sick joke and the gun isn't even real. And then, finally, I hear the van pulling into the driveway, the door slamming. Go time, I think. Like a movie hit man.

I don't want to kill him, but the way I see it, he's giving me a gift. When you pull the trigger, he had said, think of freedom.

The key slips into the lock of the front door, catching slightly. Freedom. The door swings open and I can see the outline of him, backlit by his dying headlights. I raise the gun without thinking about it. I pull the trigger and it explodes in my ears. I've never heard anything so loud. When I was a kid, I went deer hunting with my real dad a few times. We used shotguns, but they were nothing like this. My ears ring. My shoulders ache from the recoil. You did it, I tell myself. You did it, Killer.

It isn't until he falls to the floor, moaning, that I realize that when he opened the door, he was carrying a suitcase. And he had hair.

I find the light switch. Flip it on. The first thing I see are the pictures on the coffee table. A couple side by side at a fancy dinner. Atop a mountain in matching backpacks. The two of them at their wedding, much younger, feeding each other cake.

The same woman. A different man.

That man, the man from these new pictures, is on the floor now, whispering cuss words through his own blood. I move over to him and kneel beside him. His shirt is covered in blood. He's on his way out. I don't know what to say or do. "You're her real husband," I whisper. "Not the bald man."

His eyes go big and glassy. "You're the . . . the asshole . . . from that video," he says. Or maybe I just imagine him saying it, as the life eases out of him and the sirens come.

It's a month later, when I'm watching TV with a few of the guys at the county jail, that I finally learn the bald man's name: Wallace Perry. "He doesn't look like a Wallace," I tell Jimbo, the big dude sitting next to me.

Jimbo says, "I'm not sure what a Wallace is supposed to look like."

"Yeah, me neither I guess."

Wallace Perry is on the screen next to his sister-in-law Denise. They're being interviewed by a morning anchor all the guys here think is hot—all cleavage and bottle-blond hair and big, sympa-

thetic eyes. She's just given us the refresher on the poor Perrys
—Denise returning home from book club to find her beloved husband, famed financier Henry Perry, dead at the hands of fugitive
Kurt Campbell, already wanted for assault after a brutal, videotaped attack on his own stepfather. "He was just coming back from
L.A.," Denise says through tears. Denise, the sole heir to Henry's
twenty-five-million-dollar fortune. "He'd been gone for weeks. I
couldn't wait to see him."

The hot anchor turns her attention to Wallace. "You've been a
tremendous source of comfort to Denise," she says.

And he nods slowly. "We both loved Henry. We both lost him. It's
a blessing we're able to be here for each other."

The anchor turns to the camera. "There's one silver lining
here," she says.

"What's that, baby?" shouts my cellmate, Little Stan.

And she looks straight out at us, with those sweet blue eyes, as
though she's answering Little Stan and Little Stan alone. "The silver lining is that Kurt Campbell is behind bars. He won't be able to
hurt anybody else, ever again."

The guys all erupt in whoops and cheers. Jimbo claps me on
the back. "You hear that, Mad Dog?" he says. My prison nickname.
"Nadia said your name! You're a superstar!"

I don't mind it here. That's the truth of it. I get three square
meals, I can work out in the gym. Nobody hassles me. In fact, I have
more friends here than I ever had on the outside. My trial's in a few
weeks, but my lawyer wants me to go for a plea deal, and I think I
might do it. I don't feel like standing in front of people, answering
questions. And anyway, I did kill the guy.

I'm not mad at Wallace Perry. I'm not mad at Larry or my stepdad or my mom or anybody. Not anymore. It's as though, when I
pulled the trigger, all the meanness slipped out of me, and I could
see the world for what it is: A bunch of fucked-up people. All of us
trying to get through the day.

"You're a hero, Mad Dog."

Remember that thing my mom said, about prayers being answered? I believe it. I really do.

GAR ANTHONY HAYWOOD

With Footnotes and References

FROM *The Darkling Halls of Ivy*

PARNELL'S FATHER WAS a hard man. One would have thought a net worth of $240 million would make him a little less so, but a man didn't make a quarter of a billion dollars by playing nice with people.

Andrew Bennett knew how to make a dollar, in and out of corporate real estate, and he was filled to the brim with lessons to convey. Over the course of his twenty-two years, Parnell had heard them all, but the two that had stuck more than any of the others were "stand by your word" and "never be the biggest loser in any deal."

The first bit of advice was tired and old, of course, just like Andrew had become himself, but it had its merits. Making good on your promises always seemed to reassure people that you could be trusted with their hearts and their money. Women, business partners, investors—they all lapped it up with equal zeal. But Andrew's second admonition was more confusing than trite, because how could you make money without occasionally losing more than the other guy? Wasn't that the simple math behind every deal gone south? Only after he was well into his teens did Parnell begin to understand what his father meant, and why it was important: fall if you must, but always leave the hardest landing for someone else.

And Parnell always did. In this way, he earned his father's affections honestly. He worked hard and made smart decisions. If he partied like a fiend and ran through his monthly allowance—a generous eight grand—as if frugality were a mortal sin, his personal life at least had produced no public embarrassment for the family. In short, he was a fine son and only child, and neither his father nor his mother had any reason to believe he would ever prove a major disappointment.

He wasn't perfect, however. When he wasn't busting his ass to achieve a desired outcome, he was cutting a fine-edged, well-calculated corner to accelerate it. Parnell disliked the word "cheat"—it made his little indiscretions sound more desperate than inspired —but he knew that was the technical term for what he did. And that was okay. Because whatever word you used for it, Parnell never circumvented the rules of order just for the sake of it. He cheated with purpose, to seize on a unique opportunity or to save his precious resources of time and energy, and even his father could find very little fault in that.

Except as it applied to Parnell's college education. Andrew Bennett would not have been happy to learn that his son was gaming the system in any fashion to make his way through the University of Southern California. Business was war, where rules were made to be bent and broken, but education was sacred. A degree from the old man's beloved USC was an honor to be earned through blood, sweat, and tears, not guile nor influence. Money could get you in, there was nothing wrong with that, but if it bought you a single step up after your first day of classes, the paper behind the framed glass on the wall wasn't worth five cents. It didn't matter what the discipline or who it impressed. Because it had been purchased under these very conditions, the diploma on Andrew's own office wall —USC Marshall School of Business, Class of 1990—was one of his most prized possessions, and he wanted—he *demanded*—nothing less for his son.

Parnell admired his father's viewpoint but found it too hypocritical to be taken seriously. College was no different from big business, it was all the same game of win or go home, and pretending one was more honorable than the other was a joke. Parnell had done all the work and made all the sacrifices necessary to gain acceptance into Andrew's alma mater, no small or uncostly feat in and of itself, but hell if he was going to spend the next four years of his life following his father's fanciful, starry-eyed playbook. He was his own man and he had his own way of doing things. He lived life on the edge and kept friends of all stripes, some of whom he found nearly as frightening as he did entertaining. And yes, he paid someone to write a paper on occasion.

Someone who knew the subject backward and forward and

could be counted on to meet a deadline, and produce something
for twenty-five hundred that hadn't been cut and pasted from online sources. Somebody nearly as smart as Parnell was himself, but
who had far more to lose if their arrangement ever came to light.

Someone like Megan Deene.

Megan knew the type. She'd seen guys like Bennett all her life.

Smart. Funny. More money than God and twice the confidence,
nearly all of it misplaced. Parnell was prettier than most but his MO
was the same. Work hard right up to the point of discomfort, then
pay somebody smarter to take you the rest of the way home.

That she was smarter than Bennett, Megan had no doubt. Just
their typical barroom banter over beer and appetizers was proof
enough of that. But being smarter than most of the male students
at USC and damn near all the women wasn't a prize that came
with any cash award, and unlike Bennett, Megan had to find every
dime of her tuition on her own. There was no Daddy or Mommy
back home in Spartanburg to cushion her fall when what she owed
and what she earned, working a half-dozen freelance gigs at once,
failed to balance out at the end of the month. So she was left to do
what she had to do, superior intellect be damned: play the com-
moner and attend to the needs of Bennett and his blue-blooded
ilk—for a price.

And that price was about to go up. Parnell didn't know it yet, but
Megan had decided her latest term paper for him was worth more
than the $2,500 she had been charging him up to now. "Vinegar
and Oil: Ethics and Mobile Application Design" may not have been
her finest work for Bennett, but it had been the most exhausting,
and Megan was all through killing herself for his benefit without
being adequately compensated. This paper was going to cost him
four grand, and every paper hereafter.

He wouldn't like it, but what was he going to do? Write a sixty-
page paper of his own overnight? Not likely. Though he probably
could, were he properly motivated. That was the great irony of it
all. Parnell didn't *need* Megan's services, not like the other losers
she dealt with; he was only paying her to do work he could just as
easily do himself out of sheer laziness. Megan didn't understand it,
she had never understood it. Nothing else about the boy suggested
such sloth; he appeared from every other angle to be industrious
and self-sufficient, if wildly unscrupulous. And yet, here he was,

outsourcing classwork to a poor girl like Megan, dropping more on a single paper than she could keep in her checking account for more than six hours.

She knew she was taking a big chance, changing the terms of their agreement without warning. Bennett would be furious and would threaten to write his own paper, at the very least. But that was as far as his anger would take him, because he didn't have the stomach for much more than talk. Megan was sure of it. Bennett had an edge to him, yes, but at his core he was soft, incapable of ever taking things to a physical level. This wasn't true of all Megan's clients; there were some she'd never dare cross in the way she planned to cross Parnell tonight. These guys would cave Megan's head in first and consider the consequences later. She'd seen plenty of their kind, too, over the years, and always handled them accordingly.

Bennett knew a few such crazies himself. His boy Ronnie Fetters was a prime example. Parnell's cast of party-animal friends was an eclectic bunch, to be sure, but Fetters was an outlier, a black mamba in a pit of garden snakes. He didn't belong in Bennett's circle, but he was there just the same. Megan could only imagine Parnell kept him around for laughs.

She wondered how much laughing Bennett would be doing after their meeting tonight.

The way it usually worked, Megan would email Parnell the first twenty pages of a paper under a generic title, just to prove she was on track, then exchange the remainder for $2,500 in cash over morning coffee at an off-campus Starbucks. But this time Megan wanted to close the deal in the early evening at the Leavey Library, and Parnell immediately thought he knew why: a man couldn't raise his voice in anger in a library without making a scene.

Parnell wasn't surprised. Megan was smart and streetwise, and people like her never stayed in one place too long. Raising the stakes was no doubt part of every bet she ever made. Had she never tried to game Parnell at least once, even just a little bit, he would have been both shocked and disappointed.

Alone at a table in Leavey, they made quick work of the small talk and got right down to business.

"I didn't bring the paper," Megan said. She showed Parnell the courtesy of not smiling.

"Yeah. I noticed that."

"I've been doing some thinking, and I've decided we need to renegotiate."

"That's funny, because I was thinking the same thing."

"You were?"

"Yes. At least, in this particular case. The item's not bad, but it's not up to your usual standards, and it's well below mine."

Megan's eyes flashed, and now she did smile, but not with any amusement. "Excuse me?"

"I'll give you two bills for it."

She waited for him to go on, but Parnell was done talking.

"Two bills?"

"Frankly, I'm being generous. I won't presume to suggest you weren't trying this time around, but your reliance on redundancy and run-on sentences was somewhat appalling. Very unlike you."

"You're fucking insane. If anything—"

"You were thinking of asking for more than the usual twenty-five. Of course you were. But my offer's two bills, just the same. Take it or leave it."

He did everything short of crossing his arms and lighting a cigarette to show her how serious he was. She sat there and watched him wait, doing a burn so slow he almost couldn't see it. But she was on fire, all right. If he couldn't see the heat coming off her, he sure as hell could feel it.

"Fuck you. Write the paper yourself. Good luck with that."

"I won't need luck. Just a few cans of Red Bull to make it through the next forty-eight. But thanks."

He started to stand.

"You're bluffing," Megan said.

Parnell laughed and settled back down in his chair. "Now, why in the hell would I need to do that? I've already got thirty pages in the bank. You don't think I can knock out another twenty-five in two days, and save myself a couple grand in the process?"

"You could, but you won't."

He almost found himself feeling sorry for her. "Megan. You're the one bluffing, not me. If I walk out of here without your promise to deliver the rest of the goods by eight tomorrow morning, you're not just kissing off two grand. You're kissing off every dollar you might have made from this arrangement in the future. End of the Bennett gravy train. Is that what you want?"

It wasn't because it couldn't be. Parnell had looked deep into the lady's background before getting into business with her and he knew how badly she needed the income he'd been providing. She wasn't going to throw it all away over five hundred dollars.

She pushed away from the table and got to her feet. Humiliation was a bitch, but starvation was worse. "Pay me. Now."

Parnell's eyes surveyed the room. There were cameras everywhere.

"Outside," he said.

A gun, Megan thought. *If I'd only had a gun.*

She would have killed Parnell for sure. That's how furious she'd been. And she was still furious hours later, curled up in a ball in bed like a war orphan, though now her ire was as much about her own stupidity as Bennett's double-cross. He'd thrown her off completely, changing the terms of their contract before she could do it first, and she'd never recovered her balance. How had he understood how weak her play was better than she understood it herself? She had entered the library thinking only in the short term, of a single sixty-page document and how desperate Parnell's need for it had to be, but *his* eyes were on the bigger picture, the one in which he, not she, held all the cards. All Bennett had to lose by ending their working relationship was a couple nights' sleep, but Megan . . . However fair or unfair the fee, she had come to rely on the $2,500 Bennett was paying her to write a paper every six weeks or so, and she would have been hard pressed to find that money elsewhere.

Somehow, Bennett knew this — he'd probably always known it — and with that he had all the upper hand over her he could ever require. Servants were a dime a dozen, but masters were few. For now, Parnell held the power between them, and she either accepted his terms of service or dropped out of school to spare herself the indignity of being expelled.

She drew her laptop to her on the bed and emailed Bennett the rest of his goddamn assignment, vowing to someday make him wish he'd never heard the name Megan Deene.

"I say kill the bitch," Ronnie said.

"Don't be ridiculous."

"Ridiculous? What's ridiculous about it?" The big man was picking his front teeth with a chicken bone. "She can't be trusted. There's only one way to deal with people you can't trust."

"Actually, there are all kinds of ways to deal with people you can't trust," Parnell said. "And killing them is way down on the list. That is, unless prison food appeals to you."

"I ain't ever going to prison. People who go to prison ain't worth a shit afterward. I'd make 'em kill me first."

"Death or prison. Same difference. Either way, you're fucked if you get caught. So let's just leave murder off the table for now, shall we?"

Parnell watched his friend light another joint, their third of the evening. Ronnie's tiny apartment already reeked, so one more cloud of smoke would hardly matter. Parnell pinched the blunt between two fingers when it was passed and took a long drag, silently admitting something he could never tell Ronnie: he'd like to kill Megan Deene too.

But that would be a gross overreaction that could backfire spectacularly. Ronnie was a thug in a Trojan lacrosse uniform who thought getting away with murder was just a matter of wearing rubber gloves and hiding the body in a ditch somewhere, but Parnell knew there was much more to it than that. You had to have the will to commit the act, first—something Parnell sorely lacked —and then you had to have a plan that was airtight, one the police couldn't penetrate no matter how many ways they tried. Given time, Parnell could come up with the plan, but time was a commodity he spent only on things that were essential. For now, there was no reason to think Megan wasn't a problem he had under control, and until she did something to prove otherwise, she was best left alone. Monitored closely and with suspicion, but left alone.

If she had the smarts he thought she did, he would never come to regret leaving the lady alive.

Megan tried, but she could never get over it. The way Bennett had played her just stung too much.

For a while, she had worried that she may have put herself in danger, making an enemy of someone who had powerful friends and more than enough resources to do her harm. But months passed, then a year, and her fear of Bennett faded to black while her resentment and outrage grew, festering like an open wound that refused to heal. Had that night at the Leavey Library been the last time she laid eyes on him, she might have been able to put the injury he'd inflicted upon her in the past, but she'd gone on working for him afterward, writing a paper here and there, taking his money without complaint. Never letting on that the sight of his face turned her stomach. Because every day was still a struggle just to stay in school and beggars couldn't be choosers about who was buying their books or paying their overdue electric bill.

Still, her anger lingered. It ate at her like a dog gnawing on a bone. And now, finally, it was time for payback. Graduation was looming; Bennett had never been more vulnerable. The few hundred he'd saved himself playing hardball with her over a single term paper was chicken feed compared to the invoice she was about to lay on him.

Megan was the one thinking long-term now.

Ronnie didn't see Parnell's girl coming until she was practically at his table. She climbed up on the stool across from him and sat herself down, pretty as you please, smiling like she'd called ahead to ask permission.

"Hello?" he said.

They'd only seen each other once before that he could recall, here at Traddies last year, having a drink with some girlfriends. She'd drifted over to his and Parnell's table and Parnell had introduced them, explaining later who she was.

"You're Ronnie, right? Remember me? Megan?"

"I remember. What's up? If you're lookin' for Parnell—"

"Actually, I'm here to see you. You and I need to talk."

"We do?"

"Yes. But first, I'm going to order something from the bar. I'm starved."

"You're making a huge mistake," Parnell said.

Megan had called another meeting, this one at the coffee shop just outside the campus grounds where they used to conduct all their business. She didn't owe him another paper—only six weeks from graduation, his need for her services was a thing of the past—and she wouldn't tell him what she wanted over the phone, so he was left to guess what was on her mind. He showed up expecting the worst and she didn't disappoint.

"Am I? I don't think so," Megan said. "I think fifty thousand dollars to guarantee you aren't called into the dean's office two months before you earn your diploma is just about right. In fact, I think it's generous."

She smiled to show she had used that word deliberately, "generous." That was what he had said he was being with her that night at Leavey, paying her two thousand dollars for a paper she thought was worth much more.

"The dean's office? Why would I get called into the dean's office?" He flashed her a smile of his own.

"Don't, Parnell. Fourteen papers in three years. I've got the emails, I've got—"

"Zilch. You've got zilch. Did you even think this through, Meg? You sent me Word docs with no titles and emails with no subject lines. Maybe I opened them, maybe I didn't. Maybe the emails went straight to my spam folder where I never even saw them. I always paid you in cash. Do I need to go on?"

"I have full copies of papers you submitted to multiple instructors under your own name, Parnell. Whatever else I couldn't prove, you'd never be able to explain your way out of that."

"I wouldn't have to."

"Oh. Because you're Parnell Bennett, right? And Daddy gives big bucks to the university. Is that it?"

Parnell shook his head, letting the grin on his face stay where it was. She didn't get it and probably never would. "I'm not going to pay you, Megan."

She shrugged. "Then you've just thrown away four years of your life for nothing."

He watched her stand up and back away from the table. "What are you going to do?"

"I'm going to go back to my apartment and hit 'send.' And if you were thinking about stopping me, you'd better get ready to do it yourself because your boy's not going to do it for you."

"My boy?"

"Ronnie's not your boy? I thought you two were buds. He thinks so too. Though, after today, maybe not so much."

"You've been talking to Ronnie?"

"Call it a preemptive strike. Insurance against fatal injury."

Parnell had to laugh. Insurance *against*, the lady said. "Go on."

"I've just given you two choices: pay me or shut me up. You don't want to pay me and you don't have the balls to do what it would take to shut me up, so what's left? I did the math, Parnell. I got to Ronnie first."

"And?"

"He's not as stupid as you think. Or as loyal. He's not going to risk everything *he's* worked for these last four years just to silence me for your sake." She gave Parnell a moment to think that over. "Pay me, Parnell. It's the only move you've got."

She waited for him to say something.

"Okay. I'll sleep on it. But do yourself a solid in the meantime," he said, "and go check the rosters for the classes you wrote those papers for. I think you'll find them rather interesting."

Of course, she didn't follow. All she said was "I'll give you 'til tomorrow, noon." And then she was gone.

". . . the rosters for the classes you wrote those papers for."

What the fuck was Bennett talking about?

She had him by the short hairs, of course he'd say anything to try and confuse her, but Megan couldn't convince herself he'd been talking just to talk. That wasn't Parnell's style. There was something in those class rosters she needed to see.

She spent most of the night in denial, eating and drinking like a fool, determined to celebrate the fifty thousand dollars of Bennett's money she planned to use to help pay off her student loans. But the minute she parked her car on the street outside her apartment building, she brought the class rosters up on her phone, unable to wait until she could crack open her laptop upstairs. To write the papers, she'd had to know the courses and the instructors, so finding the classes on the school site, and the roster of students assigned to each, posed no problem for her. It just took a little digging.

But her stomach was already turning by the time the first list appeared on her phone, because it had finally dawned on her what significance the rosters could possibly hold for her. Parnell's name wasn't on this list, and it wasn't on any of the others, either. He hadn't been enrolled in any of the classes he'd paid her to write papers for. In four of the seven, however, somebody else had been, someone they both knew, and his name leapt off Megan's smartphone screen like an icy bolt of lightning.

"Oh, Jesus," Megan said.

She was about to get out of the car when Ronnie Fetters jumped in on the passenger side. There was a knife in his right hand, maybe the biggest knife Megan had ever seen in her life.

"If you scream, I'm gonna kill you right here," he said.

Megan looked around in a panic, didn't see a living soul anywhere to save her. She took her chances and screamed anyway.

Parnell hadn't needed the money, but selling Megan's writing services to Ronnie and two other Trojans of his acquaintance had been a quick and easy way to pick up a little spending cash his parents never had to know about. A thousand off the top on each paper—Megan hadn't realized how underpaid she really was.

But the girl was shortsighted in so many ways. She thought Parnell was just a rich, lazy frat boy and that Ronnie was nothing but a dumb jock without ambition. She'd been wrong on both counts. There wasn't anything lazy about playing the middleman in a mutually profitable enterprise of your own invention, and not every muscle-bound college athlete lacked postgraduate intentions outside of sports. Ronnie was crude, to be sure, but his parents were nearly as well off as Parnell's and about twice as demanding of their son. Ronnie's father had plans for him to join the family business upon his graduation, and he wasn't going to be disappointed. He had two other sons besides Ronnie, each with degrees of their own, and Ronnie's only ticket in was a diploma from SC. Getting expelled from school was no more an option for him than it had been for Megan.

Now the poor devil had much bigger problems than expulsion to worry about. He'd wanted to kill Megan the moment he'd heard she was trying to game Parnell for more money—"*There's only one way to deal with people you can't trust*"—and now that she'd proven him right, he was going to put her in check in the most permanent way possible.

Parnell had been surprised when he didn't kill Megan last night, after she'd made the fatal mistake of trying to win him over to her side of a blackmail scheme of which Ronnie, not Parnell, was the actual target. Ronnie had called Parnell right after, more just to say "I told you so" than to seek any advice. He'd already made up his mind what he was going to do, and when.

"I don't want to know any details," Parnell told him.

Because the details would not be necessary. It was past midnight. By now, Megan Deene was likely dead and Ronnie was still in the process of cleaning up his mess. All Parnell had to tell the 9-1-1 operator was that he feared a murder was about to be committed, and he thought he knew who was going to commit it. Maybe all of Ronnie's talk about preferring death-by-cop to prison was a lot of hot air, and maybe it wasn't. But Parnell figured it would be worth his while to find out. Either way, Parnell Bennett would not be the biggest loser in this deal-gone-all-to-hell.

Daddy would be so proud.

RAVI HOWARD

The Good Thief

FROM *Alabama Noir*

FOR HIS FINAL meal, all Thomas Elijah Raymond asked for was the cake, the one he remembered from Rachel's Luncheonette in Phenix City. Prison rules would not allow food brought in from the outside. Safety concerns. So if Rachel Walker said yes, she would have to come to Holman on the day of the execution and make it there. How to feel about such a thing. Reluctant but somehow compelled. When the day arrived, the warden's assistant greeted Rachel and escorted her to the kitchen. She could now match a face to the familiar voice she'd heard so many times over the phone in the few weeks before.

"Mrs. Walker, the warden will be here in just a minute. Can I get you anything in the meantime?" Francine asked.

"No, thank you. I believe I'm fine." Rachel wanted to sound more certain, and to dismiss any worry on her behalf. She wanted to manage that on her own.

As Francine disappeared out the swinging metal doors, Rachel watched her through round windows. The secretary walked past the corrections officer stationed outside and made her way down the corridor. The sound of her heels on the concrete was muted by the thick steel doors that had by then stopped swinging. Rachel was alone now, in the newly constructed wing of Holman Prison. It was the biggest kitchen she had ever seen.

The smell of her restaurant kitchen had always given her comfort. It was not the smell of any particular dish, but instead, the slow, thin layers built up over the years. There was always cinnamon near, even if it wasn't needed for a recipe. Bowls of it curled like scrolls used to write down histories. She wished she had brought some with her. This place smelled of bleach and ammonia. It whispered nothing.

Stainless steel shelves lined the freshly painted walls. Ceiling lamps spread a dull glaze across the metal fixtures. Fluorescent bulbs gave a uniform pale, except for a single lamp that flickered, blinking rays the color newspaper turns. A dozen parallel steel islands rose from the white tile floor, wrapped in thick blue plastic pulled taut over narrow shelves and secured around the edges of the counters. Two adjacent counters had been uncovered and arranged for her use.

Francine said that the new wing had been finished just a few weeks ago. The men would arrive soon, and from this kitchen they would be fed. In the meantime, the warden had arranged for her to work here. According to Francine, the warden thought the space would be ideal. Out of the way. Clean.

Rachel had dressed for a warm autumn evening. She was not prepared for the cold confines of the prison kitchen. It seemed the temperature was set for a space full of toiling and heat, so the cold air, unchecked, was too much. The place wasn't walk-in cold, but damn near, with air washing over her feet in waves, snaking around her ankles, and running along the floor. She placed her purse on the counter and removed a black apron, RACHEL'S LUNCHEON-ETTE: 35 YEARS IN THE BAKING in silver lettering. The silver blouse beneath her black suit matched the silver in her hair. This was how she dressed for the events she catered. Yet she had taken pause when readying for this occasion. There was no proper dress for preparing a last meal.

She'd made the three-hour drive alone. Told her family she was driving to Atmore for the weekend. Her daughter and son-in-law were busy running the kitchen, had been for years. A few days a week, she would walk the dining room and the lunch counter, speaking to the first-timers who had her cookbooks, had seen her on television here and there, and she greeted her regulars as well, trying to dole out the same welcome to any and all. She could come and go, be there without being there — her face on the menus, and the sides of buses, and the coffee bags and cookie tins they sold in the gift shop. So when she told her family she had a small job in

Escambia County, a repast for an old acquaintance, she'd saved herself the strain of a lie she may have to remember later. The truth itself was troublesome enough.

The prison kitchen was empty except for the ingredients. Francine had requested them a week before. Shortening, sugar, molasses, salt, baking soda, and flour had been lined up in a perfect row, labels turned outward. Someone had seen fit. Perhaps an eye for detail, but certainly a nod toward normalcy in a place where there was little.

On a nearby table sat an antique mixer. In the kitchen of a prison, the comforts of home seemed strangely out of place. She flipped the power switch on the mixer, and the familiar hum rang out.

She remembered having a similar one years before. Its heavy body and thick insulation produced a hum unlike the rattling of the new ones that cost more than they should.

Chrome, as beautiful as it could be, was hard to keep clean. Working folk had no time to worry about fingerprints and smudges. The matte metal about the kitchen reflected indistinguishable masses of light and dark, but in the chrome she could see herself.

She examined her reflection in the mixer's oblong body, getting closer to it until the moisture of her sigh obscured her image. With one of the neatly folded dish towels, she wiped the chrome clean.

"It was my mother's."

She had barely grown comfortable in the silence when his voice rang out.

"I'm sorry. I didn't mean to frighten you, Mrs. Walker. I'm Lionel Peters. The warden here. I'm sorry I haven't had a chance to meet you previously."

He walked over to greet her but waited for Rachel to extend her hand first. An old-fashioned stance that she hoped would fade; indeed, Lionel Peters looked a few years her junior. Set in his ways, she was sure. But he carried himself a little older than he was, and his clothes didn't help. His suit surely had the right cut and hang before the years settled into it. He was conscious of his posture, but the slouch in his jacket remained.

"Did Francine offer you anything when you came in? Excuse me if she didn't. We can forget our manners working in here. Can I get you anything, coffee or something?"

"She offered, but I didn't need anything."

"Well, everything you asked for is right there on the counter. Your perishables are in the refrigerator over there. The ovens are behind you. Officer Earle will be right outside. Holler if you need anything. He can escort you to the facilities if you need to use them. I apologize we didn't build a ladies' room on this end. You sure I can't get you anything, coffee or something?"

She shook her head.

"What else?" the warden said while flipping through a deck of papers on the clipboard he tapped against the counter. "I feel like I'm forgetting something. Oh yes, the list. I want to make sure we got everything. Shortening, eggs, sugar, cocoa, flour . . ."

"There is one thing. I realized much too late that I left something off the list: my vanilla syrup. We make our own to sell in the gift shop, so I'm just so used to having it around and not buying it. Coming down here's out of the ordinary, to say the least, so clarity has been a little challenging."

She knew they had rules about bringing things in, but she prayed they could look the other way. The warden was killing a man, and he had made a show of this little bit of kindness, so certainly he could see fit to say yes. She took from her bag a bottle and set it down gingerly, almost like a beg-your-pardon for it being there against the rules.

The bottle rested between them, and the warden walked a bit closer and turned it so the label faced outward like the rest of the ingredients. He smiled a bit then, looking from the label to her, the pattern in the design the same as the embroidery on the apron she carried. Good branding. Her smile in the photograph was clockwork, perfected after years of showing her teeth because she had to, and then because her enterprise made it worthwhile.

"I understand. I got no qualms with it, considering."

He was decent enough, but Rachel could tell the warden wanted no part of this. The letter in two places said he would understand if she said no. She could just send a recipe, and they'd honor his wishes. But if she'd said no, she would still know Thomas Elijah Raymond's execution date, and she would probably look at the clock well aware of the hour. She would have wandered there in her mind even if she had said no to making this drive.

"We pick a fine time to pay attention, don't we," she said. Rachel was looking away, but the edge to her voice was unmistakable.

The warden said nothing.

She paused before she spoke again. "Nobody looking after him for years, and he's got all kinds of eyes on him now. More this evening, I suspect. Spectators."

"Witnesses. The family of the victim." He pressed the clipboard flat against his waist, a stance that seemed automatic. "He doesn't deny what he did."

"I'm thinking about what *we're* about to do. Me and you both. Trying to wake up and go about my business tomorrow and thinking back on this here."

A hand on the counter then, like candor needed a different sort of balance before the words came freely. "You'll probably feel worse about this tomorrow than you do today. I always do."

"Why do it then?" she said.

And there they were on the other side of the nicety. She saw in the warden a decent man, but maybe that was part of the problem. What decent folks were willing to go along with. He was quiet for a minute, and he breathed in and out with too much intention. He glanced away in a room with no windows, and he seemed too accustomed to conjuring some good memory, a little daylight stored away for days such as this one. The ease in his face said as much.

"My wife reminded me this morning that we ate at your place a while back. We were on our way to see some of her people in Tuskegee. Enjoyed it immensely—just a good meal on a good afternoon. I didn't mention it to Raymond, because it's rude to reminisce on things. Get casual with the outside world. Do you remember him?"

She shook her head. "So many kids over the years, it's impossible to say."

"Well, in any case, you're appreciated."

"Please tell your wife I said thank you. To you as well. Like you said, it doesn't sit easy, so—well, thank you."

It was quiet for a while again, except for the lights and the freezers, and the sound of Lionel's wedding band against the countertop, a little sonar to bring him back to whatever was next on his clipboard.

"You sure I can't get you some coffee or something?"

"No, thank you. You've done just fine with the mixer."

The warden excused himself then, and as he made his way down the corridor, the metal doors swung to silence. Rachel was alone

again, her mind holding vigil. She had lied to the warden about
Raymond. How could she not remember?

The boy couldn't have been more than six or so, because she remembered him sitting at the table with what looked like his grandparents, coloring the children's menu with the Crayolas she passed
out in sardine cans. His family was on the way to Huntsville, the
space center they said, and he had lined up the salt and pepper
shakers, the Louisiana Hot, and the Heinz bottle as rocket ships
taking off from the tabletop. To get dessert, he had to promise
to finish the green beans, alone on the plate where the chicken
had been, the wing and drumstick reduced to gristle and bone.
He chewed with purpose but not enjoyment, like he was practicing handwriting with his jaws. But the booth they chose was across
from the cake display, so he did a bit of window-shopping while he
finished the last of the beans. Rachel was on the other side of the
glass, loading the shelf of red velvets. She remembered him studying his options. He didn't like the green beans one bit, but he'd
kept his word and intended to make the most of it.

He asked for the molasses cake, while his grandparents had red
velvet and buttermilk pie. They thanked Rachel as they left, and
then she looked away and didn't see the boy fall to the ground.
A child on the floor raised no alarm at first. Kids were prone to
go from dillydallying straight to sprinting and stumbling. And the
tantrums. But something was wrong because when Rachel finally
noticed the boy on the floor, his eyes were widening as he struggled
to breathe.

In the commotion, his people thought he was choking, but
there didn't seem to be any obstruction in his throat. He held his
mouth open wide, still searching for air. Rachel got to the boy first,
the allergy syrup from the first aid kit in hand. He coughed up the
first dose, but she gave him more while his grandmother rocked
him, his grandfather fanning with a napkin. By then the boy was
breathing easier, and the gentle wheeze faded a bit.

After taking several deep, full breaths, the boy cried some and
peered around. He hadn't lost consciousness, but his eyes looked
beyond them, apparently seeing nothing. Then he finally recognized them—Rachel, his grandparents—and it seemed he had to
lock eyes on everyone gathered around him to fully return to the
world. And then it was over, the scare behind them.

Rachel was always careful about nuts and other common allergens. But the boy's reaction to molasses was a rare occurrence. People like to sue over such things, but these folks sent her a letter of thanks. She would find out later that the grandparents were guardians, new to his care, and they hadn't known about his condition. She wondered then about his parents, what tragedy or rift had brought him to the care of his elders.

It was a blessing to discover his condition in caring company. Beneath the cursive of the grown-up handwriting, the boy had signed his name: *JoJo.*

In what she read about him during his trial, she discovered that his grandparents had died. He had made his money as a day laborer, and Thomas had killed a man who refused to pay him. He had gone through the victim's pockets for the money he was owed. Murder in the commission of a robbery.

There would be no clemency. As part of the death decree, the state of Alabama would use three chemicals for his lethal injection. After the first drug, he would lose consciousness. The second would shut down his muscles. The third would stop his heart.

What Rachel carried in her bottle would do the same, answering the young man's request for a final and private mercy. All he asked for was the cake like the one that showed him what his body could not take, what in the right dose might knock him unconscious or even kill him. Molasses had stopped his breathing once, but he'd been a boy then. She knew it wouldn't be enough for a man, so she had turned to her garden.

She had years ago planted a small plot of cassava in her greenhouse and used it for her baking. The lined skin of the cassava felt as rugged as cypress knees, but the flesh, handled carefully, was a wonder to be fried or roasted or used in her baking. She took the time to learn how to prepare it safely. Cassava carried its poison in the coarse skin and the leaves, the parts exposed to the world. And perhaps that was how it should be, a shield to survive in a certain kind of world — to thrive even. To carry out JoJo's request, Rachel had saved what was meant to be discarded, the cyanide in the pot liquor, thickened with the starch of the root.

During his trial, Thomas Elijah Raymond had been shuttled back and forth from the new county jail to the new courthouse. Depending on the road they took, he may have passed the hillside where Russell County did their lynching, out on a hill they named

Golgotha. The name had confused Rachel when she heard those stories as a child. The killers had tried to sanctify their work, but it was nothing more than blasphemy. She knew that hilltop from the Easter hymns, New Testament scriptures, and the Sunday school books. Three crosses. The Bad Thief cursed it all, and the Good Thief asked for grace and mercy.

Thomas had asked her for the same, and she'd brought his grace and his mercy, and it floated there in the thick sweetness of her bottle, a dose large enough to claim his body. He would die that evening, but she wouldn't let them make a carnival of him. The spectators would have nothing to witness, because he could do his dying, make his peace, in private.

She turned the dial on the oven to 350 degrees. The perishables, she retrieved from the refrigerator. The other ingredients, she opened, poured, and measured. The pans, greased and floured, lay waiting for the batter. When the time came, she turned on the mixer and listened to its baritone hum as it folded the necessary elements, one into the other.

Everything Is Going to Be Okay

FROM *Lockdown*

JOANNA COUGHS TWICE and turns over yet again. Then she coughs again. She groans. The sound and her shifting wake Pablo up. He doesn't move. With his eyes closed, he sends a prayer up to his Virgencita, asking her to make the fucking cough go away. *Por favor, Madrecita santa, haz que mi mujer deje de toser.* He accepts the prayer won't work before he's even done praying.

Joanna coughs once more, wheezes, moves again. She's looking for more than a comfortable position. She's looking for something that won't come. The old springs underneath her creak loudly as she adjusts her legs under the covers. She won't go back to sleep. Pablo groans. The coughing, like a tide, came and went all night long. It was just as bad as the night before. Pablo wonders how long it'll take for her to crack a rib.

Pablo hates himself for being so pissed at her. Poor thing would love nothing more than to stop hacking up a lung, but that seems to be out of the realm of possibility. The cough is now always there, and there's apparently nothing anyone can do about it. The hospitals are packed. There is no medicine for this. They can't even afford some of the Clorox shit the orange idiot has been talking about. They're stuck, the glue of poverty holding them down and making them powerless the same way it's always done.

Pablo tilts his head to the right and stretches his neck. Thirty years of working his ass off on the deck of commercial boats has taken a toll on his body. Everything hurts. Everything's wrinkled. Everything aches. His joints and lower back push him to stay put as much as possible, but the coughing pushes him out the door and onto more boats. Everything's shut down but people still have to eat. As long as people have to eat, his ass will be on a boat, his busted fingers smelling like fish despite the gloves he wears.

The calluses on his hands sound like sandpaper when Pablo rubs his face. The skin on his arms, face, and neck is leathery enough to make wallets from it. He feels older. Then he remembers half a joke, something about sleeping in the fridge and putting a bit of WD-40 in his morning coffee to stay young. Maybe the funny part is the half he doesn't recall.

Getting out of bed quietly is easier said than done. Pablo lets his legs slip off the edge of the old mattress, finding a pool of cooler sheet along the way, and then uses his arms to push himself into a sitting position. Joanna coughs again. This time it doesn't stop. She coughs and coughs. She sits up on the bed, a hand on her chest, her eyes bloodshot. Pablo knows she's struggling to breathe. His powerlessness smacks him on the face and slices his soul in half.

The coughing subsides. Joanna stays like that for a few seconds, gasping for air. Pablo hasn't left the bed and he already feels tired. He has to do something. He needs to get Joanna some help. Medicine. One of those ventilator things everyone keeps talking about on the news.

He stands up and walks over to the chair whose sole purpose is holding his clothes. He steps into a pair of dirty jeans and fishes out a bent cigarette from a pack that will be empty before noon. He refuses to get on a boat without enough smokes, so buying a few packs goes on his mental to-do list, half of which he knows he'll forget until the boat is far from shore. The bent cigarette looks like a yellowish worm in the dimness of the room. Pablo wants to light it and suck some warm smoke into his body. That might scare away some of the aches, maybe smooth his anger a bit. But he can't light up. Joanna's cough can be triggered by smoke. She doesn't need that, so he steps out, crosses the hallway and living room in the dark, and opens the door to the front porch. Behind him, Joanna coughs again.

There's an old wooden chair that was white a few decades ago and a table with a yellow ashtray sporting the name of a beer Pablo doesn't recall ever drinking. A small radio sits next to the ashtray, looking like a black smudge in the predawn darkness. Pablo walks to the apparatus and feels around for the iPod he knows is stuck in the slot in the top of the machine. His son, Roberto, gave it to him a few birthdays ago. The small rectangle weighs next to nothing and contains more music than Pablo ever owned. He scrolls using the wheel and finds some Roberto Roena. Maybe a small tribute to his son. Pablo replaces the iPod on the machine and clicks PLAY.

A percussive explosion blasts through the tiny speakers and Pablo quickly lowers the volume. No need to wake Joanna up. There's a chance she has finally fallen asleep again.

A sound in the dawn-soaked street makes Pablo look up from the iPod. A fat Mexican on a bicycle is slowly pedaling down the middle of it as if he were driving a large car. The motherfucker is probably up to no good. Only hardworking men and criminals are up at this hour, and the Mexican doesn't look like he's on his way to a business meeting. Pablo remembers a time when living in Galveston meant you could leave your door open. Now it only means you're closer to the polluted, brown water and have to put up with drunk, annoying rich kids a few times a year. While Roena sings about santos blessing him, Pablo thinks about his upcoming gig. In a day he'll be jumping aboard the *Carol Sue,* a fifty-one-foot white boat, to trudge through the dark waters of the Gulf of Mexico, trying to catch as much red snapper as possible. It'll be his seventh trip with Captain Joseph "Big Joe" Weiss. They'll hit some fishing spots seventy miles off the Galveston shore. It'll take them a day to get there. Then they'll spend two days fishing and one more day coming back.

All his life, leaving for four days was no big deal. Now it feels weird. Everything feels weird nowadays. The world has changed. The damn virus changes everything in a matter of weeks. Everything is closed. The stores aren't open. They are using fucking cheap toilet paper Pablo stole from the last boat he was on the previous week. Pablo wants to leave, to be in the open ocean and forget about this damn lockdown and all the people dying, but now that Joanna is sick, the trip is a pain. Pablo wants to be as far from home as possible and wants to spend every minute trying to make his wife feel better. He suffocates in her presence because the coughing won't stop and he feels guilty that he hasn't caught it, but he can't breathe when he's away because worry crushes his chest. A lot of people survive, but he guesses those people have access to hospitals. They probably have health insurance.

Pablo gets the urge to call Big Joe and tell him he's no longer available. Then he remembers he needs all the money he can get if he's going to try to get Joanna to a hospital soon, and any thoughts of politely bowing out evaporate with the last of the morning fog. Inside the house, Joanna starts coughing again. Pablo winces, takes another drag, and starts thinking about the beers he'll be having tonight at Big Joe's place with the captain and whoever else will be joining them on the water.

Big Joe's meaty, calloused paw is wrapped around a large glass full of dark, heavy beer. He's addressing Pablo and three other deckhands from the comfort of a gigantic green chair that's been stained with every possible food.

Pablo is sitting in the left corner of Big Joe's ugly beige sofa. Next to him is Nick, a quiet, short man who's somewhere in his fifties; Alex, a thirtysomething bald Cuban with a dark goatee who's always talking about golf and cars; and a pudgy young man named Steve who Pablo hasn't seen before. They'll leave from Katie's Seafood Market on pier 19 at noon the next day. The place is closed because of the lockdown, but Big Joe has a key to it.

"Get ready to do battle," Joe says. "I wanna come back with those coolers full of fish. Ice, bait, gut. You know the drill. Everything else can wait. We'll work long hours. Two-hour shifts, teams of two. Stay fresh and we can work around the clock. I wanna come back to this fucking place as soon as we can. The government is butchering this thing. I wanna be with my family and know most of you feel the same way." He looks at Pablo when he says this.

"Y'all know the fish ain't biting like they used to, but we need pounds to bring in the dough. My contacts sound desperate. If we don't work, people don't eat. I told everyone we'd bring back some fish and that's exactly what I plan to do. As always, I don't want any booze on my boat. Save that shit for when we come back. I don't want one of you going overboard on my watch. Take care of yourselves and each other. Watch the hooks. Hospitals are a fucking mess right now. You fuck up, that's on you. Work clean and fast and we'll be okay. Any questions?"

Big Joe stops talking and looks at them. Pablo sees the worry in the captain's eyes. Fishing in the Gulf of Mexico is a billion-dollar industry, but not much of that lands in their pockets. Folks like them catch shrimp, oysters, blue crab, and several species of finfish, but the big money happens elsewhere and ends up in hands that have never held a net or a fishing hook. Big Joe has three kids, two of them in college. They all came back for spring break a couple days before everything went to shit. Now they are living with Joe and taking their classes online. They're probably eating everything in the house. The captain needs money as bad as Pablo does. That's why they're going to focus on the American red snapper, the iconic Gulf fish. Its market price goes up every season, and that's a good thing. With the way things are now, their price is even higher. Everything is flying off the shelves and into refrigerators. They will sell everything they bring back at a decent price. Too bad the number of fish they catch has been going down in the past few years. If all goes according to plan this time, they'll catch ten to twelve thousand pounds of red snapper on this trip. That's about fifty thousand dollars for Big Joe. Each crew member will be paid a couple thousand dollars, depending on how much they individually catch. Pablo plans on working overtime and packing his coolers to the gills. He knows it won't be enough, but it might be enough to get them to a hospital. Steve interrupts Pablo's thoughts.

"What do you guys do when you get bored out there? This lockdown shit has me going crazy at home. I don't wanna also go crazy on the boat." At the beginning of the meeting, Big Joe said something about having a greenhorn on the boat and smirked. Everyone knew he was talking about Steve.

Pablo looks at Steve's hands. They look like he's never seen a gaff hook. He has the loose mouth and shiny eyes of a drunk.

"You won't have time to get bored," Pablo says. Big Joe finishes his beer and taps the glass against his leg. That signals the end of the usual speech. Everyone mumbles a good night and suddenly Pablo finds himself standing around with Steve and a lukewarm beer. He wants to talk to Joe about maybe getting a bit extra from his next check.

Steve gets up and approaches Pablo. He starts telling a story about his father, a man who owns a used car lot in El Paso. Pablo tries to tune out. Big Joe is by the door, cracking a joke about social distancing on a boat being a trip to the can. When Joe comes back, Steve keeps talking. He's one of those men who process alcohol by flapping their gums endlessly. Joe says he's gonna check on a few emails, pulls out his phone, and walks to the kitchen, leaving Pablo with Steve.

Twenty minutes later, Steve's recounted his past six years working for his father and the fact that he swindled forty-two thousand

dollars in small bills and ran away because his dad is an asshole.
Steve keeps saying he refuses to sell used cars for the rest of his life.
That, he says, is the life of a fucking loser. He's been living in his
car and cheap motels since he ran away. He smiles as he says this,
apparently proud of having stolen from his father. Pablo knows re-
venge is a powerful thing only made more vicious by sharing the
same blood, but says nothing. Steve keeps talking.

"I don't like having the money in the car, but I can't take it to the
bank because all of the banks I've seen are fucking closed. And I
can't carry that shit with me, you know? I need to keep it close until
the old man gives up looking for me. I'm gonna jump on some
boats and make a few thousand bucks while this whole lockdown
thing blows over and then use the money to open up my own business in Portland. I have some buddies up there. It's also fucking far
from El Paso. Ha ha! I'm gonna open up a coffee joint specializing
in exotic blends. Portland is full of hipsters, man. They're gonna
flock to this place. I've been there before and Portlanders love coffee. I'm gonna be swimming in money in no time."

Pablo looks at Steve's eyes and sees the pudgy man is sauced,
his words pouring from his mouth fast and slurry. He hears Joanna
cough inside his skull, sees her sitting up in bed and gasping for air
like a fish out of water. "Listen," Pablo says, "Katie's garage is a small
place, just an old shack right on the pier. You don't want to leave
your car there with the money inside. Take my garage. I'll drive you
down to the pier. You can find some other place to stash it when we
get back, but it'll be safe while you're gone."

Steve pats Pablo on the shoulder and thanks him before asking
for his address. Pablo realizes for the hundredth time in his life
that youth and stupidity are synonymous.

When Pablo's cooler has enough ice for the morning's first haul of
snapper, he moves to a wooden workstation attached to the edge of
the boat. His spot is beside one of the ship's six hydraulic bandits,
mechanical reels that allow them to catch thousands of pounds of
fish in a matter of days. It's six in the morning—only orange glowing lights from neighboring oil rigs shine in the darkness. Pablo's
head is buzzing. They've been on the water all night. They're starting the trip back home in a few hours. The lack of sleep has made
Joanna's cough louder in his head. He imagines coming home and
finding her dead in their bed and something thick and warm grows

in his throat. He can't check the news, but he reads a bit of his phone when he takes a shit. The lockdown is getting worse. People are dying. Hospitals are getting full. New York is fucked. Pablo knows it's now or never.

Knowing they're about to start reeling in the hooked line, Big Joe switches on the boat's floodlights and, after an audible thunk, the bow of the boat is illuminated in a bright-yellow glow. Pablo and Steve are working together. Big Joe said that was the only way they'd keep the greenhorn from fucking up the equipment, the boat, or himself. Pablo feels something tightening in his chest. The feeling makes him think about Joanna. He hears her coughing again. Before leaving, he sat out on the porch, smoking a cigarette and listening to Roberto Roena while wondering if his son was okay. Inside, Joanna, after giving him the kind of kiss that still made him feel things after a life spent together, was coughing again. The memory helps the tightening in his chest to subside.

"You ever eat a snapper tongue?" Steve asks Pablo, his hands struggling to unhook a fish from his line. "They don't have tongues," Pablo says dismissively. Then he thinks about Joanna again and changes his tune. "That thing coming out of their mouths when we pull them up? That ain't a tongue, man; it's their stomach. They get the bends, just like divers. The decompression blows their stomachs out through their mouths."

Steve looks at the fish in his hand, turns toward the ocean, and vomits. Pablo sees the man's silhouette against the orange-tinged sky and drops his line. In a second, he thinks about getting the car keys from Steve's rucksack half an hour earlier as the man slept through their two-hour break. That was the first move. He also took his flotation vest and placed it behind a cooler. Steve woke up and got to work without asking for it. All greenhorns do it. They forget. It's normal. Now Pablo only needs to do the damn thing. He takes two steps and grabs the buoy hook from the wall next to the cabin's entrance while looking at the door to the cabin. The others are probably sleeping. Big Joe is in the wheelhouse. The coast is clear. Pablo turns to Steve. The man is spitting into the ocean, coughing a little. The coughing is almost too much.

Pablo knows he has to put everything he can into the swing. Steve has to hit the cold water completely knocked out or he'll scream. Pablo pulls the buoy hook back and swings with all his strength. The thick metal pole hits Steve's head with a loud thunk that shoots pain down to Pablo's elbows and makes his shoulders feel like they're about to pop out.

Steve's head snaps to the side, and his left arm flies up. He stays there for an endless second before exhaling a strange moan and going overboard, his legs stiff.

Pablo leans over starboard and peers into the water. Steve is face-down, bobbing in the dark water and already drifting away from the boat. His clothes will soon pull him under. Pablo will head inside and use the bathroom. He'll sit down and take a shit. Let a few minutes go by. He'll read about the lockdown while he's in there. He'll send Joanna a text saying he loves her. Then he'll come back out and scream for Big Joe. Steve is just another idiot who made a mistake. He slipped and slammed his head. He wasn't wearing his life vest. Happens all the time. Fucking greenhorns. That's why there are ads for commercial fishing accident attorneys all over Galveston. This is a dangerous job and many fishermen lose their life every year. The floor is slippery with water and blood. Lack of sleep makes them sloppy, careless. A tired greenhorn drowning is no biggie. The story is not new or weird or unique. Steve slipped and cracked his head before going overboard. Everyone has heard of stuff like that happening before. It happened while Pablo was inside taking a dump. He had to. It's nature. No one will blame him for taking a few minutes to hit the can.

Pablo replaces the buoy hook on the wall and looks to starboard again. He keeps expecting to hear a scream or to see Steve's hand grabbing the boat. Neither happens. He walks into the cabin and heads to the small bathroom. He remembers the fat Mexican on the bicycle. Maybe he was just going somewhere early. Maybe he was going back home after having sex with some chola a few blocks down. Maybe he lived nearby and was out for a ride because being locked inside drives people crazy. Everyone has a fucking story. Pablo just wants this one to be over. He wants to hold Joanna and tell her they're going to be okay. He has the money to take her to a hospital now. Yeah, everything is going to be okay.

CHARIS JONES

Green-Eyed Monster

FROM *Wild*

YOU THINK I killed my wife because I was jealous? Not at all, officers. First of all—if you'll forgive the correction—the word you want is *envious,* not *jealous.* Envy is the desire for something that belongs to someone else. Jealousy is the fear of losing something that belongs to you. I wasn't jealous of the great Martina Rybek, I was envious of her—and wouldn't you be, if your wife were up for a Nobel Prize in Physics while you were still struggling for tenure? But that isn't why she's lying upstairs waiting for your forensics team to get here. What happened tonight had nothing to do with our lopsided careers at MIT. It—well, it all started with that tennis ball.

Right, the yellow Dunlop that's floating in the bathtub. Yeah, I know it's a strange thing to find . . . Yes, I realize it wasn't the *only* thing floating in the tub. I'm sure the ball is dead too, and believe me, the poor thing deserves a proper burial. On your walk-through, maybe the two of you noticed the string dangling from the ceiling of our garage? That tennis ball spent nine years at the end of it, just waiting for me to come home every night. It was like a faithful dog that always greets you in the same place. And, except for tonight, I always met my fuzzy buddy in precisely the same spot. Even the nights I drove home a bit hammered. I'd turn the car into the garage smooth as oil, ball hits the red dot on the windshield, bam. Mission accomplished. But when I pulled in tonight, I was dead sober. And dead tired. And damned sick of jumping through hoops.

Did I mention that Martina was something of a control freak?

You've seen her name in the news, so you know she was smart . . . but all that extra neural circuitry comes with a price. Of course, I didn't know that when I met her; I was too blown away by her visions and ideas. Caught up in her brilliance, I could feel the walls of reality getting thinner and more transparent, until it seemed that anything was possible. Now maybe I look like any Joe Schmo standing handcuffed in his kitchen talking to the police, but I've been a neurobiologist for twenty years, and I can tell you that when one part of the brain is overdeveloped, it asphyxiates some other part. In my wife's case, the part that got squeezed was her ability to let the world turn on its own. From the day I met her, she was the twitchiest person I ever saw—always wanting to fix, change, or control something. I didn't realize how deep her compulsions ran until we'd been married about a week and I found Martina on a stepladder, hanging that tennis ball from the ceiling of our garage. Why? Because I wasn't parking the car in quite the right place.

"Sometimes it's too far to the left," she explained, "and I can't get to the recycling bin. And sometimes it's too far forward and I have to go around the back of the car just to get in the house."

I gave her a look that said, *You can't be serious,* but Martina only shrugged as she uncapped a tube of paint.

"I know it looks a little weird," she admitted, "but it'll make things so much easier."

"All right, honey," I said, because I'm a pretty easygoing guy. Not the sort who wants to start fighting just a few days after tying the knot. So I let my bride paint a red dot on the windshield of my old Honda, thinking I was a good man for humoring her.

But, as they say, no good deed goes unpunished. That tennis ball was just the first pebble in an avalanche of household rules—rules I came to realize had only one explanation. Simply put, Martina had to have things a certain way or she came unglued. If the car wasn't parked right, if the milk was sitting where the OJ should be, if the trash in the bins hadn't been pushed down as far as it would go, if the tea bags were not standing at attention like soldiers at drill, she couldn't concentrate. And she didn't trust me to get any of this right. Have you taken note of the labels and instructions on every bin, drawer, and cabinet in this house? Notice how the salt goes in three different places, depending on type and size? And God help you if you put the fancy pink or green or black lava salts in the cabinet with the dry goods! One sound that will haunt me forever is the patter of her heels as she canvassed the house, checking and reorganizing, straightening edges that were already straight, and wiping up invisible dust.

You're probably wondering how on earth she managed a successful research lab. Well, the same way she managed her home. Geniuses are supposed to be eccentric, and it seems like the weirdest ones have the most illustrious careers. Maybe that's my problem — the lobes of my brain are the right size and all the neurons are firing quietly without getting in each other's way. Maybe I'm just too plain-vanilla normal to sail my ship to the stars.

What's that? Right. Stick to the story. Well, I was tired when I got home from work, okay? Theoretical physicists like my wife can play in the cosmic ether without leaving the house, but there's nothing theoretical about biology. Wet labs are messy, demanding places. Cells and explanted tissues require constant feeding, and so do cages of rats. Unlike my wife, I can't afford to hire an army of minions to carry out my grand plans. My technician and I do all the work ourselves. Seven days a week, gentlemen.

So, when I wheeled into the garage tonight and the Dunlop hit the windshield two inches left of the red target, I was surprised and a little annoyed. I backed out and tried again. This time the wretched ball landed three inches to the right. That's what's called *overcompensation*, in case you officers were wondering. Probably you know all about it, with those big guns you're packing. Well, third time's the charm, right? Only this time, it wasn't. On my third try, the ball came to rest maybe a centimeter and a half away from the red dot. Now, I can hear what you're thinking. *A centimeter and a half? Who cares? Close enough for government work.* But that's where you're wrong. *Martina* cared. *Martina* would check — she always did, as soon as I walked in the door. She wouldn't yell or throw a fit, no. She would make this agitated noise somewhere between a groan and a sigh, and her eyes would scrunch shut as if she suddenly had a migraine. And she'd say something like, *George, please, the car's not in the right spot. Would you mind parking it again? It's not too much to ask, is it?*

I gave my parking job one more try, only to miss by a finger's width yet again. Then I killed the engine and got out. I slammed the door so hard the Dunlop bounced. On the other side of the garage, my wife's gray Lexus sat smug and aloof, its unmarked windshield gleaming. Wherever she was in the house, I knew Martina would have heard my car door slam. I could already see her wincing, fingertips kneading at that place above her right ear where all the neurons were misfiring.

I have to float the boat for both of us, whispered the Martina in my mind. She often spoke to me this way in my darker moments. *Since your start-up funds ran out, my endowment is the only thing keeping your pathetic career alive. I pay for all of your rat colonies, your enzymes and petri dishes and ballpoint pens. I pull strings for you. You don't need tenure; I am your tenure. And what do I ask in return? That you keep the house neat. Put things back where they belong. Park the car in the right goddamn spot!*

It was a mistake to imagine her saying these things. A red fog clouded my vision, turning the garage into a darkening world where a faded yellow sun hung low in the sky. I reached out and squeezed that sun. The feel of it, tired and pancake-flat after almost a decade of lighting my way home, sparked my empathy. Here was something that had come off the factory line fresh and ready for life at 100 mph, and instead it had been suspended in a gloomy garage to molder away. Suddenly all the seconds and minutes and hours —hell, years—I'd spent catering to Martina's demands rushed in to fill every nook and cranny in my brain. The combined weight of all that dead time made me stagger.

My life was a sham. I loved my work, and God knows I worked my ass off, but I didn't have the funding to survive on my own. I labored within the cage of my wife's success. I had to ask her—*Ask her!*—for every single thing I needed. She owned me, and I hated her for that. But I hated myself more for staying in the cage.

Standing there in the garage, I imagined Martina sighing and saying, *Is it too much to ask?*

"Yes," I told the tennis ball. "I think it is." Before I could talk myself out of it, I gave the ball a sharp tug and felt it come loose as the old string gave way. I stared at the emancipated orb in a daze. I imagined cramming it down my wife's throat and whispering in her ear, *It took four thousand tries, but I finally hit the right spot.* With a mad laugh, I slipped the ball into my pocket. Then I went inside, closing the door as gently as a thief.

The house was dark. No light spilled down the stairs, as it did when Martina was working in her office. She always kept the door ajar so her antennae could sample the air for signs of disorder. But her car was in the garage, so she had to be home. Maybe she had gone to bed early. Maybe she was sick.

Only . . . my wife never went to bed before 1 a.m. And she had never, in all our years together, suffered from the slightest illness. Some of her circuits might be jammed, but she was apparently immune to human pathogens. So, where the hell *was* she?

I flicked on the light in the entryway and headed into the kitchen—and even in the semi-dark, I could see that something was terribly amiss. The mail on the counter lay in an *ordinary pile,* as if a normal person had brought it in.

"It's a wonder the earth is still spinning," I muttered, straightening the mail by force of habit before remembering that I'd already committed high treason. The ball, after all, was no longer attached to its string. I had torn the sentinel down from its high place and *put it in my pocket.* Tomorrow would be time enough to repent and crawl back into my shell, but tonight, by God, I was going to revel in an orgy of vandalism.

First, I arranged the stack of mail so the big flyers were on top and the smallest envelopes were on the bottom. Then I pulled some gobs of plastic packaging up from the trash bin and let them dangle artistically over the edge, like transparent flowers in bloom. I moved the soap dispenser three inches to the left. I knocked down the column of tea packets—*At ease, soldiers*—and laid one of them facedown, as if he'd been shot in the back by a sniper. Opening the fridge, I moved the butter from its proper compartment to—wait for it—the produce drawer! I shivered at the delicious blasphemy of it. Seeing the butter dish canted at a drunken angle on top of a head of lettuce made me realize what a dry evening it had been. So, I poured myself a double Scotch and violated three home ordinances by leaving my dirty glass at the edge of the table *sans* coaster. Then I went through the house in search of my wife, turning on every light along the way.

The first floor was deserted. Martina's upstairs office was just as empty, her computer screens dark, her desk covered with manuscripts and journals in pristine piles. Her white-noise machine, which migrated between her office and the bedroom, was absent from its daytime place of honor. If the tennis ball and I were fellow inmates, that noise machine was more like a spoiled pet. The little demon was the size of a jewelry box and as black as the vacuum between the stars. It said whatever Martina wanted to hear, but in a voice like rain falling, or distant monkeys howling, or waves pounding some digital shore. It canceled out the noise of real life so she could work or sleep, and most nights, the soft racket drove me to the sofa downstairs.

Peering into the bedroom, I saw no sign of my wife or the noise machine. Then I noticed a faint, flickery glow under our bathroom door. Emboldened by the whiskey, I crossed the room and turned the doorknob. The door opened silently, of course; nothing in our house ever dared to creak.

"Honey—" I began, and then whatever brash declaration I was about to make slid back down my throat, forgotten.

Martina lay in the claw-foot bathtub, which until that point had been purely decorative. All I could see was the hardwood sheen of her hair, which had fallen across her face. Candlelight from an old stub of wax played over the gleaming porcelain. By the side of the tub sat a remote control, a bottle of merlot, and a half-empty glass. Dry thunder from the noise machine echoed through the room. Martina looked up at the sound of my voice, and I was struck by how beautiful she was. Inhumanly beautiful, like something machine-crafted. You could see the fine shape of the bones under her skin. Her hazel eyes shone bright green in the candlelight.

She muttered something I couldn't make out over the rumble of thunder.

"What?" I said, moving slowly into air that was thick with the scent of jasmine. I still couldn't believe what I was seeing. Martina rarely drank, and she *never* lounged in bathtubs by candlelight.

"It didn't get renewed," she said, reaching down to fumble with the remote and send the programmed storm packing.

"What didn't get renewed?" I asked.

She gave me her patented impatient look, but there was a thread of something else beneath it. Was it fear? Uncertainty? It was like a breath of wind blowing through a familiar landscape, turning it briefly into unknown territory.

"My endowment, George," she said.

For a moment I basked in the miraculous, unbelievable knowledge that the exalted Dr. Martina Rybek had been *rejected*. Her infallible force had somehow stopped short! Then I realized what she was talking about—her endowment from MIT. The money that was keeping me in business.

The news should have been a terrible blow, but I felt only a kind of numb relief. Martina shifted in her shroud of bubbles and the smell of night-blooming flowers intensified, adding to the impression that I was in a bizarre dream.

"I don't understand it," she mumbled, reaching for her wineglass. "I hired five new people last year . . . published twenty-two papers . . . gave three keynote talks. I let them prance me around every time there's some promotion for women in science. A show pony that can do physics! Let's see them fit old Swaggerstein into a dress and have him make flirty small talk with the fat-cat donors. I go to their idiotic social functions—even showed my face at Melman's holiday party. I bring in over a million dollars a year for them. What the hell do they *want?*"

"Maybe they figure you already have more than you need," I suggested mildly. "Or maybe they figured out what you're doing with a good chunk of that endowment."

The look she turned on me was full of frustrated contempt. "They knew I was siphoning money to you for years. Besides, the funds in that endowment are untagged—I can do whatever I want with them!" She gestured angrily with her glass, sloshing red wine onto the tiles. I gaped at the impossible mess as silence stretched out like the path to a strange new world.

"So, who are they giving the endowment to?" I asked at last.

"They won't say," she replied. "But you know they're using it to woo someone who already has a Nobel Prize. Just what we need, another fossil whose best years were half a century ago." Martina paused to take a long swallow of wine. "They know I'm not going anywhere . . . not with *you* in tow. They've got me by the balls, and they know it." She put the glass down and stared at the wall. The expression on her face was so unfamiliar, it was like looking at another woman. She appeared utterly lost. This might have been the first time she had ever failed at something.

"Well, our employment opportunities have just opened up," I said brightly. "Since I'll be putting in applications for Wendy's and Burger King, which are everywhere."

Martina turned her bewildered gaze on me. I don't think it had occurred to her yet that this event marked the end of my career. All this tub-languishing and wine-swilling was because a piece of her world had slipped out of her grasp. Note, gentlemen: the biggest piece of *my* world was the very smallest piece of hers.

It took a few seconds, but eventually my point of view sank in and she rolled her eyes.

"Oh, for God's sake," she snorted, flicking at a presumptuous bubble on her arm. "You could try submitting a grant application before you decide to lie down and die. Some of us do it all the time."

I moved a few steps closer to the tub, to where that puddle of merlot gleamed darkly on the floor. It looked like an old sun—a blood-red sun on the brink of supernova. I reached into my pocket and gave the tennis ball a squeeze.

"I had an NIH grant, Martina." Speaking was suddenly difficult, as if I were forcing words through someone else's mouth. "You know that, and you know it wasn't renewed. I guess now you have an idea what that feels like."

She gave me a disgusted look. "You need to learn to play the game, champ. Would it kill you to get to know your program officer?"

"Schmoozing with your PO over cocktails might work at NSF," I said acidly, "but you know NIH sticks to grant scores."

"Are you suggesting that I *schmoozed* my way to the top?" She barked a short laugh. "You biologists are all the same—*poor me, everyone is out to get me, no one understands how important my little experiments are!* If any of you worked as hard as you whine."

"I'm not whining," I said through my teeth, fingers clenched around the tennis ball. I forcibly unclenched them, then collared the bottle of merlot by its scruffy neck and took a swig. The wine tasted like every bitter thought I'd ever jammed into the back of my skull. "I'm just telling you how it is. That money from your endowment kept me going, and I'm grateful. But without it, I have to close up shop."

"It's too bad you're not a physicist," she said, eyeing me speculatively. "Still, you could always come work for me." She said this as if it were the world's most generous offer—as if I would be an ungrateful ass to refuse it. "Jeannie's getting ready to retire, and I'll need a new assistant. You're not as organized as she is, but you know how to push paper and cut through red tape, all the administrative stuff." She took another nip of merlot and raised her eyebrows at me. As much as I hated her, I had to laugh—I couldn't help myself. Her condescension was just so predictable.

"Thanks, honey," I said, leaning over to top off her glass, "but at the end of the day, I think stuffing fries into little paper sacks would be more rewarding."

"Don't be ridiculous," she scoffed. "You're not doing any such thing."

"No?" I said, still wearing what felt like a death's-head grin. "Why the hell not?"

"Because you're my husband," she said, "and my husband is a *scientist.*"

"You just offered me a job as your secretary," I pointed out.

"You would still have the title," she snapped. "Research Associate Professor, Senior Scientist, whatever. Something respectable." She hiccuped, and the hand holding her glass shook. More wine spattered the floor in a trail of bloody drops.

"Martina," I said quietly, pointing to the tiles. She followed my finger and her eyes widened in horror. But when she set the glass down and tried to get up, I put a hand on her shoulder. I wasn't done messing with her yet. A latent perversity had woken up inside me, and it said the evening wasn't over. Not by a long shot.

"Tell you what," I said. "If you can stay in this bath for another ten minutes—just ten minutes—I'll schedule your appointments and bring your coffee. I'll do it with a smile. I'll even wear a skirt."

"What the hell are you talking about?" she hissed, still scrabbling to get out of the tub. I almost let her do it—the sight of my inebriated wife cleaning the bathroom floor in the buff was one I had never seen before and would surely never see again—but I had to stay focused. So, I picked up her wineglass and perched on the edge of the tub to block her escape.

"What's the rush?" I said, waving the glass in her face just to show her what a loose cannon I was. "That wine's not going anywhere."

"It'll stain the tiles, you idiot!"

"You painted a spot that color on my windshield," I reminded her, "the first week we were married. Remember?"

She wasn't listening. Her eyes darted around, looking for a way out, but I was leaning over the tub with her glass of merlot, and she didn't dare push me away.

"Was it really necessary to deface my car?" I went on. "You could have just used a sticker."

"What is with you tonight?" she muttered, then seemed to notice that a cloud of whiskey fumes had overpowered the scent of her bath oil. "Are you drunk?"

"Well, if it isn't the pot talking," I said, sipping her wine and belching for good measure.

Something dark flickered in the depths of her eyes. Tipsy or not, she was recalculating, deciding on a different approach. Suddenly she arched her back so the foam slid off her perfect breasts, then eased down until the sudsy water reached her chin. Her eyes softened into pools of liquid jade.

"I know this is hard," she murmured, reaching up to stroke my neck with one wet finger, "but we'll find a way to get you funded. I'll figure something out."

"There's nothing to figure out," I said hoarsely. "I'm done. Out of the game."

Her hand wandered down my arm, then crept south of my belt, caressing as she hadn't done in years. I stared into the lagoon of her eyes, hypnotized. Snicker all you want, gentlemen, but every man is a prisoner to his own lust. When that need goes unsatisfied—say, for months on end—he's even more of a fool. I had to catch myself before I put the wine down and surrendered my upper hand.

"You're not done," she said, squeezing a groan out of me. I leaned forward to kiss her, but just before our lips met, her gaze darted downward. Toward the spilled wine. And when she looked up again . . .

How can I describe this so you'll understand? Somehow, the curtains of her eyes lifted and I saw *through* them. Not to her soul. What I saw inside was a rat. An insane rat in a lab cage, chittering madly. At that moment, it was busy counting up the minutes, calculating how much time was left before the damage to the tiles was permanent. As brilliant and independent as she was, Martina was a slave to that creature. She would do anything to appease it.

I stared at the rat and it stared back at me, through my wife's green eyes. I shriveled and went cold all over, and my brain—fogged with drink and desire and frustration—finally cleared.

"You're worried about a little spilled wine?" I said, lurching to my feet. My voice was as shaky as my knees, but I spoke clearly to the rat. "That's nothing. Just wait'll you see the party going on downstairs. It's a holiday for *everyone* in the Rybek compound—I even gave the tennis ball the night off." I pulled that newly freed minion from my pocket and tossed it into the tub. Martina froze, staring at the floating Dunlop as if it were a snake.

Put it back.

The words were soundless, an order issued directly into my mind. Still, I knew exactly who—or what—was speaking. I could see it loping back and forth, back and forth, in the dark cage behind my wife's eyes.

Not a chance, I replied in my head.

Put it back. Mop up the wine. Clean up the mess downstairs. Do it now!

Not a chance in hell, I clarified. My long-held resentment toward Martina suddenly shifted its focus. I remembered that even with all her baggage, the old Martina was someone I'd fallen in love with. In the early years of our relationship, we were comrades and good companions. But the prickly sweetness of her personality eroded over time, leaving her cynical and contemptuous of everyone. And this creature giving me orders from behind her eyes . . . this creature was responsible. *As soon as I sober up, I'm going to find a way to get rid of you!*

A chuckle sounded in the depths of my head.

That might have been possible twenty years ago, said the rat, *with drugs or electroshock therapy or a really good psychiatrist. But it's much too late now. I've taken over in here.*

I looked deeper into the rat's cage and saw that what appeared to be bars were not bars at all. They were a meshwork of nerves trailing bright, pulsing axons. Some were frayed and some were dark and severed, as if they'd been bitten clean through. Black eyes gleamed from a jungle of synapses.

How did you get in there? I demanded. *Where did you come from?*

I was born here, the rat answered. *Of course, I was much smaller then —hardly more than an urge or two—but she made a little nest for me and fed me scraps until I was big enough to fend for myself.*

Fend for yourself? I said with dawning horror. I could only think of the rat's teeth, the rat's claws. *Are you trying to kill her?*

Of course not, said the rat. *I know which connections are essential, and which are expendable. Her scientific acumen will remain intact. Other things, like her affections, which were always weak at best, have made for many a good meal.* The creature nosed between the hanging vines of two thick axons, sniffing and questing. Following one up to its source, it took hold of the plump cell and licked its chops.

But won't you starve when you run out of . . . disposable neurons? I asked.

The rat grinned at me. *You're a neurobiologist, aren't you, George?*

You know that neural pathways don't replace themselves quickly, but they do grow back. In the meantime, there's plenty to snack on. As if to illustrate this point, the rat munched delicately at a fringe of dendrites along the cell's surface. Martina shivered, and all the lines of tension on her face disappeared for a moment. Suddenly I saw a trace of the little girl she must have been—as bright and impatient and headstrong as ever, but *free*. Free of this thing that had turned her mind into its meal.

So far, you've done your part to keep things in order, said the rat as it toyed with the denuded cell, batting it lightly from one paw to the other. *Is that going to change? Are you going to clean up the mess you made? Because I have all the tools of persuasion right here.* It bared ancient teeth at me, then dropped the neuron and scampered through the thicket of my wife's brain, toward regions that were still glowing and untouched. *A mind is like a buffet, George. I can stop nibbling on her desire center and she might want to have sex more than three times a year. Or I can start feeding on her sanity, or her sense of human decency. I can make things better for you, or I can make them much, much worse.*

As the rat tore through a web of luminous neurons, I felt something for Martina that I'd never felt before. Pity. Sick with it, I looked away and her noise machine caught my eye. It was sitting on the low shelf above the tub, plugged into an outlet so close that its long cord was bunched up behind it. I turned it on and thunder rent the air, cutting through steam and the stench of alcohol. The power button under my hand was as warm as a running engine. There seemed to be a deadly energy coiled inside that little black box.

I felt a pair of eyes boring a hole in the back of my head. Beady eyes, dark and feral and unblinking. The skies above our house cracked and boomed, and ozone electrified the air, turning the spit in my throat metallic. A recorded thunderstorm never felt or sounded so real.

CLEAN UP THE MESS, shrilled the voice in my head. *CLEAN IT UP, CLEAN IT UP, CLEAN IT UP!*

I swallowed hard, fighting the imperative to obey. The part of me that had always bowed to Martina was trying to drag me toward the tennis ball and the spilled wine, toward fresh string and the scourge of bleach. It was like the thirst for a drink at the end of a long day, like the crippling need for a woman who is only using you as a puppet. But in the steamy mirror, I saw the face of another puppet behind me—my wife enslaved and trapped in the prison of her own mind. I put the wine down and gazed at the source of the storm, that throbbing box under my hand. There was an answer there, if I could only see it.

In the lab, there are times when your mind's vision is true and your hands are golden—the brain and its tools in perfect sync. As the thunder rolled, I felt that power coursing through my fingers, working its way up to my brain. And all at once, I knew how to set her free. I just had to do one last experiment with a rat.

Sliding the noise machine toward me, I rotated it so the left corner overhung the shelf. Martina's favorite device was now precarious, misaligned, an offense to the eye . . . in flagrant violation of the one true law that governed this house. You can never be sure how an experiment will turn out, but that feeling of inevitability was so strong. The alcohol she had consumed, the moisture slicking the shelf, and the box itself were all colluding with me to bias the outcome. As I turned and walked away, I knew exactly what would happen in the next few seconds. And I may not be a physicist, gentlemen, but I know what a ground-fault circuit interrupter is—and I know this old house doesn't have one.

Behind me, I heard the swish of water in the tub, then the squeal of a startled rodent. I turned just as the noise machine struck the bath, hissing like oil on a hot griddle. Martina shrieked and jerked like a marionette, stirring up a maelstrom. Her face contorted, and there was nothing human in her eyes. They seethed with the frenzy of a doomed creature, clawing and gnawing in vain. Smoke rose from the bathwater as the noise machine sank beneath the waves. The wineglass had overturned on the shelf, and a Red Sea flooded the bathroom floor, but my wife no longer cared about such trivialities. I had baited a trap for her master, and the rat—well, the rat had choked on the cheese.

You're looking a little pale, gentlemen. Would you care for some refreshment? I'm sorry to say I finished off the whiskey before you got here—and we're all out of wine—but there might be an old bottle of pineapple rum in the cupboard. No?

Well, I guess that's the end of the story, then. By the time I see a lawyer I'll probably wish I'd kept quiet, but right now I just want you to understand. Tonight, for the first time, I didn't envy Martina. I finally saw her as she was, the most helpless prisoner in the

Rybek house. But I managed to free both of us. Even standing here in handcuffs, I feel liberated.

Would you believe that I feel empty too, because I've sacrificed everything I hold dear? Everything I fell in love with . . . true genius, unshakable confidence and willpower, the ability to blaze a path through all of life's obstacles. Even when thorns grew thick around those virtues, I still clung to them. I hoarded them for nine miserable years, because they were things I couldn't bear to lose.

So, I guess maybe you were right. Maybe I was jealous of Martina, after all.

Potato Sandwich Days

FROM *Rock and a Hard Place*

THE MAN WITH the mustache really wanted a potato sandwich. Dan had spent the last half hour alone at the counter, giving decent people their burgers and chicken. Just fourteen minutes to closing on a Thursday night.

"Sir, we no longer offer the potato sandwich. We have other fine—"

"I got a coupon, says good through January 31. What day is today?"

"I'd be more than happy to serve you any other—"

"What-day-is-today?"

It was January 29. Fat Lad's HQ had miscalculated demand, and they'd run out of mix last night. A lot of people were upset— *Oh, hell, no.* They pointed to the promotional poster, insulted the shape of Dan's head, knocked over the chairs that weren't bolted down. And all for a nasty mash of potatoes and gloppy white sauce inside a stale roll. Dan thought the food in prison was better, but some parts of the country had riots over the potato sandwich. People breaking in at night, some teenage girl in a paper hat fending off a mob, on the news with a thousand-yard stare, talking like it was some old Nam documentary— *I have never seen such inhuman evil in the eyes of men.*

The guy with the mustache had been in four or five times a week since Potato Sandwich Days had begun.

"We just don't have the ingredients for the potato sandwich," Dan said.

"Can you read the sign above you? Can you read what it says?"

Dan didn't have to look—*Enjoy a potato sandwich today*—but he glanced up where the man pointed.

"Today. Says *today*, don't it?"

It was quiet enough that maybe Dan could go back in the kitchen, grab a bun and a fistful of fries, squirt in six packs of mayonnaise and a touch of hot sauce. That's what he was going to do. It might just be enough to satisfy this pushy bastard.

"I got a coupon. I got eleven of these." The man spread them out on the counter. "I want six tonight. You better have five ready tomorrow."

No, he wasn't going to jury-rig six potato sandwiches.

"I'm sorry, sir, but we cannot honor these coupons."

"You're going to honor them. Some Kennedy Center shit better happen for my coupons."

"Sir, there are many other fine dining experiences you can have at Fat Lad."

"Why the fuck are you talking like this?"

It was a fair question. When he was nervous, Dan fell into passages from the training book. He knew it made him sound ridiculous, but it really did keep him from leaping over the counter and beating people senseless.

"Is there anything else I can help you with?" Dan asked.

"Step one: you are going to make me a goddamn potato sandwich. Step two: you are going to love, honor, cherish, and obey my coupons. That's what's got to happen."

"Hey, Mario Kart. Don't talk to my staff that way," Annette said.

Dan hadn't heard her come out of the kitchen, but she was all the way around the counter, moving in on the little man.

"Fine. *You* get my potato sandwiches. I want six."

Annette swiped the coupons off the counter and onto the floor. Then she pointed a finger very close to his face. "You abuse my staff, you don't get shit."

The man with the mustache spoke quietly. "You just made a very bad mistake."

He picked up his coupons and left the restaurant. A few of the other patrons looked up, but no one was too concerned.

"Why you let him talk to you that way?" Annette asked. "Guy like that? You could pick him up with one hand, dip him in the deep fryer."

"Why you think I didn't do that?"

"Because you're a huge pussy?"

"Yeah, that's why."

"I know the situation, but you don't have to let them talk to you that way."

But he did have to let them talk to him that way, because he really loved his life. Okay, maybe *love* was a little strong, but he liked having his own room, his own car, his own shower. He could come and go when he wanted. Sometimes Annette spent the night and made eggs the next morning. He was doing everything right, and he wanted to keep on doing everything right.

At the end of the shift, Dan took the trash out back and hurled it up into the dumpster. This was probably his favorite part of the job. He got to throw objects roughly the size and shape of small humans ten feet up in the air, off a brick wall, into a big metal box. Annette was coming home with him tonight. She gave him shit about his car and his room, but she liked his big, rough body, and she liked telling him how kind and gentle his eyes were. He studied them in the mirror sometimes. He thought they looked slow and scared.

The only light in back came off the illuminated FAT LAD sign, a leering, drooling child. Dan could just make out his car across the lot, the only one left—something looked wrong. When he walked over, he saw the tires were slashed. Not just one. All four were stabbed in multiple spots. And the hood wasn't shut tight. Just replacing the wheels would cost more than he had. If the engine was wrecked, then what? He'd probably have to pay someone just to tow it away. And how was he going to get to work?

He climbed into the car. It still stank like metal and cheese—the smell it had had when he'd bought it used from a friend of his PO. Cheapest car he could afford; he'd paid off about half of it. In the back seat were the bright-green Fat Lad's training manual and a pamphlet on how to get a GED. Glossy pictures of young people with bright futures. Crisp haircuts and neat clothes, they were all smiling because they knew they were going places—*Commitment, Achievement.*

Dan put the key in the ignition. Maybe he could roll home, then spend the next morning tracking down cheap tires, but the engine wouldn't come alive. When he told Annette what had happened, she pulled the parking lot security tape. It wasn't great footage, but there was no doubt that it was the little guy with the mustache who'd wrecked his car. For all he knew, it was a customer's car, or someone leaving it there overnight, but the little guy had decided that it must belong to an employee. And he'd been right.

"Look at him go at it like Freddy Krueger." She laughed.

"So what do we do?"

"He's got a lifetime ban from this store. Comes back in, I'll beat his ass. I will do that with pleasure."

"Sure, but—"

She called her ex to come pick her up.

Some guys would rather be in prison than live on the streets. Dan was not one of them. What he really wanted was to be a clock-puncher with a room and a TV, but that had all fallen apart quickly. By April, he was homeless and in violation of parole. The summer days were long and hot, and he had a few spots where he could sleep outside at night. He could feel himself losing touch with the world, becoming less and less useful or capable of accomplishing anything beyond surviving the day. For a while, he hung out in the park with a guy named French, until French got really paranoid and took a swing at him. Dan also had a few talks with cops, but all they did was move him along when he was loitering in the prettier parts of town. Eventually, he'd get taken in, someone would run his prints, and then he'd be back in prison, but so far, he wasn't worth the trouble.

In October, the nights started to get crisp, and Dan had to think about winter. He hated shelters. While he was scouting for indoor locations, he saw the advertisement on the side of a bus stop — THE POTATO SANDWICH IS BACK. STARTING OCTOBER 21 AT PAR-TICIPATING FAT LADS. There were two Fat Lads in town: the one Dan used to work at, and one out on Oakland Avenue. On Octo-ber 21, Dan started hanging out in front of the Oakland Avenue restaurant. They shooed him away from the entrance, but there was a bench under a stand of trees about fifty yards away. He sat there and watched the door. For three days, nothing, then on the twenty-fourth, he saw the little man with the mustache, hesitating, looking around as he made it to the entrance, where he waited about two minutes, then turned and started walking away again. When he spotted Dan, he came right over.

"Hey, man. I'll give you twenty bucks; go in there and buy me three potato sandwiches."

He didn't recognize Dan, but that wasn't surprising. Dan had a full beard and no plastic visor. He wondered if his eyes looked kind and gentle. There were bushes behind the bench. The easiest move might be to pop the little guy in the face, then drag him back there. Someone might see, probably not. And who knew how tough the guy was. There were muscled-up dudes who went down with a tap, and little old men with beef-jerky bodies who'd take shot after shot, cursing and screeching for years before they'd go down.

"Get one for yourself."

"I don't like the look of it," Dan said.

"Hey, I *know* what it looks like. Lumpy discharge. Chlamydia hoagie. I don't care. Fucking tasty." He gave the chef's kiss straight up to God. "Plus tax, it'll come to about thirteen bucks. You bring them to me, you keep seven dollars."

"Why can't you buy your own sandwiches?"

"You don't want seven bucks?"

If the prices were the same as they'd been last January, three sandwiches would go for $14.33. Easy money for a few minutes in a Fat Lad.

"Give me the cash," Dan said.

The man hesitated. "I'll be back tomorrow. Probably be back most days as long as they got the sandwich. You wait here, we can do this every day."

Dan nodded and took the bill.

This Fat Lad looked exactly like the one Dan had worked at. There were five people waiting in line and two kids at the register, punching buttons indifferently. He stood behind a small woman who glanced back at him once and tensed up. She kept her place another half minute, then left the line and went over to the condiment area to read a pack of mustard. The manager came out just before Dan's turn. Dan had to show him the money before he okayed the girl to get the sandwiches. But that was the worst of it.

The man with the mustache smiled when Dan handed him the food. He didn't get up, just set the bag in his lap. He'd sat in the middle of the bench, so there wasn't enough room for Dan on either side. Lined up perfect for a kick to the face.

"They don't let me in there," the little guy said. "That ever happen to you? You do something in a place, get banned?"

"No."

"Some girl is an assistant manager at a Fat Lad, thinks that makes her some kind of fucking aristocrat?" He laughed. "No. I put her in her place."

"What you do?"

The man shrugged.

"That happened here?" Dan asked.

"No, it was a different place, different Fat Lad."

"So, what, they got your picture up on the wall in every restaurant?"

"Man, I'd kerosene them all. Light them all on fire. But I love the potato sandwich too much."

For the next month, Dan bought three sandwiches for the little guy every weekday. He also found a spot to sleep just two blocks from the Fat Lad. It was a narrow wedge between two buildings, sheltered by the tin overhang of a paint store. No wind, no rain, but it got cold. Dan bundled up and he was fine, but it was only November.

"Hey, want to see something?" the man asked one Thursday.

He showed Dan a video on his phone. Two women straight from church in white dresses and hats, slugging it out over the last Fat Lad's potato sandwich.

"Look at her, look at her. *Bonk.*"

The man laughed as one of the women crashed hard onto a plastic table. Punching, clawing. Dan shook his head.

"Ladies in lace, tearing each other apart." He looked over at Dan and seemed disappointed that Dan wasn't laughing along with him. "Yeah, eleven million idiots, we got nothing better to do than watch this crap. What's wrong with us?"

"You have to do something with your time."

"Yeah." He nodded. "There was a lot of pressure on me growing up, you know? Pressure to achieve. You know how I mean that?"

"Sure."

"And I think about what I've actually done. What I got to be proud of. My job's all right, but there's not much more room for advancement. I'm almost forty. What have I done? What have I achieved, really?"

That evening, Dan went all the way across town to get rat poison.

"You got rats? In your— *house?*"

The man was snide. If you didn't have a home, you didn't have to protect yourself from vermin. You were vermin.

"Whereabouts do you live?"

"Why?"

"I want to know where you're going to use it."

If the counter had been a little less wide, he might've grabbed the man by the neck. Please, just sell me my poison.

"I'm at a halfway house over on Mason," Dan said. "We got rats big as Thanksgiving turkeys. Staff don't care. They don't sleep there."

"So you get a few bucks together, and the first thing you do is buy rat poison out of your own pocket?"

"That's right."

"You could get some shampoo. Clean pair of pants."

Most people didn't want to talk to you, but there was a certain kind of guy who'd bust your balls for no reason.

"How about you just sell me my rat poison?"

"Don't talk to me that way." The man stepped back, and his hand went under the counter. Provoke the big homeless dude, get him to threaten you, shoot him in the head? It was possible that this man could justify all of that—justify it to himself, to the police.

Dan tried to remember some of the old lines from the Fat Lad's training manual—*How can we work together to resolve this issue?*

The man got the rat poison off the shelf and rang it up.

The last day of the potato sandwich was the twenty-third of November. The Fat Lad on Oakland Avenue had kept up with demand, and they had product all the way to the end. The man with the mustache showed up a little early on the final day. He wanted eight.

"It's not as good reheated, but it's better than nothing," he said. He gave Dan a hundred-dollar bill. "Keep the change, like always. It'll probably come to seventy bucks for you. Something like that."

Dan shook his head. "They're not going to take a hundred from me."

"Yeah, you're right." The man took back the hundred and gave Dan three twenties.

When Dan brought the food out, the little guy was standing up, jangling and clapping his hands to keep warm.

"Long line?" he asked.

"No. I think they had to fix the fryer or something."

"You were in there so long, I started to think you'd stiffed me because it was the last day."

"I wouldn't do that."

"I know. I know, you wouldn't." Then the man got very sincere. "I'll tell you something—I deal with a lot of people. You're a good dude. People want to tell you who's important, who's got value. Man, you're real, and you're one of the good ones."

"Thanks. Means a lot," Dan said.

"So I wish you all the best. And, you know, Potato Sandwich Days will come again."

They shook hands, and the man walked back to his truck and drove away.

It only took one death to end the potato sandwich. They closed both the Fat Lads in town. The CEO went on national TV—*this cowardly act stands in direct opposition to everything the Fat Lad family believes in*. Dan didn't see it, but he read about it in one of the discarded newspapers that he collected and slept on. Some mornings he woke up numb from the cold, unsure whether or not he still had feet. They hadn't even had a deep freeze yet, those subzero nights. When it came, he wondered whether he'd make it through, but he didn't feel like he had much more to achieve.

AYA DE LEÓN

Frederick Douglass Elementary

FROM *Berkeley Noir*

KEISHA WAITED UNTIL everyone else left the office. It was Friday night and nobody seemed to be working late. Still, she shoved her sweatshirt up against the bottom of the door, in case any light could be seen. Only then did she turn on the fluorescent light in the windowless copy room.

A few weeks before, she had swiped a contract on letterhead from a real estate agency. Earlier that day, she had borrowed a co-worker's computer to write the fake lease for a rental apartment. She had copied the language off the Internet but was anxious about any spelling or grammatical errors. Especially because she couldn't save a forged document on a company computer. She had sat at her data-entry cubicle during lunch, reading the words over and over until they blurred, proofreading it to the best of her ability.

That night in the copy room, she cut and pasted and made copies of copies, until she had a reasonable-looking forgery on fine linen paper. She squinted at it in the glaring fluorescent. It looked legit. It "proved" that she rented a two-bedroom apartment in Berkeley.

Keisha and her seven-year-old son, Marchand, lived in Holloway, a few towns north of Berkeley, just past Richmond at the end of the BART line. Holloway's student population was nearly all Black and Latino, but the teachers were predominantly white. All of the schools were performing far below the national average, and the district was on the verge of bankruptcy. Her son had been bullied by bigger boys, and one of the teachers had been fired for hitting a student. Apparently, the administration had tolerated it for years, but one of the staff had caught it on video, and it had gone viral on social media.

That was the last straw. Keisha wasn't going to allow her son to be in a school where white teachers were physically abusive. But she couldn't afford private school. Even a partial scholarship was out of the question. Bay Area rents were exorbitant.

When she first got pregnant with Marchand, she and her boyfriend had a great one-and-a-half-bedroom apartment in Richmond. She was working at the law office doing data entry. Her boyfriend was working as a security guard at the mall. They had enough income to save for the baby. But one night, her boyfriend got stopped by the cops for no apparent reason. Ultimately, he was hauled off for resisting arrest and battery on an officer. The dashboard cams, however, had been turned off. They beat him badly enough that he was in the hospital for a week. Then he was locked up.

Keisha gave up the apartment and moved in with her mom in Holloway. She was numb with grief for the first couple weeks, then she cried for another month.

"Girl," her mother had told her two weeks before her due date, "you need to stop all that crying and get ready to have this baby."

Her ex-boyfriend's mom called after the video went viral of the teacher hitting the student. "One of my friends from church called me," said the woman who would have been her mother-in-law. "She asked me, *Isn't that your grandson's school in Holloway?*"

The two of them talked, and Marchand's grandmother offered Keisha the use of her address to get Marchand into the Berkeley public schools. They had much better test scores, and Berkeley was the first district in the United States to voluntarily desegregate in the 1960s. They wouldn't have crazy racist white teachers hitting the kids.

The mother-in-law put Keisha's name on her energy bill to document her residency, and Keisha breathed a sigh of relief.

But when she went into the district office to figure out how to register her son for school, there was much more documentation required.

All proofs must be current originals (issued within the last 2 months) imprinted with the name and current Berkeley residential address of the parent/legal guardian. A student can have only one residency for purposes of establishing residency.

Only personal accounts will be accepted (no care of, DBA, or business accounts).

Group A:
  __ *Utility bill. (Must provide entire bill.)*
  __ *PG&E*
  __ *Landline phone (non-cellular)*
  __ *EBMUD*
  __ *Internet*
  __ *Cable*

Group B:
  __ *Current bank statement (checking or savings only)*
  __ *Action letter from Social Services or government agency (cannot be property or business)*
  __ *Recent paycheck stub or letter from employer on **official** company letterhead confirming residency address*
  __ *Valid automobile registration in combination with valid automobile insurance*
  __ *Voter registration for the most recent past election or the most recent upcoming election*

Group C:
  __ *Rental property contract or lease, with payment receipt (dated within 45 days)*
  __ *Renter's insurance or homeowner's insurance policy for the current year*
  __ *Current property tax statement or property deed*

Keisha was bewildered by the list. She wouldn't even be able to document her actual address in Holloway, let alone her baby daddy's mother's address in Berkeley.

As she stood there in the empty entryway for the Berkeley Unified School District, a mother and daughter walked in, a matching pair of strawberry blondes. The mother was talking on the phone, pulling the girl behind her. ". . . which is exactly what I told him," the woman was saying. "The rest of the PTA needs to get involved, because this is absolutely unacceptable. Hold on—" The woman stopped in her tracks and the girl, who was looking off into space, nearly collided with her. The woman turned to Keisha. "Where's the Excellence Program office?" she demanded.

Keisha blinked, confused. "I don't work here," she said.

The woman stared at her for a moment, taking in Keisha's multicolored extensions, tight jeans, and low-cut top. Then she turned away without a word and put the phone back to her ear. "Where did you say the office was?" she asked whoever was on the other end, and headed down the corridor, dragging the girl behind her.

The strawberry-blond woman was the only parent Keisha saw that day. Obviously, this white lady wasn't going to let her daughter get smacked by a teacher. Or go to an underperforming school. Keisha was determined to beat the list.

At work, she canceled her direct deposit, and started having her paychecks sent to her mother-in-law's house. It was incredibly inconvenient to have to take public transportation across three cities twice a month to get her check two days later than usual. Yet she and Marchand managed it, and his grandmother was delighted to see more of him.

But the rental agreement? That had proved to be the most difficult to fake.

"Number seventy-two?" The full-figured woman behind the counter at the Berkeley Unified School District office had large brown eyes, a neat bob hairstyle, and a weary smile.

Keisha stepped forward with her paperwork. After the look the strawberry-blond mom had given her last time, she'd had her braids done without colors and dressed in her interview suit. She wanted to look like she worked in San Francisco's financial district or Silicon Valley. Like someone who could afford a two-bedroom apartment.

But now it was registration. The district office was full of Berkeley parents wearing jeans and T-shirts, cotton separates, and ethnic fabrics. Keisha felt overdressed. Still, she filled out the various forms to enroll Marchand in second grade.

When the woman called Keisha up to the counter, she pulled out her paperwork with what she hoped looked like confidence. Marchand's birth certificate, her driver's license, and each of the required documents from the list. Two were real, but the third one was the forgery.

The woman inspected each of them carefully. Keisha's heart beat hard as the administrator's sharp eyes got to the rental contract. As the seconds ticked by, Keisha grew increasingly certain the woman would call her a fake, or worse yet, call the police. Could she be arrested for this? But just as she began to brace for the worst, the woman smiled and said she would make copies for the file.

Keisha smiled back, relief washing over her.

The woman brought back the originals, stamped her copy of the registration form, and stapled it to a packet of papers. They were in.

Two months later, she got a letter at Marchand's grandma's house stating that the boy had been assigned to Frederick Douglass Elementary.

The first day of school dawned overcast and chilly, like so many Bay Area August mornings. Keisha and Marchand rode a BART train and a bus to Frederick Douglass. It took longer than expected, and they arrived twenty minutes after the start of school. Keisha found Marchand's name on a list and hurried him down the hall to room 126.

The hallway was wide and bright, with daylight streaming in through the windows. At their old school in Holloway, there were always late families rushing in, parents hissing at their kids about what they should have done to be on time. But this school's corridors were quiet and orderly. Keisha vowed to catch a much earlier train. She would get Marchand to school on time from now on.

The numbers of the classrooms were getting higher. Room 118. Room 120. Along the hallway wall hung a big banner that read EVERY MONTH IS BLACK HISTORY MONTH, between pictures of Harriet Tubman and Rosa Parks.

When they got to room 126, there was a poster of Frederick Douglass on the door.

Marchand tugged on Keisha's hand. "Mommy," he asked, "do they sometimes hit the kids here too?"

"Oh no, baby." She kneeled so she could get down to his level and put one hand under his chin. "Nobody gets hit here," she said, glancing up at Frederick Douglass. It was the classic unsmiling portrait in a bow tie, with his salt-and-pepper hair combed back and a dark goatee. "That's why Mommy worked so hard to get you into a good school. Now come on, sugar, we got to get you into your class."

She opened the door with an apology in her mouth—full of *late BART train* and *I promise to do better*—but she was startled into silence. Twenty-three faces turned to her, expectantly. All of them were white.

Keisha felt disoriented. This was the first school district in the nation to voluntarily desegregate? This was a school named after the great Black abolitionist?

Keisha looked closer. No. Not all white. That girl by the window with the blue hair was Asian. That boy on the far end might be Latino. And that girl looking up at her, with the sandy hair and the missing tooth, was definitely mixed with Black. But every single kid in the class would pass the paper-bag test.

"You must be Marchand," the teacher said warmly to her son. She was a slender young woman with a messy blond bun on her head. Miss Keller.

Keisha watched her son walk shyly forward into the class.

"Give Mommy a hug goodbye?" Miss Keller prompted.

Numbly, Keisha hugged her son and stepped out into the hallway, wondering what she had forged her way into.

KRISTEN LEPIONKA

Infinity Sky

FROM *Tough*

THEY WERE CALLED the Speed Dragons. Jeramey first laid eyes
on them in the lobby of the Columbus Hotel, four smug guys in
nearly identical Affliction T-shirts dragging their gear across the
polished floor. They made a beeline for Chess, her boyfriend, who
lounged with Jeramey's guitars on a leatherette ottoman, and the
band members engaged him in conversation for several minutes
before Chess finally shook his head and pointed to Jeramey standing in line at the front desk, like it was just then occurring to him
that they were looking for her. Jeramey felt a stab of irrational hatred for the Speed Dragons as they gazed at her, blank. But she was
forced to turn away, her attention pulled into this new indignity.

"No, there's been a mistake. I'm supposed to be in the penthouse suite, with the view of the river," she said, shaking her head
at the room keys in their little paper sleeve. The wedding planner
told her it had all been arranged. "It was all supposed to be arranged."

The desk clerk nodded. "We've had the *tiniest* change of plans,"
she said, then dropped her voice to an unapologetic whisper. "We
have some *very* high profile guests in the hotel this weekend."

Jeramey considered. So no one recognized her here — fine, even
though she still looked as good as the girl in that white miniskirt on
the cover of *Touch and Go*. Or, at least, that girl's slightly older sister. More or less. But that was beside the point. She could feel her
personal equity receding, like soil erosion of the spirit. As it was,
she'd already compromised by flying coach. *There isn't a first class on
a Chautauqua Airlines regional commuter flight,* the wedding planner

had told her, getting a little snippy. *It's only for two hours. Is it that big of a deal?* But Jeramey was the one who had to buy Chess three bloody marys on the plane just to make him shut up about it. Nine dollars each, and she could smell the cheap vodka from two seats away. It was getting to be a bit much to endure, even for ten grand.

Now the Speed Dragons were heading her way. Jeramey didn't need to meet them in order to distill this band down into their essence: there would be a Brad among them, and a Wesley or a Corbin, a weekday-afternoon radio DJ, and an ad agency project manager. The quiet-looking one in the fedora would be the only real musician of the group but he would avoid any kind of direct attention, terrified that someone would discover his terrible secret — bald at age twenty-eight. The wedding planner had passed along their LP so that Jeramey could learn the songs in preparation, but she hadn't. "Listen," she said to the hotel clerk, wanting to be done with it before the Speed Dragons knew all about her business. "Forget it. The seventeenth is fine."

"It's a lovely room," the clerk said. "Great views of the insurance building!"

After the wedding, Doug Beavers rode the sad little shuttle back to the hotel and fumed. It was almost funny, how some smug assholes just *think* they're the center of the universe, but others, even though it hurts to admit it, actually *are* — they somehow know everyone that you know, they've already been anywhere you could hope to go, they even turn up at your cousin's stepdaughter's wedding and charm the pantyhose off every woman there. Bennett Langdon was one of those assholes. It transcended coincidence. It was just the way things were. Beavers bet Langdon had a private driver to take him to the reception. No way a guy with that much cash would ride on a shuttle bus, with its stained gray-brown seats and sticky floor and vague chemical blueberry deodorizer in the air, which gave the impression that someone had, recently, peed inside the vehicle.

At least Langdon had come to the wedding alone. "I bet he didn't get an *and guest*," his cousin murmured sympathetically when they both discovered the horror, that Langdon was some peripheral friend of the groom's family. It would have been undeniably worse if he'd turned up at Beavers's cousin's stepdaughter's wedding with Celia Beavers on his arm. This was not out of the question — it had only been a year earlier that the whole affair went down, his plain, good-hearted wife and the cap-toothed charmer who taught the six-session self-actualization seminar that Beavers himself had paid for Celia to attend. It was hardly a fair fight; Langdon, silver-tongued devil of the self-help aisle, versus Doug Beavers, Weeble-shaped middle manager. The affair was long over by now, but the divorce was forever and Beavers was the type to hold a grudge.

"I really wish you could just relax and have a good time," his cousin said when he stalked back to the table with a plate piled high with bacon-wrapped water chestnuts.

"Oh, I'm having a great time," Beavers said. Langdon was currently holding court near the wedding cake with two of the bridesmaids, who were giggling behind their wrist corsages. "I just want to keep my eye on him. No surprises."

"But Dougie, he probably doesn't even know you're here."

"Then it's even more important to know where he is," Beavers said. He set down the hors d'oeuvres plate and headed in the direction of the bar.

". . . penthouse," he heard Langdon say to the women. "It's got an incredible view."

So it was not the worst performance of her career. No, that honor would have to go to the gig in Berlin when her bass player puked on one of the tube amps and shorted out the entire sound system. But it was, quite frankly, a close call. The Speed Dragons played angsty garage-rock versions of "The Electric Slide" and "Butterfly Kisses" while Jeramey faked along. If not for the weed that Chess had procured from a bellhop, she would have been in tears. As it was, she wondered how many more times she'd be able to play "Infinity" without her head exploding. "*Sweet forever sugar,*" she sang as the newly wedded couple swirled around the ballroom during their first dance, "*infinity sky.*" This was the whole reason she was here—the rich, dim, Midwestern bride having always dreamed of dancing to the tune played live, by Jeramey Jones herself, at her wedding. It was a wildly inappropriate choice, nothing but a heroin-soaked ballad about, well, heroin, but the masses, with their endless capability to misunderstand, had turned it into a mainstream love song, rocketing Jeramey out of the indie punk world and into the spotlight for a moment in time. The moment had since passed—long since passed—but the song endured.

"I just can't even tell you," the bride gushed at her afterward. "Having you here, omigod! I want you to stay all night!"

"Totally!" Jeramey said, accepting a clammy hug before departing immediately.

She sought refuge in the lobby bar, where two bourbons filled in the cracks left by the mediocre weed. She sat against the wall and half watched a silent baseball game on a television mounted to the wall and willed no one to speak to her, but she was only midway through the second drink when a large, oniony presence appeared to her right.

"Don't I know you from somewhere?" the guy asked with a blast of gimlet breath.

Jeramey looked at him. He was fat and fiftyish, sloppily buttoned into an odd gray tux, the bow tie of which dangled from one shoulder like it was trying to get away from him. He had hair the color of nothing and pale-gray eyes that seemed to have trouble focusing.

"You're not famous or something, are you?"

"No, I was just at that wedding," Jeramey said.

"Which side," her new friend said, "bride or groom?"

"Bride."

"Yeah? Me too. My cousin's—"

"Can I just watch the ball game, please?"

At this, the guy laughed way too hard. "The *ball game?*"

"Yeah," Jeramey said. "I want to watch the ball game."

"You're interested."

"I am."

"Okay, Abner Doubleday, who's playing?"

"For the love of God," Jeramey muttered. She slid off the barstool and tossed a crumpled tip next to her half-empty glass.

"For such a baseball fan, you're a pretty poor sport," the guy said. He spun around on his stool and grabbed her ass.

Jeramey bristled but walked away without looking back. "Ohio fucking sucks," she announced as she exited the bar, to a few mutters of agreement and one whooping cheer.

Chess was sitting on the bed with the bellhop when she walked into the room. "Wow, are you her?" the bellhop said.

"Yup, this is Jeramey Jones, 1997's Best New Artist nominee," Chess said in a fake-announcer voice. He held a smoldering joint with one hand and sifted through a pile of minibar snacks with the other.

"Nineteen ninety-eight," Jeramey said, shooting him the finger. "If you set the sprinklers off, I'll kill you."

"Don't worry," the bellhop said. He was a lanky kid with reddish hair buzzed into a fade. "We got it covered." He pointed up at the smoke detector, which was shrouded with a dripping wet washcloth. He offered her the weed, but Jeramey shook her head.

"I'm exhausted," she said. "Can we wrap up this party?"

"It's only nine-thirty," Chess said.

"Seriously?" She flopped onto the edge of the bed. The room was beige and claustrophobic. It had an anonymous quality to it, like a shared cubicle at the phone company. "I think time is messed up in Ohio. It's stuck or something."

"Tell me about it," the bellhop said. He unscrewed the cap on a tiny bottle of Baileys and chugged it.

Jeramey lay down on the edge of the bed and selected a whiskey bottle from the pile, drinking it without sitting up. Then she rolled off the bed and went to the window. "Great views of the insurance building!" she muttered. The building in question was a concrete void with a blinking radio antenna on the top. "Hey," she said finally. "You don't have keys to the penthouse suite, do you?"

"This has to be the worst idea ever," the bellhop whispered as they padded single-file off the eighteenth-floor elevator. "But I'm just high enough to go along with it."

"I just want to see the view," Jeramey whispered back. She steadied herself on the wall with one palm. The night was getting silvery, like she was viewing herself through a window streaked with liquid diamonds.

"Do you think the minibar has better shit up here?" Chess asked.

"What, like tiny bottles of Cristal?"

"That would be *awesome*," the bellhop said. "Okay, this is it."

They stood in front of the door. It looked pretty ordinary. The bellhop rapped sharply on it with a knuckle and called out, "Room service!"

No response.

"Room service," the bellhop said again, knocking louder this time.

Nothing.

He turned to Jeramey and gave her an impish smile. She decided that she'd sleep with him, if it came up.

"Let's do it," she said.

The bellhop inserted a plastic key card into the slot and pushed the door open slowly. Jeramey practically heard angels singing. The room was at least twice the size of hers, decorated in plush navy blue instead of beige, with a whole separate living room area and kitchenette. Chess made a beeline for the minibar. "Shit, there's macadamia nuts in this one," he said.

Jeramey headed for the window but froze just after she crossed into the bedroom. The room was not, as it turned out, empty.

"Fuck," Jeramey said.

A dark, lumpy shape was snoring quietly from the bed.

"Fuck, fuck."

"Oh, man, we need to get out of here," the bellhop said from behind her.

But the window, with its view of the river, was right there, just a few feet away. Jeramey darted toward it and parted the curtains, but it was too dark to see anything other than the ghost of her own reflection.

"Okay," Jeramey whispered. "We can go."

As she crept back past the snoring lump, it stirred and emitted an oniony belch. "Wait a minute," she said, turning back. She squinted in the thick darkness at the man's face. "No fucking way," she said. Of all the *high-profile guests* in the hotel, this asshole from the bar was the one who took her room?

"Come on, let's go," the bellhop whined.

Jeramey held up a hand. She wished she had a Sharpie—the man's dumb, doughy face was just begging for a freehand mustache. He twitched and rolled to the side, his jacket flopping open. Jeramey saw the bulky square of a wallet peeking out of the pocket. Even better.

Doug Beavers had a problem. More accurately, he had several problems, but with varying degrees of urgency.

One: his head felt like a malfunctioning Tilt-A-Whirl

Two: his mouth tasted like onions

Three: his pants were spattered with Bennett Langdon's blood

Things had gone bad pretty fast. He'd sat in the bar for a long time, drinking overpriced gimlets and working up a stormy rage over Langdon and the bridesmaids. Somewhere in there he decided that it was his moral obligation to intervene—those nubile, satin-sheathed maidens needed protection! Langdon was a predator. But when Beavers got up to the top floor of the hotel, Langdon had opened the door with a quizzical smile, and it was clear he was still alone. It was also clear that he had no idea who Beavers was, which somehow made it all worse.

"I, uh," Beavers stammered, losing his nerve within two seconds, "I went to one of your seminars. Last year."

Langdon had just loved the sound of that and invited Beavers in for a drink.

Which was more or less the last thing Doug Beavers needed.

But halfway into that drink, Langdon disappeared into the bedroom and reported that he had to get ready to meet up with a young lady he'd met at the wedding. "Women at weddings are just so *game*," he called. "Are you getting lucky tonight, my man?"

That was enough for Beavers. A tingling in his chest traveled down his arm and into his fist.

Reactivated, he was on his feet in a second, aimed like a surface-to-air missile toward his enemy. He threw the punch before he even realized he was in the bedroom, and what a punch it was: a glorious right hook that connected with Langdon's jaw just as he turned away from the bathroom mirror, looking alarmed. Airborne for a second, Langdon tumbled backward into the shower, sputtering blood. Beavers moved in for the coup de grâce with a primal yell: a kick to the chin. It sounded awful, an unnatural wrenching of bone and skin. Langdon went instantly slack-eyed and still.

Wigging out, Beavers backed out of the bathroom and sat on the bed. But there was blood on the mirror, on the sink, and it turned his stomach. Did that really happen? He peered back into the bathroom—yes, it had. He pulled the door closed. Now he *did* need that drink. He went for the liquor bottle with both hands.

A few hours later, he'd come to on the bed, a sharp line of sunlight from the windows across his torso. He sat up halfway and rubbed his face. A plastic room key was stuck to his cheekbone in a slick of gummy dried drool. At first it felt like a dream, until he realized that dreams, no matter how vivid, don't actually bleed on you. A glance at the clock revealed that it was ten in the morning. He had to piss, but there was no way he was opening that bathroom door. He looked through the peephole into the hallway and saw a housekeeping cart three doors down. "Motherfucker," he said.

He flung open the closet and flipped through the items hanging there, settling on a pair of flat-front khakis. He dropped his own bloody pants and pulled Langdon's on—or tried to, a plan that might have worked eighty pounds ago, but not now. Beavers clutched his infuriatingly large belly and kicked the pants back into the closet.

The housekeeping cart was now two doors away.

He had no choice but to pull on the fluffy terry-cloth bathrobe hanging on a hook on the back of the bathroom door. It smelled like hotel and Langdon's obnoxious Old Spice, but it did, at least, fit. Beavers grabbed his room key off the bed and darted out into the hallway, his bloody pants tucked under his arm like a football.

But down on the tenth floor, he inserted the room key into the slot and was met with a blinking red light. He inserted the key again and again, not understanding. The key on the bed must have been Langdon's, he realized—his own key was in his wallet, which was—

Which was—

Which had formerly been in his jacket pocket, but was no more. The wallet, he concluded, had to be back in Langdon's room. Beavers banged his head on his own locked room door, cursing the day he ever filled out the little RSVP card for his cousin's stepdaughter's wedding in the first place. He tried shouldering the door open, the way you see hero spies do it in the movies. He tried jamming Langdon's key in and out of the lock in the hope of confusing the electronic gatekeeper into submission. Eventually he just headed back to the elevator and hit the UP arrow, but when the doors slid open, two uniformed cops blinked out at him.

"I, uh," he mumbled. There was no way he could go back up to the room now. "Sorry, I was going down."

Jeramey woke up devastatingly hungover. The inside of her mouth tasted like campfire and Cheetos. She was fully clothed, her head resting on the bellhop's stomach. Chess was spread-eagled on the floor, the bedspread tangled around him. She had a vague memory of buying round after round of drinks for everyone in the lobby bar, using Abner Doubleday's American Express. This explained the hangover, but not the Cheetos. She closed her eyes again.

When she woke the second time, it was afternoon. She moved to the floor and smoked half a joint with Chess while the bellhop took a shower. "What the hell should we do here all day?" she said. "Our flight isn't until five."

Chess waggled the joint at her. "Isn't this entertainment enough?"

Jeramey took a drag. Back in the *Touch and Go* days, the morning after a gig had held a wild, raw magic, her fingers sore, her voice hoarse. Champagne for breakfast. Although she knew it was impossible, she couldn't remember ever being hungover on that tour. "Yeah, I guess," she said.

The bathroom door slammed open then. "You guys," the bellboy said.

Jeramey turned. He was brandishing his cell phone.

"There's a *dead guy* upstairs."

Jeramey didn't understand at first. "What?"

"In the penthouse! There's cops everywhere."

"What?" Jeramey repeated, then it hit her. "Wait, no, that guy was passed out, not dead. What the fuck happened?"

"My friend says there's homicide detectives and everything," the bellhop said. "They're talking to everyone who tries to leave the hotel."

Jeramey dropped her head to her hands. It was certainly going to be hard to explain how she happened to be in possession of that American Express card last night. "Fucking Ohio," she said.

Still clutching his bloody pants football, Beavers lurked around the second-floor mezzanine and watched from behind a pillar as a coroner's stretcher arrived and then departed with Langdon inside a rubber sack. When the lobby seemed to reach a momentary lull, he descended the stairs and tried to cross the polished floor with confidence. He imagined he was Bennett Langdon — *Look at me, I'm an asshole millionaire, I'm walking around a hotel in a bathrobe but it's okay because I fucked your wife.* The effect of this was more unnerving than empowering. By the time he made it to the front desk, Beavers was shaking.

"Um, excuse me," he said timidly.

The clerk turned to him, wiping her eyes. She was clutching a balled-up tissue. She did not appear to notice his robe. "Sir?"

"I, uh," Beavers said, "I seem to have misplaced my room key. Can I get a new one? It's Douglas Beavers, room 1016."

The clerk nodded. "I just need to see your ID, Mr. Beavers." She wiped her nose. "We've had an incident in the hotel this morning, so we've been asked to be extra cautious."

"Cautious," Beavers repeated. "Well," he added, improvising, "as it turns out, my ID is in my room. Which I cannot access."

The clerk considered this. Beavers smoothed the lapel of his bathrobe meaningfully.

"Of course, sir," the clerk said finally. She gave him a small smile. "You probably want to get out of that bathrobe," she added.

"Oh, yes," Beavers said.

Safely inside his own room, Beavers took a shower and contemplated his next move. The wallet must have been stuck between the cushions of the leatherette sofa or under the bed or somewhere else out of sight, since he hadn't seen it when he had been up there. And reason had it that the police hadn't seen it yet either, since their first stop after finding it would have no doubt been his room. He developed a new set of plans.

Plan A: Wait until the police were gone, and go back into Langdon's room for the wallet. They had to leave eventually, he figured, and it had been a couple hours already. He couldn't get very far without the wallet, given that he had an hour-long drive to get home to Springfield and his car was hovering on E.

Plan B: Live forever in room 1016.

He figured that he had a few dozen hotel nights' worth of available credit on the American Express he used to book the room. Well, maybe not quite that many, he realized as he ordered two twenty-dollar cheeseburgers and a beer from room service. He needed sustenance if he was going to stay sharp for his mission.

At some point during the day, it became imperative to Jeramey that they return the wallet. Though getting high in the middle of a crisis had never had any other effect on her, she started to get panicky and decided it was the fault of the wallet and not the weed.

"Look," she explained to Chess and the bellhop. They'd already missed their flight due to being too freaked out to leave the hotel. There were cops talking to everyone in the lobby. "I used his card to buy I don't even know how much liquor last night. I need to get rid of it. What if they come here and do a search?"

"I think it was something like eighteen hundred dollars," the bellhop said, unhelpfully. Jeramey regretted that she ever considered sleeping with him.

Chess, suffering from sympathy paranoia, nodded along. "But we can't just dump it somewhere," he said. "Because as soon as they find it, they'll start trying to trace who dumped it, which makes the whole thing worse. Maybe we could destroy it."

"Like how?"

Chess flicked the lighter.

Jeramey pointed at the smoke detector. "I don't think the washcloth trick will work if we set a wallet on fire."

"Maybe we could cut it apart," the bellhop suggested, "and flush it down the toilet."

After sending the bellhop out into the hotel for a pair of scissors, the three of them stood around the low-flow toilet as Jeramey cut an experimental corner off Doug Beavers's driver's license and let it fall into the bowl. She pressed the flusher and held her breath.

But the low water pressure wasn't even enough to make the plastic triangle flutter.

"Fucking conservation," she muttered.

She cut off a larger chunk and dropped that into the toilet too, but no dice. Finally she reached into the water and retrieved the driver's license pieces, shoving all of them back into the little plastic compartment.

"The police have to leave eventually, right?"

Chess nodded. "They do."

"No," the bellhop said. "No. That's an even worse idea than going in there in the first place."

Jeramey shrugged. There was no other way. The weed made her feel certain of this. "We're going to have to put it back in the room," she said.

Beavers conducted some light recon. First, he waited until evening fell, then crept down to the lobby to look for cops. Everything appeared normal again, though.

Phase one, check.

Then Beavers sat down on a leatherette ottoman and faced away from the desk as he dialed the hotel's main phone number from his cell.

"Good evening, Columbus Hotel, how can I help you?"

"Yes, uh, I'm in room, um, 1610," he said quietly, "and I've been burgled."

"You've been what?"

"Burgled."

"Sir?"

"I think I might have seen someone going into that poor man's room last night," he tried next. "Can you send the police down to talk to me? Ten—I mean, 1610."

There was a muffled pause. Beavers resisted the urge to look over his shoulder at the desk to see what was happening. "Sir, if you have information about the incident in the hotel, you should contact the police immediately. They're no longer in the hotel, but I can give you the investigator's phone number if you have a pen?"

"I'll call back when I can find a pen," Beavers said.

Phase two, check.

He rode the elevator up to the eighteenth floor, alone this time. Once the doors slid open, he cautiously stepped out and looked around. The hallway was deserted, and the only indicator that anything unusual had happened was a neon-green seal over the frame of Langdon's door. THESE PREMISES HAVE BEEN SEALED BY THE COLUMBUS POLICE DEPARTMENT. ALL PERSONS ARE FORBIDDEN TO ENTER UNLESS AUTHORIZED BY THE POLICE OR A PUBLIC ADMINISTRATOR. Beavers let out a short sigh and slit the seal with his Swiss Army knife.

The room had a garbage-y smell, but there was no time to contemplate it. He searched the sofa first—no wallet. Then he looked under the bed—no wallet there either. He went back to the door and retraced his steps: doorway, kitchenette, sofa, bedroom, bathroom. He retreated quickly from the bathroom after seeing all that blood again. Langdon's head, Beavers could practically swear, contained more blood than a normal head, Jesus Christ. He closed the bathroom door again and looked out at the room. He couldn't remember being in any of the other areas, but then again, he had quite a few unaccounted-for hours. He crossed to the window and drew open the curtains, and it was then that he heard the unmistakable click of a key being inserted into the door.

Jeramey screamed. "Oh my God, I thought you were dead."

Beavers screamed too. He got a little worried. *Was* he dead?

The bellhop screamed and ran out of the room.

Jeramey threw the wallet at the guy. "I don't know what is going on here, but I don't want anything to do with it."

"Where did you get this?" Beavers said.

"So no one died?" Jeramey said. She looked over her shoulder for explanation but the bellhop was gone.

"Well, I wouldn't say that, exactly," Beavers said.

They both spun around as the door opened again.

"There he is! The ghost!" the bellhop said.

Two cops followed him into the room. "Okay," one of them said. "Which one of you would like to explain?"

Beavers folded immediately. "It was an accident," he blubbered. "He fucked my wife and I just, I don't know, I went crazy for a second. And I thought I left my wallet in here, so I came back in to get it, but it turns out she had it, and I don't even know—"

"Who are you?" the cop said to Jeramey.

"Hey," the other cop said. "You're Jeramey Jones, right? *Touch and Go?*" He strummed a few notes on an air guitar. "That album defined my twenties."

"Wait, what?" Beavers said.

"Yeah, that's me," Jeramey said. She cocked her head at him and smiled. Out of the corner of her eye, she caught a glimpse of the river beyond the window.

That view, just, wow.

LAURA LIPPMAN

Slow Burner

FROM *Hush*

Hi, it's Phil. New phone, who dis, ha ha. I got a second phone.
  Pourquoi
Going to use regular # for business, this # for trying to bring you up to
speed on seminal films of the 1980s and '90s. Welcome to the friend
zone, matey.
  Funny
No parking in the friend zone—remember when I showed you the
movie Airplane! that time in Santa Monica?
  Yeah
Thrilled to be working with you again. You are absolutely aces, the best
in the biz. Would have been devastated if you didn't want to work with
me again but not surprised. I'm really sorry I crossed the line. Crossed
the streams, if you will.
  ?
Ghostbusters reference.
  Loved the new one. Never saw original
Opposite for me.
  Misogynist
Hey!
  JK
I'm in SF next month, maybe dinner?
  Lemme check date

LIZ IS GATHERING the laundry when the phone slides out of
Phil's khakis' pocket. It's a cheap basic model. It looks like a toy,
but why would Phil have a toy? Liz and Phil don't have kids; they
don't even have friends with kids.

She looks at the phone on the bathroom floor. What to do with it? It seems natural, innocent even, definitely innocent, to pick it up and manipulate its buttons until this text thread comes into view. Liz has found several lost phones in their Logan Square neighborhood over the years, and she has always done her best to reunite them with their owners. She assumes Phil has found someone's phone while walking their dog, then didn't follow through on finding the phone's rightful owner.

Only—Phil is the not-so-rightful owner, hiding behind a Utah area code. His correspondent—San Francisco area code—appears to be the contractor, HW, who almost wrecked Liz and Phil's marriage eighteen months ago. That was the code Phil used for her in his contacts, HW. A private joke, one Liz never sussed out.

Now what? Liz cannot put the phone back in Phil's pocket and then put his pants in the wash, because the phone will be destroyed and he will replace it with another phone, one he will safeguard more carefully.

Yet she also cannot ask Phil about the phone, much less the text. She promised she would never spy on him again. It was an easy promise to make and keep because she believed they were happy again and there would be no reason, going forward, to doubt him.

She believed they were happy until a strange cheap phone clattered to the bathroom floor.

It is early April in Chicago, and the only thing predictable about the weather is how unpredictable it is. Phil left his denim jacket slung over the sofa when he came home last night, a habit of long standing, and headed out the door this morning in a peacoat. He had to walk ten steps past the hooks in the vestibule to avoid hanging up his jacket, but he does that almost every day. Liz has tried everything to encourage Phil to hang up his jacket. Finally, at great expense—Phil's expense, to be fair, but he runs a venture capital firm and she's a private-school teacher—she hired a carpenter to come to the house and restore the vestibule that a previous owner had dismantled, the final renovation in their home of almost twenty-five years.

Their house was built in the early twentieth century, a sturdy stone home for one of the financial whizzes of *that* era, then divided into apartments in the 1970s. The Kelseys rented the first floor as newlyweds, bought the house fifteen years later, and eventually began to restore it, floor by floor, room by room. One now enters a toasty vestibule with a mission bench, hooks for coats, cubbies for wet shoes, and an antique umbrella stand. Almost every day, Phil sits on the mission bench and takes off his shoes; he puts his umbrella in the stand—then pushes open the heavy oak door with the stained glass window and throws his jacket on the sofa.

Liz puts the phone in the denim jacket's right breast pocket. Phil is a man who is forever losing keys, wallets, phones. (This absentmindedness is deemed proof of his genius.) Clearly, he is not in the habit, not yet, of taking this second phone everywhere he goes. He won't remember that he left it in his khakis. All he will feel is relief at finding it.

Later that night, she notices him roaming the house, fidgeting, picking up piles of magazines and newspapers, poking under the mission bench in the vestibule.

"Are you looking for something?"

"I thought I left . . . my keys in my pocket."

"I hung your keys by the front door." There is a charming iron arrow by the front door with multiple hooks for keys. Phil never uses it.

"Oh." He continues to pace, poke, search. At some point, he must slide his hand into the pocket of his denim jacket and find his new friend waiting for him. At any rate, he comes into the den, where Liz is reading, suddenly jovial and relaxed.

"Do you want to watch a movie?"

"Sure," she says, although she doesn't. She curls into his side on the sofa. Their pug crawls into her lap, snuffling wetly. Phil chooses *Ghostbusters*, the all-female reboot.

"How old were we when the first one came out?"

"I was ten, you were nine." She has never minded being older than he is. It's only a year, and Liz knows she looks good for her age.

She also knows the old saying that cautions men to remember, whenever they meet a beautiful woman, that somewhere, someone is tired of her.

Throughout the movie, Phil's fingers twitch as if yearning for purchase, the feel of the new phone. *Who you gonna call? Who you gonna text?* He will write about this later. The movie, his memories of the original.

*

You were right about Ghostbusters. I love the original, but the all-female reboot is better.
<Thumbs-up emoji.>
I can't believe all the misogynist crap it had to withstand. Not to mention the racist stuff. You were right. Sometimes, I'm so embarrassed to be a man.
Love Kate McKinnon!

"No bread for me," Phil says at dinner. "And no potatoes."

Dinner is roast chicken, with carrots and potatoes roasted in its pan juices, homemade cheddar biscuits, and a salad. It's a perfect meal for the blustery night. Phil eats only white-meat chicken and preempts the salad course.

"Are you doing . . . keto?"

"Nothing that formal. Just cutting out bread, starches. They make me logy. And you know I'm never really off the clock because I'm working with people across time zones. London's six hours ahead, San Francisco is two hours behind. I have to keep a clear head. Been reading this book, *Grain Brain*. It's interesting."

"You used to say that all diets were frauds, that every eating plan was, at bottom, just a gimmicky way to reduce caloric intake."

She liked that Phil. She misses that Phil.

"I still think that. But I also find my head is so much clearer now. Giving up alcohol helps too." He takes a sip of LaCroix.

Liz pours herself another glass of wine. It's a pinot noir, which pairs better with chicken than most white wines. There's no way she's going to give up alcohol right now.

I ran five miles today.
   Ouch
Started again a few weeks ago. Gotta get fit. I'm an old man in a young man's game. Gotta keep up.
   You're not old
Says the 29-year-old who looks like she's 22. You can't imagine being old. But you know what? I can't imagine you being old either. You will never be old.
   TY
Hey I had a meeting with Willoughby.
   That guy
Did I ever tell you how I came to meet him? It's a funny story. Three

years ago, I was in Seattle and I had to take a meeting with him what a pig. He made us meet him for this dreadful vegan food, then insisted on going out for gelato and when someone said gelato wasn't vegan, he got so angry, argued about it all night. That's Willoughby in a nutshell. His type—that's the reason we need people like you. We have to move away from this idea that having a great business model is a license to be rotten to people. The hubris on these guys—and they're all guys.

[*twenty-four hours later*]

Just seeing this sorry

He has left the phone in his jacket pocket, but the April day is mild, a classic Chicago tease, so his jacket is once again on the back of the sofa. Liz finds it when she comes in from a walk with Pugsley, and she can't help patting the pockets as she hangs it up. Ah, a lump! It makes her sad, embarrassed for him, to see the inequity of the exchange—Phil's logorrheic style, the girl's terse replies that she can't be bothered to punctuate.

This is how it happened before, eighteen months ago. He became conscientious about food, exercise. He bought new clothes. Liz started snooping, found his love letters to HW, who clearly was keeping him at arm's length but also wanted to continue working with him. He was a pipeline for future contracts, after all.

Liz and Phil went to counseling. Liz admitted all her flaws and then some. She had been angry; she had been resentful of the chasm between their worlds, the high-flying venture capitalist and the high school English teacher. She had been cold.

But she'd changed, become more solicitous, realized that the world's ego stroking meant nothing to Phil if he didn't feel attended to at home. She had saved their marriage.

Or so she had thought.

Got my own burner
  New phone who dis
Haha
  Why are you using a burner?
It's . . . fun. Like a secret club, walkie talkies like that TV show you're always talking about
  The Wire

That's it
   I can't believe you still haven't watched it. Everything OK at home?
   J saw that you were texting me again
OH
   Life's just easier if you don't pop up on my screen when I'm with J.
I get it. Liz is the same way—I feel like she needs to stir up drama be-
cause she doesn't really have that much going on. She blows everything
out of proportion. Or she renovates. And now that she's renovated ev-
ery room in our house, she's buying art. She's always on me to pick out
something for my office, like I care. She's bored.
   Sad

"Miss Kelsey?"

"Ms.," she corrects absentmindedly, her thoughts far from
this classroom, her thoughts locked on the 2.8-inch display
of a Samsung flip phone, wondering what messages might be
flying back and forth. "Msssssssss. Mrs. Kelsey is OK too. But
not Miss."

"*Msssssss*. Kelsey—why was Zeus so awful?"

"Awful?"

"He's a *rapist*."

Liz has been teaching a Greek mythology unit every spring for
ten years now. She begins with Demeter and Persephone; Chicago
Aprils make it easy to imagine a world where spring might never
come again. It's a private school, a progressive one verging on what
her mother called hippy-dippy, and her students have always been
quick to recognize the vagaries of the gods.

Since #MeToo, however, they are even more disturbed by how
the gods behave. Hades is a kidnapper, plain and simple; why
should Persephone be punished for eating a few seeds? Why is
Medusa demonized for being raped? Why does Zeus force himself on unwilling women? (Liz has always encouraged that inquiry,
teaching Yeats's poem "Leda and the Swan," which recognizes how
frightened Leda must have been, carried skyward by a swan. Liz
leans hard on Yeats's choice of *terrified*.) To teenagers, the gods
are like adults, taking themselves much too seriously, demanding
respect they have not earned, changing the rules as it suits them
while torturing the puny mortals in their care. Gods are hypocrites
and bullies.

The students are not wrong.

"As a god," Liz says, "Zeus believed himself entitled to what he wanted when he wanted it."

"Why does Hera put up with him?"

"There aren't a lot of choices for gods when it comes to marriage."

"She's his *sister.*"

"Gods can't be married to mortals. Mortals can't even look at the gods in their authentic state. Remember what happened to the mother of Dionysus when she asked to see Zeus in his true raiment."

"Hera tricked her into asking that. Why does Hera go after the women? Why doesn't she kill Zeus?"

"Because he's immortal."

Phil is not a god, but he is often treated like one because he gathers and allocates money for ideas that might change the world. He does not force himself on young women. He does not take on disguises to seduce them, nor does he turn them into creatures to hide his dalliances from his wife of almost twenty-five years.

Phil's weakness—his Achilles' heel, Liz thinks—is that he cannot resist the delight of being new to someone, anyone. To tell the stories that Liz already knows, having lived through many of them.

Did I ever tell you about the time that I realized I was sitting in front of David Foster Wallace at the theater?
    ?
It was in New York. A production of Lysistrata that had been a big hit at the Edinburgh Fringe Festival had been brought over. It was a hot ticket. They set it in the 1970s—the design, the look was borrowed from a satire of Marin County life, called The Serial.
    The podcast
No, not Serial. _The Serial_. It ran in newspapers in San Francisco, just like Tales of the City by Armistead Maupin.
    Gesundheit
Haha. Anyway, they took the humor really low. Scatological even. There was this running joke about a woman with bulimia. It was gross. Maybe it worked in Scotland, but it was dying in New York. The third or fourth time the character fake vomited, the theater was dead silent—and then this big, booming laugh came from behind me. Turns out David Foster Wallace loved a good vomit joke.

*

It wasn't David Foster Wallace, Liz thinks, staring at the phone. *It was William Styron.* How could he confuse the two? Then she realizes —HW wouldn't be impressed by Styron. But DFW is a writer her generation might know. Phil is not only changing the story; he's tailoring it to make it more appealing to HW.

And, of course, there is no mention of Liz, who was the one who recognized Styron in the first place, who chose that production over the musical she really wanted to see because Phil hated musicals. It was her thirtieth birthday weekend. She felt so old. She was so young. In the wake of Alexander Hamilton's indiscretions, his wife sings that she's taking herself out of history. But Phil is taking Liz out of his. If she doesn't exist in Phil's stories, will she eventually not exist in his life?

She's surprised Phil even remembers *The Serial,* a book that was quite dear to her. As for *Tales of the City*—he never read those books, but he watched the PBS television adaptation with her. He liked Laura Linney. "She's my type," he said to his brown-eyed, brunette wife. "I mean, my type before I met you."

HW is blond and dimpled, like Linney. Liz has watched her TED Talk, multiple times.

Liz closes the phone. They say eavesdroppers hear no good of themselves, but that's the point of eavesdropping. It's a form of espionage, a device, used by the Greeks and Shakespeare and daytime soap operas. The difference is that nowadays the device is done via device. A flip phone, a laptop. What device will she use to spy on Phil next time?

And there will be a next time, Liz realizes. She's not the only one in need of drama in her life. Phil works twelve, fourteen hours a day and is immensely prized within his world. But he's not one of the tech CEOs who receives ceaseless public attention. He's the money guy behind the "geniuses." Phil goes to TED Talks, but he will never be asked to give one.

What's up?
  Not much. Work. Life.
Same here. Work. Wife. Life.
  Damn autocorrect.
Yes, last I checked, you don't have a wife, but you young people are so what's the word fluid. Or maybe J told you he's going to transition?
  That's a weird thing to say. Kinda transphobic

Sorry. If J didn't exist—would that change things?
For me? Of course
And me? What would it mean for me?
We're friends
We are. But things can change. I'm sorry if this lands on you unwanted.
But things could change, if we both wanted them to change.
Don't cross the streams
Now you get it.

Liz flicks through her phone, looking for a selfie taken on their trip to Barcelona last year. It's blurry, unflattering. A shadow mars half her face. (Bad foreshadowing, shadow! Too obvious. Too on the nose. THE SHADOW IS LITERALLY ON HER NOSE.) But she loves this photo of herself because she looks insanely happy.

Loved, she *loved* the photo, past tense. Now the photo is simply evidence of how dumb she was to believe herself happy. The trip to Barcelona had been a business trip for Phil but also a celebration. They had survived the darkest days of their marriage. It hadn't been easy. Phil did not see how his emails to HW could count as a betrayal when there had been no sex. A kiss, yes, just one kiss, and they had agreed the next day it was a mistake and it had never happened again.

"Agreed?" Liz had said in counseling. "She basically stopped answering your emails after you kissed her, and you took it out on me for weeks."

That had been a mistake, because it wounded his ego. It also reminded Phil that Liz had spied on him, and he insisted her invasiveness was as egregious as what he had done. He rejected the term *emotional affair.* His needs weren't being met at home; he should be praised for *not* cheating.

That was August 2017. October 2017 brought #MeToo, but Phil had a clear conscience. He hadn't masturbated in front of anyone. He hadn't lured vulnerable young women into his hotel room and taken off his clothes, or dangled quid pro quo deals in front of them. He had fallen in love, but it was a first-act *Camelot* kind of love. He loved her in silence.

Then Phil's company began working with a start-up that desperately needed the exact service HW provided, a sophisticated psych test that identifies and treats problem personalities. She wanted the contract. If she didn't get it—well, who knows what might happen? Phil hadn't understood at the time that he had done anything wrong, given that she was no longer under contract when he started mooning after her. In fact, the kiss had occurred after a simple wrap-up dinner to commemorate the project's end.

Now he gets it. *Now.* He understands that the patriarchy never sleeps, that he might have ceased to be HW's supervisor, but he still had power over her, which forced her to be polite about the kiss, which was awkward for her, as she too had a spouse. What could he do? He had to give her the new contract or she could go public with his blunder.

By the time he told all this to Liz, he had, in fact, already given HW the new contract.

"Here's another fine mess you've gotten us into," Liz said when Phil came clean. He didn't even recognize the reference, much less its significance. Their first real date had been to a Laurel and Hardy film festival.

Well, it was a very long time ago, so long ago that it might have been a different place. The Chicago of their college days has been replaced by something shinier and more generic. Or maybe Chicago is the same and they're the ones who changed.

Good morning, what city are you waking up in?
   W-ville
   ?????
   I don't visit cities. I occupy a series of interchangeable W hotel rooms.
If there was a city outside your room, what would it be called on a map.
   Checking. Double-decker bus, traffic on the wrong side. All our instruments agree: London
London! Oh, I have a great restaurant suggestion. Wait—you don't eat meat.
   Nothing with a face.
But you can do Indian, right, you upright millennial? There's this amazing place in Mayfair that I stumbled on a few years ago. Hard to get a res, but there's a communal table and a bar . . .

Knightsbridge, Liz thinks when she reads this exchange. *It was in Knightsbridge, Phil. And I was the one who found it.*

Their therapist had a word for the stuck-in-second-gear nature of the emotional affair, but Liz has forgotten it. Besides, #MeToo changed the emotional affair. Why is no one talking about this? People thrown together in work environments, hyperaware of the new rules, are probably more likely to have emotional affairs now. Perpetual anticipation, as the Sondheim song warns, is not good for the heart.

Liz used to love musicals. Lately not so much. They are too linear about love. People fall in, people fall out, but they seldom fall in and out and in again. She doesn't like rom-coms anymore either. Has anyone noticed how easily people jettison their partners in rom-coms? Liz has.

At any rate, she recognizes Burner Phil, as she thinks of him. It is the Phil she knew when they first started dating—solicitous, eager to share, impress. Solicitous Phil wanted to recommend restaurants and books and obscure films. Solicitous Phil wanted to take you on adventures! "Let's get in the car," Solicitous Phil would say. "I've got a surprise, I've got something to show you."

They had been together ten years when Liz realized that the whole point of Solicitous Phil's surprise quests was that he determined the agenda. They went where he chose to go, ate what he preferred to eat. By casting his plans as surprises, he was always in control. Heck, she made him go to that awful production of *Lysistrata* just because she wanted, on principle, to be the one who made the plan for once.

Still she loves him. That's what rom-coms get right. Love isn't logical. Only in rom-coms, the two people seem mismatched, then find their antipathy is really just their way of fighting their mad attraction to each other.

Whereas in real life, the mad attraction feels logical and then these rifts are exposed, yet you go on loving the other person anyway.

What's up? Who's up? Who's on first? What's on second?
  I'm up. Body's in California but thinks it's in London
You do get around.
  My carbon footprint :(
Oh, I'm sure you have the daintiest of carbon footprints. In fact, I bet there is a prince out there with a glass slipper, trying to find whose sooty sole it fits. Did I ever tell you the story about when I was 7 and I insisted that the story of Cinderfella was the "real" story and Cinderella

was copying it? I was adamant that it was about a guy, that everyone else was wrong.

Now, this is Phil's own story, and Liz knows it well. It's a first-date story. Maybe second or third. Again, this is what happens when a relationship is stuck in the second gear of "friendship." Chug, chug, chug. Charm, charm, charm. Has he not noticed that HW never responds in kind? Her texts are short and to the point. Of course, she's younger, a millennial. Her generation grew up with texts. (Part of her TED Talk centered on an excruciating experience with AOL Messenger, in which she claimed to have a terminal disease and traumatized her entire eighth-grade class.)

Phil is a Gen Xer. Like Liz. Not old enough to be HW's father. Just old enough to be her creepy uncle.

She almost feels sorry for him. Almost.

I'm going to be in SF next month. Lunch? Dinner?
OK
Where do you want to go? Your town, your pick—but I pay
No
It's a write-off for me. You're my contractor.
I'll wear a tool belt

It's not spying to read something in plain sight, Liz tells herself. It's normal; it's human nature, like walking down an alley and stealing looks into lighted windows. Liz had been strangely disappointed to find out that other people did this. She had thought herself unusually sensitive as a teenager, the Jane Eyre of Mount Lebanon, Pennsylvania.

As a teen, Liz was a lonely, gawky girl, convinced of her own unattractiveness despite the insistence of those around her that she was lovely. Her mother was a great beauty, a fate Liz wouldn't wish on anyone. Except, possibly, HW.

She met Phil senior year of college. She worked at the information desk in the student center. He bought a Friday *New York Times*, sat down in a nearby easy chair, and worked the crossword puzzle in forty-five minutes, then put it in front of her.

"What do you think of that?"

There's a line in a novel that haunts her. She can't remember the novel. She can't remember the exact line, and she worries that it's a bad novel, that she would be embarrassed to have one of its lines stuck in her head for eternity. But the line is about how everything that would come to characterize a relationship, for better or worse, was there from the beginning. Liz wishes she had said to Phil: "I think I'm not your mother." Or: "I think you must be very good at crossword puzzles." Maybe: "Have you mistaken me for your second-grade teacher?"

What she said was: "Wow—I can't even do Wednesdays by myself."

And because it was 1994, they slept together that night and that meant something then. Not a lot but a little. He told her all his stories. She told hers. But they were young when they met, and they ran out of stories quickly. So they made stories together. The hilarious mix-up in Mérida. The Indian restaurant in Knightsbridge. The handsy tailor in Turkey who cupped Phil's balls when measuring him for a suit and said, when Phil objected: "But this is the most important part."

What they didn't make was a child. By the time they got serious about it, Liz was almost forty, shades of Lichtenstein. Her body wouldn't make a baby and Phil started the new company and adoption was hard and he met HW and who needs a baby when a twenty-seven-year-old wunderkind is batting her baby blues at you, explaining to you that a person's "tech type" wasn't just a random collection of tics and social inadequacies, but a particular kind of emotional intelligence that can be harnessed to make companies more competitive *and* more compassionate.

Really, what kind of man-boy brandishes his crossword puzzle at a stranger and demands her attention? The one that Liz married, the one that Liz loves, the one that is stuck in this permanent not-quite-a-betrayal-but-definitely-a-humiliation loop. How will they ever get out? How does this end?

But Liz knows the answer to that question. It's never going to end. Phil needs to be new, and that's the one thing he can never be with Liz.

What happened? I was so worried about you when you didn't show and then I got the message at my hotel that you couldn't make it.

Sorry! I lost the phone! And then J surprised me with a reservation at our favorite place and what could I do? I totally spaced that it was our anniversary

Freudian slip?
    No one wears slips anymore Freudian camisole, maybe
But you have yr phone now?
    OBVIOUSLY ;)
Glad you're safe. I was just disappointed. Was looking forward to seeing
your face.
    It's aging rapidly
Don't be silly.
    I spend $175 on face cream.
Again, don't be silly. Anyway, I'll be back in San Francisco next month,
staying at my usual place. We can try again.
    Can't wait

Oh, Phil. You're being played. Can't you see? But Liz knows he cannot, that men have no understanding of the subtle ways in which
women keep them on hold forever.
    When Phil is home in Chicago, he's careful with the burner
phone, keeping it in his desk. Sometimes, she notices him absentmindedly stroking the drawer while he's talking to her. Maybe it's
the phone he's in love with, not HW. He's in love with the idea of
love; he's in love with this eternally puerile game. His texts might
as well read: *Do you like me? Yes. No. As a friend.*
    There should be a fourth alternative: *You're just another horn-
dog man I tolerate for my job, but if you want to think this is mutual, go
for it.*

So it's a wrap
    There will be more projects, more companies that need your unique
    skills.
I don't think there should be
    Why not? I love working with you.
Maybe too much
    What?
It was OK for you to use a burner. Your wife is crazy jealous. But when I
got a burner—we both know this isn't right
    We're FRIENDS.
Right. Friends who hide our friendship from our spouses
    I don't. Liz knows everything now. EVERYTHING
Srsly?
    Srsly

But that doesn't make it right. This is not right
    I'm leaving her.

Liz breathes in so sharply it feels like a little knife in her diaphragm. *This is not true, this is not true.* Phil has said nothing of the sort to her.

But even after this exchange, she is not prepared when Phil announces he wants a divorce.

He doesn't ask right away. There are several days of stormy moods, blowups over nothing. He's still texting, but no replies are coming back. Liz is sure of it. You wouldn't need access to a phone to know something is up. He has been cut off. He has been used. Liz has been waiting for this day to come. She assumed he would be happy to run back to the safe haven of their marriage, to the woman who has always stood by him, no matter how much he humiliates her.

Only Phil doesn't know that, does he? He really believes Liz knows nothing, believes she has given up spying. And she can't tell him what she knows unless she's willing to tell him *how* she knows, and that's unthinkable. She has to keep the moral high ground. Especially now that he's saying he wants to end their marriage.

Of all the scenarios she imagined, she never thought that he would see this as a sign that he needed to leave her. Had HW really made him that happy? Is the thought of being without her that devastating?

"I know—" she begins that night at bedtime, then stops. What does she know?

He doesn't even seem to notice that she spoke.

This isn't about you, but—I'm definitely leaving Liz.

[*a day later*]

Did you really give up the burner? Or are you just ignoring me?

[*eight hours later*]

Do you talk to other people on this burner? Do you have other burners?

[*a day later*]

Dammit, HW, I'm going to call you on your other phone.

[*one minute later*]

Please don't.
　Are you seeing these messages?
Yes.
　OK.
I don't know what to say.
　My marriage has been over for a long time. Again, this has nothing
　to do with you.
I'm married.
　I know.
I'm happy.
　If you say so. Clearly some need was going unfulfilled.
Still open to working with you
　I wouldn't want to make you uncomfortable.
You usually don't
　I don't want to be one of the shitty men. So many shitty men out there.
You're telling me

They go back to therapy. Liz literally doesn't know what to say. She has been spying on Phil for so long, it's hard to remember what she does know, what she might know, and what she can't know. She isn't temperamentally suited to this level of deception. By nature, she is an honest person. Whereas Phil has always been in favor of the judicious lie, the lies people tell while rationalizing that they are sparing someone else's feelings but are really mainly sparing themselves the inconvenience of the truth.

Liz says to the therapist, "He seems very distracted to me. Since this spring."

It's summer now. She has too much free time. She exercises more, she gets a new haircut, adds highlights, window-shops at galleries, looking for things to fill all the walls she added to the house during its renovation. A house with walls needs a lot more art.

Phil says: "She's so cold. All I want is love and affection. When I walk through the door, I feel as if I'm just a giant imposition, a wallet for her to plunder, like Jane Jetson."

"He travels a lot."

"For my job."

"You don't have to travel that much."

"You could travel with me."

"I have a job."

"You don't have to have a job."

Without a job, who would she be, what would she do? There's nothing left to renovate, not in the house, not on herself.

Hi?
  Hi
How are you?
  Fine How's therapy going
Ok. I guess I owe it to her.
  To yourself too.
Thanks. You're a good friend.
  We're better as friends, don't you think?
Shrug
  I'm happy with J
What changed?
  I was taking him for granted. If you really love someone, embers are always there.
I feel that I'm taken for granted. She doesn't even have a real job! Our lifestyle, our house — she just takes that as her due.
  Maybe she feels taken for granted?
Maybe. Hey did I ever tell you the story about the time my father tried to teach me how to score a baseball game?

It's a funny story, yet a sad one too. Liz knows it, of course.

They had been together for three months. She and Phil were in bed in her room in the apartment she shared with three other girls. Her room was the largest, but it wasn't well insulated. That was the trade-off. Huddled beneath two blankets and a quilt for warmth, they began telling new kinds of stories, the tragic stories that people think define them when they are young. She talked about her father, a serial cheater who was forever sneaking out to meet up with other women. "The dark end of the street," Phil warbled mournfully. She had never heard the song before.

Then Phil told her about *his* father, who wanted to do the fatherly things but always botched them. The day he tried to teach Phil how to score a baseball game he ended up screaming at him, calling him a moron.

Touched by Phil's vulnerability, Liz did what women were never supposed to do: she said "I love you" first. Phil then did what nineteen-year-old men were not supposed to do three months into a college romance: he asked her to marry him. They were engaged for eighteen months, married a week after their graduation. How smart they had felt in their certainty, how lucky.

Now here is Phil's familiar story, text box after text box, with barely a comment back. Her husband is preening for this other woman, strutting with his feathers in full view.

According to the Greeks, the peacock owes its appearance to adultery. Hera asked the watchman Argus, with his one hundred eyes, to keep guard over a white cow, Io, one of Zeus's loves that he had tried to disguise to keep her from Hera's wrath. It was Zeus's solution to send a disguised Hermes to Argus. He talked and talked and talked until finally all one hundred of Argus's eyes closed.

And Hermes killed him.

Argus's eyes were added to the peacock's tails. And what became of Zeus's love? Hera sent stinging flies to torture her, until she ran all the way to Egypt and regained human form, one of the happier endings for a lover of Zeus.

Liz loves Phil. She loves him so much that it hurts, watching him make a fool of himself in front of a young woman who clearly has no interest in him. How can someone not love you when you love him this much?

She and Phil have the exact same problem. If only she could tell him that.

I'm going to be in SF again at month's end.
  Oh
Dinner?
  I don't know
We're friends. Friends have dinner, right?
  No one has dinner anymore except Insta influencers
Funny
  [curtsy]
No, seriously, can we have dinner?
  Where are you staying?
Fairmont
  Nice. Old school, but nice.
I'm old school. But nice.
  <g>
So dinner?
  Date?
NOT a date! DINNER.

Haha You know what I mean
Oct 30.
That works J will be in Shanghai
If he were here, would you tell him you were meeting me?
Does Liz know you're still talking to me?
We're separated as of last week.
Oh
Not that it's relevant to you.
I don't know what to say.
I'm going to be happy. This has nothing to do with you. I deserve to be happy.
You do. Everyone does.

They are not separated. He floated the idea of a trial separation at their last counseling session. Liz refused to discuss it. The only way to save a marriage, she believes, is to stay and fight. Once Phil is out the door, he will never be back.

But he also will never stop straying. And she is no Hera. She cannot send stinging flies after the poor girl trapped inside the white cow. It's not this girl's fault, and it won't be the next girl's fault.

Oh God, there's going to be a next girl—and that's the best-case scenario.

He whistles as he packs for San Francisco. Liz realized long ago, the first time, that he is kindest to her when he believes his relationship with HW is going well. He must think that she is going to leave her husband for him, despite the denials. Phil has always gotten what he wants. A short man, boyish and charming, he has a big personality. He's irresistible. It's only a matter of time before he gets what he wants. What he thinks he wants.

He whistles and packs, packs and whistles. The blue Thomas Pink shirt Liz gave him for his last birthday, the handmade Italian shoes from Christmas. Of course, his money really paid for those gifts. He owns everything.

It seems to Liz that he's packing a lot for a two-day trip to San Francisco.

"Do you want me to go with you," she blurts.

"You're working."

"I could use my sick days. They'd never suspect a thing."

"Not worth it for this kind of trip. Wall-to-wall meetings. Maybe next time."

*

Let's have dinner in your room.
   Really?
For discretion's sake. It's a small town in its way. I live here, remember.
People know me.
   Whereas I'm nothing but a face in the crowd.
It's my hometown. Text me your room #
   I'll behave.
What if I don't want you to?
   2110
Leave the door unlocked so I can slip in. I don't want anyone to see me
knocking on someone's hotel room door.
   The Dark End of the Hotel Corridor.
What
   A reference to an old song. I'll play it for you.

Winter comes early to Chicago that year, with measurable snowfall
the second week of November, then an unending string of icy rains,
which are worse than the snow. Still, Liz likes to walk after dark, no
matter the weather, and Pugsley is happy for the extra exercise. She
walks and walks and walks, and the neighbors who recognize her
give her space, respect her need for solitude.

Besides, no one knows what to say to a widow, especially a widow
in these circumstances.

Once upon a time, the story of Phil Kelsey's death might have
been kept to the circumspect old-school media coverage. *Prominent
Chicago investor killed in hotel robbery.* Those were the facts. He was a
prominent man, a rich man. Someone had entered his hotel room
—no sign of forced entry—and shot him as he came out of the
shower, then left with his wallet and his watch.

The Internet, however, was happy to indulge in speculation and
gossip. The flirtation between PK and HW was well known in the
incestuous world of tech; she had confided in her friends, after
#MeToo, how confused she was by his attentions. Yet she had cho-
sen to go back to work for him less than two years later. Friends said
he promised her he would be professional, and for the most part,
he was. That's what friends had been told.

Phil's phone, the second phone, yielded a different story. Although he had been diligent about deleting all the texts from HW
within a day or two, nothing ever really disappears. There it was, the

history of their communication—a man pushing, a woman pulling away—their plan to meet. She denied it all, professed amazement, and her husband stood by her.

The texts didn't matter to the police, however. HW's husband was not in Shanghai; he had never been in Shanghai. He had returned earlier that day from Seattle. The happy couple had been at dinner together when Phil Kelsey was shot.

A door was left unlocked. A man with a gun walked through it. Or maybe a woman with a gun. A watch and a wallet were taken; two phones were left behind with tantalizing clues, but—Occam's razor. It was a robbery. Phil had surprised a burglar and been killed, his body left on the bathroom floor, the shower still running. It was a random crime, not a crime of passion. HW and J were miles away, having dinner in San Mateo.

As for Liz Kelsey, the sad cuckquean—the term for a female cuckold, seldom used, perhaps because betrayal is presumed to be part of the female condition—she was at a school event two thousand miles away, a showcase for students' artwork. One of her students from last year had, at Liz's suggestion, done a series of pastel profiles of the collateral damage of Zeus's infidelity. Io and Argus and Echo and Callisto and Leto—it was quite a gallery.

Liz walks and walks and walks. Every night she walks until Pugsley begins whimpering to be carried.

Deep in her down coat's right-hand pocket, a phone vibrates.

"It is time to discuss your invoice."

"Of course. And you will invoice me for—"

"Item #2728. It's an oil painting from the midcentury. Unsigned, but in the style of a mid-Atlantic artist whose bigger canvases have gone for as much as $250,000. He's back in vogue because he was featured on some movie star's Instagram account. All you have to do is hit the 'Buy Now' button. You won't be able to use a charge card, but we're set up to take bank transfers. In a few weeks, you will receive the painting. It's a very pleasant landscape. We do recommend hanging the work. Don't try to resell it or insure it."

"May I ask—where did you get the painting?"

"We have a young woman who scouts flea markets and garage sales for items that could credibly be works of value. She assumes it's a simple art scam."

He is assuring her, Liz realizes, how few people know just what, exactly, Vintage Works LLC sells to its customers, those canny art lovers who are enterprising enough to enter the dark web to find what they really need.

She is on the bridge over the northern branch of the Chicago River. "It runs backward, you know," Phil had told her on one of their early dates, and she hadn't known and had been so impressed. As students at Northwestern, she and Phil had loved coming downtown. They felt so grown-up, with their fake IDs and true love. And when they actually could afford to buy their dream house, that had been more amazing still. It was their forever house in their forever town, where the river ran backward, but they were going forward. *A city so old-fashioned that you might, as the song had it, see a man dance with his wife.*

"Well, goodbye," she says.

"Pleasure doing business with you."

She has been speaking to her "art dealer" on a flip phone that is the exact same model as Phil's burner. She powers it down and throws it in the river. There will be no record, no proof that she is anything but the grieving widow she appears to be. And she is grieving; that part is true. That will always be true. Next week, $125,000 will go out of her bank account, but an oil painting believed to be by a somewhat fashionable midcentury painter will arrive at her home. She will hang it in Phil's office. She will tell people that Phil admired the painter and had asked her to try to find one of his works.

She pulls a second flip phone from her left-hand coat pocket.

This was her first burner, the one she obtained a few weeks after she found Phil's secret one. She had, after all, promised not to spy on him. So she bought a burner phone and texted her husband, pretending to be the woman with whom he was infatuated. Then she watched her husband woo the other woman.

Eavesdroppers hear no good of themselves, fair enough. But Liz also had to bear witness to her husband's excitement and concern and affection for another woman, a flame that couldn't be extinguished as long as it burned inside his phone. Then the fire leaped, as fires do, threatening everything.

Liz gets to be almost everyone in this story. She is Hera; she is the cow chased by stinging flies until she regains human form. She is Leda, swooped up, then dropped, *terrified.* This story cannot be told without her, but what does that matter when a story can never be told?

Zeus and Hera, Hera and Zeus. How much damage they caused to everyone around them. Why, her student asked, did Hera hurt the women and not Zeus? Because Zeus is immortal, Liz said. Why does Hera take him back? Because gods must marry gods.

Phil was not a god. Neither is she. But for a few months, she seized the gods' prerogatives in order to survive. To spy, to fool. To kill.

Liz throws the second phone in the river, picks up the exhausted Pugsley, and heads back home in the stinging rain.

Mr. Forble

FROM *Salamander*

THE TREES SEEMED to hunch closer as darkness fell. Something —a mouse, or maybe a squirrel—emitted a high-pitched shriek, and Marta startled. An owl, she thought. The notion of being seen by something invisible, a creature swooping noiselessly onto its prey, unnerved her. Owls could rotate their heads due to special contractile reservoirs in their cephalic arteries; she'd learned this fact at a natural science center event she'd taken Teddy to when he was little, and it had been one of the facts he'd repeated to her for some time afterward, during a brief obsession with raptors. The path she followed now was washed out, rippling and uneven with knobby roots, so she moved with care, picking her way forward. In daylight, the tree trunks rose white-blond to the sky, filtering golden light, but now the shapes surrounding her had turned inky and strange.

"Teddy?" she called.

The sound of Marta's own voice was alarming, too loud.

The birthday party guests would all be home by now, safe in their pleasantly lit houses. There would be evening news reports, light dinners, the rinsing of plates and cups followed by the loading of dishwashers. Back under the park pavilion, the remnants of Teddy's double-layer Funfetti cake listed on the picnic table. The icing was probably studded with mosquitoes and gnats at this point. She'd been in such a hurry that she hadn't even covered the cake, and the thought wouldn't have occurred to Doug, eager as he was to usher his own daughter away. All the other parents had stood there, dopey-eyed, useless, hands resting protectively on the shoulders of their own children for those first few seconds. Wary. You could feel it in the air, or at least Marta could—everyone was looking out for his or her own. The chatter had stopped, the party suddenly over. Later, they'd recovered themselves, the other parents, in a flurry of perfunctory offers to help, but by then, she wanted none of it. She'd dismissed them all, brusquely. Her thoughts were only on finding her boy. You could say this for Teddy: he knew how to make an exit.

Marta walked across the little wooden-plank bridge that she remembered from other visits during daylight hours, recalled how it crossed a little creek in which springtime minnows darted. The creek dwindled to almost nothing in the summer. "Where do the fish all go?" Teddy had asked her once, the water then nothing but a reddish-brown thread. She'd shaken her head: "They disappear."

Marta's face was starting to ache already. Gone was the numb feeling, and now she felt a dull throb, the sensation of her flesh starting to swell like fruit past its ripeness. She touched her nose and cheekbone lightly, wondering if something was broken. There were fourteen bones in the human face: another fact she knew because of Teddy. She could picture him, only a few years earlier, his face boyish still, beaming up at her, offering these morsels like a cat presenting its owner with dead mice. Facts pleased him. *How precocious he is!* everyone said to her. At a certain point, Marta had realized that *precocious* was a word that carried its own malicious little twist. What at age six is precocious, by age thirteen becomes simply odd.

Up ahead, there rose a set of steps carved into the hillside—an ascending series of large, smooth stones laid into the packed earth. Marta and Teddy and Rick had taken the dog out here many Saturdays back when Teddy was younger, back when Rick was still living and they were a unit, a family. They'd watched as the dog scampered joyously ahead of them, leaping two paws at a time, snuffling underbrush. The path was a loop. There was a little bench at the top of the rise where the three of them would sit together, drinking water from canteens and eating bagels Marta packed. It was some of their best time together. Teddy had enjoyed it, or so it seemed. He'd enjoyed it as much as he enjoyed anything; it became part of their weekly rhythm. This was before Rick's diagnosis, before his long decline, before Teddy had started spending every minute he had alone in his room, going wherever boys went on their comput-

ers these days—online games featuring bright terrain and anach-
ronistic weaponry, chats with friends in Sweden, message boards
cluttered with cryptic messages. Places she did not want to know
about.

She'd tried. Therapists, tutors, parenting books. No one could
fault her efforts.

Marta almost expected to find Teddy sitting there at their old
bench, waiting for her. Crying, maybe. When was the last time
she'd seen him cry? Probably in third grade, after Kaitlin Richard's
boy played that prank. One of many he'd endured, but this one
could have killed Teddy. Kids didn't appreciate the seriousness of
allergies. Kaitlin had called her, of course, apologetic. Kaitlin had
punished Michael, done everything a good parent ought to do.
And Marta had understood on some level. Teddy invited prankery,
mischief; he stood out among the other boys in his class, a serious
little old man, long-jawed and morose. Puberty had hit him too
early, rendering him a halfling, more satyr than human boy. His
responses, even to her, were always slightly offbeat. Sometimes she
got the feeling he did it on purpose, taking a perverse satisfaction
in provoking meanness out of others, like it proved him right.

Recently he'd become more obstinate, refusing family dinners,
burrowing away in his bedroom. She offered to take him for haircuts, new clothes. He declined, barely looking up at her, his face
awash in the bluish light of his laptop. So when he'd asked her
for a birthday party, the first in years, she'd been delighted. There
he stood in a yellow-pitted T-shirt, his hair mussed, a line of dried
saliva visible down his chin. She'd been so delighted she'd hugged
him, not even minding how he stiffened, or that smell of his: sour
and faintly murine. A birthday party. Of course. He would have a
birthday party. She would make sure of it.

But did thirteen-year-olds still have birthday parties? Marta was
vaguely aware that the other kids Teddy's age had transitioned to
inviting a couple of friends out to dinner, or to the new cineplex
with plush reclining seats, or over for a pizza and game night. She'd
asked him if he might not like to invite some friends for dinner and
a movie night instead, if that's what his classmates were doing.

"I want a party like when I was a kid," Teddy had told her. "Like
when I was little and Dad was here."

She'd winced when he'd said this. Doug had been over at the

time, grilling salmon on the patio. Perhaps that was what led Marta to respond so enthusiastically.

"Of course," she said. "We can go to the park just like we used to. Your favorite cake and everything."

Teddy looked back at her blandly.

She recalled a moment a few years earlier when she'd found Teddy in her bedroom, poring through his father's prized baseball card collection, the old photo album of their honeymoon open on the floor beside him. A photo of young Rick in bathing trunks beamed up at her. Rick had treasured those baseball cards, would have been thrilled to see his son admiring them. Teddy was a good boy deep down.

On the porch, Doug and his daughter, eleven-year-old Emmeline, were laughing while the fillets cooked. They looked like an advertisement for something summery, fabric softener or clean white bed linen. Oh, to have such a normal child! Doug always corrected her gently when she said this. He was a family therapist, and quick to point out the diversity of individual gifts. *That's easy for you to say*, she would respond, *seeing as you have a normal child*. The air was delicious with the scent of salmon on the grill, teriyaki glaze. Teddy, of course, refused to eat salmon. There were basically only three foods he ate: Goldfish crackers, hot dogs, and oatmeal. She'd stopped fighting him on it. It wasn't worth the battle.

"Marta," Doug said, entering from the porch with the grill tongs still in hand. He pecked her on the cheek, and Teddy flinched.

"We're planning a birthday party," she said brightly, gritting her teeth into something like a smile.

"Fantastic!" he responded, always game. Doug was, on the face of it, a very good sport.

But the party had been the opposite of fantastic, and now here she was in the woods, alone, as it grew even darker. There was a bit of ambient light from a distant neighborhood, and a sliver of moon was up, but even so it was difficult for Marta to see more than a yard ahead. Her face pulsed steadily, like a living thing she carried separate from herself, bruised and humming.

"Teddy! Let's go home, please!"

Something grabbed her foot—a cruel, hard hand jerking her downward—and she flew forward, smacking the ground so hard that her breath was knocked out. She lay there, stunned.

She'd prepared so hopefully, with the cake, the streamers, the snacks Teddy had requested: Sun Chips and cotton-candy ice cream and Mountain Dew, things he said the other kids liked. But then, for the entirety of the party, Teddy had appeared aloof, distracted. He'd barely talked to the other boys, sitting by himself on one of the park benches. His eyes rose expectantly every now and then, surveying the parking for some late arrival. It was like none of it, none of her efforts, even interested him.

At one point, when the other guests were playing corn hole and badminton with more enthusiasm than she'd expected—because the rest of these boys and girls, his classmates, were not such bad kids, really, when it came down to it—she'd grabbed Teddy by the elbow, jerking him toward her.

What? What's wrong? she'd hissed at him. *What are you waiting for?*

Nothing, he'd said, pulling away, his voice gruff with tears. And she knew then he'd been wishing for something she was incapable of providing, incapable of even fathoming. All this—the party and streamers—was for naught.

Marta let the good side of her face rest on the ground where she'd fallen. Maybe she would just lie here all night. She had no idea where she'd left her phone; it probably sat, useless, beside the remains of the cake. She could feel the looping tree root that had snagged her foot, her ankle turned at such an odd angle that she could barely consider it without feeling queasy. Already she could tell it would not bear her weight.

The woods around her held a foreboding kind of quiet now. Marta felt the steady throb of her face and ankle but refused to cry. A sound like firecrackers went off somewhere in the middle distance, puncturing the silence.

Then came a crunching of leaves—footsteps, someone coming up the path behind her—and she could tell from the heaviness of the tread that it was not Teddy, but rather someone fully grown. Whoever it was, she could hardly lift her head to look at him.

It was Teddy's thirteenth birthday. All at once she felt very old.

After the party stopped abruptly—not the way he'd planned, but still—everyone stood there like morons with their plates of birthday cake and cups of soda, their sugar-sticky mouths hanging open like dummies, plastic spoons poised midair. Teddy had looked at them, wanting to howl in amusement, even though he could feel the tears welling up in his eyes. He'd shouted something stupid — the first words that came to him — about his mom being a bitch, an idiot, forcing out a hoarse laugh. Before anyone could respond, he'd fled. He'd run up the familiar path, agile and sure-footed. They'd come here all the time with the dog when he was little. Then he sat there for a while at the top of the rise, hidden just behind a cluster of trees, catching his breath and waiting for his mother to come find him.

None of it had gone off. Nothing he'd planned. He was uncertain what he wanted now. For his mom to come and wrap her arms around him, murmuring words of comfort? *Oh, my sweet Teddy, my special one.* Even though he'd hit her. Hard. She loved him stupidly and could not help herself. Teddy attributed this to some fixed rule of evolutionary biology, the cell's love for its cellular line: bullshit. He hated her for it, hated himself for craving solace from her. It felt pitiful, the way he lapped up his mother's soothing — something written into his genes, a dumb biochemical inheritance over which he also had no choice.

Maybe she would understand implicitly, not even expecting him to apologize. Or maybe she would be accompanied by Idiot Doug. Doug of the graying hippie ponytail and all-season Tevas, with his kabbalah bracelet and therapy-talk. Everything with Doug was about *appreciating dialectics* or *wise mind.* It was all enough to make you want to punch him in the face, an urge which Teddy had always resisted. Punching Doug in the face, however satisfying, would have accomplished nothing.

Teddy had learned to watch Doug with the same immobile calm he'd beheld in the copperhead they'd once found sunning itself in their front drive: slit-eyed and motionless, biding its time. The less he reacted, the more Doug danced, desperate for friendship, approval, any reaction. It was pathetic. In a small way, withholding made Teddy glad. Of course, ultimately, he'd ended up punching his mom instead.

He was growing bored sitting there. It was a little surprising no one had come to find him yet. A crew of ants had been hauling the dead body of a wasp near his feet. He watched for a while, studying the elegant machinery of the wasp's wings, its beaky proboscis, the up-close tiny horror of its face. Teddy placed his hand down nearby, letting the ants crawl over his fingers. It was a strange sensation, not unpleasant.

An evening bird gave a hiccuping call off in the distant under-brush. Maybe his mother had given up. Maybe she wasn't coming, just like the guy hadn't come. You couldn't trust half of what you found on the Internet. His mom always said that. And yet he'd always had good luck sourcing things online in the past: weed, acid, a surprisingly realistic-looking Russian passport, some kind of sketchy supplement called Dick Enhancer that came in a little white envelope with a crude sketch of a rearing stallion on it. Why not expect that the guy would come through too?

He'd had excellent customer reviews: *Trouble. Havoc. Mayhem. Your hands kept clean! Mr. Forble delivers.* Naturally, the listing had caught Teddy's eye. The guy had a felon's inventiveness—nothing too large or too small. All for a fee. Teddy could get the money; he had his dad's old baseball card collection. *Take good care of these,* his mom told him, way back when Teddy still wore footie pajamas. *They're going to help us pay for your college.* But the guy online had taken Teddy's money and no-showed. The reviews were probably all fake. Although maybe, apart from having lost the baseball cards, it was for the best that he hadn't come. Teddy considered this, poking the anthill with a stick. And yet—the thought of their faces. For one satisfying moment, he could have sat back and just watched. He would have called things off before it went too far.

Flicking the ants off his hand one by one, he heard her voice.

"Teddy!" his mother shouted, and the way she said his name made something hurt inside of him, like a hard crust wedged in his throat. Reflexively, he froze behind the nearest tree, as if he were still a child and they were playing hide-and-seek.

He'd hit her hard, his fist landing on her face with a sickening smack. It had felt exhilarating, just for a moment, like a release of some pent-up bodily need—finally taking a piss after holding it so long, your whole gut ached. Something like that. Even after the guy hadn't shown up, even with his disappointment that the whole thing hadn't gone off as he'd envisioned. Hitting his mother hadn't been part of the plan. But afterward he'd felt a physical high for a split second. She'd flinched, turning away and pressing a hand to her nose. When she'd turned to look up at him afterward, though, he'd seen the worst thing of all: she wasn't surprised. She'd been expecting this from him his whole life. There was a resignation on her face that he recognized. Resignation, and dumb, bovine, unimpeachable love.

He'd watched Doug tighten his arms around smug little Emmeline. Emmeline with her straight A's and summer musical camps and too-cheery voice. Emmeline, who sang to animals and said hello to every passerby, like a nauseating cartoon princess. There was the way Doug's lips curled upward then too—the look of someone who found the whole thing slightly amusing, someone suppressing an I-told-you-so.

Teddy should have finally punched Doug as well and been done with it, but instead, he'd thrown the jug of lemonade against the wall and ran. The jug—plastic and half-full—landed with a heartless *thwat* that even Teddy could appreciate was anticlimactic.

A low rumble passed overhead. It could have been thunder, but he knew that there was a backroad just over the rise, beyond where the trail ended. A truck, he thought, and for some reason he shivered. It was getting cooler now that the sun was setting. He'd left his jacket in the car.

His mother appeared on the path below.

She was moving slowly, unsteadily, off into the brush away from the trail. She looked winded and baggy, and this only made him angrier at her, her weakness a personal affront. He squinted to bring her into his sights, pulling back his trigger finger on an imaginary rifle and letting his bullet find its target. Bull's-eye. He nodded to himself.

As if on cue, she stumbled, smacking the ground with a heavy thud. He sucked in his breath, fighting the urge to call to her. He felt a pang of something that wasn't quite sadness.

There was a *pop-pop-pop* in the distance, like an engine backfiring. His forehead went cool and slick, as if he were coming down with the flu, his armpits gone sticky.

It was hours after the time they'd agreed upon, but he was struck with a sense of certainty.

Mr. Forble was coming after all. Mr. Forble was already here.

Michael sat in the front seat of his mom's car, fiddling with her satellite radio. He had a sick feeling, a mixture of the cake and caffeine and carbonation roiling his gut, but probably also because he got a kind of sick feeling whenever he saw that kid Teddy. He'd tried to explain it to his mom, but she didn't understand, or else felt too guilty. She was still so hung up on that prank they'd played with the peanut butter in Ms. Pendergraff's third-grade class. It

hadn't even been his idea, but he'd been the one designated to
carry it out. How were they supposed to have known? They weren't
trying to kill anybody. It was a joke. And look at Teddy—he turned
out fine. Or, maybe not *fine*, but peanut butter wasn't his problem.

Of course we're going, Michael's mom had said when the invitation
arrived. *We're going, and you're going to be happy about it.*

Sometimes, when Teddy looked at him, Michael could swear he
was wishing him dead. That's what Carter Blanchard always said:
Teddy Yarborough over there shooting death beams out his eyes again.
Then they would all laugh, him and Carter and Tyler and Dylan
and Griff, releasing the tension, and it would feel okay, but seriously, that kid Teddy could give you a creepy feeling. He was too
big for his age, all hunched up in the classroom desks like a weird
narc. He already had facial hair, or at least a dark line of fuzz over
his upper lip. Michael was an avid and jealous student of the signs
of puberty in others. His own underarms were still perfectly hairless and smooth, like nectarines, but he'd learned to laugh and
deflect.

He could see his mom walking in a loop over by the trash cans,
near the big sign that showed a map of the intersecting trails and
trailheads. She was on her phone. *It's work*, she'd said. *I might as
well take this here. We can wait a second, just to make sure Teddy's mom
finds him. Just in case they need anything. You sit tight.* It was never just
a second, though. He watched her, pacing around the recycling
bins, gesturing with her hands. He could see the nervous way she
kept brushing her hair back, a tic of hers. All the other party guests
had already left. The only other car in the lot belonged to Teddy's
mom.

Michael turned the radio to NPR, his mother's preferred station, and let the smooth voices comfort him. He never bothered
to listen to what they were saying, but it was pleasant hearing the
familiar chiming musical interludes, the voices polished and calm,
intelligent-sounding. Verbalizing the world into a kind of order.
Sort of like his mom. She was all right, really. She did important
work for the school board, and people in town respected her for it.

Once, when Carter and Dylan had both been at his house spending the night, Carter had said to him, like it was a revelation, *Dude,
your mom's actually kind of hot.* And he'd tackled Carter, rolling with
him like two puppies on the floor until finally things had resolved
into breathless laughter. It was true, although uncomfortable to

admit: she *was* kind of hot. But Carter was just saying it the way he said a lot of things, to get a rise out of people. Carter had also told them that Teddy was having sex already—with Ukrainian prostitutes he hired online, big-titted sluts with hairy legs, according to Carter, which was hilarious. A lie, certainly. But with Teddy, you could almost believe it.

Michael's mother was sweeping one hand through the air in a slicing motion now, a gesture he recognized. He was aware of a dull rising ache from his pelvis, a fullness in his bladder from all the soda. Walking back to the bathrooms over by the picnic shelter seemed an impossible task, though. Maybe he would just hold it until he got home.

He wondered if Teddy's mom had found him, if Teddy had apologized. He'd heard a crunch like a seashell under the heel of a shoe when Teddy had hit her. *Damn, son!* Carter had whispered under his breath, and ordinarily, Michael would have laughed obligingly, but he hadn't felt like it.

Prior to that, the party hadn't been so bad, really. It reminded him of the parties they'd always had in elementary school—wholesome fun, the entire class invited. There'd been that awkward moment when he'd run into Teddy in the bathroom. Michael, baby-faced and good-natured, a little chubby even, was well aware of which way the power tipped. His only advantage came when he moved en masse with the other boys. Man-to-man, Teddy was more imposing.

Teddy was leaning against the wall near the urinals when Michael walked in. He'd glanced up, nodding curtly at Michael. The bathroom was bare and cold, filled with spider webs and the husks of dead insects piled in the corners. Michael wanted to pee and get out.

Teddy moved away from the urinal to the sink, focusing on the video playing on his phone. Michael stood for a few seconds, nervous, trying to relax his mind. He always got pee-shy. Finally, he went. Zipping his fly, he walked over to the sink.

"Happy birthday, Teddy," he offered feebly.

Teddy continued to concentrate on his phone. At little intervals, he laughed, and Michael could see orange bits of food caught behind the tines of his braces.

"If you want soap, there isn't any," Teddy said without looking up.

Michael shrugged. He rinsed his hands off anyway, wiping them on his jeans.

"Whatever. I think your mom brought sanitizer."

Teddy's gaze was still locked on his phone. He grinned, amused at something Michael couldn't see. Flashes of color reflected off the lenses of his glasses. Michael wanted to leave, but Teddy was blocking the door. The others would be wondering what was taking so long. Carter tended to crack jokes whenever someone spent too long in the bathroom. *Trouble changing your tampon?* he'd say, which was stupid, but always left Michael red-faced.

"Look," Teddy said, thrusting his phone in front of Michael. "Tell me what you think."

It took him a second to piece together what was happening in the clip. Movement, flashes of color, fleshy shapes—once he was oriented, he could identify the specific body parts in motion. Then he saw someone sitting in a chair, begging to be let go. The video was grainy, the lighting poor. A jangly soundtrack. Laughter at one point, a goading voice.

Michael was growing increasingly uncomfortable. He wanted to look away, but Teddy was very close to him, so close that Michael could smell his unwashed odor. The phone was right in his face. Michael shifted himself away.

"Wait for it," Teddy said, moving closer, his breath in Michael's face. "There."

"Oh, God," Michael said, pushing the phone back reflexively. He leaned away from Teddy, pressing his hands to his knees, breathing like he'd just finished a race in gym class. A wave of clamminess passed over him, his vision narrowing so that he blinked hard, trying not to pass out. "That's not real, is it?"

Teddy was full-on grinning now, the entirety of his silver orthodontia revealed. He slipped the phone into his back pocket, opening the bathroom door so that the late afternoon sunlight fell in an oblong shape onto the cement floor.

"You're not so bad, are you?" Teddy said, his expression inscrutable. "Spineless. But gentle."

Michael didn't answer. Were Carter Blanchard saying this, it would clearly be mockery. With Teddy, he wasn't so sure. Michael wanted to leave. And never watch that video again.

"Anyways, have a good birthday," he muttered.

He was halfway out the door when Teddy grabbed him by the shirtsleeve.

"Hey, I like you, so I'll let you in on a little secret," he said, and he whispered into Michael's ear, his breath ticklish. "Tell your mom you want to leave early. Before the cake. Before the piñata. Tell her you don't feel good or something. Trust me."

He released Michael's shirt and winked.

Michael had barely seen Teddy for the rest of the party. He'd whispered to his mother at the first opportunity that he wanted to leave, that he felt sick and needed to go home, but she'd shaken her head. *Uh-unh, sir. Not today. We're staying.*

And so they stayed. The singing of "Happy Birthday" had sounded a melancholy note in Michael's ear, and the lighting of the candles on the cake added a touch of menace. He'd felt jumpy, overly alert, ready to bolt.

But then nothing had happened.

He saw it in Teddy's face, though: Teddy had been expecting something. It hadn't just been a joke, what he'd whispered in the bathroom. It had been a genuine warning. And after whatever it was hadn't taken place, after the candles and the cake, Teddy, in frustration, had punched his mother. Boom. Right in the jaw.

You had to feel bad for Teddy's poor mom, the way she'd looked, bug-eyed and afraid, and yet, Michael had experienced a wave of relief. The party was finished. Done. They could all go home.

He could go home, that is, if his mom would ever finish up her phone call. It was dark now. The lights over the parking lot came on with a pop and a click. Michael could see his mother, still pacing over by the picnic hut, phone pressed to her ear. He pressed the radio button again, finding a pop station. Some cheesy song was playing, a happy song about being happy, and since no one was around, he turned it up.

The music was loud enough that he didn't hear the truck pull into the lot. When he glanced up again, there it was: a rusted, reddish Ford one space over from him. He turned the music down, careful to keep his eyes straight ahead.

In the side-view mirror, he saw the driver's-side door of the truck open and a very tall man slide out. The man wore jeans, a dark shirt, and boots. Michael could see that he walked with a mincing sort of limp. He carried a long stick—a baton? or some kind of cane?—that was black and gnarled. He waved to Michael, but Michael kept his gaze straight ahead, pretending not to see.

And then the man was rapping on the passenger-side window with the stick. Michael wasn't sure whether to answer or to call out to his mom, who had moved out of sight. He remembered a snippet from the video Teddy had showed him—one specific and horrible frame—although why this should enter his mind at just that moment, he couldn't say.

He took a breath, turning to look him directly in the face. Before the man even spoke, Michael felt a tingling in the soles of his feet. The man had arrived like an answer to a question Michael hadn't realized he'd even asked.

"Hello, little guy," the man said through the window. "I'm late."

Emmeline's roommate is scraggly-haired and morose, a techy kid from some rural backwater who, instead of going to class, forever sits in their dorm room wearing noise-canceling headphones and cackling over YouTube videos. While Emmeline is out forming friendships, trying out for the fall musical, meeting up with classmates for study sessions in the library, Emmeline's roommate posts comments: on video clips and Instagram posts and Reddit threads and multiplayer gaming sites. Her name is Flo. She has long, pale, mosquito-bitten legs—a wonder, since Emmeline has never seen her go outside—and large, unblinking eyes. *Psychopath eyes,* one of Emmeline's friends said, although Emmeline shushed her, because Flo is not so bad really, and because Emmeline believes she has known a true psychopath, although she does not mention this. When people ask Emmeline about her roommate, she shrugs. "She's an Internet commenter," Emmeline explains, like it's a vocation. For Flo, it is a vocation. All hours of the day, Flo's face is bathed in the bright light of her laptop screen, aglow as if she's in the presence of something holy.

It is freshman year: first-year, as they're supposed to call it. For Emmeline, the university is something from a dream—lush green lawns, stately buildings with columns and domes, libraries filled with a solemn quiet as pages are softly turned. It all inspires in Emmeline a kind of awe. She is bright and well-adjusted. She has earned this; this is what her father, three hours away, tells her over the phone. She can hear the whistle of their pet cockatiel in the background and knows her dad is in the kitchen. She pictures him:

ponytailed, in jeans and sandals, like an aging community-theater Jesus. It is just the two of them, plus the cockatiel, whose name is Petey. She wonders if her father is lonely. It has always been her tendency to wonder about the inner lives of others, even if she is careful to conceal this, to appear buoyant and harmless so as not to make people uncomfortable. Her life has been more or less charmed; she knows this, and she knows too that this makes her curiosity a little unfair.

So one warm fall night when she comes home to the dorm crying after a cast party, she hopes that Flo won't notice — not because she is ashamed, but because it feels like a thing over which she ought not to trouble Flo. Her sadness is genuine, but it is also mundane, and even from within it, she can hold on to the awareness that it is small. It will pass. She will feel happy again.

Flo glances up when Emmeline walks into their room. The room is dark, Flo's side a morass of empty potato chip bags and stray articles of clothing. A video is playing on Flo's computer. Emmeline, stubbing her sandaled toe on a massive sociology textbook, cannot help but kick the offending book out of her way, issuing a great, frustrated moan. Insult on top of injury.

"What's wrong?" Flo asks, pushing back her headphones so that Emmeline can see her ears for once. They look raw and pinkish, almost private, Emmeline is so unaccustomed to seeing them. The sight fills Emmeline with tenderness.

"Oh, nothing," she says, wiping under her eyes, where she can feel her mascara running. "Dumb boy stuff."

Flo nods knowingly, then pats the corner of her bed.

"Here," she says. "I'll show you something interesting." She types into the search bar on YouTube and a number of videos pop up in the results.

She turns to Emmeline and clasps her hand, as if it is a thing Flo has studied in theory but not had opportunity to practice. Emmeline appreciates it, nonetheless.

"You've heard of Mr. Forble, right?"

Emmeline can see in the YouTube results the thumbnails and descriptions of videos: *Mr. Forble Visit 1, Mr. Forble Visit 27, Mr. Forble Comes to Kentucky, Mr. Forble Takes Manhattan*. Now she recalls. It is one of those recent viral memes, another Internet hoax, like the one about a horrible bird-faced woman daring children to commit suicide.

But looking at the results on Flo's computer, something funny and familiar pulls her. Flo pivots the laptop toward Emmeline, and she leans closer. She rests her hand onto Flo's touchpad and selects one video in particular. There is something in the frame: a face she might have seen before, or an expression she recognizes. It is nothing, but she hesitates.

"Mr. Forble," Flo says, nodding toward the screen. "People say he's all about vengeance."

Emmeline clicks on the clip, and it is blurry, a chase scene through a field, someone running after someone until there is a muffled sound, the footage swinging wildly from sky to darkness, followed by a strange, low laughter.

"Weird," Emmeline says, and she has stopped crying now. It's the laughter she recognizes. It is the laughter that's familiar.

"There are better ones," Flo says, and she brushes Emmeline's hand away gently, scrolling down through more results. *Mr. Forble Comes to Dinner, Mr. Forble Airport, Mr. Forble Prom, Mr. Forble Office Party #3, Mr. Forble Meets the Parents.*

Emmeline has placed the laughter now. It is the wild, angry laughter of someone trying not to cry. It is the laughter of her former stepbrother—or her former almost-stepbrother, the son of her dad's girlfriend—creepy Teddy, who disappeared after he punched his mother at his birthday party. Teddy had legitimately scared her, Emmeline recalled, and when he'd run away, she hadn't been as bothered as maybe she should have been. Things ended between her dad and his mom not long afterward; relationships cannot withstand certain stressors, certain losses, her dad had said. The truth is, she'd sensed tension between her father and Teddy's mom long before the disappearance. Weeks had passed, months, with no trace of him. *Poor Teddy,* her father said, but she could tell that he'd been a little relieved.

"They say Mr. Forble always comes when you call," Flo says, and she smiles a little sadly. "But there's always a catch."

She selects another clip and shifts in her chair so they can both easily see.

It is a bare room, empty but for a chair. A boy sits, his hands bound. The video is well-done, Emmeline must admit, authentic-looking and eerily reminiscent of a recurring nightmare from her own childhood. What happens next looks almost real. Emmeline recoils, but forces herself to keep watching. She hates watching stuff like this. But it's nothing—a simulacrum, a deep fake, low-fi guerrilla horror.

Flo exhales. "See?"

Emmeline swallows before she speaks. Her tears have dried now. She's pleased with herself not to have been duped.

"Play it one more time."

DELIA C. PITTS

The Killer

FROM *Chicago Quarterly Review*

AT 8:15, THE sawed-off man burst through the restaurant door.

Other men had finished their breakfasts and cleared out, headed for work or mischief in the late-August humidity. That left me and Burt at the counter of the Dominion Country Diner. Burt wiped the stainless surface, then pointed at my empty mug. Before I nodded, he filled it with coffee for the third time.

The little man took a stool at the counter, five seats to my right. He glanced at the laminated menu, which added "Melba's" to the name of the diner. "You do eggs over easy?" No greeting, no small talk, no smile. New York style straight up.

Burt blinked, but the customer was always right. "Yes, sir. Sure do. They come with home fries. You want coffee?" Burt slid a mug toward the new man and poured without waiting for an answer. "Your pick of toast or buttermilk biscuits comes with 'em."

"No toast. No biscuits." The man sipped coffee, scrunching his nose at the smoky bite. "I'm in a hurry."

Burt yelled the order to George, the cook, in the kitchen, who barked a reply, "I heard ya." Same answer he'd given when Burt bellowed my scrambled eggs order fifteen minutes earlier. "Keep yer wig on."

I pushed the cold fries to the edge of my plate. Dragging the last half slice of rye, I corralled another lump of egg and pitched it into my mouth. At least the air conditioner worked. And the coffee was decent.

The sawed-off man had a story I needed to hear.

*

This was my second, quieter, visit to Melba's Dominion Country Diner.

The previous evening, I'd had two cranky women and a toddler in tow. Sabrina Ross was my girlfriend and the owner of the Harlem detective agency where I worked. She was my boss, but on this road trip, Brina played sidekick with natural flair. The other woman was Crystal Figueroa, leader of a mob murder squad and mother of a two-year-old girl. My job was to drive Crystal and her daughter, JoJo, from New York to Tampa. They were running from rival gangsters, collateral victims of a festering war in the criminal underworld. My job was keeping Crystal and JoJo alive until we reached her relatives in Florida. Driving was the easy part.

Our first day on the road, we'd driven past Petersburg. Pushing to the Virginia/North Carolina line made sense, but Crystal insisted we take an early break. Her baby was cross, she was jumpy, Brina was fed up. No use pressing the argument until we all exploded. The Dominion Country Diner was on the main street of the little town. Easy access on and off the interstate. The restaurant was a narrow railroad car set above street level on a concrete platform fronted with blond bricks. Four steps up to the aluminum-framed glass door. Turquoise panels of peeling wood flanked the entrance.

In the shallow room, still sunbaked at seven, blue-and-white linoleum tiles encouraged JoJo to scamper beside the booths. There were five customers in the diner. Entering a new space, the racial calculations came naturally: two white couples shared a booth; a lone Black man perched on a stool at the counter. The two women smiled as JoJo's giggling play carried her past their table. All three men kept their eyes on the pork chops and pot roast cradled in their platters. Our noisy arrival altered the racial balance for everyone in the diner: three Black adult strangers and a brown-skinned baby girl tipped the scales. No way to predict how the locals would feel about us.

In the bathroom, Brina splashed her face and Crystal tamed her long black ponytail. While they washed, I checked the Dominion Country Cocktail Lounge attached to the diner. The saloon was dark and musty as an attic. It was empty of patrons, but stocked Coors in cans. I drank one standing at the bar and brought the second can to the restaurant. I didn't ask the women if they wanted drinks. When I returned, they'd already ordered Cokes and the Black man had gone. The white couples were wrangling over who would cover the bill. They reached a settlement, paid the waiter, and left.

Beyond the long counter, a rectangular slot in the back wall showed the cook at work. The waiter called him George when he shouted our order through the kitchen door. George was a tall Black man who carried his weight on his chest like a slab of sod. His thick pork chops, homemade applesauce, fluffy biscuits, and mashed red-skin potatoes filled our stomachs.

The server's name was embroidered in red script on the breast of his pale-blue shirt. Burt was a thin white man with straw-thatch eyebrows over hazel eyes. His head hair and lashes were the same chaff-yellow color. The veins and sinews of his arms tightened under hairless flesh. As waiter, cashier, busboy, and manager, Burt might have had his hands full. But we were the last customers for the night.

For the opening three minutes, Burt's climate patter scraped my nerves. "You folks brought the first dry weather we've had in quite a spell. Nigh on to eight days of rain. Enough water to choke a duck's uncle. Cleared just before you arrived."

No reply from me. Burt filled in the silence. "Y'all's good luck, that's for sure. Must be dry up north where you come from."

I didn't answer. Burt kept up the babble, soothing and low like the rumble of a well-tuned car. Though the temptation must have been great, he limited questions about our hodge-podge party to the most basic.

"Where y'all from?"

"New York City." I was the designated talker for our group.

We looked the part. Brina's Afro was almost shoulder wide. She wore a navy blouse with yellow-and-red embroidery over skinny denims. Crystal and I wore black jeans and T-shirts; hers were tight, mine not. JoJo brightened our show with bubble-gum-pink shorts, shirt, and sneakers. The headband over her black curls was dotted with pink knit flowers.

"New York City? Woot, that's a fur piece from here. Where y'all headed for?"

"Savannah." No need to give him the truth.

"Savannah's more than a hoot and a holler from these parts. You looking to stay overnight here?"

"Yes."

Burt recommended the Host Motel. "Not more 'n one hundred

yards from here. On the right. You can't miss it. Blue-and-white sign out front. Says WELCOME HOST MOTEL. Nothing fancy. Simple cabins. Clean and quiet is how Emily runs it. You tell her I sent you. She'll fix you up right. You'll be needing one, maybe two rooms, I reckon."

"Thank you."

No need to feed his curiosity about our sleeping arrangements. We'd ask for a single room with two double beds, queen if they had them. Crystal and JoJo could have one bed. Brina and I'd use the other bed, taking turns on guard duty through the night.

"Y'all come back for breakfast now. George flips the best pancakes in the county and his fried chicken is second to none. Ask Emily. She'll tell you."

No promises. But the coffee was decent. The air conditioner belted a merry racket. And it was close. We could be on the interstate by seven.

The next morning started slow. At eight, as the women finished washing, dressing, brushing, and packing, I walked to Melba's Dominion Country Diner for a return visit.

When the short man's egg platter arrived, he stabbed the yolks with a thrust of the fork. They bled yellow to the lip of the plate. Burt's head jerked at the sharp gesture, but he said nothing.

The stranger was Latino, tawny skin pulled tight across his cheekbones under eyes that slanted toward his ears. His black hair was slicked from his low forehead without a part. His brown fake-leather jacket was zipped despite the early morning heat. A net of fine scars draped across his right wrist and hand. His arms were thin, the muscles bunched and wiry. His torso bulged with uneven lumps: a weapon was stuffed into his waistband.

I reached for my wallet, but when the man spoke, I placed it on the counter next to my plate and lifted my mug. Hearing what he wanted could be crucial to our survival.

"You seen a woman come through here yesterday?" No pleasantries or misdirection, the man jumped into grilling Burt without preamble. "Had a little girl with her?"

"I don't know if I remember rightly." Burt's blond lashes screened his eyes.

"You'd remember her if you saw her. She's tiny, light-skinned, with long black hair pulled into a ponytail." The man scowled as if his description of Crystal Figueroa tasted sour. "The little girl looks like her. Only smaller."

"Now you mention it, I do come to think I saw a woman fits that picture." Burt's smile stretched over his large teeth. "Pretty little bit of a thing with that long black hair all shiny like in a magazine."

"That's her. She come through here?"

"Sure did."

I drilled my eyes into the side of Burt's head, but he kept a steady rhythm polishing the counter with his wet rag. Never turned to catch my glance or pause his wiping.

"When?"

"Just about noon yesterday. Lunchtime, it was. I remember 'cause she ordered tuna fish sandwiches for her and the little girl. White bread, not toasted. Light mayo. They washed them sandwiches down with two big glasses of sweet tea. Got a bag of potato chips for the little girl."

"Lunch, hunh?"

"Yes, sir. Lunchtime it surely was. You want me to call George out the kitchen? I bet he remembers too. Not often you see two such pretty little things as that around here. Say, what you want with them two anyway, mister?"

The short man fidgeted on the stool as he fixed his story. "Diamond's my wife. Run away from me and stole my baby girl too." His mouth drooped at both sides as if this were true. Limited imagination led him straight from Crystal to Diamond. He was hired for the muscle on his arm, not the sponge between his ears.

Burt played along. "Awful sad to hear it. Awful sad." As he spoke, George's massive head rolled into view in the window separating the dining room from the kitchen. A white kerchief stuck to his bald scalp, sweat patches staining the hem.

"I'm hoping if I can just talk with Diamond, I can get her to come home." The short man poked a blunt finger into the corner of his eye as if a tear had leaked out.

"Course you do. Any man with more than a feather in his pants would want what you want, mister." Burt screwed his mouth into a tight purse. "Bet you miss your little girl too. What'd you say her name was?"

"Jasmine."

"Pretty name for a pretty little girl. Jasmine."

"You see which way Diamond drove after lunch?"

"More than saw it."

"How do you mean?"

"She asked me for directions."

"Directions to where?"

"Showed me the address on her phone." Burt closed his eyes as if summoning the memory. "Don't rightly remember the street. But it was in Jackson. I do remember that."

"Jackson?"

"Sure, Jackson. You want me to call George? I bet he recollects better 'n me." Burt tilted his head toward the kitchen but kept his eyes on the stranger.

The short man's face flushed. "Which direction is Jackson from here?" He was hooked, squirming, and eager to be landed.

"Not far. Twenty-five miles due west as the crow flies. By road, forty."

"On the interstate?"

"Oh, no, sir. You fly right by Jackson if you stick to the highway. You need to follow the county roads."

"Where do I go?"

"From here, take a left onto Main Street. Then three blocks till you come to a four-way stop. Turn left past the old bank building. The one with the fancy columns out front." Burt used his index finger to sketch a map on the dry flesh of his palm. "Then four more blocks. You'll see signs for County Road 355 on your right."

"Left on Main, then left again at the stop, then right to the signs for County Road 355. That it?" The pupil eager for approval from the teacher.

"You got it in one, mister. Head due west and you'll hit Jackson by lunch. Can't miss it."

The short man shifted on the stool again, adjusting the waistband of his jacket where it dug into his belly. I could see the outline of his weapon's handle pressed against his pocket.

He rested three fingers on the hidden gun butt, then zapped his eyes at me. "You enjoying this conversation, fella?"

"I couldn't help but hear." I raised the mug and took a deep draft of coffee. No longer hot, the brew tasted brackish, like well water.

Burt swished the damp cloth toward my plate with his left hand, lowering his right shoulder and arm as he moved. His right hand stilled in the shadows below counter level.

The short man stared at me. "Well, you forget you heard anything. Understand?"

I nodded and set the mug on the counter next to my plate.

Against my silence, the short man raised his voice. "Better for your health the sooner you forget."

"Already forgotten, pal."

Burt laid a paper slip next to the man's platter of cold eggs. The man stood, eyed the receipt, then tugged his jacket until it settled below his belt again.

"Good. Then you won't mind paying for the entertainment." He stepped toward me and slapped his receipt on the counter at my elbow.

Muscles along Burt's pale jaw flickered. I stabbed the receipt with an index finger and pulled it toward me. "Sure. Happy to. Pal."

The stranger looked to Burt. "Thanks for the breakfast." Then a quick exit, the door shushing on rubber guards as the man left.

The cook pushed through the kitchen door. He pulled his white kerchief from his head, wiping his eyebrows. The three of us watched the man back his low-slung black Nissan sedan over the curb. The scrape of bumper against concrete drew a twitch of a smile from Burt.

George was first to speak. "What you figure he wanted with her, Burt?"

Burt looked at me. "Mister, that tiny woman you traveling with, she's riled some mean folks, that's for sure." When I didn't answer, he swiveled his head toward George to continue his speculation. "Maybe she's mixed up with big-city gang types. Killers and whatnot."

"You got that right, Burt. No way that rough customer was looking to round up a stray wife. His intents was murderous. No doubt about it." George curved an index finger across his upper lip, ladling sweat, which he flicked onto the floor. "What you figure she done?"

"That little lady crossed a big boss for sure. Maybe stole drugs. Or money. Maybe killed somebody."

"And the big boss sent that hit man who come looking to kill her, you figure?"

"That's how I make it. Guess we'll never know." Burt looked at me. I studied the egg crumbs on my plate.

George kept talking. "Unless he circles around here again."

"Why would he come back?" My question let me off the hook for explaining. "You gave him good directions, didn't you?"

"Oh, my directions were plumb straight." Burt hung a smile on the last word, then let it drop. "As far as they went."

"What's that mean?"

George elaborated. "Burt said she was headed for Jackson. But he didn't say *which* Jackson."

"There's more than one Jackson?" The squeaky rise in my voice sounded more chump than Harlem smooth.

"Sure." Burt's small smile expanded at last. "There's Jackson Spring, Jackson Ridge, Jackson Pass."

"Don't forget East Jackson, North Jackson, and Jackson's Ford. That's just in this county." George ticked the names on his giant fingers, dough specks flying as he tallied. "And then there's three more Jacksons in the next county west of here."

His friend nodded. "How long you figure before he realizes he's never going to track down his Diamond or whatever she's called?"

"Might take him the rest of today and into tomorrow, Burt. He didn't look all that smart."

"Maybe he'll be too shamed to show his face around here again."

"Maybe so."

Burt turned on me again. "Whether he comes back here or not. You know you got him on your tail now."

"Yes."

"George, bring them shears you keep in the top drawer next to the stove."

The cook disappeared into his kitchen, returning thirty seconds later with a huge pair of scissors.

Burt laid the scissors next to my plate, handle end forward. "You help your woman cut off her ponytail. Soon as you get back to the motel. Just snip it right off. She's going to want to argue. Want to wait till she gets to a beauty salon. Claim she needs a fancy do. You know how women get. But you don't have time for that. She needs to cut off her long hair. All of it. And do it fast."

George added more advice. "And buy your baby some blue jeans at the Walmart on your way out of town. You need to dress that child like a little boy. Ditch all the pretty pink clothing and get her into some plain T-shirts and dungarees."

"Point taken." I reached for the scissors and slipped them into the waistband of my jeans against the small of my back. "It'll be a tough sell. But I'll make it stick."

"You'd better."

"What'll you do if the killer comes back?"

Burt shifted his right shoulder and flexed his elbow. He slid a shotgun onto the counter. He pushed its blunt nose against the plate of half-eaten eggs left by the short man.

"I'll handle him. If he comes back." Burt stowed the shotgun in the shadows below the counter.

I pulled two twenties from my wallet. "This cover the bill? His and mine?"

"That'll do a handsome job of covering. Thank you, mister."

"The name is Rook. And the thanks are on my side." I leaned an elbow on the counter, my voice low under the air conditioner's rumble. "Why'd you help?"

"Didn't like the look of his face." Burt tilted his head toward George.

The cook expanded. "Me neither. Didn't sit right with me. Coming after women and little babies like that. Plain wrong, that's how I seen it."

I reached a business card from my back pocket and laid it next to the twenties. Its shiny black face shouted, "The Ross Agency / Private Investigations / Lost? Missing? Cheated? / Your Problems —Our Solutions." I flattened the card's bent corners against the counter. "You ever need help in New York, call me. My number's on the back."

The door swooshed open. An elderly couple stepped into the cool interior of the diner. With a smile and wave at Burt, they took seats at a table to the left of the door. George folded my card in his heavy fist and rolled toward the kitchen.

"How you doing, Mr. Anderson? Be right with you, Miz Anderson." Burt gathered two laminated menus and swept from behind the counter to tend to his new customers.

I jerked the door. A gust of air, like an oven's breath, rushed past me into the diner. In the hot sunlight, I turned toward the Host Motel. The sharp tip of the kitchen shears scratched my spine as I hurried over the gravel driveway.

ELIOT SCHREFER

Wings Beating

FROM *Tampa Bay Noir*

I GUESS I should have figured a Florida vacation would have lots
of cars in it. This trip has been red arrows, four-way stops, ogling
the rare pedestrian, hailing a car on this app or that, or waiting for
a crusty cab with a crustier driver. How much of a life around here
is spent wallowing in seats, hands at ten and two or a pinkie at six,
waiting for a light to tell you when it's time to act?

I'm driving around all the time in Maryland too, don't get me
wrong. On Darren weeks I'm chauffeuring him plenty. Violin lessons or swim practice or trips to the mall food court with his girlfriends. Darren's a busy kid — the only thirteen-year-old I know who
uses his calendar app — but driving with him back home means not
having to talk. Now we're on vacation so we're pressed in the back
of these hired cars, not me in front and him on his phone, but right
next to each other, shoulder to shoulder, like we're sweethearts on
a date. Like we're me and his mom, back before the split.

We're done with the sightseeing part of the vacation and onto
the spa stay, the whole point of this trip. I'm no spa guy, but I was
the third-place-out-of-three winner of an episode of *Guess It Now,*
and this spa trip was my prize. I thought Darren and I could bond
a little. Maybe we can laugh about it.

That's why we're in the back of a car whose upholstery smells
like nightclub cologne, driving down the main street of this town
called Safety Harbor, even though there's no ships here. Pretty safe
though!

"Nearly there, kid," I say. "The glamorous resort and spa."

Darren puts his phone away—he's pretty good about that stuff, not an addict like most of them—and casts his liquid staring attention toward the spa. I guess it's the same place as the cutaway graphic on the game show: curved brick drive, blue rectangle of a pool behind the front windows, a restaurant that looks like the conservatory from Clue. There's something a little seedy about all of it too, which I definitely didn't expect. Hard to put my finger on. There's probably microscopic grime between all the tiles.

Valet boys in polo shirts lounge in front. One says, "Good afternoon, sir," when I pass. It's in this put-out way, though, like his mom just made him say it.

The other boys look at Darren, with his skinny jeans and gay or at least rainbow-spectrum-y designer eyeglasses, and I can feel the smirks they're all hiding, each and every one.

I don't know, maybe I thought the game show would have called ahead, said, *Hey, a prize winner's coming in to stay for a while, give him a congrats when he gets there*, and Darren could have had a moment of being proud of his dad, but I guess we're just like any other guests, because the lady behind the counter says, *Enjoy your two nights with us*, as she gestures me and Darren toward our room.

The hallway's covered in aggressively ugly carpet, a blue-green run through by ship's wheels and nautical rope. It saps the sound from our feet and our luggage wheels.

The room is perfectly clean. It's also perfectly stale, like a mock-up that was never meant to be lived in. While we slot our clothes into drawers the window air-conditioning unit rattles and chugs, goes quiet, rattles and chugs, goes quiet. I open the blinds, see the license plates of the cars parked right in front, the gas station on the far side, and close the blinds again.

It's a third-place-winner sort of joint, I guess.

Darren's messaging on his phone for a while. When the air conditioner's off, I can actually hear the sound of his thumbs on glass. I wonder, not for the first time, if he's cruising nearby guys. A little young, sure, but I'd have taken up any chance to have sex at his age, though willing girls are harder to find and I didn't have apps or anything.

It's not like he's come out to me, but I'm operating on the assumption that my son is gay until proven otherwise. I work with three gay dudes—maybe four, actually—and I find it hard to keep up with their fast and mocking conversations, but they're good guys. My son has their same armoring wit, the same tendency to check his hair, the same examined life.

Darren looks up from his phone and asks if I want to go for a walk. My son has made a request that involves spending time with me. I try to play it cool—but yes, I would like to go for a walk!

We haven't said much during our days working on our sunburns on Clearwater Beach. We don't ever talk much, to be honest, but I think that's what we both want. At least I know it's what *I* want, or at least it's the only way I know how to be. Darren, though—when he's with his mother he can't shut up. The number of TV shows they manage to watch and then discuss, it makes me wonder if he's ever sleeping when he's in his bedroom with the door closed.

There's an old pier right near the spa, and we walk along its curving and pitched wood. The constant sea air's made the surface waxy. Our sneakers tilt and squeak. At the end of the pier is a fisherman, a young guy with a University of Florida T-shirt who I figure is plucking fish out of their water for kicks and not for food. He doesn't catch anything in front of us, thank God; Darren would not be into that, but I can feel my kid getting withdrawn as he smells the blood and scales.

Darren dutifully plucks up any scraps of loose fishing filament we come across, balls them into his pockets. He doesn't want them flying into the sea and garroting mermaids or whatever he's worried about. He doesn't want to see things that aren't even human get hurt. He's an absurdly sweet kid, my son.

Amelia called me a week ago, saying Darren had been moody until he'd finally explained to her that I'd said it didn't matter if he was gay, or if he was green-skinned or ate babies or was a terrorist. Did that seem like the right way to talk to him about that? she wondered. I told her that I was sure I didn't put it that way, and if I did it was a joke because I was nervous because I love the kid so much. Of course I don't think being gay is the same thing as being a terrorist, but how am I supposed to find the words to tell Darren that? And now it's like we're never allowed to discuss the topic ever again.

I stop to talk to this nice woman in a tight top about where she's from and whether she knows good places to eat near here, and when I look up Darren's gotten away from me and he's almost back at the spa. He's a fast kid, his skinny legs made twitchy by all the swimming. I say goodbye to the lady, she was probably too young for me to be flirting with anyway, and catch up to my kid.

He's at the entrance, where there's this two-lane road clogged with glossy cars pumping out exhaust while they wait for the four-way stop to clear. Something's caught Darren's attention, but I can't tell what. On the other side of the road is nothing special, just a six-story apartment complex that's under construction. The earth around it is ripped and raw, and the apartments aren't finished or anything. It seems like a nice enough place to live, though. I'd take it.

Darren looks upset, and I get worried that all the dried fish guts we saw on the pier are going to make this spa stay go blammo. I'm sure he'd be telling his mom just what was the matter, but I don't know how to get him talking. I like everything he says to me; I just don't have a lot to say back, that's all. I scratch at the sweaty small of my back. "Something wrong?" I finally try.

"Nothing, Dad," he says. But I know there's something. It would be a bummer if your view got blocked by that new building, but I can't see why he'd get upset about that.

He's looking toward the spa, like he's ready to go back and chill in the room, but I focus on where he was looking before, and see there's an egret, a white spindly thing, pretty and harmless unless you're a fish. It's fluttering beside a stopped tractor, beating its wings uselessly against the side of the machine. It's only going to hurt itself. That tractor's not going anywhere until the crew returns on Monday.

What does a bird have against a tractor?

We have nothing to do with ourselves anyway—I'm at a get-away spa with my kid, and the awkwardness is hitting me more and more hard core—so we wander into the construction site. We poke around the boundary of the scalloped orange tape, check out the derelict backhoes and the homes without doors as we make our way to the bird. If you don't count the line of stopped cars or the egret or the ladies in white jeans going to the Starbucks on the corner, we're on our own. Eventually Darren and I make it to where we both know we're heading: as close as we can get to the tractor and the egret.

The bird goes all still when we get near, like it's trying to camou-flage itself into the tractor. It seems to me that something spindly like an egret should fly away if a couple of humans approach. But it doesn't, and the wrongness of that leaves me fluttery. Darren, too, he gets this posture like, *Let's leave, Dad,* but he doesn't say any words, he just folds his arms over his slight chest and stares at the bird.

Look, I'm not a knucklehead, I had enough smarts to get onto that trivia show in the first place. I put it all together quick enough: new construction, maybe getting ready to show a model apartment to prospective clients, first-time landscaping around the building, someone knocked down the bird's tree or whatever, and its nest and its eggs—or God, little birds?—are gone now, but it's still fighting the tractor, like it can get the babies back. Maybe the dead birds are still under?

"All right, Darren, let's not bother the bird anymore."

"What do you think happened?"

"I don't know, but we've upset it, look."

"I don't think we upset it," Darren says quietly. "It was already upset when we were back across the street."

"Okay, but it's not going to calm down with us around. Come on, let's check out the pool."

I walk away, but Darren doesn't move. He's like a kid in a horror movie sometimes, his attention gets so focused that all other things fall away.

"Can we help it?"

"I don't think so," I say. "Whatever it's upset about is over now."

"Poor egret," he says in a whining way that makes me worry about how guys treat him at school. But he's always tight with the girls in his violin section, chatting away, and I bet they'd all be making friendship bracelets for this egret right now. I decide my kid's life is fine. In general, at least. For the next two days, I'm not as sure.

"You hungry?" I ask.

He shakes his head. I don't need to look to know that his eyes are wet. "Okay, we can just stand here and look at the bird, if that's what you want."

That's what we do. Cars are going by, sweat is dripping down my back, more ladies in white jeans are going into the Starbucks, and the egret is still freaked out, but not about us, and I wonder how long it's been there, fighting this metal thing, and it's making me sad too, even though my emotions are cinder blocks, so I go and try to investigate, like maybe if it can show me the broken eggshells the bird will feel better, but it flutters its wings at me, with its beak open, and that's when Darren says, "We can go check out the pool, Dad," so we head back to the spa.

While we walk I ruffle the hair at the back of his neck. It's limp and wet. I know he's gotten sad. He and his mother have always had plenty of melancholy in them, and I've never been able to do much about it for either one. They're just not sturdy, but my own dad made me be sturdy above all else and I've come to realize that sturdy isn't an especially healthy thing for a person to be.

"Maybe there's chicken fingers at the spa restaurant," I say.

No reaction to that one. He's always loved chicken fingers. But thirteen is different from twelve.

The valet kid welcomes us back in that same go-tell-Aunt-Bertha-thank-you tone. By the time we're at the indoor pool and steam room, my sweat has chilled.

The pool was probably something to behold back in 1980. It's hidden away from any natural light, occasional tiles darkened like age spots. An old lady in a bathing cap is doing slow laps, and two more are sitting on chaise longues around one of the little tables with pebbled-glass tops. The ceiling is dentist-office low.

"Nice, huh?" I say.

The kid's staring at a landscape with ceramic vases painted on it, which makes it look like we're in a low-res Greece or maybe Rome or something. He taps the fakey-jake sky and looks back at me smiling, like he's finally figured out the answer to some frustrating question.

We lie on our striped towels in the chill AC around the warm pool, and take turns diving in. He keeps his T-shirt on, like I'd have done at thirteen. I display my padded hairy belly to the world, then we go back to the room and put the TV on and drop into our phones. Someone can't figure out the software licenses in accounting, but otherwise everything at work seems to be going along fine without me. Amelia asks how Darren's getting along and I text her back a pic of him staring at his phone on his drooping hotel bed, and it all feels nice, like we're still married. I compose and delete a few texts to her, then finally put the phone down to stop myself from sending any of them.

I say it's time for dinner, and Darren doesn't change out of his T-shirt, so I tell him it's a special occasion. I'm grateful I don't have to explain that I want the game-show prize to be something special. He puts on a button-down shirt, pleated khakis, and a clip-on tie —it's a bit much but also pretty damn sweet.

We go tripping along the nautical hallway, my kid's loafers—

loafers!—squeaking on the plush plastic-y fibers. When we get to the restaurant there's a printout taped to the window, seventy-two-point Calibri telling us it's closed for a private event.

Kid and I peer in anyway. He's on his tiptoes to see what's going on, bringing his white-athletic-socked heels right out of the backs of his loafers. At first I think it might be a wedding, but then I see that it's probably a work event. There's an easel with some poster board I can't make out through the foggy glass.

I'm not the kind to go places I'm not wanted, so I bring Darren to the host desk and ask where the spa's other restaurants are. The lady explains that there's just the one, and sorry it's closed for a party, someone should have told me. I ask what else is within walking distance and she explains that there's nothing unless we want to get a sandwich from the Starbucks. That's when I start getting really mad, but Darren's there so I swallow it all down. He heard enough of my yelling back when I was married to his mom.

We stand in the hallway and I pull out my phone, but just looking at the car apps, imagining sitting in the back of a Camry in traffic, pits my stomach. I don't want to get back on the highway, don't want to wait at lights and pass three Applebee's on the way to what other chain restaurant we've chosen. I put the phone away. "Come on, we're going in," I say to Darren, and before he can protest I've pushed through the doors and gone into the private event.

"Whoa, Dad," he says under his breath as we step to one side, into the shadows. I crashed enough weddings back in my crazier days to know that you stay as still as possible until you've picked your strategy.

Looks like the event has been underway for a while already—maybe it's technically a lunch?—and the conversation is drunken, the buffet mostly picked over. There's plenty of waxy little cheese cubes, though, and some raw broccoli, and, no way, what looks like chicken fingers! The placard is in French, but I know a chicken finger when I see one. Darren can eat around the creamy blue-cheese center.

I tell him to wait at the quiet end of the buffet while I grab some plates, since that'll bring me close to the nearest clot of drunk office-party guys—this office does seem to be all guys, at least the ones who've stayed this late. I nod to four hair-wave polo-shirt bros with their napkin-wrapped beers, like to say, *Hey, office stuff, that work we all do, crazy, amiright?*

I get four nods back, then return to my kid with the two plates, their porcelain scuffed gray from innumerable meals. Feeling the office bros' eyes on the back of my head, I hand Darren one and ask him if he doesn't want to make up his own dinner and has he seen the chicken fingers yet? I'm hyper-aware of these guys' focus, am sure they're passing around theories about us, because they're in that late-party zone where no one has anything to talk about, but they're intimate and cheerful and a topic you've discovered together is proof of how amazingly everyone gets along, them against the world. Them against me and my kid. Potentially. I dunno where this is all going to go.

We get our food and then find an empty table where I can move enough smudgy wineglasses and napkins to one side so that we can eat together. Darren's laying into his chicken fingers and I'm eyeing the bucket with the open wine bottles and we're just being peaceful and companionable until I sense those guys nearby.

"Hey, are you two with—" Here they say the name of their company, which I honestly can't remember, but it was one of those full-name-of-a-hometown-guy kind of small-fry investment joints.

"Nope," I say, keeping my eyes on my plate.

Darren keeps his eyes furiously on his food too, but in a maybe overdramatic way, like we're in a black-and-white movie avoiding Nazis.

"We were thinking this little guy could be a new junior analyst or something." It's the same bro speaking, and he's probably the one drunk or naturally aggressive enough to make this confrontation happen. Not that I think they're going to start an actual fight —they just want to make us feel shitty for a while so they can feel un-shitty together. I get it. I've done it before.

I look right into them. "Look, guys, we're just trying to have dinner here. We're not causing any trouble."

They make side-eye at one another, and that's how I know I've taken the wrong tack. Now I've turned from a foreign adventurer to a freeloader taking handouts. I could have explained that the spa rented out its restaurant without thinking about its guests, and that's why I'm here eating food they don't want anymore anyway, but I don't feel like I owe these bros any explanations.

"Guess you didn't see the sign," lead bro says. "This is a private party."

"We're not doing any harm," Darren mumbles.

I raise an eyebrow at him. He just said that? My kid?

"What did you say?" lead bro huffs.

"We're minding our own business," Darren says. "You should try it." He takes a preposterously large bite of chicken finger and starts chewing.

Maybe it's called cordon bleu, this chicken?

"*We're just thinding our own thisness,*" lead bro says, with an extravagant lisp. "Well, this is a private party, and you're not on the list, so you being here is our business, faggot."

My world clanks and drops. Blood buzzes through my ears.

"They're not causing any trouble, man, just let it go," says one of the other bros. They suddenly come into focus, a trio of pastels —pink, green, and blue—behind lead bro's orange. One of their hands is on lead bro's shoulder.

"They're not done ramming themselves down our throat on every TV show, now they're coming to our parties and eating our fucking food."

For the sake of Darren, I will myself motionless despite the rage pushing my limbs to move and fight. Do these douchebags think we're together? Me and my thirteen-year-old kid? Whatever version of the truth lead bro is thinking, it's not working for me. I push back hard from the table, enough to send my chair clattering to the floor. A couple of other guys in blazers look over, and go back to their conversation.

Pastel-blue bro picks up the chair. Maybe this is going to work out fine.

Lead bro puts down his beer and rubs his knuckles. Maybe this is not going to work out fine.

I've been in my share of fights before, and the whipsmack of this lifetime-achievement-prize trip being so sucky has definitely given me the urge to connect my fist with something that'll scream back, but as I start to do my chest-forward-bumping-the-air toward lead bro, I catch a glimpse of Darren and he's got this look on his face —not scared, exactly, but more tired, like he'd give anything to be surprised by what's about to happen.

If I'm a good dad, my priority should be getting us out of here.

For the sake of my kid, I put my hands up and turn away from the bros. They start chuckling and victory-snarking, and it makes my shoulders square off and the hair on my forearms rise, but I still walk away. Darren stands up, looking all meek and lanky, but he takes one last chicken finger from his plate and waves it like a Potter wand. "Faggot out!" he says, before sauntering after me and out of the restaurant.

The fight fury fades. It's replaced by a queasy middle zone, where the pastel voices join together behind me and I'm waiting to feel a beer bottle or a hock of spit hit the back of my neck, things men have done to me and will do to my son for decades to come, but also my mind is skimming along the new reality that my meek sensitive kid stands up for himself, has developed a whole gay arsenal of zingers. Who taught him how to do that?

We're out of the room, and I've got my arm around him, rubbing his birdlike shoulder, and then I'm laughing. "*Faggot out*," I say. "Amazing."

"I dunno, that just came out of me," Darren says.

"I should use it," I chuckle. "*Faggot out*. Awesome line."

"You don't need to use it, Dad."

That can mean ten different things, and I try to ask him to tell me more, but the words stop before they get to my mouth.

Darren looks back where we came, to the closed doors. "I'm glad those guys aren't following us. They were total assholes."

"Yep," I say.

Without quite meaning to, we've wandered back into the pool area. I lean down and slap the warm, slightly cloudy water. "Want to take a swim again?"

Darren shakes his head. "I think I want to go back to the room."

I knew that would be his answer. We don't even have our trunks and towels with us or anything, and after nearly getting gay-bashed, neither of us is exactly inclined to any father-son skinny-dipping.

We walk past the steam room, and since it's still barely sunset and we have a whole night of sitting on our hotel beds on our phones ahead of us, I drag my feet by looking inside. Narrow tiled box, dingy without officially being dirty anywhere. It's like sitting under a giant hand dryer that blows wet. I've never gotten the appeal of those rooms.

Darren's waiting for me, worrying his fingers and tapping his knees, so I close the steam room up and walk with him down the corridor of nautical carpet. We get to our room, and he's immediately absorbed in his phone, unclipping it from the charger and hurling himself onto the bedspread. I take a piss, then waffle in the doorway. "Did you get enough to eat?"

He nods and pats his belly.

"I'm not sure I did," I say. The hair on my forearms has risen again. "I might go back out there and see what I can scrounge up."

He nods again.

"Sure you don't want anything?"

Headshakes.

"Okay, see you soon."

I step out and press the door closed behind me. My palms are sweaty, my mouth full of a metallic taste. All I hear beyond my racing heartbeat is the feeble roar of air conditioners behind closed doors. Where are all the other hotel guests? In their cars somewhere, out to dinner, I guess. But not here.

My feet bring me to the restaurant. I could do with another beer, a cracker, a leaf of lettuce, anything, whatever I can steal from those assholes. I want them to see it, and I want to see the consequences. I listen to the door, then crack it open. There's just a server left there, cleaning the tables and putting chairs up. She gives me a *Hey, stranger* smile and I give one back. There's still some food left, so I could get some, but since the party bros aren't there it wouldn't count as stealing, and stealing is what I want to do. I do grab a beer, though, and start it going down quick. That gets a genuine smile from the server. She might like me.

She's way too young, though, so I leave the restaurant and lean against the door, drinking my beer and listening to the nothing happening all around me. Male murmurs in the distance, the sigh of the steam ticking on and ticking off, the constant hum of the pool pump. An old lady in a bathrobe shuffles down the hallway. I nod and smile at her, she nods and smiles at me. Think she's the same one who was doing laps in the pool.

I wish I had a cigarette. But I don't smoke anymore unless it's at a party. This is not a party.

The question that got me was geography. I wasn't stuck in the moment; I wouldn't have gotten it even from the comfort of my living room. I wasn't meant to be more than a third-place contestant on *Guess It Now*.

The Amazon River passes through Peru before entering Brazil.

How hard is life going to be for my son?

A roaring janitor passes me, his industrial vac advancing and retreating, advancing and retreating. He dips into the pool room, keys jangling. He comes out a few minutes later, closes the door, and flips a sign on a chain.

The vac roars back to life, then fades as the janitor passes around a corner and out of view.

My fingers flick over my phantom cigarette. Alone again.

Until I'm not. Voices approach from down the hall, voices I recognize.

I don't hide, but I do go still.

The bros, only two of them now, orange bro and pink bro, lurch along the hallway, coming from the same direction where the janitor disappeared. Pink has his arm around orange's shoulders, and the pressure of his heavy limb makes orange trip as much as he walks. They're staying upright, but only just.

My fingers drop the phantom cigarette and make a fist instead.

The bros go right up to the glass door to the pool area, peer in. They totally ignore the CLOSED sign and push through.

Their voices fall away beneath the hum of the pool pump. I'm alone in the hall. It's as if the bros were never here, as if they dropped into the water and were sucked away.

I stand there for a moment, resisting the urge to check my phone, just wondering about people being here, people being gone.

I step toward the pool entrance.

I'm totally silent, not from any special source of elegance, but because the carpet is so plush and so thick. I reach the door and peer in.

In soft focus through the blurring glass, the bros are doing midnight laps, laughing and splashing as they kick against either side. Their polo shirts stick to their torsos, and as they pull themselves out of the pool, their shorts cling. Would my son enjoy the sight of this? The bros probably wouldn't want to be seen by my son, and tonight that matters.

The lights are out, but the streetlight silhouettes the bros as they jostle and push, as they scamper along the edge of the pool, frantic and agile, like little boys at a sleepover.

They head toward the door, toward me. I tense, ready for a confrontation. My fist on a jaw might just be the answer I need, the thing that will clear this murky unease.

The bros turn before they're at the exit, though, and head into the steam room. I hear the crank of the knob, the clink of the heater, the whoosh of the steam.

I walk toward the entrance to the pool area and lay my hand on the doorknob. I push it, and head into the chill, chlorine-tanged air.

The bros are mere smudges of pink and orange behind the small fogged window of the steam room. If they looked toward the window, I think they might see me, but I'm also sure that they won't. I can hear the barks of their drunken laughter.

Darren's waiting for me back at the room. I can almost imagine him here next to me, the stew of desire and self-consciousness he would be feeling.

I place my hand on the looping handles of the steam room's double doors, consider opening them, enjoying the shock of the bros as I confront them, as I lay into them with my fists until they turn the tide on me.

How would I explain the blood and black eyes to Darren?

Instead I look to the pool, to its painted scenes of meadows and vases, and finally to the bug net lying along the tiled wall. I pick up the net, test its metal pole between my hands. Hollow, but strong.

The pole passes right through the handle loops, holds there at an angle, one end pitched into the wall.

Unaware that they're trapped, the pink and orange smudges continue their jostling and laughter. Drunk as they are, the bros will probably stay too long before they try to leave. Before they find that they can't leave.

I want to see it happen, want to see their shock at their sudden powerlessness. But I also want to get out of there, get back to Darren, watch whatever horrible show he's found on the room's greasy TV, lie there in quiet in our shared space.

I give the steam room door a kick.

The bros go silent, and the smudges near, resolve into shirts below red faces. Voices shout, but I can't make out the words. I back up, in a horrible kind of awe at what I've done, what I'm doing.

I head to the exit, give one last look at the steam room door, at the narrow rectangle of the window. Pale arms beat at it, like wings.

ALEX SEGURA

90 Miles

FROM *Both Sides*

November 12, 1992

JOAQUIN CARMONA TRIED to close his eyes. He knew it was a bad idea. Everything he'd been told said to do otherwise. Keep your eyes open. Don't lose sight of the horizon. Marta had said these things before they set off, knowing her husband, unlike her and their son, Manolo, was not a water person.

Had the circumstances been better, he would have laughed at the memory—of beaches, uncomfortable dips in Cuba's crisp blue waters; of his son's bubbly laughter as Joaquin picked him up and tossed him into the air, the sun casting half his small olive-skinned face in shadow. But laughter was for another time.

Now they were in hell.

Rigoberto, the older man, was at the front of the small, rickety boat. He was the captain of their doomed vessel. A raft, really. A tiny flotation device of his creation that was supposed to carry the four of them to freedom. Actually, freedom didn't matter anymore. It was about safety. It was about land and feeling their toes in the sand or on concrete. Anything, really. Joaquin didn't care anymore. He wanted off this maldito boat and to be anywhere else.

Joaquin felt the raft lurch left, and his stomach turned right. His empty stomach. There'd been some tostadas before boarding but he couldn't bring himself to eat. Couldn't bring himself to do anything even mildly celebratory before they reached the other side.

Freedom. Miami. Or so they were told.

Manolo was nestled next to Marta, his tiny toddler face buried in her armpit like a tiny bird waiting for food. His mood was a blend of fear, anger, and sadness. They'd woken him up suddenly, rushed him outside their tiny house, rushed him down the empty streets —sliding into alleys and dark corners if they caught wind of any-one. He was a smart boy. He caught on quick. He knew something was wrong. They weren't leaving *de vacación*. There were no bags. Plus, he knew—had known for years—that vacations and trips and adventures like that were for other families. Families with more.

Joaquin felt a sharp jolt of regret as he met his son's eyes—for a moment, before Manolito's dark-brown pupils turned back to his mother. This was on *him*. He'd made this decision. He, in a fit of anger at their lot in life, had reached out to Rigoberto.

The bar—La Bodeguita del Medio, on Empedrado—had been dark and empty when Joaquin stepped in and met Rigoberto in the back. A cold beer was waiting for him. It was a tourist spot, that bar. The checkered floor, the writing on the wall, photos of American celebrities hanging everywhere. Joaquin didn't belong here. Would get kicked out if he stuck around too long. But this beer. This frigid dream materialized in front of him. He felt the dirt on his palms mix with the condensation on the bottle and he could almost taste the Presidente before he brought the bottle to his chapped, peel-ing lips. Desperate for the cold liquid to help fend off the tropical heat that had coated his body for what felt like a century. The bar's sputtering air conditioner felt like an arctic paradise.

He slurped it down with gusto. Barely savoring the refreshment. Barely feeling the alcohol pulse through his brain. Joaquin hadn't had a drink in at least a year. Not since Marta told him it was her —and Manolo—or the bottle. Bottles, rather. As life got worse, as their lives became more about scrounging and scavenging just to survive, Joaquin found himself turning more and more to release. Sipping his friend Osvaldito's gualfarina—the homemade, illegal liquor—with a frequency that bordered on obsession. It had got-ten bad. Well, worse. He barely remembered those days. Stumbling into his tiny house, reeking of sex, sweat, drink, blood. He didn't know what he had done. Who he had met. How he had survived. Marta was having none of it. She knew they were in hell. She felt it too. But she hadn't forgotten their son. She would not allow Joaquin to forget him, either. So the line was drawn: drink again, and we leave. No middle ground. So, Joaquin listened. And for a year, up until that moment in the bar, with the cold beer coming alive in his hands, he'd listened. He'd done what he was told. He went to work as a janitor, cleaning office buildings and government spaces when there was work to be done, sitting at home feeling his world fade into red when there wasn't. He bid adios to Osvaldito. He taught his son about baseball. He had sex with his wife once a month. He tried to remember the sound of his mother's voice, and a time when Cuba was a place where he wanted to be.

"Osvaldito told me you wanted . . . help," Rigoberto had said, his sun-crackled skin giving his appearance a wraith-like quality. He was a skinny old man, his body frail and rigid. But his face had an unexpected expressiveness that alarmed Joaquin. A serpentine smile and tiny obsidian eyes that seemed to pulse to their own rhythm. His hands were mangled, clawlike, from decades of working the fields and little medical attention. His teeth—what few Joaquin could see—were a dull yellow, the incisors sharp and vampiric.

"Yes, yes," Joaquin said, swallowing down the last bit of the beer. He tried not to look around the bar, not out of worry, but out of a need for another drink. He was not the type to have just one. To sip a rum and take a nap. No, Joaquin drank hard and long, like his father and his abuelo before him. He didn't know any other way. He didn't want to.

"Bueno, then tell me, hermano," Rigoberto said. "We are only briefly outside the eyes of the people who frown upon this kind of conversation."

"I understand."

"Do you, Joaquin Carmona, hijo de Salvador? I knew your father. He was a hard worker. Loved to sing and dance and drink. I have fond memories of him," Rigoberto said, his eyes glazing over slightly, the deep blackness now a cloudy, murky gray. "So when your friend called me, I came. I want to help the son of my friend, you see? I am a helper. I can get you where you need. But it's not free."

Joaquin felt the boat—the raft—lurch again. He felt Rigoberto's stare before he dared meet it. The dark, sludgy eyes on his, then trailing over to Marta, and settling on Manolo.

"It's just you and your wife?" he'd asked Joaquin as they walked back toward el Centro, where Joaquin lived. The first beer had blended into six more, and Joaquin felt wobbly. There'd been a time, not long ago, when six beers was an appetizer. A primer for the night. A necessity. But that was long ago. His tolerance was gone. He felt the rough edges of a brownout creeping into his vision.

"Just me and Marta, yeah, just two," he'd said, nodding fast. Why was he lying? Was it the cost? Was it habit—to lie, to deflect, to dance around the truth? The alcoholic habits came back fast, like sliding into comfortable slippers found in the back of the closet. It should've scared him, the ease with which the lies spread. But something inside him wanted these words, wanted this to be the truth—and that shook him to his core. Or, it would. Later.

"Está bien," Rigoberto said, slapping Joaquin's face softly as they parted. "Anything more and we'd barely make it off the island, mijo. My boats are strong, but not that strong. They have to be fast too, you know? To get past them."

"Them?"

Rigoberto laughed, a dry, crusty laugh that sounded like sandpaper on asphalt.

"Los tiburones, Joaquin," Rigoberto said. "The sharks."

Joaquin had heard the stories—of what men and women traversing the waters between Cuba and Florida had seen. The deep blue waters masking a deadly darkness. Sharks were fearless, and Joaquin had heard many a story of the giant predatory fish snatching balseros from their rafts. He'd heard stories of bloodstained waters, arms and legs floating past. But that was just the sharks, Joaquin knew.

He'd stopped outside the rickety front door to his home and felt a jolt of clarity electrify his body. If the sharks didn't get them, there were many other paths that led to a painful, brutal death. If they were captured—if they didn't make it past the twelve-mile area surrounding Cuba that preceded international waters, they'd be arrested. At best. Joaquin had also heard stories of balseros not making it back home, shot point-blank on the boats ferrying them back to the island. If they did manage to get past Cuban waters, and if they did manage to avoid a deadly encounter with a shark, they'd still have to navigate the waters—the massive Caribbean waves, some clocking in higher than fifteen feet—that could easily flip and destroy the kind of boat he envisioned Rigoberto captaining.

"What have I done?" Joaquin asked himself as his hand wrapped around the chipped and rusty doorknob, careful to not make any noises that could wake Marta. He cursed softly, remembering the drinks. Sure she'd sniff the alcohol on his breath as he slid into bed.

"What have I done?"

He made a beeline for their mildew-infested and cramped bathroom, sloshing water from the sink into his hungry mouth, rinsing and gargling in a vain attempt to clean up the stains of his behavior.

Rigoberto had laid out the plan as Joaquin worked on his fourth beer. He, unlike many on the island, owned a fishing boat, he said. And while he worked in the fields to this day, he earned a healthy income as a smuggler—ferrying people like Joaquin from Cuba to Miami. But the journey wasn't over once they hit international waters, explained Rigoberto. No. They needed to dodge nature's traps and man himself—notably, the Coast Guard. The United States had enacted a "wet foot, dry foot" policy specifically designed to prevent another mass exodus along the lines of the Mariel swarm that hit Miami in the early eighties. Now, if balseros were caught on their way to Miami, they could be sent back. And a trip back to Cuba was certain death. No, they had to reach land. Their feet had to touch the ground. That made the Coast Guard the enemy, and it made international waters just as dangerous as the twelve miles surrounding Cuba.

Joaquin blinked, and he was back on the raft. Lying down now, his eyes staring up into the bright Caribbean sky—the sun bearing down on them, roasting his tan skin. His mouth was dry. His body limp. He heard Manolo whimpering behind him somewhere. He wanted to get up, but he couldn't.

"Halfway there," Rigoberto said, his voice a ragged croak.

How long had he been out? Joaquin had no idea. It couldn't have been that long. His mind drifted back to the morning— boarding Rigoberto's boat, just a few bottles of water, a bag of food, and nothing else. They were going fishing. At least that's what they wanted anyone who saw them to believe. There was nothing wrong here. Just a family paying an experienced fisherman to show them the waters.

Rigoberto's entire expression morphed once he set eyes on Manolo. The kid was pudgy, big for his age. But enough to create a problem on the old man's boat? Joaquin had tried not to worry, had tried to ignore the lie he'd drunkenly spat out at Rigoberto the night before—but now it all came back, and he saw the older man's eyes flicker with a flame that could only be pure hatred.

But they were out, in the open, and the old man couldn't deviate now. The plan had been set. People were watching. They'd boarded, and he felt Rigoberto's hot, angry breath on his face as he helped Joaquin onto the raft, the last crew member aboard.

"Pendejo mentiroso," he hissed. "Now we all die together."

Joaquin tried to ignore Rigoberto. Now, his back flat on the boat, the entire vessel bobbing up and down with a ferocity that he'd never imagined, he could care less about the old man's petty concerns. He was worried too, but it had little to do with a fat toddler. It had to do with *survival.*

Then they sprung the first leak. A small tear near the front of the raft—near where Rigoberto was seated, his makeshift captain's seat really just a cooler at the front of the cheap, man-made raft. *Owned a boat,* Joaquin had thought when he and Marta caught a glimpse of Rigoberto's vessel. Who was the real mentiroso?

The water came into the boat slowly, but Rigoberto danced to his feet like a child stung by a bee, stepping back from the leak as if singed by flame.

"No, no, no!" he said, his voice an octave higher than Joaquin thought possible. "Now we die! Now it's over!"

Joaquin felt blood pump through his body. Felt life come back to his limbs. He saw—felt—himself sit up, yank his shirt off, and stuff the tattered white cloth into the tear, trying to stop the flow. It seemed to work for a second, and his heart slowed, and he almost sighed in relief, but then he felt his shirt soaking in his hands and he knew it was over.

"Papi, no!"

Manolo's scream, shrill and desperate, didn't come soon enough to prevent what happened next. Joaquin felt the blade slide into his back, long and fat, the hilt touching his sunburnt skin. Then another scream—Marta—followed by a scuffle. Marta was strong. Forceful. She would not die quietly. And she would not die at the hands of some pendejo viejo, as she'd described Rigoberto that last night, as she angrily poured Joaquin a glass of water to sober him up.

"What have you done, Joaquin? To us? To our family?"

The raft bobbed up again, a larger, more powerful wave tossing the tiny boat up and off the water for a few seconds—and Joaquin felt like they were gliding on air. He fell backward, his face now watching the struggle: Rigoberto standing over Marta, his hands wrapped around her throat, Manolo cowering behind the old man.

"Puta maldita," Rigoberto spat, his body shaking from the effort of trying to keep Marta down. Joaquin felt the knife dig deeper into him, and he knew if he was going to act, it had to be now.

He was dying.

He stood, the lurch and lunge of the waves underneath them balancing out his own dizziness, giving his blood-drained body a brief moment of control as he grabbed Rigoberto's shoulders and pulled the skinny, jagged old man back and toward the edge of the raft—the raft that was now filling with water, the crystal blue ocean no longer something that surrounded them—now something that would consume them.

Joaquin felt his hands wrap around Rigoberto's scaly, tan throat, felt his fingers tighten around it, his thumbs pressuring the bones and muscle and life that took up space in there. He saw Rigoberto's eyes bulge open, a look of surprise and hate steaming off his eyes, like the exhaust from an old Ford.

"Estas muerto, cabrón," Rigoberto said, the words a sizzling whisper, a last gasp.

Joaquin felt the burning now. His back. The blood coating him. His hands hurt. His body was buckling. He couldn't hold on. He just felt so . . . so alone. So empty. So tired.

He'd tried, Martica, he really had. Even after everything—after prison, after that first failed attempt, she'd stayed with him. She'd cared for him even when the work disappeared. He'd tried this to save her, to save them, their life . . . their son. And now what?

He felt the crack in Rigoberto's neck before he heard it, a soft, wet krrk sound that he might have just imagined. But then the old man stopped fighting, though his eyes—red, the vessels burst and spreading—remained awake, as if looking for a final corner to cut, a last deal to make to ensure their survival.

Joaquin stumbled back. That's when the shark popped up, its sleek, gray-blue form sidling up to the raft, its mouth hooking onto Rigoberto's head and dragging him into the water, almost silent in its execution—a predator accustomed to scavenging for meals between an island and a peninsula.

Joaquin wanted to gasp but found it hard to breathe. He felt a hand on his shoulder as he dropped down onto the floor, the water sloshing as he fell back, Marta next to him. She was crying. Manolo was crying. He could still hear them, but he found it hard to make words, to respond.

"Perdóname, Dios," he muttered. God, forgive me. Forgive me for what I've done.

He didn't mean Rigoberto.

"Think we got something, Lieutenant," the ensign said as he approached the edge of the small Coast Guard cutter and peered into the calm teal waters of the Florida Straits. He felt his commanding officer, Lieutenant Osman, approach from behind.

"Already? Shit, we just left dock," she said, under her breath. She stood to the ensign's left and followed his gaze.

"You sure?" she asked. "Just looks like a bunch of wood . . . and some clothes?"

They'd anchored the cutter at the first sign of something. They'd expected a small craft or a boat in need of assistance. But this? This looked more like someone's overturned laundry bin.

Then they saw the red.

The kind of red that could mean only one thing. The kind of dark maroon that wasn't meant to be seen on the outside. At least not in these quantities.

"Shit, shit, shit," Osman said, more out of annoyance than genuine fear or concern. This wasn't her first trip off land. But as the image she was recording in her brain lingered over the next few months, it would, for all intents and purposes, be her last. "What the hell happened here?"

"Usual shit," the ensign — a good ol' boy from Pensacola named Gilbert — spat. "'Nother bunch of dead spic rafters, trying to swim 'cross these shark waters to get a taste of American freedom, y'know? Maybe next time, kids. Stupid."

Osman blinked, trying to reject the words slithering into her ears. She turned to face Gilbert, her expression immediately telling the junior officer he'd fucked up. Big time.

"Call it in," she said, straining to keep her tone calm and aligned with her job as a commanding officer, not shrill and enraged, which is how she actually felt. "People died here, ensign. Do you understand? *People.*"

Gilbert nodded nervously and seemed relieved to be heading back to the comm station.

Osman looked down at the wreckage, at the bobbing debris that had once been something else—a ship, a construct. But not just that. It had been something more important. Something primal. Something good.

It had been hope.

BRIAN SILVERMAN

Land of Promise

FROM *Mystery Tribune*

HE SAT ON the park bench covered in dirt and ash. A light, late spring rain shower began to streak the dirt on his arms. People stared at him as they hurriedly walked past. His body ached and his throat was raw. He was on the east side now, close to the 4, 5, and 6 trains. The subway entrance was just a few blocks away. He could make it there and then get a train uptown to the Bronx. That was his hope.

There was a crowd gathered around the entrance to the subway. Two cops stood vigilant on either side of it. Thick yellow tape was spread across either side. People peered beyond the cops at the blocked stairs leading to the subway.

"System's closed," one of the cops said.

He started walking uptown. He stopped in a deli for a bottle of water. He drank it down and then continued walking, along with so many others. He checked his phone again. There was still no service. He knew his wife would be worried. He knew she probably was trying to reach him as he was trying to reach her. He wanted to get home to her but that wasn't going to happen anytime soon.

He trudged uptown, almost in lockstep with the crowds escaping the city the only way they could. His legs ached, but he kept them moving. The rain ended almost as quickly as it had begun. He stopped when he was close to the Williamsburg Bridge. He could continue walking uptown and then into the Bronx and home. Or he could cross the bridge and get to his car parked in the garage near the bar he owned and managed on Grand Street. He realized that was what he had to do. He needed to clean up. He had a change of clothes in his small office in the back of the bar. He couldn't go home covered in dirt. He wouldn't want his wife to see him the way he looked now.

He walked with all the others across the bridge. Once, along the way, he stopped and moved to the edge of the bridge that was protected by sturdy wire netting. He tried to look down at the turbulent water of the East River, but it was hard to see because of the netting. He put his hands on the wires and pushed. There was no give. He had heard of jumpers off the Brooklyn Bridge and even the George Washington Bridge, but he couldn't recall ever hearing about someone jumping off the Williamsburg Bridge. Now he knew why. He moved back into the procession of people trudging toward Brooklyn.

It took an hour and a half, but he finally made it to the bar. He had his key and opened the sliding grate that covered the bar's entrance. He went inside and pulled the grate down behind him. He didn't want anyone entering.

He found the remote control behind the bar and turned one of the televisions on. Every station, even the sports stations, were covering the explosion. He tried his phone again. Still there was no service.

He washed in the sink in the bathroom and changed into his other set of clothes. He looked in the mirror. His eyes were bloodshot and they stung. He wished he had eye drops for them but didn't. Had he been crying? He didn't even know.

"You're better off walking," the lone garage attendant said as he finally unearthed his car and drove it to the exit. "Roads are jammed from what I hear. And bridges are closed for the time being."

"Maybe I'll get lucky," he said as he took the keys and got into the car.

He stayed on the local roads in Brooklyn parallel to the parking lot that was the Brooklyn-Queens Expressway. After about an hour and a half, he made it to the Grand Central Parkway. To get to the Bronx he had to cross the Triborough Bridge. He eased onto the ramp for the bridge and then stopped. No one was moving. He had the radio on in the car. The talk was of all the dead. He tried to find anything but that.

Bom bom bom . . .
Dang a dang dang
Ding a dong ding
Blue moon blue moon
Blue moon dip dip dip

He almost smiled when he heard that. The song his Uncle Frank used to play on the little tape recorder he carried with him almost all the time. "Blue Moon." The city was on high alert and some station was playing ancient doo-wops. He listened to the end of the song and then went back to the news of the day.

He tried to call his wife again, but the coverage was still down. He sat in his car near the ramp to the Bronx-bound side of the Triborough Bridge. He looked out the window at the pedestrians walking across the bridge. He noticed that there was a high fence above the walkway. You would have to climb the fence to jump into the water below. It was almost too much effort, even for the suicidal, he thought. Or maybe not.

After over an hour sitting there, the traffic, almost mysteriously, began to move. And at the same time the traffic moved, his phone began buzzing with text messages and voice mails. He didn't bother to look at or listen to any of them.

As he drove across the bridge he heard on the radio that the bridges and tunnels had reopened and that some of the subway lines were back up and running again. The gate was open to the small driveway of his three-bedroom home not far from the Throgs Neck Bridge. He pulled in and before he could get out of the car, his wife was out the door and running to him, followed by his two children.

"Jesus, Len." His wife was crying. "You're safe. Thank God."

She hugged him tight. His wife Kathleen. Blond, beautiful, Kathleen, whom he had met at the Chase Bank almost ten years earlier when he was financing his first bar in Brooklyn. Who he fell in love with almost immediately.

"Everything was jammed up," he said. "The subways were down. And the traffic . . ."

"I know, honey," Kathleen said. "It was horrible not being able to reach you. But the service came on a while ago. Didn't you get my messages?"

"No . . . I . . ."

"It doesn't matter," she said. "You're home."

He stared at her and then nodded. Yes . . . he thought . . . I'm home.

His seven-year-old daughter curled under one of his arms while his five-year-old son pushed himself under his other. He hugged both his children, and with his wife alongside, he and his family made their way into the house.

His wife slept close to him that night; her head on his chest. He could hear her slight snoring, and he could see the glow of her blond hair in the darkness. Looking at her hair made his stomach lurch. He got out of bed quietly so as not to wake her.

He wandered into the living room and sat in the chair in the dark. He stared at the dark television until the sun came up.

The next morning he checked in with his staff and partners at the three bars he owned in Brooklyn, all in Williamsburg. He knew he had to get back to work, but he didn't want to go to Brooklyn. His legs were achy and his shoulders sore. His throat was still raw and he had a headache that would not go away. But that was the least of it. He had a bare, empty feeling inside that seemed to be consuming him. He knew his face was clouded. He felt as if he was in a trancelike state that he couldn't shake.

He did his best to hide what he was feeling from his wife. He tried to keep the calm, steady demeanor that attracted her to him and that also helped him succeed in the cutthroat, high-pressure nightlife world he was in. His many years studying the martial art Muay Thai and practicing the mental flow state that complemented his physical training helped him focus without stress on what really mattered. That demeanor was a calming influence on his staff and sometimes his hot-head partners.

After the phone calls, which took almost all morning, his wife made him lunch.

"You're not going in today?" she asked him as she sat down opposite him at their kitchen table.

"Not today," he said. "The others can handle everything without me."

She took his hand and focused her blue eyes on him. "That's good, 'cause you're not yourself. Maybe you're coming down with something. I know what happened yesterday was horrible, but I don't remember you taking it this hard back when the towers fell."

He finished his sandwich and stood up and shrugged.

"I'm gonna go take a little nap. Wake me if I'm still sleeping after a half an hour."

Her eyes were on him as he moved to their bedroom.

There was a buzzing sound he heard faintly in his stupor, just loud enough to bring him back to the edge of consciousness. He was in that somnambulant state when the door opened, letting in bright light. He felt a nudge at his hip.

"Len, there are people here for you," his wife said.

"Huh?"

The incessant buzzing was coming from his phone that was on an end table next to the bed.

"You have to get up. They want to talk to you. I don't know what it's about, but there are a lot of them."

He pulled his body up and grabbed the phone. There were over a dozen messages.

"What people?" he asked.

"Outside, Len. Trucks. Reporters. Something happened. They want to talk to you."

She had his attention now. He got out of the bed and headed to the front door. As soon as he opened the door, voices shouted to him coming from multiple directions from people holding microphones.

"Are you Len Buonfiglio?" they asked in unison.

They were standing on the other side of the fence of his front lawn. There were vans with satellite dishes on them. His wife was standing close behind him.

"What's going on, Len?" his wife asked.

"Are you Len Buonfiglio?" they asked again.

His neighbor, rotund Victor Casale, pushed himself to the front of the fence. He was smiling broadly at Len.

"Of course that's Lennie Buonfiglio! That's our local hero!" Casale said.

"What?"

He slowly made his way to them at the fence. He looked at Casale. And then looked at the mass of reporters.

"Yeah, I'm Buonfiglio. Why?"

One of the reporters up front had a tablet. He held it up to Len and pressed the screen. He watched what they showed him but showed no expression.

"Was that you?" the reporter asked.

Len just stared at the screen.

The reporter pressed the screen again.

"Look again," he said. "Is that you?"

"Oh my God," he heard his wife mutter as she stood close behind him, looking at what the reporter was showing him. Seeing what he was seeing.

Len stood there.

The other media barked a flurry of questions his way.

"Why did you do it?"

"Are you a paramedic?"

"What made you risk your life?"

He said nothing. He didn't expect this. He didn't want this.

Victor Casale extended his hand over the fence to Len.

"The video is all over the news, Lennie. I knew it was you right away when I saw it. You've made the neighborhood proud," Casale said.

Len stared blankly at his neighbor's hand but did not shake it.

"Len?" his wife whispered. "I don't understand."

Tears rolled down her cheeks. He didn't know what to say to her.

"I don't understand at all," she said, and then ran back into the house.

The press remained camped in front of his house all afternoon. The phone calls on his cell phone were from friends and relatives who had seen the news. He listened to a few of the messages. They all wanted to talk to him. To tell him how proud they were of him. He didn't call any of them back.

His wife retreated to their bedroom and shut the door. He could hear her sobbing in there. He should have known this would happen. After a while he went into the bedroom. She had the shades pulled down and it was dark. She was sitting on the bed with her hands on her lap.

"I didn't want you to freak out or anything," he said to her. "I didn't want you or the kids to know how close I was to it."

She picked her head up to look at him. Her eyes were red. "I'm your wife, Lennie. You don't tell me something like that? How could you do that to me? How could you let me find out like this?"

"I didn't know it would turn out like this." He waved his arm toward the front lawn and the media circus camped there.

"No? How could it not?"

"I'm okay. It's all okay," he said as he sat on the bed next to her. He took her hand in his.

"Is it?"

He knew it wasn't. And she knew too.

"What were you doing down there anyway?" she asked. "You said you were in Brooklyn and staying at the bar. What were you doing in Manhattan so early? You never told me you would be in Manhattan. You've been doing that a lot lately and I never said anything about it. Should I have, Lennie?"

He didn't answer her.

"Are you going to tell her today?" the woman with the long, dark hair who lay naked by his side asked him. Her hand was on his burly chest as they lay there. She turned her big brown eyes on him.

"Today. I promise," he said and then caressed her hair, looking down at her, wondering how all this happened and where it would ultimately go. There had been plenty of temptations at work, but he never succumbed. He never indulged like some of his partners had. He was faithful to his wife and to his family. He loved them too much to risk losing them.

And then he met her. It was innocent at first. She would come in early and they would talk before the bar got crowded. She was an immigrant from Lebanon. She was smart: an associate art professor at Columbia, the youngest in the department. He had studied art too but gave it up a long time ago. Maybe that was a reason why he felt such an attraction to her. She pursued what he always wanted and never did. He just didn't know. So when she came to the bar, they would talk about art. But not just art—they talked about everything. They talked about things he never talked about with his wife.

She knew he was married and had children. She knew it from the beginning. Though he wanted her very badly, he couldn't do it. He would not cross that line. He didn't want her to think of him that way: as a man who betrayed his family for a fling, an affair. She knew he was holding back, that he was trying to be honorable. But it was a lost cause—for both of them. Still, it had to come from her. He would never make the move. It took a while, but one night, after maybe one glass of wine too many, she finally said: "Come home with me."

He knew what it would mean to his life. He always tried to stay strong. To do the right thing. To be a man of honor. But when he heard those words from her, he did not hesitate.

He gave it time to see if it was just a temporary affair, a midlife crisis, something like that. But it wasn't. He was sure it wasn't.

"I hate this," she said. "I hate that your children will be hurt. I hate that your wife will be hurt, but I need you in my life, Len. I need to see you every day. Do you feel the same way? Please don't do this if you don't. I may be tiny, but I'm fierce. I can take it."

He couldn't say it. He couldn't express himself like she just did, but the feelings were the same. He knew it would be very hard on Kathleen and his kids. He knew what it would do to his life, but he couldn't live like this: cheating on the sly.

"Today, Len?"

"Yeah, today," he said.

They dressed and walked out of her apartment together, stopping at a Dunkin' Donuts for coffee. She had an English muffin with an egg and cheese. He had a bagel with cream cheese. They sat at a small table and ate quickly. They walked to the subway with their coffee. She had to get uptown for a class she taught. He hadn't showered and knew he had to before he went home. He would go back to her place, shower, and then go back to Brooklyn to get his car before driving back to the Bronx. He wanted to be home well before the kids were back from school. He didn't want them around when he told his wife what he had to tell her.

"Your hand is all sweaty," she said.

It was. His mouth was dry too. His mind was on what he was going to say to his wife. How he could possibly explain his betrayal. How he could admit to her, the mother of his children, that he wanted to be with someone else.

"Just think of that land of promise," she said, sensing his discomfort.

He grinned at her. "You mean the 'Promised Land,' like that song?"

She loved her reggae music, and he knew there was a song with that title on a mix she downloaded for him onto his phone.

"No, I mean the Land of Promise."

"Oh, that one?" He smirked.

"Yes, funny man." She pinched his bicep. "I mean it. Somewhere small and beautiful and always warm. I hate the cold. It's better when it's warm. It's going to all work out, Len, isn't it?" She looked up into his eyes.

"It is," he said, but he wasn't so sure.

They were in front of the subway entrance. She stopped and hugged him. Her smile radiated brightly as she took both his much larger hands in hers, squeezing them. She wore big blue-rimmed glasses. Her dark hair was in a ponytail. She got up on her toes; he was over a foot taller than she was, and he bent to meet her lips. They kissed, and then she started down the subway steps, turning to him, smiling tentatively before disappearing into the station.

He walked away from the station and put on his earbuds. Her talk of the land of promise, or whatever it was, made him want to hear that reggae mix. He played it on the sound system of the bar whenever she came in. He was hoping it would soothe him. He was anxious about what he had to do. That tune, "Rollin' Down," or was it "Rain from the Sky," was the first track.

He was a block and a half away from the subway station when, over the music, he heard what sounded like a bomb go off and felt the ground shift under his feet. He froze for a moment and then, no longer thinking, just reacting, turned and sprinted back to the subway. He saw others running in the opposite direction. He almost knocked a woman over as he ran. Smoke was fuming out of the subway entrance. Without hesitation he ran down into heavy darkness.

"Nura," he shouted.

He heard cries and groans. There were bodies on the ground, blocking him from getting farther into the tunnel and even to the turnstile. From what he could tell through the dense smoke, there was a pile of bodies scattered around the entrance to the train tracks. A train was stuck in the station; there were no lights from inside. Some of the bodies were moving. Most weren't. One of the moving bodies was blocking the turnstile, slumped against it. A woman. But it wasn't Nura. The woman was coughing. His first response was to move her to the side so he could find Nura. He had to move her to get into the tunnel and the train that lay broken on the tracks. She was in there. He was sure of it. He had to clear a path. That was what he wanted to do. For no reason he could comprehend at the time, he picked up the woman and carried her up the subway steps to the street, and after setting her down gently on the curb, he ran back down into the station.

"Nura!" He screamed now.

A voice called for help. Was it her? He wasn't sure. He looked at the dazed open eyes of one of the bodies. He picked that one up too, heavier than the last, and carried it up out onto the street, placing it next to the other and then went back down again. He did that four more times; each time his calls to Nura were more frantic. The smoke in the tunnel was thicker. His eyes were burning and so was his throat. Still, he had to go back down there. The next one would be her. He was sure of it. He had to get her out.

He sucked in the air outside and started toward the subway entrance again, but this time he was blocked by an army of police, paramedics, and firemen, who seemingly appeared out of nowhere. They were streaming down into the subway. He knew he was struggling with someone; he wasn't sure if it was a cop or someone else; two of them held him tight. He tried to land a roundhouse kick to one of them, but his legs were heavy. He couldn't lift them that high. They wrestled him away and then kept an eye on him. He wandered around for a few moments and then ran back and tried to get down into the station again, calling her name. Again he was blocked by a cadre of first responders. He couldn't get back down. He couldn't get to her. They wouldn't let him.

When the victims were identified, the newspapers published pictures of them all. He stared at the portrait of Nura Azar provided by Columbia University. In it she was smiling, beaming. The photograph made her skin look darker than it really was. Or than he remembered it was.

He wondered what he should do. He felt obligated to do something for her. As far as he knew she had only one living relative, a sister who lived in Paris. He called the coroner's office to find out details, whether her remains were picked up. The coroner's office would not talk to him. He wasn't an authorized family member. He called Columbia University and inquired about her there and got the same blowback. They wouldn't talk to him. He tried to identify someone, anyone, with the Azar surname in France. There were hundreds, and he started to make some calls, but he couldn't speak French so got nowhere.

In the weeks after, he was contacted by movie producers, book publishers, literary agents, television networks, and others who wanted to sell his story. He talked to none of them.

It took him a while to go back to work, and when he did, his partners wanted to exploit him, to promote the bars by using his tabloid name, "The June 1st Hero," in connection with the bars. He never went back after that and did his business with them from home. But really, he didn't do much of anything.

It was late summer when he sat with his wife and children on folding chairs set up just below the steps to City Hall. He wore a navy-blue jacket, a white dress shirt, and dark sunglasses. The heat was intense and he knew he had sweated through his dress shirt. His wife wore a dark-green dress and the children were immaculately attired and groomed as if they were going to Easter Mass with their grandparents. They were just a few blocks from the site of the explosion. The mayor was going on about Len's bravery that day. How he risked his life and saved six people. He was going to present him with the keys to the city for his bravery.

He had resisted. He didn't want this, but the mayor had been persistent. He and his staff put the pressure on him to hold a ceremony to honor him. They pressured his wife.

"It has to be done," Kathleen said. "But promise me, Len, that you never, ever tell them the truth as to why you were there that morning. That's all I ask from you. For our sake. Don't humiliate us by telling them the truth."

She didn't have to ask. He knew that secret was something he would have to keep inside him. That was where it belonged. Along with so much else he could never let out.

Now he had to stand up there with the mayor, who gushed about his heroism. As if he rescued those people because he was brave. The survivors were there, assembled close to him. They hugged him in gratitude. If they only knew that he didn't care about them. There was only one life he wanted to save. They were in the way. And they were lucky they were. He carried them out of there to clear the way—to get to her. That was what he told himself. He was convinced of that. And now he was being called a hero. The thought made him sick.

He glanced at his wife as he stood next to the mayor. He marveled at how beautiful she was. She looked back at him and then quickly looked away. He stared at his children. He lived a charmed life, he thought. He wasn't sure when, but knew now that life was coming to an end.

The mayor smiled and shook his hand firmly and handed him the key to the city. He played along as best he could. He even smiled when he took the key.

The city provided a limousine to take the family home. They were quiet in the car. His son slept against him. The air conditioning was drying the sweat on his shirt. They were on the Bruckner when he stared out the window. Dark clouds were forming north of the glorious ugliness of the South Bronx. There would be a thunderstorm soon. He could see the Throgs Neck Bridge in the distance. He looked at how high the bridge was elevated above the water. His eyes went from the bridge's apex down to the water below; he estimated it to be a very long drop.

He looked away and instead stared at his beautiful daughter and son. He tried to get the image of the bridge out of his mind. He closed his eyes tight and thought about being somewhere else. He tried to think about the Land of Promise.

When they got home, his wife went with their son to help him change out of his clothes and hang up his jacket. He went into their bedroom and took the leather case that held the key to the city out of his pocket. He opened it up and removed the key from the case. He looked at it closely. It was gold and had the mayor's name engraved in it. He studied the key a moment more and then shoved it deep down in his dresser drawer under a pile of socks and underwear.

One Bullet. One Vote.

FROM *Low Down Dirty Vote*

IF YOU HAD a mind to walk up on them at that very moment, you'd think that maybe Lionel had just hauled off and smacked Emma a good one across the face. Maybe his brain, for some reason, got so addled that he forgot who *he* was, who *she* was, and exactly *where* he was. Hitting on womenfolk may be okay where he came from up north, but striking a Southern woman in her mama's house in Byrd's Landing, Louisiana, in early '64 was liable to get you an unscheduled meeting with a pan of hot grits.

"What you trying to do, Lionel?" Emma said. "Get us all killed?"

"No. I'm just trying to say we got a chance to show these white folks something."

"Maybe we don't need to show them anything. You ever thought of that?"

Emma pointed a long brown finger at her grandmother, the woman who raised her, Willie Mae Brown.

Willie Mae sat at the head of the Sunday dinner table wrapped in skirts and shawls even in the boiling heat of the dining room. *So old and so cold even in summer,* Willie Mae thought, *as if a body's getting ready for the grave.*

Emma was right. They got along just as well without making trouble with white folk, point of fact being the roof they were arguing under. Willie Mae had made so much money delivering a few white babies and doctoring all kind of folk since her husband died that pretty soon she was able to build a side room here, a screened-in porch there, and another floor atop the kitchen. They were lucky enough to celebrate God's grace every Sunday, and never once had to worry about money to pay for the chicken.

And now there was this voting thing brought expressly to them by her new grandson-in-law. He met Emma about a year ago when he had come to Byrd's Landing along with a friend who was visiting kin. Lionel took one look at Emma and decided to stay. Only eight months married, with a pregnant wife, and he was already feeling like Louisiana was the top half of a grave. He just couldn't get a grip on how things down here needed to be.

"We show them that they can't keep us from voting. The package—"

"Hell, the package, the package, the package. That's all you been talking about for weeks. We got it good here. Nobody bothers us," Emma said.

"Everyone isn't as lucky as you and your family. We got a chance to make things better."

"By getting my grandmother killed? And getting us burned out? How's that going to make things better?"

"Ain't nobody killing nobody," Willie Mae said.

She wasn't surprised that they didn't pay her any mind. People had a way of making a ghost out of your walking, talking body when you lived past their expectations.

"She's everything," Lionel said. "She can read, write, and she's got that memory thing going. She's smarter than God."

"Don't blaspheme," Willie Mae said.

"Nobody dare do anything to her, or this family," Lionel said. "They need her too much."

"They touch me or my blood and I'll hex him," Willie Mae said with a chuckle, trying to lighten the mood.

Again. Ignored. She sighed. Just as well. Even though half the town thought she was a witch and the other half thought she was a freak of nature, she really didn't know any hexes. She just read a lot, that's all, and most things she read stuck. When she was younger, she followed Mama Anna, the old midwife who also did a little doctoring for Black folk, like a shadow. It was pure luck that the ole white doc came up to the house one day, talking about the town needing a new doctor because his mind was going bad.

"I guess that'll have to be you," he had said.

She laughed and said, "No white folk going to let no Black

woman touch them other than to help deliver babies when they feelin' desperate."

"They won't have a choice," he countered. "No self-respecting doctor wants to come to this godforsaken town."

He taught her some while his mind was still good. When he died, she was all the town had for a while. Some white folk used her, but a lot more didn't. A good many died while going for help outside of Byrd's Landing. A white doctor eventually came, but the man liked the bottle more than he did the stethoscope. Willie Mae found herself guiding his shaking hands with the knowledge in her Black head. Lionel was right. No one in this town would be stupid enough to mess with her.

"Lionel, do I have to remind you what happened to my grandfather?" Emma said.

That knocked the wind out of him. He sat back in his chair and sighed, picked up a fork and then threw it down again.

"That was a long time ago."

"From a tree."

"That's not now."

"They burned him first. Alive. Then they strung him up and cut pieces off him so they could remember it by."

"You'd think his screaming was enough for them to remember it by," Willie Mae said, the memory making her blood rise. Ever since he died, she stayed on the right side of white folk. Now at the end of her life maybe she could give them something to chew on once she was no longer around.

"And he wasn't trying to register to vote. He was just trying to get a fair price for his crop," Emma said.

Emma, done with the talking, got up and started stacking the empty plates. But Willie Mae wasn't at all done. Hell, she hadn't even started. She lifted her old polished hickory cane and thumped three times on the wooden floor. They turned to look at her. Finally.

"How y'all finished talking and nobody asked me?"

"Emma's right," Lionel said, wiping his hands over his face. "Too dangerous. Time's not right."

Willie Mae laughed. "Being Black and living is dangerous. What I have to do?"

"According to the package—"

Willie Mae waved her hands. "Stop all that. You make the laws those scoundrels passed sound like they fair. Just say what the white folk want for our God-given rights."

"You have to register," Lionel said slowly. "But there are rules."

"Rules?"

"We'd have to hunt down the registrar first, Big Mamma. They change them all the time. And they hide out so Black people can't find them," Emma said.

Willie Mae didn't miss the tiredness in her granddaughter's voice.

Emma knew as soon as Willie Mae thumped her cane that she had lost.

"Don't worry about that. I'll find the no-account. What else?"

"You have to take a test," Lionel said.

"I've been taking tests all my life, son."

"And be of good character."

"What in the dog's hell is that supposed to mean?"

"No kids out of wedlock, no breaking any laws, not even to protest," Lionel said.

"Never protested a damn thing. Too busy keeping folks already here alive, and bringing in the new ones. Besides, if I ever need something they don't want to give me, I get it through sneak. They don't even know they givin' it to me."

"Well, as long as your sneak didn't get you arrested, and you pass the test, you can register to vote."

"What kinds of things on the test?"

"Stuff about the United States, the government."

She sat back, her cane leaning between her legs. "Well, that don't sound too hard to me."

Both Lionel and Emma sat there not talking. Willie Mae fancied she could smell something on the silence, and it wasn't the leavings of Sunday dinner. Blood. Grief, maybe.

Somehow Lionel caught a whiff of it too because he said, "You sure you know what you getting into, Big Mamma?"

She looked him in his young eyes. "I always know what I'm putting on the line, son. Do you?"

For the next week or so Willie Mae sat outside the courthouse from can-to-can't see. After the first two days she made Lionel haul her rocking chair to town and sit it at the bottom of the courthouse steps. She wanted to rock while she waited on that no-account registrar, Fat Tommy. His real name was Thomas Oleander, and he was so busy hiding from Willie Mae when he heard that she was wanting to register that he hadn't been to work in a week.

She sat in layers of granny skirts and shawls while the sun beat down. For once she wasn't so cold. She rocked nonstop, read nonstop, and when she was tired of reading, which wasn't often, she hummed. Fat Tommy would eventually show his sorry face. He'd have to come to work one day, and she didn't think he was fool enough to walk right by her and ignore her, not with his wife so sick and all.

One day she looked up to see the sheriff standing there in all his glory. Big hat, shiny badge, and smiling like a Cheshire cat.

"How you, Sheriff?" she asked.

"Right fine, Willie Mae," he said. "I think we need to have us a talk, though."

"How's that?"

He brought his big old boot up and put it right on the rocker's seat by her hip, not bothering, or caring, that he was stepping all over her skirts. Before she could say anything about it, he was talking.

"Now, why you want to go and cause all this trouble, Willie Mae. This town's been good to you."

"I don't want to cause no trouble. I just want to register to vote. Y'all said I could."

"Now, nobody said no such thing. You know that."

"Yes, you did. You passed some laws that said all I had to do was show up at the registrar, take a test, and be a good person. I'm just doing like y'all said."

He pressed his foot down on the seat of the chair until it tilted. Any farther and there'd be a heap of old woman on the sidewalk.

"I can't let you do that," he said with a big ole smile on his face. "People might get hurt. You don't want that to happen, do you?"

"I certainly do not. All I want to do is register like the law says."

"Willie Mae . . ."

But she didn't want to talk about it anymore. She was straight tired of his foolishness.

"Now you look," she said, "while you go about disrespecting me, don't forget that I'm the one who pulled you out of your mama."

That big smile vanished like somebody blew out a candle.

"And it wasn't no easy birth, or easy waiting for her. When she found out that you were coming into this world, she asked me to put a stop to it. And when you were squalling and wet with after-birth, she asked me to take you down to the river and drown you like a kitten."

He didn't say anything, but he was so mad that he hissed like a snake.

"This is just what people been speculating on over the years," she went on. "But I can turn their speculation into fact if you don't get your foot out of my chair. And what will your mama and all her meeting club friends say about that?"

He took his foot down and hooked his thumbs in his gun belt.

"All right, Willie Mae," he said in a voice so deadly quiet that her heart jumped a little. "You got this one. But no matter how many stories you may have to tell, ain't no way you're going to be allowed to actually vote."

She inclined her head. "I thank you kindly, Sheriff. Fat Tommy sneak in the back?"

"Mr. Oleander is at work, yes."

Fat Tommy didn't even look at her when she came into the reg-istrar's office. There was a chair in front of his desk, but he didn't ask her to sit.

"Willie Mae," Fat Tommy said, as he was scribbling on some pa-pers in front of him. "I hear you want to register?"

"You heard right, Mr. Tommy."

He looked at her then, probably searching for sass. But she kept her face blank like she had been long used to.

"Your full name?"

"Willie Mae Brown."

"You got any proof of that?"

She grinned and said, "I'm the same Willie Mae that birthed your two children and the same one that come by your place every two weeks to see after your wife."

"I'm sorry, Willie Mae, the law says I got to have proof."

"All right. Here you are."

He shuffled the papers she had handed him for a moment or two before looking up at her.

"A real birth certificate. Not many Negras your age have one of these. You sure you didn't get somebody to make one of these up for you?"

"I didn't," she said, "but my mama did by filing for one when I was born."

"These other papers, letters from folks around town to declare who you are. They white folks?"

"As white as you, as I'm sure you can already tell by reading the names."

"Okay," he said. "Real fine."

Your face don't look like it's real fine, Willie Mae thought but didn't say out loud. She didn't want him riled any more than he already was.

"How old are you?" he asked.

"It says—"

"I got to hear you say it," he said.

"I'm eighty-five," she said.

"I need the months and days."

"I'm eighty-five, eight months, and twenty-seven days today."

He made some scratching noise on his paper as he worked out the equation. "That's right."

"I know it's right."

"Now we need to ask about your character . . ."

"Mr. Tommy," she said. "If you filling out the LR-1, you best just give it on over to me, seeing how I can do it quicker than you can write it for me."

He took his time pushing both the paper and pencil over to her.

They wanted to know had she ever been arrested, lived in sin, or had any children without a husband. She answered all the questions and pushed it back to him.

Like Lionel had told her, the test wasn't that bad. She didn't really need what he called that "memory thing." Any Black folk she knew could take it with a little studying. She answered some easy questions, like the three branches of government and who's in charge of an impeachment trial. Fat Tommy's face became worried as he checked her answers. When he was done he sat back in the chair and looked at her, his fat belly almost busting his shirt open.

"Now you need to do an oath."

"Do I have to?"

"You do if you want to be registered in the state of Louisiana."

She raised her right hand, like he told her to do.

"Do you swear that you are well disposed to the good order and

happiness of the state of Louisiana and that you will fully abide by
the laws of the state?"

She told him that she was, and she would as long as they were
fair. But of course she kept that last part to herself.

"Congratulations. You are registered to vote."

"Thank you, Mr. Tommy."

"I can't say you're welcome. You should know that if you do vote,
you'd be the first Negra to vote in this town. There'll be trouble as
sure as sunshine in June."

The night before the vote, Lionel kept playing this record by a
man named Sam Cooke. The entire record was called *Ain't That
Good News*. Willie Mae wouldn't know about any good news because
Lionel insisted on playing one song over and over again that kept
talking about something being a long time a-coming. All Willie
Mae knew that if he played it one more time, the only thing that
would be coming would be her brains exploding right out of her
old head. She finally told him to shut it off and put on the television. He was fooling with the antennas when they heard the cars,
a lot of them, zooming and racing around in the dirt front yard
with their white lights flickering and piercing through the window
curtains. Willie Mae wondered what took them so long.

"Well, Lionel, I guess you better get on upstairs for hiding."

"Hiding? Why? Where?"

After they lynched her husband, Willie Mae had a hiding place
built in behind the closet. It was no bigger than a traveling trunk,
but big enough for a man to fit if he made himself real small.

"I'll take him, Big Mamma," Emma said.

"I don't understand, what makes you think they are here for
me?"

"Because you ain't blood, son," Willie Mae said, "and you come
from up north. They figure you the one stirring up all this mess."

"Hurry, Lionel, hurry," Emma said.

Lord, Willie Mae didn't like the fear in her eyes. But true to
her girl's strength, even seven months pregnant, she bodily moved
Lionel up the stairs.

"Send him on out, Willie Mae."

The sheriff's voice. Good Lord, and he was using a bullhorn.
Don't that beat all, Willie Mae thought.

She opened the door, then the screen door, and walked right up to the porch railing. They were all dressed in pointy hats and white robes, but she recognized all the cars, sure enough.

"You can't be serious, Sheriff," she said. "How bold do you have to be?"

"We're looking for Lionel," he said. "We ain't going to hurt him. We just want to keep him as an insurance policy."

"An insurance policy for what?"

"To make sure you don't go down there and vote tomorrow morning. Once the vote's done with, we'll bring him back to you and Emma without touching a hair on his nappy head."

Emma had come out the house to stand beside her.

Willie Mae could feel her granddaughter tremble.

"He ain't here," Emma said. "Go on now."

The sheriff pulled the hood from his head. He walked up to the porch with a rifle in his hands. Two other men came to join him, but they kept their hoods on. No matter, though. Willie Mae could recognize Fat Tommy anywhere. The other one was ole doc's son. He never saw eye to eye with his father.

"Now, we gone have to search the place, you know that, don't you?"

Willie Mae folded her arms across her chest. "Search all you want. Me and Emma going back to watch *Gunsmoke*. She likes Matt Dillon, but I'm kind of partial to Miss Kitty, myself."

"We can stop all this foolishness if you just agree not to vote tomorrow," he yelled to her retreating back.

"Can't do that for you, Sheriff," she said as she walked back into the house.

The sheriff followed Emma and Willie Mae into the house. Emma took Lionel's place, fiddling with the antennas. Willie Mae knew that she was doing it only to keep her hands busy while ole doc's son and Fat Tommy clumped through the house.

"Search it real good, boys," the sheriff called after them.

Willie Mae broke off a bit of Spark Plug tobacco and tucked it in her cheek. She ignored the sheriff, staring at her the entire time, trying to make her jumpy. Her hand was steady as she spit a long black stream into an empty green-bean can.

"Turn that left antenna toward me, Emma. That's better," Willie Mae said.

"You know we're going to get him, don't you?" the sheriff said.

"I don't know nothing," said Willie Mae.

She heard Fat Tommy in the master bedroom, pulling drawers from the chifforobe. Sounds of glass shattering floated down to them. She hoped Fat Tommy was spending so much time breaking things that he would forget to search the closet. Ole doc's son was throwing pots and pans around in the kitchen.

"They have to destroy my home?"

"You lucky we don't burn it down. You brought this on yourself," the sheriff said, leveling the rifle at her.

She didn't flinch. "You going to shoot me, or are you just trying to make a point?"

"You'll see what point I make if I see your ass at the polls tomorrow."

Fat Tommy clumped down the stairs with the hood pushed to his forehead so they were all privy to his fat, sweaty face. Ole doc's son came out of the kitchen.

"Anything?" the sheriff asked.

"Nothing," Fat Tommy said. "He ain't here."

"Why you spend so much time in the bedroom?"

"Searching good just like you said. Had to make sure they ain't got no secret room."

"They ain't smart enough to build a secret room. If they did you'd still have a husband. Ain't that right, Willie Mae?"

Willie Mae didn't let herself react. Eventually the sheriff got tired of waiting for one and left. She sat rocking and chewing until she saw the yellow light leave from the windows and heard the last car drive away.

The whole time Emma fiddled with the television antennas. She stood there a long time before finally saying, "I'll go get Lionel."

But Willie Mae shook her head. "No, chile. That's his bed for the night. They'll set somebody to watch the house."

"All night?"

"All night."

"He can't sleep all scrunched up like that all night."

"He's going to have to make do."

"And then what?"

Willie Mae got up and pushed the curtains aside.

"They'll probably leave Fat Tommy as punishment for registering me in the first place. With his sick wife and all, he'll fall asleep in his car probably going on two or three o'clock in the morning. Around four, you take Lionel and get him over Jack and Melva's place. Tell Jack to get Lionel out of town. Tell him to drive fast and far. Then you come on back here to take me to the polls."

"Maybe if you don't vote . . ."

"Too late for all that, Emma."

"I'm going with Lionel."

"No. You have to take me to the polls."

"But you can't still be thinking about voting!"

"If I don't vote then all this will be for nothing."

"Even if they kill my husband?"

"They ain't going to kill him, because he won't be here. Now do what I tell you. I'm going to get some sleep."

But Willie Mae didn't sleep that night. The first half of the night was putting the clothes back in their drawers and sweeping up glass, righting things as best she could. When she finally did get to sleep the witches rode her back all night long, and she had to claw herself up from sleep to wake up for another day in this world.

As Emma drove her to the polls, Willie Mae couldn't but help thinking about that song Lionel kept playing the night before, "A Change Is Gonna Come." But it wouldn't come all by itself. It needed to be ushered in like a newborn baby, but in this case by lots of folk making that first step. Folk like her. She started out midwifing, and here she was midwifing again.

"I can tell it's going to be a boy by the way it's sitting," Willie Mae said to Emma as Emma guided the Buick to the courthouse.

"Yes, ma'am," Emma said, and then nothing more.

Willie Mae sighed. The only thing keeping that child moving right now was fear. She was just about to tell Emma to turn the car around, to go back home. Enough foolishness and back to living —such as it was. But before she could open her mouth, Emma said, "Well, I'll be."

In front of the courthouse, where the voting was to be taking place, was an entire crowd full of Black folk. What spooked Willie Mae was how quiet they were. But also how expectant. It was like they were waiting with one heart, with a single soul for the change that was about to come.

"Emma, I can't . . ."

"No, Big Mamma. Like you said, it's too late no matter how scared we are."

Willie Mae usually made her own way without a lot of help. But right now, her heart was beating so fast, and her stomach dropping so far, that she was mighty glad she could lean on Emma. She knew down in her bones that the Devil had been up to something evil.

Everybody was so quiet. Even the white folk, who had come out to vote themselves and see the first Negro in Byrd's Landing vote. She would have felt better if they had been hooting and hollering. But they were as quiet as death. She did hear an old rattling voice saying something about "Go home, nigger," but right behind that came another saying to hush.

And then, again, silence. Just the sun beating down on her old hat and Emma's strong young legs matching her weak old pace. Willie Mae had to stop a time or two and gulp air as if she had forgotten how to use it. Her chest hurt again something fierce as she climbed the marble steps.

"You all right?" Emma asked.

"Right as I'll ever be, chile. Let's keep going."

They finally reached the front door to the courthouse. Emma pushed the heavy doors open.

"Willie Mae."

Just her name, in a voice that made her back stiffen.

She started to turn around, but Emma beat her to it. The wail coming from her granddaughter cut through the silence like a scythe cutting through the wheat.

There was the sheriff. That bastard child its mother wanted to drown before her husband found out that it wasn't his. He pressed the barrel of the biggest gun Willie Mae had ever seen to the side of Lionel's head. Willie Mae closed her eyes. *Yes, ma'am,* she thought, *I should have drowned him when I had the chance.*

Emma, still screaming, fell to the ground. Blessedly one of the older Black women from church came to help her stand and move her out of the way.

"I told you, didn't I? And you just had to be so hardheaded," said the sheriff.

Willie Mae didn't answer him. She was too busy looking at Lionel. He was scared, had to be, but he was looking at her as if trying to tell her something.

"If you go through that door, I'm going to blow his brains out."

"You're not right, Sheriff."

"Then come on down from there."

She waited with her eyes on Lionel. He didn't whine, or beg for his life. The boy wasn't even breathing hard. She had seen many people on their deathbed. She knew when someone had made up their mind. Even though he was from way up north, Lionel always knew the price he'd have to pay for speaking out. Her husband did too, all those years ago. Lionel nodded to her. She nodded back. And there came a little smile that she was sure only she could see peeking around the corners of his mouth.

She turned. Emma screamed in words so wrapped up with sobs that Willie Mae couldn't make them out. As soon as she placed one foot over the threshold, the shot rang out. Through her tears and sorrow, Willie Mae said in a whisper, thinking about all those Black voters that would be after her, "One bullet. One vote. It's the price we pay."

LISA UNGER

Let Her Be

FROM *Hush*

I MOVE BRISKLY down Second Avenue in the crisp autumn afternoon. The city hums, and the leaves are turning. My body pulses, my senses on high, taking it all in. The car horns, the chatter of people on their phones, pretty women striding to and from this and that, the aroma from Veselka, the church bells from St. Mark's, even my own footfalls. It's only recently that I've realized how precious is the mundane, the day-to-day.

In fact, the sad truth is that I didn't understand a thing about life until mine was spilling, black-red, onto the white tile of my bathroom floor. Maybe no one does. Maybe we *can't* grasp the gift—the crazy, mixed bag of tricks—until it is being wrested from us. My shrink says that most of his patients who survive a suicide attempt report a moment of clarity, that there's deep regret, a clawing back toward the light. I'm here to tell you that it's true. You cling at the end, realizing too late the blessing of it all, even the pain.

Unfortunately, I've never been one for half measures, or for leaving myself an escape hatch. I'm all in. So by the time I realized my mistake, it was too late.

I turn onto St. Mark's Place, where there's a sudden quiet from veering off the avenue. Trees, pretty stoops, plants in window boxes. Closer to Broadway, this street is a circus of shops and cafés, but as you head east, it takes on a quaintness that I love. To think I might never have walked the city again.

Most men shoot themselves, from what I understand. But I don't have a gun, and like many urban millennials of privilege, I had no idea how to even get one. Online? A gun shop uptown? What kind of gun might I need? Too much. Also, it seemed a little distasteful — loud, so goddamn inconsiderate. I mean — my parents.

Or they jump. Buildings, bridges, cliffs, I guess. Certainly there are plenty of iconic places in Manhattan to do the deed in a spectacular final leap, to make a gruesome point with my untimely death. But truth be told, I'm a bit of a wuss. That final step — the vertiginous spin, the anticipation of impact — can you imagine?

A straight razor was easy enough to come by. A good one can be found online for about sixty-five bucks. No permits or background checks. It's a hipster thing, apparently. You can get a straight razor, a badger-hair brush for shaving cream, all the cool accoutrements for the old-school shave.

Sharpness is key. Razor sharp, literally. Then, a long cut from the middle of the forearm to the wrist, deep, fast. Horizontal across the wrist is a cry for help. Vertical is for real.

It's amazing how fast life drains, how the light around you dims, and that indefinable force that keeps you moving, striving, wanting, loving — it just slips away. A shade. A trick of light.

By the time the regret set in, I was immobile in the warm tub, my body limp, all strength gone. In those final moments, I thought of my mother, the novel I was almost finished writing, my childhood dog. I thought of writers' retreats and children I'd never have, of martinis on balconies in European cities I wouldn't visit, and the sound of a fireplace crackling inside while snow falls outside.

And I thought of what it felt like to love her.

That feeling — nothing to do with her or with me really. That miraculous lift of the heart, that buzzing in the brain that is wild, romantic love. If I'd lived, I thought in the waning light, if I could have just found a way to let her go, I might one day feel *that feeling* again.

And that's when Anisa burst through the bathroom door, face pale, phone in her manicured hand. She wore that black coat I like, the one that ties at the waist. I think. The details are blurry. The whole thing felt like a dream at the time, and it feels even more like one now.

911. What's your emergency? I heard the voice, tinny on the air.

My fr-friend. She stumbled over the word, and rightly so. I had never been a good friend to her. I was a shitty boyfriend. A worse ex. *My friend, he* — she gulped back a sob — *slit his wrists. Oh God. There's so much blood.* She started crying. There was someone with her, someone who pulled her back from the pool of blood and bathwater on the floor.

Who was that? He stayed in the shadows.

Was it *him?* The new man in her life?

The memory brings an unwelcome rush of anger, darkens my mood. Dr. Black tells me to focus on my breath when this happens, to examine the anger. *Why are you so angry? What story are you telling yourself?* Then release it. Let the feelings, the thoughts, pass like ships on a river. I do that. It works sometimes.

And so, today, by the time I get to the café, the rush of feeling has faded. I stop at the entrance and hold the door for an elderly woman exiting. I gaze past her, looking for my friend Emily. Maybe I'm early.

But thoughts have a life of their own, don't they? They're not always ships on a river. Sometimes they're gremlins.

As I'm searching for Emily, still holding the door, a young mother pushes a weeping toddler by in his stroller—his face a mask of unhappiness, wet with copious tears. And his sobs remind me of Anisa crying. Which, sadly, became a familiar echo in our final weeks. I made her cry *a lot* as our relationship entered its death spiral.

Once, I made her scream. *Just stop, Will,* she shrieked. *You're hurting me.*

I still search for the details of that now-distant evening, as Dr. Black encourages me to do. What did I say? Why was I so angry? Did I get physical with her?

But all I can remember is the fear on her face, the dread and despair in her voice. I have no memory of myself in that moment at all. I wish I could recall, because that's the last time we were together before my suicide attempt.

All I know for certain is that the authorities were called that evening.

Not to save me from myself.

But to save Anisa from the man I became in that moment.

I remember afterward, though. The long, miserable hours in a city holding cell—wow, talk about how the other half lives. Before that very long night, I'd never met a person who thought it was a good idea to tattoo his whole face. My father bailed me out, looking old and confused. *What happened, son?*

Apparently, assault was on the table. Stalking. Anisa didn't press charges, but she took out a restraining order against me.

That's when I knew for sure that it was over between us. And this world? Without her? No thanks.

But when I called her, even after the horrible things I did and said, she came. *Anisa,* I told her voice mail before I put the razor to my skin, *I'm sorry. I can't do this without you. I just wanted to say goodbye.*

Pathetic, I know. Downright maudlin. But that's what I was, a suicide cliché.

She saved my life. I hadn't been a good friend to her. But in the end, she was a good friend to me.

I slip into the warmth of the café, unwrap my scarf.

My phone pings in my pocket; I pull it out to look. My mom. Understandably, she worries. *Hope you're taking care of yourself, sweetie. We love you.*

When someone's life really goes badly—drugs, suicide attempts, breakdowns—everyone looks at mom and dad. What did *they* do wrong? How did *they* fuck up? But don't blame my parents. They are kind people who love me well and always have. They were *there*, covering the bills and taking turns sleeping in the chair by my bed. After the acute crisis had passed, there were six weeks in a psychiatric hospital upstate, and that wasn't cheap. They stayed in a vacation rental nearby, but they didn't hover. They came in for the family sessions, but otherwise they let me work my shit out with the doctors. There was some detox; I'd been drinking too much.

My mother, of course, blames herself: *I softened too many blows. We always came in for the rescue.*

Okay, yeah, I see that. But how can you fault your parents for wanting to airbag the big, ugly, hard-edged world? Especially when they'd already lost a child. *I am responsible for my life. I am doing the work I need to do on myself.* It's a mantra my shrink gave me.

There she is, tucked in at a corner table, facing out across the restaurant. I nod to the hostess and make my way over.

Today is a new day, I remind myself. And I'm a new man. That dark night of the soul, when I thought the world wasn't worth living in without Anisa, it has passed. And I see clearly the mistakes I made—in my relationship with her, in my life before that. I'm in therapy, on medication. I have nearly finished my novel and have some interest from agents. I'm on my way to being that best version of myself. The one Anisa and I always talked about.

I've written to her, to tell her about it.

But she won't respond to my emails. Or return my calls. Not even a text.

Okay. Yeah. I get that. She's moved on. We both have. It's probably for the best.

She might not forgive you in the way that you want, my doctor said sagely. *And you don't need to hear the words to have closure. Sometimes silence is the only answer we get, and we have to accept that.*

That's hard, though, isn't it?

Emily is the sweetest of Anisa's friends, my ally against the others, who quickly turned against me. Truth be told, I think she might have had a little bit of a crush on me. Emily's a poet who works in children's publishing—bookish with round specs, flowy clothes, leather satchels. She moonlights as a social-media maven for authors, helping her clients create their online presence. I hear she's pretty great at it.

This coffee date is about, ostensibly, my novel. Emily has an agent friend, someone she thinks will like my work.

I stand beside her table for a second while she frowns down at the blank page before her. Her face brightens when she finally looks up and sees me.

"Will," she says, rising. "You look great."

"So do you."

She does. She's lovely with her strawberry-blond curls and constellation of freckles, her icy-blue eyes. She wears a rose-colored peasant blouse that highlights her coloring. The neckline gapes a bit, offering a tantalizing glimpse of flesh.

I take her into my arms, and we hug mightily, like people who have almost lost each other. And I guess that's the truth of it.

I hear my dad's voice: *Anisa was not the last Coca-Cola in the desert, buddy. Move on.* My dad is a practical guy, not one to cling to the past. The fact that I'm noticing how pretty Emily is—the first time in a while I've looked at anyone that way—makes me think he might be right.

"How's everything?" she asks, pulling away, sitting. "How are you feeling?"

I hate that question.

It has such an inherent heaviness to it, almost an implied judgment, don't you think? Like: *Here I sit on my pedestal, looking down at you drowning. From this distance, I can offer only a sympathetic wince.*

Who's kidding whom? We're all drowning, aren't we?

I don't want to be peevish. People mean well. Most of them.

"Better," I say, sitting across from her. It's warm inside, a lovely contrast to the cool fall weather. "Getting there."

This answer seems to make people happy. Because, really, there's nothing anyone can do for you in this life. They can't haul you out of the mire of your own dark thoughts or circumstances or ease your suffering. Only you can do that.

Emily watches me with a poet's eyes, kind and seeking truth. Her smile is bright and sincere. A friend. Truly.

"I'm so glad, Will," she says, puts her hand on top of mine. It's warm and soft. The noise around us—hushed voices, spoons against saucers, low ambient music—swells a bit in the warm silence between us.

"So," she says.

We chat a little about my novel, about her poetry. She slides a business card across the table, the agent she told me about. A guy she knows from college who's looking for "literary thrillers" like the one I'm writing. Though she hasn't read my novel yet, Emily's a fan of my short fiction, reads my blog. I enjoy her poetry—it's smart and dark. She has a keen eye, an unexpectedly sharp wit.

Emily has had a smattering of publications in small but notable journals. Her poetry echoes back to me sometimes when I least expect it. Like this one:

> *dismay sits*
> *at my breakfast table*
> *a noxious guest*
> *spilling the coffee and getting jam in places*
> *i'll have a hard time cleaning.*
> *i hope she doesn't invite herself to lunch.*
> *and dinner too.*

She's saying something about my blog now. How moving she found my entry on clawing my way back to some kind of normal after my—what are we calling it? My break. That's how Dr. Black likes to refer to it.

As if I decided to take a hiatus, a sabbatical—from being alive.

"Speaking of blogs," I say. "Have you seen Anisa's?"

Emily raises her eyebrows.

"Who hasn't?" she answers after a beat. "She's on fire. I think she's on the verge of a big book deal. That's the rumor, anyway."

"Oh?"

There's a lash of something dark, which I quickly quash. It's that thing inside. When it rears its head, that's when I make my worst mistakes. Dr. Black and I talk about it endlessly, this part of me that becomes activated when I'm angry. I breathe through it now. I'm getting better at that. In fact, since Anisa and I broke up — or she broke up with me — I haven't felt it much at all until now. That spin. That feeling of not being in control of myself. *She wasn't good for you,* my mother has said more than once. It's true that she brought out the worst in me at the end. But that's not the whole truth.

"I love her post from this morning," Emily says, her voice an octave higher than normal. "She just looks so . . . *happy.*"

But the word darkens her a bit, makes her go internal. She holds out her phone.

There's Anisa's face. Angelic. Thick russet waves of hair frame the valentine of rosy cheeks and dimpled chin. Big, thickly lashed eyes, full lips. And yes, that smile. Radiant with happiness. I know that look very well, better than most, I'd venture. For a while, *I* was the one to put it on her face.

Just a year ago, pretty Anisa writes, *I was in a dark place — a rat in a maze. Today, the day dawned clear and crisp, and I greeted the rising sun on my yoga mat. Then, for two uninterrupted hours, I wrote. This is the dream. You can have it too. #yogaatsunrise #lovethesimplelife #amwriting*

"Yeah," I say. The word catches in my throat a little. "Amazing."

Emily turns the phone back and stares at the screen for a minute. Seems to rethink her actions. That dark place — Anisa doesn't just mean the finance job she hated or the writing dreams that lay fallow. She means *me.* Our relationship. She called it toxic. I was poison, she said. Of course, she was right. I see that now.

"I'm sorry," Emily says.

I lift a hand and shake my head.

"I'm happy for her," I say. "Really."

Love the Simple Life, that's her very popular new blog, soon to be a book, soon to be a podcast, possibly a television show — according to a whirlwind of social-media rumors.

So since that *dark day* when she found me bleeding out in my tub, Anisa has changed her life.

She left her soul-crushing — but oh so very lucrative — job in finance and has moved away from the city. She and her new boyfriend, Parker, have built a tiny house, of all things, and are apparently living said simple life. They've pared down to just thirty-three possessions apiece. They're growing their own food, composting. Anisa has taken up knitting.

She posts one inspirational saying a day, one brief yoga practice (*You can do it anywhere, anytime!*), which she sketches in black and white, and one writing exercise (*You have fifteen minutes for your writing, don't you?*).

Parker posts vegan recipes and money-saving advice. His blog: *Parker Pinches Pennies*. (If that doesn't make you want to puke, we can't be friends.) They have nearly a million followers between them on Instagram, and they are apparently "simple life" influencers. Their website, lovethesimplelife.com, gets—according to one of Anisa's giddier posts—thousands of unique visitors a day.

"Me too," Emily says. "I'm happy for her too."

She takes a sip of her herbal tea. The waitress hasn't come again since I sat, so I haven't ordered anything. Emily, noticing, offers me a sip of hers, but I wave her away.

"Have you talked to her?" I ask, trying to sound casual. My shoulders are tense; I try to release them. Emily stows her phone, her face going a bit still.

"Actually, you know," Emily says, leaning back, "no."

"Not at all?"

She stiffens a little. Is she lying? Or just uncomfortable with the conversation?

"Brianna and I were just talking about that the other night," Emily says carefully.

The waitress, a slender tattooed woman with eggplant-colored hair, stops by, and I order a cappuccino, though I'm supposed to avoid caffeine. People who have trouble managing their anger don't need stimulants of any kind.

"You were saying . . . ," I prompt Emily when the waitress is gone again.

"Well, like, no one's *talked* to her in ages. The occasional text, an email here and there. But it's like she's just trying to shed everyone and everything from her old life. You know she just left? No goodbye gathering or anything like that. She just made the announcement one day on Insta, and by then they'd already left the city."

"Anisa and Parker?"

She frowns. Something in my tone, maybe.

"Yeah," she says. She pushes up her glasses. "Maybe we shouldn't be talking about this, Will. Right? Let's talk about you. Your book."

"It's okay," I say, leaning in. "I've done a lot of work on myself. I get that I made mistakes—big ones. She's moved on, and so have I. I'm . . . glad she's happy."

"That's great." She seems relieved, offering a sweet smile and reaching for my hand again. Then she pulls her hand back, checks her phone.

"It just seems a little strange, doesn't it?" I venture. "You guys were so close, more like sisters. Living the simple life doesn't mean you shed your friends, does it?"

"I wouldn't think so," Emily says. "But she did this big post about clutter clearing, leaving behind old, dead relationships that hold you back. She said something about how even people you love can hold on to outdated versions of you, causing you to cling to that part of yourself."

I offer her a laugh. "Don't worry. I'm sure she was just talking about me."

But Emily doesn't laugh with me. "Some of us were kind of hurt by that. Especially since none of us have spoken to her."

"None of you?" I ask.

She shakes her head, now looking like she might be tearing up a little. "Like, not for almost a year. Since, you know, all that happened."

I clear my throat. It's awkward to have survived a suicide attempt; people become very *careful*—about what they say, how they refer to the event. I wear long sleeves, of course. The scars are quite pronounced still, marks of my pain, my instability, which will not fade quickly.

"Well, what about this Parker guy?" Breathe. Keep it light. "What did you think of him?"

"I never met him in person. Brianna met him once at a bar. She said that Anisa didn't seem *that* into Parker. And then, a few weeks later . . ."

Was it him? Was this Parker the one who'd pulled her back from me as I lay dying? That darkness in me, it wants to cling, to yank her out of the shadows. More than anything, I told Dr. Black, it wants to hold on tight.

"It happens like that sometimes, doesn't it?" I say, trying to sound carefree and in the know about these things. "When it's right, it's right?"

"I guess," she says quietly. "But I miss her."

You have no idea what it means to miss her, I nearly snap. But I bite it back. She sips at her tea. I keep breathing.

"You know, Will, I probably shouldn't say this. But I miss *you.* The way it was then, before it got—bad."

The flash of anger passes.

"Me too," I say. I mean it.

I glance down at the wood grain in the table between us, then up at a framed picture hanging on the wall behind her, a grainy photo of a crow on a branch. "I really fucked everything up."

Because Anisa and I—we were happy. Not just *Instagram* happy.

We were Sunday-walks-to-the-market, inside-jokes, turkey-chili-Tuesday, soul-baring happy. We were fight-and-make-up, rub-each-other's-feet-while-we-watch-TV, go-out-at-ten-to-buy-her-tampons-without-a-second-thought happy. We were the real deal. True love.

Emily reaches across the table again for my hand. "We all make mistakes coming from our place of pain. When we know better, we do better."

I let the words hover a moment.

Thanks, Oprah, I don't say.

She means well—I know she does. But I'm full up with shrink-speak. Both of us stay quiet, the café noise around us seeming to grow louder, the energy between us tensing a bit.

"So where is it? The tiny house," I ask.

It's misplayed, and Emily draws away, that worried frown that Anisa used to love crinkling her brow. *Her Piglet frown,* Anisa used to call it. Sweetly worried. Kind but wary. *Is he one of the Fiercer Animals?* Anisa used to tease Emily, mimicking Piglet from *Winnie-the-Pooh.* Any teasing between the two of them, though, was from a place of purest love. A loving, laughing acceptance of each other's flaws.

"Will," she says, "I don't know where the house is. But even if I did, I don't think I could tell you."

I lift both palms, pull my face into a mask of patient innocence.

"I get that, really. I was just going to suggest that you go find her. Go talk to her. She can't be far, right?"

I pull out my own phone and open Instagram. "Those are northern trees, right? Autumn colors?" I look out the window to our own urban autumn afternoon, leaves amber, sienna, scarlet.

She nods her assent but still looks uncomfortable. She gazes toward the door, starts packing up her things.

"Look," I say, "I still care about her. Of course I do. It just all seems a little weird to me. That she meets some guy that no one else really knows. She just takes off, doesn't even say goodbye. No one has heard her actual voice or seen her in person for nearly a year."

I realize that I'm leaning across the table, talking a little too fast, too loud. I catch myself, breathe, pull back. I can tell she's hearing me even though she looks uneasy.

"What about her mother?" I say.

Emily blows out a breath. "That woman," she says. "She's useless at the best of times."

That's true. Anisa's mother was the biggest part of her problems. A drunk. Alternately neglectful, then clingy. She actually came on to me the night Anisa introduced us. We laughed about it, because what else could you do with that? Anisa's father died when she was a toddler. This shitty childhood was why Anisa was empty inside, always looking to be filled—by her work, by her relationships. It also made her a victim to shitty men—like me. And probably this guy Parker.

"Or Brendan?" I toss it out there, earning another eye roll.

"Anisa hasn't talked to her brother in, like, five years. The last I heard, he was in jail. Cooking meth or something totally fucked like that."

Yeah, her family is crap.

To be honest, that's why I'm worried. She has no mooring. No place where she's safe. It could have been me. I could have been that port in the storm of her life. We could have built a foundation where she was loved and cared for, where we could both grow. That was what I wanted. I just blew it, massively. Worse than the anger is the regret. I really hope I didn't hurt her that night I wound up in jail. I guess I could ask Emily. But a big part of me doesn't want to know if I'm the kind of man who could put his hands on a woman he loves in anger. Dr. Black and I talk about this too. *Have you ever hurt anyone before, Will?* Dr. Black wanted to know. *Have you ever hit a woman?*

No, I told him, never. And that's the truth.

I'm sorry, Anisa.

"Neither of them has seen her, talked to her?" I say. The silence between us has grown long.

"I don't know, Will," Emily says. When the waitress brings my cappuccino, she asks for the bill.

We sit a moment. The coffee is too hot to sip. I blow at the foam.

"It just all seems a little strange to me," I say, trying to catch her eyes. "Something's not right."

Emily shrugs, stares at her phone. "It looks pretty right to me. Her face—she's glowing. Read her words; she sounds grounded and wise. She looks healthy and strong."

She points the screen back in my direction. There's her beautiful body, a lean, arching silhouette against the rising sun. Did Parker take that photo?

"In fact," Emily says, wistful, "she might be better than she ever has been."

The room seems dingy suddenly, overcrowded. There's a garish smear of Emily's lipstick on the pale mug. The woman behind me is coughing fitfully. The table between us wobbles.

This is my point. The world. The *real world* is fraught with imperfections. It's messy and complicated, often uncomfortable, awkward, painful, dull. It's not curated and filtered for consumption.

"But that's social media," I say. "It's not . . . *true.*"

"Isn't it?"

"No." Again, too emphatic, a little too loud.

Emily's eyes widen, just for a millisecond. Then she stows her phone, clutches the bag to her middle. She dips her head and shifts. I think she's going to scurry out without another word. *You can be frighteningly intense, Will.* Anisa used to say this all the time. *Scale it back.*

"I'm sorry," I say, to soften the awkward tension.

"What's *true,*" she says after a breath, "is that she left us."

It's almost a whisper, like she's trying not to cry.

"Not just you, Will, but all of us, and this life we were living together. And that sucks."

The woman behind me. She will *not* stop coughing.

Emily goes on over the din. "But if she wanted us to be a part of whatever new version of herself she's creating, she'd call or visit or invite us to her goddamn tiny house in the woods."

Now it is Emily's turn to take a moment to calm herself. I will say this about Anisa. The people who love her, really love her. They care. They want her in their lives. I wonder if she knows this.

"We may not like it," she continues. "It may hurt. But that doesn't make it *less true*."

I nod, trying to give the impression that I'm not just waiting for my turn to talk.

"But that's my point," I say, jumping in when she's done. "I can see why she'd ghost me. I screwed up. I was jealous, possessive, a total dick. I drove her away. Then I basically stalked her, okay? I . . . menaced her. She was so afraid of me that she called the police and took out a restraining order. I lost it, tried to kill myself. She was right to move on from me."

I'm reaching for Emily, but she's pulling away. I often feel like this—reaching, trying to make my point, my case, while others draw back.

"But what if—stay with me—she didn't leave her life, all her friends, by her own *choice?*"

Emily gives me a confused, uncomfortable squint, looks toward the door again.

"I mean—what if something's wrong? Like—*really wrong.*"

When our eyes meet again, there's naked pity there. Emily has seen me at my worst. I wondered why she would agree to meet me. Why she's helping me with my career. She knows how bad it got with Anisa, that my life is in shambles. I see now that she just feels sorry for me. She's the rare nice person in the world who wants to help someone who is clearly struggling.

"Will, she's finally happy. Maybe she'll reach out to us again when she feels more, I don't know, *solid* in her new life."

I issue a laugh that sounds more bitter than I intended. "Not to me, I'm guessing."

She stands, pulls a twenty from her pocket, and puts it on the table for the check that hasn't come. I should offer to pay. After all, I invited her. But the truth is, I can't afford it. Ashamed, I let her leave the wrinkled bill and lift my cup in thanks.

"Will? Just—" She shakes her head. "Just let her be."

She leaves, and I'm alone. The normal state of things. Pity party.

Under the menu, I spy the black corner of a Moleskine. I grab it and run out onto the street after her. But she's nowhere to be seen.

I text her.

She doesn't answer.

She'll probably ghost me now too. When I open the notebook, its pages are filled with her notes and poetry. The voyeur in me experiences a dark thrill. What would I learn about sweet Emily in these pages? Not that I'd rifle through her private thoughts. I snap it closed quickly, tuck it under my arm.

I walk home, not even wanting to spend money on the subway. It's a hike, nearly ninety blocks. But it's okay; I like to ramble through the city, watch the neighborhoods change, see the haves and have-nots mingle, hear buses hiss, listen to horns bleating, observe the endless construction of ever-taller gleaming towers for the megarich, while steam rises from manholes, nuts roast in sugar, and wood burns in someone's fireplace, putting the scent of smoke in the air.

I live in my parents' Upper East Side town house now. Nice, right? Three floors, working fireplaces, an outdoor space, original fixtures and wainscoting throughout. Shelves of rare books, art from all over the world. They've had this place since their thirties, inherited from my mother's parents. It's worth a fortune now, though it's a bit run-down and in need of work here and there. The pipes clank; the lights flicker; the floors creak terribly. I think they should sell it, but they won't hear of it.

Where in the world would we go?

Anywhere, I tell them, *anywhere in the world.*

But they're lifers, Manhattanites to the core. *They'll carry us out of here feet first.*

Anyway, they're away on one of the trips they take—these kind of hiking, educational things. Basic accommodations, good food, but nothing fancy. They're all about substance, my parents. I have no idea where they are, though they've told me multiple times, their itinerary buried in my email somewhere. I'll have to check my mom's Facebook page. Idaho? Something about bird migration. My father has made it clear that this—my living with them—should not be seen as a permanent solution. I don't blame him. It's been a year. I'm truly better, solid, on my feet. And I'm ready to be on my own too. No one wants to live with his parents, right?

I enter the foyer, close the door. The quiet of the place greets me. My mother usually has the television on or music playing. She can't bear silence. My father is usually in his study, working or having a soft-voiced conversation with an author. He could have retired, but he still works as a freelance editor. He too has offered to help me get published—or to make the connections, anyway. But I want to do this myself. The help of a peer is one thing; getting your dad to make calls is quite another.

I'm confident that you'll be on your way to having a situation when we return, Dad said. A situation? Who am I? Jane Eyre?

They're not going to kick me out, though. That much I know. The room upstairs is mine and has always been my refuge, the place I return to when things go badly, as they so often seem to.

I look at the card Emily gave me—Paul Stafford of Writers Space—stuff it back in my pocket. That's a good thing. I'll focus on that. Write a query letter, send those very polished first three chapters, using Emily's name. Maybe. Maybe this is my first step forward into a real life.

My sister, Claire, would have been a better adult child, I'm sure. She was my superior in every way. No one ever says so, but it's quite obvious—she was the smart, beautiful, sweet one. There was *so much promise.* Whereas I was always the difficult one, the problem —colicky as a baby, bad grades through middle and high school, worse behavior, then a general failure to launch, multiple career "setbacks," recently my very serious suicide attempt.

Again, my parents would never say so—perpetually singing my praises and overinflating my meager accomplishments, making excuses for my failings. *The world is too much with him,* I overheard my mother tell her friend on the phone. *He's creative, such a sensitive spirit. That girl. She just bled him dry.*

Interesting turn of phrase.

Yes, Anisa just bled me dry.

Or was it I who bled *her* dry, bled *us* dry with my insecurity, my accusations?

Looking back, knowing that she loved you, that she was always faithful, what led you to doubt her? Dr. Black asked.

It always seemed true. *There was always a* real thing *that sent me into a froth.*

Once it was some text messages that seemed suggestive. Another time I was sure I saw her kiss a man in the dark hallway outside the bathrooms in a club. Once she said she was with Emily. But she hadn't been. I still don't know where she was that night. She was already pulling away from me then.

But even if it were true, the doctor said, *do you recognize that you don't, can't, possess another person? Even if you were married, it's not a crime for her to be unfaithful. It doesn't give you the right to spy, snoop, follow, to violate her boundaries. Can we agree on that?*

I know that. I do.

But—how can you keep that jealousy from causing you to do things you know are wrong? How can you keep from clinging to things you don't want to lose? When they seem to be slipping away?

Dr. Black suggests, of course, meditation and mindfulness exercises, deep breaths, a calm and respectful query, if necessary. Yes, that seems right.

I want to tell Anisa all of this. How it took me nearly throwing away my life to finally understand it. Maybe she can forgive me.

Not take me back. No. I know that.

I'm just looking for forgiveness, for closure.

You have to be okay with not getting that from her. You have to forgive yourself.

If ever there was a shrinky non-phrase. What the hell does that mean? Forgive myself. Of course I forgive myself. Isn't it all too easy to do that?

My parents have another house too. Upstate, on twenty acres, deep in the woods. Another inherited property, this one from my father's side. Grandpa's old hunting cabin that they've built upon and modernized over the years. That's where my sister died. They don't go up there anymore. It sits empty, going to seed, as my father likes to say. I'm the only one who ever goes there—to check on things, meet with the handyman when there's a problem. Sometimes I go there to write. Anisa and I visited a few times.

My mother thinks I should go up there permanently, do the fixing up that needs doing instead of the handyman, take care of the property, get a job in town while I finish my novel and try to get it published. I think she wants me to exorcise its demons, make it a happy place again.

Anisa never liked it there. There's a sadness there—in the walls, in the lake, in the trees, she said. It's true. My sister drowned there in the lake behind the house. An accident.

Claire was older by three years, a beautiful sylph of a thing. In pictures, she looks ephemeral, as if she was never part of this world. I remember her always just out of my reach—with sunlight for hair and a galaxy for eyes.

She was babysitting that night, fifteen to my twelve—well, not really babysitting. She was supposed to be with me, keeping an eye on things, the older, more responsible sibling. Why did she go out there in the dark? I remember hearing the door, that slapping of the screen so common in summer. The whisper of her voice. The melody of her laughter. Another tone too, the youthful baritone of a boy. There were always boys—on the phone, sitting awkwardly in the living room with my parents. It didn't mean much. She wasn't allowed to have friends over when she was babysitting, but she knew I'd never tell on her.

There was no evidence of foul play. The police ruled it an accident, a careless nighttime swim. She drowned. But who was the boy that night? We never found out. People wondered if I'd dreamed it, that other voice.

Somehow thinking of Claire makes me remember that shadow behind Anisa again, the one who pulled her away from me. Why was there always someone taking them away? Again that ugly lash. If I let those thoughts take their course, I'll get angrier and angrier. But I use one of Dr. Black's mantras: *I acknowledge that there is anger arising in me. I accept it and release it.* At first it seemed like pure bullshit. But it actually works, most of the time.

I creak up the stairs, down the hall to my room. I lie on my bed and scroll through Anisa's Instagram feed—again.

Today her blog post is about "Letting Go."

We cling to the past, don't we? To versions of ourselves, to people we tried to love, to dreams we have outgrown. But there's only one moment. Now. And the only true self exists here.

There are prettily staged images scattered throughout the blog—a colorful stack of notebooks, a steaming cup of tea, a picture of her hand curled around a pen, poised over a blank page. More than two thousand followers have offered their "likes" on the Instagram post where she sits in half lotus, hands in prayer at her center. I used to love the soles of her feet, even when they were dirty from walking barefoot on the hardwood floor. They were always so soft.

I stare at the slope of her shoulder, the swell of her breast, the way that wisp of hair always escapes her bun. The light touches her face, making her skin glow. I spend too many hours scrolling through her feeds, reading her words. Time I could spend moving on. Working on my novel. Getting a real job. The days seem to disappear. I lie to my shrink, to my parents, to myself about how I'm spending my time. The truth is I crawl through a digital portal and swim through the dream world there, trying to find my way back to her.

I touch my finger to the screen. It's cold and flat. There's nothing there but hard glass, beneath that tiny mazes of circuitry, wires. No matter how badly I want to climb inside, I can't.

It's not real. Not true. Anisa is not there.

In the corner of the picture, I see a shadow. Someone tall and slim, unmistakably male. Must be Parker taking the photo, lucky bastard.

Wait.

I sit up quickly, start scrolling back through images taken on my phone.

The whole catalog of us exists there. Funny moments, private ones, a few X-rated, the curated ones we posted on social media to show everyone how deeply we loved each other, how special we were.

Not on here: the night I grabbed Anisa's tender wrist too hard when she tried to leave after an argument. The day I made her cry while I grilled her, ceaselessly, possessed, about text messages that turned out to be from her cousin. The afternoon she realized that I had been following her while she was having a girls' day with her friends. That look on her face—the disbelief, the anger and sadness. Not something I want to revisit. The night she piled all my stuff outside the door of her apartment and I banged and banged and yelled, Anisa sobbing inside, until a neighbor called the police.

No, we don't share those things, the ugly moments between the beautiful ones.

There. I find it. Anisa sitting in half lotus. Same top, same strand of hair prettily falling, same light on her face.

That shadow in the photo, slim and dark.

The lucky bastard is me.

Okay. What does that mean?

Is she just recycling old images? Or—is it? Is it a sign maybe? She must know I'm watching her blog, her social feeds; it's not the first time I've suspected that she's sending me veiled messages. Which I would never say out loud, especially not to Dr. Black, because it sounds . . . batshit crazy.

Or—is someone *manufacturing* these posts? Using her catalog of old photos—cropping, filtering, photoshopping. It's all too easy to do, to create a new reality from the old.

I zoom in on the photo and see that she's wearing the Tiffany infinity necklace I bought her for our first anniversary. The sight of it sends a jolt through me.

Our first anniversary. One year—it made our love seem so real. I knew we weren't ready for the big step. We were still living in our separate apartments. Her job in finance kept her exhausted, run ragged. I was working for a temp agency—publishing my short fiction in small journals, working on my novel—heavily subsidized by my parents.

Even though I knew it wasn't time for a ring, I wanted *so much* to get her something in that little blue box. I could afford only the smallest version of the necklace, in sterling. Still, I made my point. Infinity, forever.

She loved it, of course. And made a big fuss over it, posted it all over her feed. All the world, our world, gushed at the sweetness.

That Will. He's a keeper.

I stare at the image on the screen. So is it the old photo? Or is she still wearing the necklace?

My phone rings then, startling me so badly that I throw it in the air. It lands on the bed beside me with a thud. Her image disappears.

Emily's face, nestled against Anisa's, appears in its place. I remember taking that picture of them. One of our many joyful outings together—this one for frozen hot chocolate at Serendipity. They both have chocolate lips and big smiles. Afterward we walked forever in Central Park. We were a cozy little threesome, like something out of a Victorian novel. Anisa and I were the young lovers, accompanied by the doting sister, cousin, ward, whatever. She, this attentive third, was a sweet, lovely thing—but just that much less lovely than the heroine of the story. Poor Emily.

"Hey," I answer.

"You have my notebook?" She sounds annoyed, as if it's something I did to keep her looped into me. I should have just left it. "You didn't—"

"Read it? Yes, and now I know all your secrets, Emily."

There's a leaden silence.

"Just kidding," I say, eliciting a relieved sigh. "Come on. I would never. I tried to catch you."

I hear the wail of a siren in the background of the call.

"I'm in your neighborhood," she says. "Can I stop by for it?"

"Sure."

Why would she be on the Upper East Side? I wonder. And did I tell her I was staying with my parents?

But how can we keep any of this straight anymore? What we said, what we posted, what other people posted about us on their feeds. A chaotic mishmash of almost-true gossip and fake news, of rumor and posturing. Anisa and I had a couple of parties here while my parents were away. Most of her friends thought it was my place; I never cleared it up unless pressed. *It's a family home,* I might say if questioned. *Oh, wow,* is the normal response. Translation: *I knew you couldn't afford a place like this.*

I try to tidy up, my head spinning with thoughts of Anisa, that photograph. That shadow. Me or the elusive Parker? The infinity necklace.

When Emily knocks on the door, I let her inside. She's let her hair down, taken off her glasses. There's something so delicate about a redhead, isn't there? Anisa used to say that Emily had fairy-princess hair — all gold and white highlights. Anisa was right. Emily's curls shine in the foyer light.

I'm practically bursting to tell her about my Instagram discovery. But I know what everyone thinks of me. When you stalk a young woman and then try to kill yourself, you lose all your credibility. It's hard to convince people that you're on solid ground.

Anything I say on this topic is going to sound crazy.

Maybe I *am* crazy.

How are you supposed to know these things? So I just hand her the notebook and hope she'll leave quickly. I want to get back to my Internet sleuthing. She flips through the pages as if she could tell by looking if I've been snooping. She tucks it possessively into her satchel.

"I'm sorry about today," I say. "I didn't mean —"

She smiles, lifts a hand. Her glitter nail polish is chipped. "It's okay. I know you loved her, Will."

Love her. I still love her — wildly, madly, deeply. As much as ever.

You don't stop loving someone just because they stopped loving you. It would be a lot easier if you could. Emily's kindness makes me turn away from her; I don't deserve it.

I wait for her to move to the door. In fact, I'm still standing by it, gripping the handle. But she stays rooted, her brow wrinkled; she chews at the corner of her thumbnail. "I've been thinking about what you said."

Hope wells. I almost leap on her with what I've just discovered, but I stay quiet. Instead of leaving, she moves into the living room and sits on the old sofa, places her bag on the floor.

I follow her and sink into the overstuffed chair on the other side of the coffee table. This furniture, it's been here since I was a kid. A lot of it belonged to my grandmother. There are pieces—a shaky secretary, an ancient chifforobe—that haven't been moved in half a century. There's a portrait of Claire and me as children hanging over the fireplace. My parents were good about stuff like that—some people want to forget. But they wanted to remember her well, with joy, once the shock and the most brutal phases of grief and loss had passed. We talk about her openly now, allowing ourselves to remember, even when it's painful.

"Did you know that Anisa just kind of bailed on her place?" Emily says. "She didn't tell the landlord. She just packed her clothes, left most of her furniture. She just stopped paying."

I didn't know that. I haven't seen or spoken to the real flesh-and-blood Anisa since she saved my life. I went straight from the hospital to the facility upstate, finally ending up here at my parents' place, where I tried to piece my life back together. *Am trying* to piece my life back together. Am *supposed* to be trying to do that.

"It just doesn't seem like her to do something so irresponsible, does it?"

I shrug, shake my head. Anisa, truth be told, *could* be a little irresponsible. She was prone to racking up debt on luxury goods like Gucci totes and Prada shoes, and then she'd eat ramen noodles for a month to pay it off. (What do you think about *that, Parker Pinches Pennies*? Little Miss Minimalist would do *just about anything* for a pair of Christian Louboutin shoes.) She could swing it because she made a fortune at that detested finance job, but she wasn't much of a saver. She'd pretend to have the flu—like really play the role for her boss—to spend a few days with me when I was between temp jobs. We'd stay in bed, order in, watch rom-coms.

"And her job," Emily goes on. "She didn't love it. Finance was not her calling. But she left without notice. Again, not really like her. She respected her boss, was happy with the day-to-day. Or so she said."

That was true. She didn't hate her Wall Street job as much as she said. She had the rare mind that was excited by both art *and* numbers. She was a poet, and she could rock a spreadsheet like nobody's business.

"I think she was happy," Emily says. "Happyish? As happy as any of us are."

Yes. But. There was a subliminal current of unhappiness there, a skein of dissatisfaction.

Is this it? Do you think this is it? she would ask me sometimes—in quiet moments after we'd made love, or walking through the park, moments when I was vibrating with happiness. *I hope so,* I'd answer. Writing. Loving her. Making a home in this frenetic candy store of a city. What else might there be? She'd drift away from me a little in those moments, as if we were on different wavelengths.

I think about Dr. Black, something he said coming back to me. *People walk away from their lives all the time. Make big sudden changes. It's not a crime.*

Emily and I sit with all of it a moment, our two different versions of Anisa. Was she Emily's friend, my girlfriend? Yes. But she was also herself, unknown in some ways to both of us. I accept that now, when I couldn't before. That's progress, I think.

The big grandfather clock that my mother hates, and that my father winds and winds, ticks off time. It's aggressive. Never lets you forget the passing seconds.

"I don't want it to seem like I'm not happy for her." Emily rubs at the bottom of her eyes. "I mean . . ." A sigh, an imploring lift of her gaze. "I'm jealous, okay? Everyone is. I thought it was that. Sour grapes, you know?"

Again, I stay quiet.

"But I guess you're right. There *is* something off about it—the whole thing. The pictures. Even her words. Maybe it doesn't— sound like her."

My thumb finds the scar on the opposite arm. It's still tender. Ugly. Frankenstein's monster, I am stitched together. Less than the sum of my parts.

Before I can think better of it, I tell Emily about the Instagram post, about the old picture in my photo albums, the infinity necklace. It comes out in a tumble, sounding manic and off.

I wait for her to regret her decision to come, to share, to listen. I wait for her body language to close up before she scurries for the door, eager to get away from the shiftless, postsuicidal stalker that I am. But she just nods thoughtfully when I'm done, touches her collarbone.

"Show me," she says.

I move over to sit beside her on the saggy sofa, and she dons her reading glasses. She stares at my phone, scrolling, flipping back and forth between apps.

"It *does* look like the same photo, Will," she says. "I mean, it's possible that it's just really similar. She's still wearing the necklace, maybe—she loved it. She loved *you*. And how many different ways are there to sit in lotus? But—the hair, the shirt, the light . . ."

Emily pulls out her laptop.

And over the next couple of hours, together, we analyze Anisa's feed, comparing images with photos each of us has on our separate devices. I am comforted by the presence of someone sane. It's not just me banging around the inside of my own head, analyzing, questioning, doubting.

We scroll through the feeds of Anisa's friends going back two years. Many of the pictures on her new feed can be sourced from elsewhere—the yoga studio where she subbed Sunday morning classes, a cooking class she took here in the city, photos snapped by friends.

We search some of the phrases in her blog that seem especially *not like Anisa* and find that much of what's there is a patchwork quilt of Zen memes, self-help books, Buddhist texts, sound bites from popular new-age writers and thinkers like Eckhart Tolle, Gary Zukav, Michael Singer—even Jung, Einstein, Thich Nhat Hanh, Gandhi.

While I brew coffee, Emily makes some phone calls. Because no one is going to talk to me about Anisa. I hear the soft rise and fall of her voice from the kitchen.

Yeah, but actually speak to her, I mean. Like hear her voice.

When was that?

Are you sure? No. Okay.

Yeah, of course. Think about it.

When I come back with our mugs, she sits staring at the portrait of me and my sister, her face unreadable.

"Is that your sister?" she asks gently. "The one who drowned?"

"Claire," I say. "Yes."

She's quiet a moment, seems to be considering her words.

"Did you ever notice how much she looks like Anisa?"

I hadn't noticed at first. We are not quick to notice these deep psychological burdens, the secret machinations of our inner pain, and how they manifest themselves in our choices, are we? It was my mother who went sheet-white when I brought Anisa home, quickly recovering, effusing warm smiles and opening welcoming arms. Only later did I find her crying in front of our portrait. Their coloring is not the same. It's all in the shape of the eyes, the mouth, the dimple in her chin. Something ghostly in the essence — not knowable, untouchable.

"Only later," I say. "After my mother pointed it out."

She looks back and forth — to my face, back to the portrait.

"You still look the same." She smiles at me. "Same killer cheekbones, regal nose, and serious dark eyes. You were an old soul."

"So they tell me."

I hand her a cup of coffee, and she takes it, puts it down on the coaster.

"So," she says. "I think I was the last one to talk to Anisa."

I settle in across from her.

"Brianna hasn't spoken to her since February of last year," she goes on. "Brent — you know Brent — has lost his phone since she left. So he doesn't have a log of their calls. Just a few texts."

She looks down studiously at the notes she's scribbled in that Moleskine with just a few pages left blank. "Chloe can't remember but thinks it was sometime after — you know, what happened." She casts an apologetic look in my direction.

"Anisa mentioned Parker to Chloe. But like Brianna thought, Chloe also said Anisa didn't seem that into him. Anisa billed him as some extreme early retirement guy — one of those geeks who lives on like ten percent of his income and tries to retire by thirty."

"That tracks. *Parker Pinches Pennies* or whatever," I say.

"According to Chloe, Anisa found that really annoying. Said he was cheap. A freeloader, basically."

She really did hate cheap people; it was kind of a pet peeve. She was unfailingly generous — showering me and all her friends with expensive gifts, picking up the tab at tony restaurants.

Outside someone leans on a car horn. Some shouting follows. Then things go quiet again.

"I probably shouldn't say this." Emily takes a sip of her coffee, closes up her notebook. "I always figured you two would get back together—even after all the drama."

My heart clenches a little.

"That's a romantic notion. If I was her friend?" I say. "I'd have told her to run and not look back. I was not my best self."

That's such a "now" thing, isn't it? My best self. Is it a goal? An ultimate destination? Or is it a fluid thing, something that might ebb and flow with the tides of our lives?

"What about now?" asks Emily. "Are you your best self now?"

"Honestly, I don't even know what that means anymore."

She lets out a little laugh, curls her stocking feet up under her.

"Does anyone?"

"Parker seems to." I hold up the phone. He's a good-looking guy —a vegan hottie with stylish stubble and cut abs. He's fast becoming a millennial finance guru—quoted all over the place. But his stuff too—lifted more or less from everything else out there. *Not spending a dollar is like earning a dollar.* Um, hello, Benjamin Franklin—a penny saved is a penny earned?

Meanwhile, there's nothing about him online. Parker doesn't have a LinkedIn profile. There's no personal Facebook or Instagram page—with pictures of friends and family, party shots, or his nephew's first birthday party. His social-media presence is on point —only about his finance blog and his *Parker Pinches Pennies* persona. The real Parker is nowhere to be found.

She leans in to stare at my phone.

"He looks like a dick," Emily says flatly. I laugh. It's funny when kind, careful people say what they're really thinking.

"She sure can pick 'em," I say.

She issues a knowing snort.

The list of Anisa's exes is long and colorful, kind of a running joke among her friends.

The tattooed bartender who smoked so much dope that he regularly passed out cold while they were making love. The hirsute hedge-fund manager who could never, ever not be looking at his phone. The off-Broadway actor who kept a picture of his mother by his bed. The timid IT guy who still had a VCR, along with a complete cataloged set of *Seinfeld* episodes that he rewatched and quoted endlessly. I never minded talking about her past, especially since I was always billed as the light at the end of the long, dark dating tunnel. The prince to all her frogs. Until I wasn't.

We decide Emily's next call should be to Anisa's mother, Jenny. There is a rule for calling Jenny. Never after six. Anisa's mother starts drinking at lunch and is pretty much on an alcohol drip until she falls asleep in front of the television at night. She is fine, more or less, until the second glass after dinner—then she might turn maudlin or belligerent, nostalgic, exuberant, clingy, or downright mean.

It's 7:02 p.m. when Emily calls her, putting her on speaker while I sit silent, and it apparently isn't one of Jenny's better nights.

"Hey, Jenny, it's Emily, Anisa's friend from college."

"Oh," she says. Anisa used to say there was a pitch, a shift in tone that she could pick up on in one syllable. Over the time I got to know Jenny a little, I became able to discern it as well. It was kind of a sloppy wobble to words, a sharpness of tone. "Hello, Emily. Do you ever hear from my daughter?"

"Actually," Emily says, glancing at me, "I was calling to ask you the same thing."

A snort, the tinkle of ice in a glass. "Would you believe it's been over a year since she called her mother? Not that I'm sitting by the phone. I have a life, you know."

"A year?"

"Well, you know she has nothing but a catalog of complaints about me. Apparently, I was the world's worst mother. The last I heard from her—a text, of all things—she was done with me. She said I was a sandbag in her life, one she had to cut loose in order to be free."

Clutter clearing, shedding the things that no longer serve, moving away from toxic people, dead relationships, the life-changing magic of getting rid of all your shit. It's another very "of the moment" thing for our generation.

But I look around my parents' place, the house that belonged to my grandparents, the same floors they walked on, pieces of well-made furniture that have aged with grace over generations, that have embraced us in times of joy and sorrow—Christmas mornings and birthday parties, the gathering after my sister's funeral. There are boxes of photos, childhood drawings and report cards, wedding china on which festive meals have been served to imperfect gatherings of friends and family. Piles of books, collected art of varying quality, notebooks of poetry and fiction that will never be read.

How do you discern between the things that hold you back and the things that hold you up? My parents have made mistakes. I have too. Maybe they *have* enabled me, softened blows, causing me to grow up unable to deal with the harsh realities of life. And I have been in trouble, was a middling student, an inconsiderate son at times.

And I tried to kill the only child they had left—myself. But we're all still here, making our way, together. I can't imagine being done with them, or they with me. Sometimes if we cut too many sandbags, we float away. Is that what happened to Anisa? Did Anisa float away? Having shed all her family and friends, did she disappear into the ether?

"I *tried* to tell her." Jenny and Emily are still on the phone, Jenny's words dipping and pitching. "She can stop. *talking* to me, stop *visiting* me. But I'll always be her mother. Like it or not."

"Yeah, I hear that. So, I am trying to locate her, Jenny," Emily says. "Do you have any idea where she lives?"

"So I'm not the only one she left at the curb? What about that nice boy? Will, was it? I knew that wouldn't last. She only wants someone who treats her badly."

"Jenny," Emily says, rolling her eyes at me. "Do you have an address? Or did she mention a town? Anything that might be a clue to where she lives."

"She lives online, like all of you kids. You think that's the real world. But it isn't."

The line goes dead, Emily's phone issuing the desultory beep of an ended call.

I dip my head in my hand. *I'm sorry, Anisa. I'm sorry for driving you away.*

I've been round and round about all of this with Dr. Black. He lets me walk the winding roads of regret and self-flagellation, of what-ifs and if-onlys. But we always wind up at the same point. Anisa has walked away from her life and any contact with me, due in large part to my bad behavior in our relationship, our breakup, and my suicide attempt. She has made clear her choice and her boundaries. Any chasing I do is boundary trampling, an attempt to control another person, the actions of an abuser. I must accept the consequences of my actions and respect her choice.

For some reason, sitting here with Emily, it suddenly becomes clear that there's no road back to what I had with Anisa. I have to let her go.

I am about to suggest that Emily do the same when she speaks up.

"I think I might have some idea where she is," Emily says.

I look up at her. She's hunched over her laptop in the dark room, the screen turning the lenses of her glasses blue.

"Look," she says when I don't say anything.

When I come to stand behind her, I see Anisa's face—mouth open, eyes on the camera, a giant glop of pink on a spoon headed for those perfect lips. It somehow manages to be totally innocent and yet highly sexualized, like all of her posts.

Organic ice cream, made with all locally sourced ingredients—milk from local grass-fed cows, strawberries from the farm up the road, sweetened with honey from an area beekeeper. Parker may be totally vegan, but I am NOT. #local #organic #yum #sogood

"We've been there," Emily says.

I look at the picture, and there on the counter behind Anisa's smiling face is a stack of paper ice cream bowls. The logo: a simple black-and-white cow with a big smile and a pink tongue. The Happy Cow. Emily is right. It was a brutal summer weekend, sweltering temperatures, and my AC on the fritz. Anisa was jealous that all our friends seemed to have left the city for rental houses in the Hamptons. Emily was going through a bad breakup. So I suggested we borrow my parents' car and all head north.

That was the weekend I told Anisa and Emily about Claire. Anisa already knew that I'd lost a sister; she just didn't know the details.

We stopped in town, had lunch, ice cream at the Happy Cow. Then we got groceries, booze, and went to the house. She loved it there at first. The house is sweet, the grounds beautiful, the town a picture postcard—a yoga studio, a little bookstore, some really nice restaurants, and tons of shops selling goods from local artisans, farmers, craftsmen.

It was only after Emily had gone to sleep and Anisa and I sat out by the firepit that she started to feel the sadness that kept us all away. My parents couldn't bring themselves to sell it, because it always felt as if we had left Claire there. But we couldn't stand to be there either.

"I'm sorry your family has had to go through this," she said that night, holding my hand. The fire crackled, and the night sky glittered with stars.

Even though Anisa was sad, I could see for the first time how love might transform the house again. We'd come up there with our friends, make a new energy field—parties and cooked meals, take the old rowboat out on the lake. Laughter and music would energize the space. Maybe my parents would find their way back. One day, after Anisa and I were married, we'd bring our own children here for lazy summer weekends. The house, the garden, the woods, the lake—it would breathe again. That was the way of it in the organic world—death and rebirth.

But we didn't go back. And strangely, that weekend lives in my memory as the last time things were really good. A few weeks later, those first clouds of suspicion started to set in and turn our relationship dark. Almost as if remembering how painful it is to lose someone, I started to cling to Anisa in unhealthy ways. Dr. Black and I have discussed at length how Claire's death changed the way I saw the world. How I discovered too early that it was wild, unpredictable, utterly out of my control.

"We *have* been there," I say.

"The Happy Cow," she says. "Anisa loved it up there."

"But what if it's just another old picture?" I scroll through my photos, but I don't see anything like it. Emily does the same.

"In this photo, she's not wearing the infinity necklace," Emily says finally. "You had just given it to her when we were there together. She never took it off. If it was an old photo, she'd be wearing the necklace."

I look more closely at the post. Her neck is bare.

"So," I say. "What should we do?"

"Do your parents still have a car?"

"They do."

"How about a road trip?"

"You mean go look for her?"

I balk. Stalking. I've been accused of stalking her. There's a restraining order, which, as far as I know, is still in force. Isn't this just more of the same? A violation of her very clear boundaries.

I express all of this to Emily.

"I get all that," she says. "Except I'm worried too. Maybe something's *not* right, Will."

"Then maybe we should just go to the police."

She blows out a laugh, points at the computer. "And say what? My friend won't return my calls. I think this online life she's living is an elaborate sham. I think—*da-da-DAH*—she might be the victim of foul play."

It does sound pretty stupid.

"Look," she says. "This is not just you. It's me. I'll vouch for that, if it comes down to it. All I'm asking for is a ride."

I wonder what Dr. Black would think of this plan. I'm going to guess he would not support this. Work on your novel. Work on getting a job. Work on yourself. Those are the three sanctioned activities. Avoid relationships right now. No alcohol or drugs of any kind. Don't social-media-stalk Anisa.

But the draw is so powerful, my suspicions so convincing.

But this is exactly the place I was in when I was certain she was cheating on me. She was lying, I believed. It was true to me in that headspace, with the evidence I thought I had. And that gave me the right to do ugly things like stalk, snoop, follow. To grab her arm when she tried to leave, maybe even worse. And my angry thoughts, my suspicions, felt real. Why is this different? I'm guessing Dr. Black would say it isn't. He has encouraged me to call him when I feel those dark impulses. Maybe I should do that.

"I think I'm going," Emily says into my tortured silence. "With or without you. You know why? Because I can live with making an idiot out of myself if we're just being totally paranoid. But I'm not going to be able to live with myself if I'm right and I do nothing."

Fair point. She stands, a bit breathless with the power of her intention. Her hair is wild and shiny, and I find her slightly mesmerizing—her sudden passion, her prettiness. It's not that I never noticed before. It's just that I had eyes only for Anisa.

"And say we go, say we *find* her," she goes on. "And there she is, all gorgeous and minimalist and in love, living her best life. Then we know for sure—she bailed. She doesn't want the life she had here. She doesn't want my friendship anymore. And then, well—"

"We know the truth," I finish. "And that's that."

It isn't long before we're in a cab heading to the garage where my parents keep their Land Rover. Then, for a while, we stand in the brightly lit drive, cars coming and going, waiting for ours to be re-trieved from the mysterious depths of urban vehicle storage.

"Where are we going exactly?" I say when I'm behind the wheel. Their car is a nice one, late model, with beautiful leather seats and a dash alive with glowing lights, a colorful GPS map. I pull out into the schizophrenic flow of city traffic.

"Well, just up to the town where the ice cream place is," Emily says.

"The shop will be closed," I say. "The whole town shuts down at nine."

Something crosses her face, doubt maybe.

"It's okay," she says brightly. "We're in the flow. We'll find our way."

She sounds sure of herself, though to me it just sounds like one of Anisa's regurgitated posts. Something illustrated and packaged for happy consumption. This idea that if we just ask the universe to fulfill our desires, it will? I'm not sure I buy it.

But maybe that's why that attitude never seems to work for me. Because in my heart, I don't believe. I know that no matter how much you love and want, no matter how much you ask and beg, sometimes things just get taken away from you. Like Claire. Like Anisa.

I share this black idea with Emily as we pull onto the highway. It's still sitting heavy in the air as the city disappears behind us.

"Jesus, Will," she says after a while. "That's really depressing. Maybe—lighten up a little?"

We exchange a look in the dim interior of the car, and then we both start to laugh. Hard. Tears streaming, shoulders shaking. It feels good, like really good. It's the first time I've had a belly laugh in a damn long time.

But then the laughter dies and we are in the dark, driving north —to find someone we've both loved and lost. Someone who may be in trouble—or not. Who may need a rescue, or who may see what we're doing as deluded, a terrible violation of the space she's claimed.

She doesn't want you, I remind myself.

We ride in silence.

"I always wonder why she came that night," I say after I don't know how long. "After everything. Why she even answered my call."

I say it out loud, even though I don't mean to. Dr. Black thinks I shouldn't attach too much meaning to it. It was the right thing, the human thing to do. And Anisa is a kind person. Of course she wouldn't just ignore my calls and let me die.

"She didn't," Emily says. Her voice is soft but clear, and the words ring like a bell in my psyche.

"What do you mean?"

"It was—me," she says.

We've pulled off the interstate and onto the smaller rural highway that leads to town, trees all around. We haven't seen another car for a while now.

"It was me," she says again.

"You?"

There's a kind of tightening in my center.

"She never answered you that night. She felt awful about it later. Will—she did. But she sent your calls straight to voice mail, then deleted them. She didn't know until later that you tried to kill yourself."

I let this sink in. But no. It's not true. I *saw* her standing there, an angel calling me back from the edge of my life. There was nothing else, no ray of light, no voice offering a choice. It was just Anisa.

"You called me when you didn't reach her." Her voice is just a whisper. "I raced to your place, convinced your landlord to open the door. The whole bathroom was flooded."

My friend . . .

There's so much blood . . .

"I called 911."

I've clung to that memory. Really held on tight, thinking that Anisa came. That some part of her still cared about some part of me. Except she didn't come. Even after she knew, she didn't call or send a note. She just—left.

"I didn't want to tell you." Emily's voice is small in the dark. "I didn't want to hurt you any more than you've been hurt already. I could tell that it meant something to you."

My hands grip the wheel too tightly, my eyes on the dark stretch of road glowing in the headlights.

"Will?"

Finally, I loosen my grip. I reach a hand out and put it over hers. She's shaking.

"Thank you, Emily."

I guess it's long overdue. I'm myopic, unable to see past my own pain these days. "Thank you for saving my life."

Her breathing is shallow now, wobbly. She laces her fingers through mine.

"Will." Her face has gone earnest, and then she casts her eyes down. "I'm glad you're still here."

I think about it a moment, watching the road ahead.

"So am I."

Of course it wasn't Anisa. Why should she answer my calls that night? Why would she take my threats seriously—or care? The restraining order forbade me from calling her, and her lawyer friend had advised her not to "engage." She used that word a lot. *I'm not going to engage with you, Will.* Boy, did that enrage me.

My addled brain saw what it wanted to see.

But Emily. Why is true friendship so often invisible? The person who is always there, the one who answers when we call, who comes when we need her. Why do we so often take that quiet presence for granted? I turn to look at her, but she's staring straight ahead. I feel like I'm seeing her for the first time.

One of her poems rings back to me:

> *Show me your crooked teeth*
> *The nose you were born with*
> *The birthmark you had removed*
> *Your childhood scars*
> *I want to see all your beautiful ugly*
> *Shed the mask you wear for everyone else and*
> *Show me*

When she turns to face me, she wears an odd smile. Something in me shivers. I am naked beneath that gaze. I tighten my fingers around hers. Her smile widens.

As we arrive in town, it's clear that we're not "in the flow." Not at all. This is a fool's errand. Every business is closed and shuttered for the night. We pull into the gravel lot of the Happy Cow and sit in my parents' car. Suddenly it feels as if all the urgency has drained from our venture.

We climb out of the car and walk around—because what else? Our feet crunch on the ground; we wrap our arms around our middles against the cold. I walk over to the storefront window, cup my hands around my eyes, and peer inside. The counter, the stack of cups. A chalkboard lists the day's fresh flavors in cheerful lettering and bright colors.

Like every place now, there are cameras mounted over the door, behind the counter. They're just basic home cameras like most people install to watch their front door, their dog, their child. We have put ourselves under constant surveillance. Never a moment when we are not watching ourselves and each other. And yet here we are, chasing those images, searching for the real Anisa, who is as elusive as a ghost.

"This was stupid," Emily says.

She wears a peasant skirt and lace-up boots, a kind of fuzzy, wrappy coat. She's let her hair go wild around her shoulders. There's a look—they all share it. Claire. Anisa. Emily. A kind of manifest disbelief that the world falls so short of the fairy tale they were sold.

"It was worth a try," I say, my voice sounding false and tight. Dr. Black suggests optimism. He says it's a choice. I'm trying, Dr. Black. I really am.

"I watch too many crime shows," she says. Her laugh disappears into the night. "I thought we'd found a clue. That we could solve the case of our missing friend."

More words of Emily's whisper back:

> *The case is cold*
> *Your secrets hold*
> *We'll all grow old*
> *Just wondering*

I move closer to her. I don't dare touch her. But I'm surprised at how badly I want to. Am I wrong? The way she's standing, body leaning toward me, eyes on mine—does she feel it too?

"There's only one place still open," I say. "Pop's, the twenty-four-hour diner."

My voice breaks the spell.

"I'm starving," she says, looking suddenly spent, depleted.

"Me too." I am. I don't remember the last time I ate. I'm thinner than I ever have been in adulthood. Gaunt, my mother says. I've always been one of those too-skinny guys, not that interested in food. I gained with Anisa. We were constantly eating.

The diner is a bit out of town, closer to the house. I haven't been there in a while, but we used to go all the time before Claire died, and a few times since. Big juicy burgers on floppy white buns, crispy fries, pillowy, creamy shakes. And a peanut butter pie that is my mother's all-time favorite. I always grab her a slice when I'm up here checking on the house. She eats it with equal parts joy, sadness, and guilt.

> *This meal*
> *Tastes like regret*
> *Salty and stale.*
> *I eat it anyway*
> *Grateful for any nourishment at all.*

Pop is there, as I knew he would be. He must be ninety years old. His son and daughter run the place now, but he's always there, greeting customers. He sits in the same booth by the door, a newspaper always open in front of him. Late at night, it's just him, a single waitress, and whatever shift worker they have in the kitchen.

"Will," he says brightly. "Long time no see."

He always says that, no matter how long it's been since I saw him last. I really cannot believe he remembers my name. Or maybe he just calls everyone Will.

"How you doing, Pop?"

"Never better, son," he answers. Every time. "How's that lovely family of yours?"

"All good," I say.

"Don't forget to bring a piece of pie to your mom for me."

He's wrinkled and nearly bald, except for some neat white wisps. His thick hands shake. He's dressed neatly in a buttoned-up plaid shirt, pressed khakis, and old-man brown shoes.

This is the same conversation I have with him every single time. He is as senile as they get, on some kind of loop that will not reset. I don't feel bad for him. I envy him. There are so many things I'd like to forget.

We order. Emily shows the waitress a picture of Anisa. But the girl just gives her a blank stare, a dismissive shrug. She doesn't ask a single question about who Anisa is or why we might be looking for her. She just sticks our order ticket through the window to the kitchen, then immediately goes back to whatever she was doing on her smartphone.

We get the same meal I used to get with Claire when we were

kids—cheeseburgers, fries, chocolate milkshake to share. In spite of our dark errand, our failure, the food is good. We talk and talk —not about Anisa but about Emily's poetry, how she applied for a writers' retreat and might go if she gets in, leaving her job. We talk about my novel and where I'm stuck. She agrees to read it. It's easy. Our friendship, even after everything, and with Anisa gone, is still intact. I take Dr. Black's advice and choose to be happy about that, at least.

I pick up the tab on the credit card my mother gave me that my father doesn't know I have. She pays the bill from an account that my father doesn't track. He'll rail at year-end when he balances the books, but he won't stop her. Softening blows. Coming in for the rescue.

On the way out, I use the restroom. When I emerge, Emily is sitting with Pop.

"Have you seen this girl?" I hear her say as I come up beside him. I didn't even think to ask him. It would be like asking an old transistor radio.

But Pop just stares blankly at the phone, then up at Emily.

"Is that the girl who died so long ago?"

Emily shakes her head. "No," she says quickly. "Her name is Anisa."

His eyes are filling, though.

"Such a tragedy," he says.

She looks stricken, horrified that she's upset the old man. "I'm so sorry," she says.

The waitress comes over and hands me my take-out pie.

"I've got my peanut butter pie, Pop," I say brightly, hoping to cheer him up. He turns to look at me, and Emily slips quickly from the booth, glad for the escape.

He seems to forget Emily and the picture.

"Don't tell your mother that I've always had a crush on her."

"Your secret's safe with me."

"Good night," Emily says.

We move away, the bell ringing as we exit. Emily is far ahead of me, out in the night. She doesn't hear him say before the door closes: "They say the brother did it. There was always something off about that boy."

I pretend I didn't hear it, don't let it upset me the way it used to. There were endless rumors then—a beautiful young girl dies by accident, and no one wants to accept that. No one wants to accept the randomness of it all. Believe me, I get it.

In the car, we sit. There's an energy between us, a tingle.

"We don't need to drive all the way back," I say.

The long trip is not an enticing prospect with a belly full of cheeseburger and milkshake. "We can stay at the house. I promised my parents I'd stop by and check on it anyway."

I figure she'll say no. Even though it's Friday night and she doesn't have to work tomorrow and probably her only plans are to write all weekend. She's very still, staring at the picture of Anisa glowing on the screen. She clicks the side of the phone, and it goes dark. She leans closer, blinks. I wait for her to come back with a list of excuses.

"Okay," she says. "That sounds good."

It's a bit of a drive, the road hypnotic and winding. No streetlamps. The exact opposite of city living. The layers fall away—light, noise, clutter—leaving a hush, a peaceful silence. I turn at the tilted red mailbox and stop to retrieve the pile of junk that inevitably collects in it.

"I forgot how isolated this place is," she says. "Total middle of nowhere."

I don't say anything. Is she nervous, questioning her decision to come out here with someone who has proven himself to be unstable?

"You should come out here more," she goes on. "You could really focus on your writing up here."

"That's what my mom says."

"You could really, you know, get quiet," she says, wistful. "That's what I always think when I look at Anisa's posts. I'm so jealous—not of Parker, not of her success or happiness. Just that she's found the space she needs to—I don't know—be."

"Hey," I say, eager to give her something. "Anytime you want to come up here, you can."

"Really?"

"Are you kidding? It's empty most of the time. My parents would love it."

Silence. This time when her words echo, I recite them out loud to her:

Why are they so afraid of you?
Boredom, why don't they seek your hidden magic?
To sit and think.
To be.
All gone the way of the 8-track.
A silly, outdated thing.

"You memorized one of my poems?" she says, her hand at her chest, her smile wide.

"They're very memorable. You really have a gift, if I haven't told you before. I have, haven't I?"

She blushes, looks down shyly. "Thank you."

The house comes into view, small and dark. The sight of it never fails to fill me with this odd mingling of nostalgia and revulsion. There's this feeling of thinking I've spotted a long-lost friend, only to realize with despair that it's a stranger, someone not very nice at all.

Emily draws in a breath. "It's beautiful here."

It's really not. Maybe it was once, when I was young and we were happy, but the house is in disrepair, the grounds neglected. Just on first glance, a shutter tilts, the porch sags. I know that doves roost in the gutter, clogging it. My parents always make it sound grand. *Our place in the country.* Designed by someone, built by someone else. Names no one knows but still nod about knowingly anyway. A mystery writer lived there, died there, wrote something in between —a book no one's ever read.

Stories, stories, stories—reality narrated, packaged, disseminated. Why can't anything just be what it is?

We climb out of the car and stand in the stillness. There's rustling in the leaves, the call of a great horned owl. It's a moonless, starless night.

"It's so"—she stops, the poet searching for the perfect word— "apart."

Yes. We could be on the moon.

I tried to give her this. Anisa. What she seems to have found with Parker. But what I offered, she didn't want. I touch the scar on my arm, snaking a finger up the cuff.

"Hey, Will?" Emily is standing on the porch. "Is someone else here?"

She's wearing that Piglet frown.

"No," I say. "Why?"

"I hear music."

"No."

She points. "And there's a light on inside."

This house is haunted, I want to tell her but don't.

I feel that rise of anger.

It's haunted by the ghosts of all my parents' expectations, their grief. By the perfect Claire, who was everywhere and everything —the shining light, the will-o'-the-wisp that you chase and never catch. And then, after she was gone, her presence only grew. She was made perfect in life by her untimely death. And all the lost possibilities ballooned. *Your sister was a talented writer; I can only imagine what she would have done.* A great beauty. A sterling intellect. An angel of kindness. Who might she have been—if only?

But that's not the whole truth.

The truth is that my sister was mean. She tortured me—teasing, getting me in trouble for things I didn't do. She slept around— there were any number of townie boys who might have done her in. She was a city cat, and they were her country mice. And you know what? She wasn't that good looking. She developed early. She had a great body for a kid. A dangerously hot body. She evoked emotions she wasn't prepared to handle.

No, no. It wasn't me. Come on.

There were whispers, of course. Rumors abounded—that it was me, my father, a boy in town who everyone thought had violent tendencies. But the police ruled it an accident. A cramp, maybe. Or she got her foot tangled in some weeds. The only evidence that someone else might have been on the bank of the lake that night were some scattered boot prints, much larger than my size, even larger than my father's. But that piece of evidence never led them anywhere, didn't link back to any of her known friends in town.

No, I didn't kill my sister. I was just a kid. And I *loved* her. And just like everyone else, I thought she was perfect. Because even though she pinched me hard under the table to make me yell, pulled the arm off my favorite bear, and told me that there *really were* monsters in my closet—she also lay on my bed when I had bad dreams, patiently helped me with my homework, and taught me how to do my hair so that I didn't go through life looking like a "total dork." It was only later, after my suicide attempt, my hours with Dr. Black, that I started to see the truth behind all the dream-weaving my parents did. She was just a girl who died too soon.

"Will?" says Emily, snapping me back. "Do you hear it?"

Yes, actually. Something tinny on the air. I come to stand beside her. There is a slight glow. As if there is a light burning somewhere in the house.

"There's a cleaning crew that comes. Maybe they left a light on?"

"Or someone knows this place is empty? And they're squatting?"

We stand a moment.

"Let's go," Emily says. "We can call the police and have them come check it out."

But I'm already moving around back, jogging.

It's her. Must be. It all makes sense now.

"Will!"

Emily's voice is a whisper-yell in the dark, but I keep going—around the side of the house, past the trash cans.

My heart swells.

She's here! All this time, she's been hiding here. All of it—her life with Parker, the tiny house, Parker himself. It's all a fiction. Such a clever girl.

I imagine coming around to the porch. I'll see her, sitting at the kitchen table with her laptop. She'll be wearing one of those long-sleeve V-neck T-shirts she favors, her hair up. The infinity necklace will lie prettily against her collarbone. She'll be shocked to see us. Amazed that Emily and I figured it out. Then she'll be angry. Then relieved. Because it takes so much energy to live a lie. She fooled everyone, except the people who know and love her best.

It will be easy to back out of it, to save face. So easy. All we have to do is create another fiction. She and Parker broke up; he was a controlling jerk. But she's still living the simple life, in a reasonably sized house in the country. Lessons learned.

But when I come around back, all the lights in the house are dark. It's the porch light that burns. It's on a timer—set to turn on at 9 p.m. and go off at 5 a.m. The music—it's carrying from someplace across the lake, which happens. Hope leaves me, a lantern floating into the sky.

Emily knocks into me from behind.

"Are you crazy?" she wants to know. "What if there had been a break-in? Some meth head living in your house?"

I have to laugh a little—at her, at myself.

"What if it had been one of the Fiercer Animals?" I suggest.

She stares a moment, that worried face freezing in place, finally dissolving into an eye roll and an embarrassed smile. Then she smacks me hard on the arm.

"Jerk."

"Ow," I say, laughing, rubbing at the spot. She's a lot stronger than she looks.

The house is a total throwback. There is no wireless. On the rare occasions I come up here, I use my phone as a hot spot to get online. But even that's wonky because cell service is spotty. There's a television, an ancient box of a thing, connected to a VCR, no cable. But there's a vast library of modern classics—*Scarface*, *The Godfather*, the Star Wars trilogy, *Pretty in Pink*, *The Breakfast Club*. And books—books in every room, on every shelf and surface—all genres, from Stephen King to Jane Austen.

It smells a little. The musty scent of old, little-used places.

There's a transistor radio in the kitchen. It picks up AM and FM stations. And yes, of course, there is a landline with an answering machine. The nineties came here and stayed.

We keep the place stocked—in case. There are good bottles of red and white in the pantry, canned goods—soups, beans, spaghetti and ravioli, nuts, chips in tubes. When I do come up, I normally stay the night, feast on junk food, go home sick.

"This place is amazing," Emily says, walking around, running a careful finger across surfaces, objects. "Time has stopped."

We make a perfunctory attempt to get online, to look through Anisa's feed for more clues, to come up with next steps, but we can't get her page to load. Finally, exhausted, we just give up.

I open a bottle of wine. Build a fire. We make popcorn on the stove. I find *The Matrix* and pop it in the VCR. Rewind. Wait and listen to it whir. Time settles when there's nothing to do but wait. Our phones, Emily's laptop, are all useless and lie dark in the other room. She puts her notebook and a slim pen on the coffee table, in case inspiration strikes, I guess.

We curl up on the couch. The lights are out, the room lit only by the screen. The popcorn is buttery and salty.

Keanu Reeves is smooth faced and svelte, caught in a web of digital deceit. Morpheus tells Neo how the Matrix is all around him. How it's the world that's been pulled over his eyes to blind him to the truth. How he is a slave born into bondage, in a prison he can't touch.

When Emily's hand finds mine, I turn to her.

Her lips are sweet, her skin silk under my hands. My need for her is sudden—urgent and real. Not a reaction formation. She sighs as I pull her to me. She yields, her arms wrapping around me, her passion a taste on my tongue. I am awake and alive, truly present for the first time since I watched my blood spill on the bathroom floor.

We tear at each other's clothes, tumble from the couch. Skin on skin; I am alive for the first time since Anisa. I shiver with pleasure. Emily's skin glows in the firelight, her eyes shining.

When she pulls at my shirt, I'm embarrassed, try to keep it on.

"Let me see all of you," she whispers beneath me.

The keloid scars are dark on my arms, two long lines. I show them to her.

She puts her lips to them, and my whole body shudders with the relief of being seen, my whole truth, no matter how flawed and ugly.

We make love, ravenous for each other. It's raw and desperate. I make sounds I don't even recognize as we roam each other's imperfect flesh. Emily cries, tears streaming down her face as she moans with pleasure. It's nothing like it was with Anisa. Emily abandons herself to the moment. Anisa always seemed to observe it. I am lost and found.

By the time we're drifting off, the television is emitting white noise and the sun is rising outside.

"Oh, Will," she whispers. "I've wanted this for so long."

"Me too," I say. It's true, and it's not true.

We just stare at each other in wonder until we fall asleep in each other's arms.

When I awake, I lie by the fire, which I guess Emily has kept going. The blanket from the couch covers my body.

For a moment, I think she's left. Or that maybe she was never here. This was a dream. A hallucination. Chasing Anisa's digital presence, I've walked right off the edge of reality.

But then I smell something. The unmistakable aroma of Campbell's chicken soup—that chemical facsimile of food that is somehow so much more than the real thing. I get up and retrieve my clothes from the floor.

In the light of day, everything looks as shabby as it is—the carpet is stained, the couch pilled, the blanket frayed. In the kitchen, Emily is the only thing of beauty. The linoleum floor peels, the Formica countertop is rife with burns, scratches. The wallpaper is yellowed.

"I love it here," Emily says. Her notebook is on the table. I can see that she's been writing, the pen tucked into the pages.

I sit. The wine we drank last night, the heavy meal, makes my head ache, my stomach complain. I am not a morning person. I remember that we came up here looking for Anisa and didn't find her. Emily seems to have forgotten that. But maybe, I'm realizing, that's not why she wanted to come up here at all. She turns to me with a bright smile, but whatever she sees on my face causes it to fade.

Silent, she pours the soup into two bowls, carries them to the table. There's tea too. With honey. We eat and drink. It's good. The food helps my darkening mood. But I realize I've missed a dose of my medication. We should get back.

Emily has gone still, internal. She feels the shift of my energy.

"You're never going to stop looking for her, are you?" she says finally.

The light of day has cast all of this differently.

I am slipping back into old behaviors. Paranoid. Delusional and compulsive. Maybe it's more than one dose I've missed. Dr. Black would not approve of this errand.

"It's really about Claire, right?" she says. "How you couldn't hold on to either of them?"

I shake my head, not wanting to hear the truth of it.

That dark place, it starts to open in me. I try to breathe it away.

"And Anisa. Even when she was with you, in love with you, you were chasing her. You held on so tight that you strangled the love between you."

When it starts, it's a rumble, an engine gunning deep within. I hear it coming like a semi in the distance.

"You drove her away. When all you had to do was let her be."

"Stop," I say.

"Look," Emily says, putting down her spoon. She looks up at the ceiling, then back at me. "She's gone, okay? Here's the truth, Will.

That tiny house? It's far from here—in Portland, Oregon. Anisa and Parker? It's real. They're happy."

I grapple with her words. "What are you saying?"

"I've helped them with social media," she says, hanging her head. "I did some work for both of them, in the beginning. Still do occasionally."

"No," I say. But the look on her face—pale, mouth turned down. Shame.

"She doesn't want anyone to know where she is. Especially you, Will. You hurt her, frightened her. That night you got arrested —you pushed her against the wall. You tried to strangle her. If it wasn't for her neighbor breaking down the door, she said you might have killed her."

I hear Anisa's voice: *Stop it, Will. You're hurting me.* I see the fear on her face. I was only the chaos of my rage; I couldn't stop.

"Will," Emily goes on. "She says it's hard enough to be stable herself without your instability."

The room, the world, is spinning.

"Why?" I manage. "Why would you *do this?* Make me think I had the same suspicions that I did. Make me think—"

"I don't know," she says quickly. "It was wrong. I'm sorry. I mean —I *haven't* talked to her. Just text and email, direct messages, for a long time now. But I just thought—if I could get you away from it all, get you alone, out here where it's quiet, maybe—maybe you'd *see.*"

She reaches for me, but I draw back. "See *what?*"

"See *me,*" she says, eyes shining. "Will, I'm right here. Flesh and bone. What happened between us last night—that was real."

"Emily."

She's right. It was real. Her flesh. Her lips, our breath, my pleasure, the closeness. Even now, her delicate beauty, her soft voice.

But the lies.

Why do they *always have to lie,* leaving me to play the fool, the one waiting for a return that never comes?

Despair, anger, they wrestle within me. I hear Dr. Black's voice, urging me to acknowledge and release my anger. But it's too late. The world is fading.

Don't tell on me, you little asshole, Claire said as she slipped out that night. *Go back to sleep. If you say a word, I'll tell Mom and Dad that you got a boner when you watched me sunbathe on the dock.*

So when I heard them come home, I didn't tell them that Claire was not in her room. I let my parents go to sleep, wake up in the morning, make breakfast. I let my dad go for his run and my mom do the laundry. And it wasn't until just before lunch that my father said, "Are we going to just let her sleep all day?"

That was when they discovered that her bed hadn't been slept in. She was out there all night, alone in the cold, dark water.

The guilt of that, it split me in two.

Why do they *always* lie?

"I'm the one who came when you called," Emily says now. "I'm the one who is still here answering your calls, helping you with your career."

She starts to cry.

"I love you." It's a whisper into her palms. "I always have."

I can see that it's true. Really true.

Through the fog of my anger, I can see how that truth motivated her to lie, to create this clever errand, to get closer to me. What a tangle. What a mess we all are. So many layers of truth and lies that no one knows what's real anymore.

She takes something from her pocket.

"That photo from the Happy Cow. It was an old one, from the day we were all up here. I sent it to her from my photos a while ago. I fell in love with this place then. And it was here that I acknowledged for the first time — to myself — that I was in love with you."

I can tell Emily is still hoping for a happy ending to this conversation.

"But she wasn't wearing the necklace in the photo, and she *was* wearing it that day." I barely recognize my own voice; it's raw with desperation.

"She must have photoshopped it out," she says. "I'm sorry."

She opens her palm. There it is. Anisa's silver infinity necklace.

"She gave it to me just before she left town. She wanted me to return it to you. But I couldn't. How could I hurt you like that? When you were working so hard to get well."

I look at it. It sits small and dull in her palm. I wanted to give Anisa diamonds — a huge glittering ring. But I couldn't. I gave her all I had to offer, and it wasn't enough.

"Why are you telling me this now?" I'm shaking. That thing, that dark, dark thing inside me. It's raging. I really need to call Dr. Black.

"Because," she says, "after last night, the raw reality of that connection, I don't want anything false between us. Just the truth from now on."

With Anisa, things used to get fuzzy. That's happening now. A kind of siren in my head blocks out all other sound, makes it hard to think. Her face. Her eyes go wide.

"Will," she says. "Will, are you all right?"

The darkness swallows us both. Then there's nothing.

I posted on Instagram this morning, a lovely sunny-day shot of the red front door of my agent's gorgeous town-house office.

This is a big day, I wrote. *Today I sign my first book deal.*

I've really been growing my social-media presence, and I had a hundred likes in the first ten minutes. Even Anisa sent me a comment, just emojis: clapping hands and some stars.

It's true; it really is a big day. My novel, which I finally finished, sold to a real publisher, one of the best—after a vigorous auction. My debut was acquired by a famous editor, one who has launched bestsellers and prizewinners.

Now I sit with Paul, my agent, the one with whom Emily connected me, as he and I page through the contract. We go over every detail in the enormous legal-size document.

Of course, even if the elliptical, purposely confusing language translated to "And upon literary stardom, you will relinquish your eternal soul," I would sign.

"This is going to be big, Will," Paul says. "Congratulations. And the book—it's amazing. Just everything it needs to be. A great hook, perfect suspense. And that ending. No one will see it coming. I still think about it."

He shakes his head in admiring disbelief. "I never once suspected the brother. Not for a second until the truth was revealed. Just masterful."

"Thanks, Paul," I say, lifting a modest hand. "I owe it all to you. Well, really to Emily first."

"That was a hell of an auction. I owe her big-time for connecting us," he says.

I feel a rise of something, a whisper, a niggle in the back of my brain. Guilt. Sadness. I push it back hard. *Don't look back,* Dr. Black always says. *That's not the way you're headed.*

"Me too," I say. "Big-time."

We stack the documents, all the copies now bearing my signature. There's a tidy pile on the varnished mahogany table. I can smell the ink. I thought the contract would be digital. But no. Publishing is still a pen-and-paper business. I'm glad. It feels more solid, more real this way.

"Hey," Paul says. "Have you heard from her? Like, actually talked to her?"

"Emily?" I say with a disappointed frown. Tension creeps into my shoulders. "Not in a while."

I can tell he's trying to be light, casual. I think he has a crush on her.

He buzzes for his assistant, and a frazzled, bespectacled young woman hurries in. For a second, it could almost be Emily. Same anxious sweetness.

"Oh," she says, breathless. She looks at me with eyes wide in admiration. I see that look a lot lately. I could get used to it. "I *loved* your book."

"Thank you," I say. "What's your name?"

"Bella." She blushes a pretty scarlet.

I take her hand and smile into her eyes. "Nice to meet you, Bella."

"Really," she says. "It was mesmerizing. Such an unreliable narrator. He hid so much from himself, we never knew what was true."

I smile. "Well, we're all unreliable narrators of our own lives, aren't we?"

She nods, sighs. "That's so right. Wow."

When she's gone, Paul is looking at me with a knowing smile.

"You are going to do very well, my man. Handsome, charming, talented. They'll be eating out of your hand."

"Hey," I say with a laugh. "I'm just happy to be here at all. It's been a long road."

"Let's grab a drink. Celebrate."

He pats me on the shoulder. I fold my copy of the contract and slide it into my satchel, right next to the Moleskine I carry with me everywhere now. And we head out.

"So a writers' retreat, huh?" he says on the street. We're still on this, I guess. I'd really like to move on from the topic.

"What's that?"

"Emily still on a writers' retreat?"

Yeah, he's got it bad. Poor guy. We push through the door of the

restaurant across from his office, take our usual spot on the corner
of the marble bar. We've knocked back quite a few here. It's elegant and dim—leather seats and smoky mirrors, black-and-white
tile floors.

"I guess so," I say, settling onto the stool. "According to her last
post."

"Where is she again?" He waves at the bartender, who doesn't
even need to take our order.

"I'm not sure. Out of the country. The Cotswolds, was it?"

"Just took off," Paul says. "Went for broke."

"That was the plan."

He clicks his phone. We're all always doing that. Checking and
checking. When everything real is right in front of us.

"I'm envious," he says, looking up. "Some days."

When the bartender brings our drafts, we clink glasses.

"To Emily," he says. "I wish she was here to toast with us."

"I'm glad she's following her dreams, wherever they've taken
her," I say. "She just published that poem. Her work is better than
ever. She's really grown."

He nods. "I miss her."

He takes a sip of his beer.

I miss them. All of them. Claire. Anisa. Emily.

I'd bring them all back into my life if I could. Sometimes regret
is a bitter meal you have no choice but to eat.

When I look down into my glass, for some reason, I flash on the
murky cold water of the lake on our property up north.

"You okay?" Paul asks. I'm not sure what he sees on my face.

"I miss her too."

I've learned something important since Anisa left me. That part
of loving is releasing. That to truly honor someone you love, you
have to let her be.

"Well," Paul says, trying for brightness, "maybe sometimes you
just have to drop out, disconnect, to really dig into your truth. Into
that real space within."

The infinity necklace, the one I gave Anisa. I carry it with me in
my pocket, a kind of touchstone. I reach for it now, feel the cold
metal between my fingers.

"Yeah," I say, patting him on the back. I know what it's like to
wish you could be with someone who has slipped away. "That's so
true."

Contributors' Notes

Jenny Bhatt is a writer, a literary translator, a writing instructor at Writing Workshops Dallas, and the host of the *Desi Books* podcast. Her debut collection, *Each of Us Killers,* was published in 2020. Her debut literary translation, *Ratno Dholi: The Best Stories of Dhumketu,* was published in the same year. Her writing has appeared on *NPR* and in the *Washington Post, The Atlantic, BBC Culture, Literary Hub, Poets & Writers, Electric Literature, Longreads,* and many other venues. She resides in the Dallas area in Texas.

• "Return to India" is the opening story and sets the tone and theme for my entire collection *Each of Us Killers.* It deals with work-life difficulties that, to some extent, I had also experienced as an immigrant worker during my first ten years in the Midwest. When I read about another immigrant engineer, Srinivas Kuchibhotla, dying in a race-driven shooting in Olathe, Kansas, I wanted to explore it in a way that went beyond the usual headlines and think pieces. At first I tried telling the story from the point of view of a particular character: the engineer, the engineer's wife, one of the coworkers. Nothing worked. It was only when I switched to a Greek-chorus style of narration, as in the film *Rashomon,* that things clicked. Everyone in the story has their own version of the crime and their genuine emotions about it. And that's all very much a part of the tragedy.

Christopher Bollen is a writer who lives in New York. He is the author of four novels, *Lightning People* (2011), *Orient* (2015), *The Destroyers* (2017), and his most recent, a gay heist thriller set in Venice, *A Beautiful Crime* (2020). He is also currently the editor at large of *Interview* magazine and a contributing editor at *Vanity Fair.*

• At the start of the pandemic, I pulled the Peter Benchley novel *JAWS* off my bookshelf, having grown up with that iconic bloodthirsty shark filling my dreams. Two very different ideas occurred to me while reading

Benchley's novel, which would braid together as the impetus for writing "SWAJ." One is that *JAWS* is the ultimate pandemic novel, with a fearsome yet largely unseen threat lurking in the waters around town and those who don't want to shut down the carnival of summer, deaths be damned. The second idea is the one I always have when reading an American classic in any genre — *where are the hidden seams in the story where queer characters live, the small roles and unmentioned bars and overlooked couples that the story refuses to reveal?* As a bookish, closeted kid growing up in conservative Cincinnati, I found myself adding a gay narrative on top of heterosexual stories, giving a queer double-life to my favorite characters. That's what I wanted to do, using *JAWS* as a template. I wanted to give voice to the gay kid in 1970s Amity who was living through the carnage and financial pillaging of his town as well. I thought of it as a missing chapter in *JAWS,* slipping the pharmacist's son into the plot without ruffling Peter Benchley's creation (although Michael ends up being directly responsible for the shark-cage murder of his lover, Matt Hooper, who, unlike in the movie, does die in the book due to the inferior cage bars). I wanted to add queerness into the American legend. Thus I wrote "SWAJ" (which is *JAWS,* backward).

Strangely enough, as much as the Great White Shark terrifies me, I also can't help but admire it. I sincerely think this might be another condition of growing up gay: I often find myself cheering for the monster or villain in a story — even the worst ones strike me as charmingly misunderstood. In "SWAJ," the protagonist, Michael, starts identifying with the shark, that shadowy threat on the outskirts of all this bright, bubbly heterosexual fun. Michael conspires with it, hoping it will keep devouring people so that Matt will have to remain in town on the hunt. After "SWAJ" was published, a few readers did write to me, saying something like this: I always thought *JAWS* was gay! The shark turns up to scare all of those straight, normal families out of their wits. It makes its own party right there on their beach!

Nikki Dolson's stories have appeared or are forthcoming in *Vautrin, TriQuarterly, Tough, Thuglit,* and other publications. She is the author of the novel *All Things Violent* and most recently the story collection *Love and Other Criminal Behavior.*

• "Neighbors" came about partly because of my obsession with broken marriages and how people lose their identities once married, along with a summer spent researching con artists and grifters. I had a vision of a happy neighborhood and happy couples with their happy kids and this very picturesque life and how easily the right person can upend things. I wanted to write about unhappy couples but it ended up being about Val and Anika, two Black women on very different paths.

E. Gabriel Flores is the author of novellas and short stories, including "The Truth of the Moment" and "La Loca Bella," all published in *Ellery*

Queen Mystery Magazine. She received the Robert L. Fish Memorial Edgar Award for "The Truth of the Moment." Flores is currently working on her first mystery novel, set in the imaginary town of San Bernardino in the Dominican Republic. Flores has lived in Africa and Latin America, and for the past twenty years she has been a geography professor.

• "Mala Suerte" is a tale of how unexpected events can wreak havoc on a well-planned criminal enterprise. The idea came from a real-life situation . . . Back in the day, my father was a street entrepreneur—a numbers runner. People would choose a three-digit number, write it on a slip of paper, and give it to my dad in an envelope with a dollar bill. Bettors won if their numbers matched another three-digit numeral published in the daily paper, like a standard stock-market figure or a horse race's winning time. Dad matched the numbers, awarded the lucky winners (if any) their money, and kept a portion of the takings. No heavy lifting, and he could spend his days engaged in two of his favorite activities: schmoozing and counting dollar bills.

In his twilight years, my dad often lamented that he could have easily retired a millionaire if not for one unforeseen misfortune—the legalization of the numbers game. What a stroke of bad luck! The government took control of the once outlawed practice and created state lotteries, and my dad ended up driving a cab. (Is it any wonder that Nevada, casino capital of the United States, has never implemented a state lotto?)

I imagined that other successful illegal enterprises throughout history had been disrupted by something nobody could have predicted. That idea led to this story about people who just cannot get a break. *¡Qué mala suerte!*

Alison Gaylin has won the Edgar Award and the Shamus Award. Her work has been published in the United States, the UK, France, Belgium, the Netherlands, Japan, Germany, Romania, and Denmark, and she has been nominated for the Macavity Award, the Anthony Award, the ITW Thriller Award for Best Paperback Original Novel, and the Strand Critics Award. Her twelfth book, *The Collective,* will be out in November 2021.

• I was in the midst of writing *The Collective* when I received an email from Paul D. Marks, asking if I'd like to contribute to *Coast to Coast Noir* (which he co-edited with Andrew McAleer). Even though I was in the throes of a novel, I'd long wanted to work with Paul, whom I met at the 2012 Shamus Awards, where we sat at the same, apparently lucky table, both of us winning in our categories. The assignment: write a very short, down-and-dirty noir story that takes place in a specific part of the United States. I quickly claimed New York's Hudson Valley (where I live), and "Where I Belong" took shape. Writing *The Collective,* I'd become immersed in a world driven by female rage—specifically that of mothers whose children's killers went unpunished. I think I came up with my young, angry-for-no-good-reason male protagonist as an escape from that world, and boy, was he fun to write. I'm indebted to Paul—a great writer and a dear friend, who passed away on February 28, 2021. The story is dedicated to him.

Gar Anthony Haywood is the Shamus and Anthony Award–winning author of fourteen novels and dozens of short stories. His crime fiction includes the Aaron Gunner private eye series and the Joe and Dottie Loudermilk mysteries. His short fiction has been included in *The Best American Mystery Stories* anthologies, and *Booklist* has called him "a writer who has always belonged in the upper echelon of American crime fiction." He has written for both episodic and long-form television, and for the *New York Times* and the *Los Angeles Times.* His most recent novel, *In Things Unseen,* was published last December and is best described as a thriller for fans of nontraditional Christian fiction.

• The act of plagiarism has always ranked high on my list of the most egregious crimes against humanity. It's the Neapolitan ice cream of assault: one part theft, one part fraud, one part invasion of privacy. I've never been a victim of it that I'm aware of, but it irks me just the same, so I knew my story for Lawrence Block's *The Darkling Halls of Ivy* anthology would have something to do with one lowlife or another passing someone else's work off as their own. I stirred in two very smart, beautiful people of questionable character vying to outwit each other on the campus of my favorite college football school—the University of Southern California —and "With Footnotes and References" was the result.

Ravi Howard is the author of two novels, *Like, Trees, Walking* and *Driving the King.* He was a finalist for the Hemingway Foundation/PEN Award and a recipient of the Ernest J. Gaines Award for Literary Excellence. His essays have appeared in the *New York Times, McSweeney's Internet Tendency, Atlanta,* and *Gravy,* and he has recorded commentary for NPR's *All Things Considered.* His short fiction has appeared in *Salon, Massachusetts Review, Gulf Coast,* and *Alabama Noir.*

• I wanted to write about a last meal before an execution, because that ritual, like the death penalty itself, is troubling to me. The story examines Rachel's life as a Black woman who fed people as a restaurant owner. I wanted to show the power and the burden of that work historically, and I also wanted to avoid the common caricatures of Black service and caretaking. I tried to find the right balance of kindness and defiance as Rachel looks for an ending other than the one mandated for Thomas Elijah Raymond.

Gabino Iglesias is the author of *Zero Saints* and *Coyote Songs* and the editor of *Both Sides* and *Halldark Holidays.* His work has been nominated for the Bram Stoker Award and the Locus Award and won the Wonderland Book

Award for Best Novel. His fiction has been published in five languages and optioned for film. His reviews appear in places like NPR, *Publishers Weekly*, the *San Francisco Chronicle*, and the *Los Angeles Review of Books*. He teaches creative writing at Southern New Hampshire University's online MFA program. Find him on Twitter at @Gabino_Iglesias.

• My fiction often explores how good people are pushed to do bad things for all the right reasons. That, I think, is the essence of noir. After the lockdown began and I lost my high school teaching job, I started thinking about the things we do when we're desperate for money. I already live paycheck to paycheck and in affordable housing . . . so what next? That is not just my question; it's the question millions of people ask themselves every single day, with more added to the list since the pandemic began. When the editors Nick Kolakowski and Steve Weddle reached out and asked me if I'd like to contribute a story to the *Lockdown* anthology, which would benefit the Book Industry Charitable Foundation, I knew someone desperate for money because of the pandemic was going to be at the center of it. "Everything Is Going to Be Okay" was my way of showing how poverty, desperation, a crappy health-care system, and crime can clash, with bloody results.

Charis (Himeda) Jones, PhD, is a research associate professor at the University of Nevada, Reno School of Medicine, and a cofounder of EpiSwitch, Rx. She has authored twenty-five research publications and reviews and filed two patents for novel therapeutics. She has been interviewed by the *Washington Post*, the *Huffington Post*, and the *Boston Business Journal* for her research, employing CRISPR gene-editing technology as a potential therapy for muscle disease. At night, Dr. Himeda doffs her lab gloves to pen speculative fiction about renegade scientists driven by their deep desire to explore and shape the world around them. She is a three-time winner of the PNWA Writers' Contest, a winner in the Sandy, the Zebulon, and the Colorado Gold contests, a shortlister for the Cygnus Awards, and a quarterfinalist in the Amazon Breakthrough Novel Awards. Her short fiction has appeared in *Antimuse*, *Eureka Literary Magazine*, the *Marlboro Review*, *MudRock: Stories and Tales*, and *Nth Degree*. Dr. Himeda is a member of PNWA and Rocky Mountain Fiction Writers, and she lives in Reno, Nevada.

• The rigors of science writing and those of fiction writing are surprisingly similar. Telling made-up stories requires the most scrupulous honesty—and it can be a real challenge to faithfully transcribe the voices in your head. Sometimes those voices are from strangers on another world, and sometimes they are the disturbingly familiar whispers of the person you might have been. When I heard about a colleague whose ex-husband had once hung a tennis ball from the ceiling of their garage so she'd park the car exactly where he wanted it, I was appalled—but the image resonated with me. I kept wondering how obsessive-compulsive a person could get while a voice deep in my head whispered the answer. My rat is smaller and quieter than Martina's, but it occasionally prowls around looking for a meal—and I do my best not to feed it. I am very grateful to Peter Jones, Steve Jaquith, Lawson Reinsch, Rachel Craft, and Natasha Watts for helping me polish, prune, and put this tale in order.

Preston Lang is a native of New York and almost entirely a product of its public school system. His short work has been published in *Ellery Queen Mystery Magazine, Thuglit,* and *Betty Fedora.* He has also published four novels and writes a regular column for WebMd.com. He can be followed on Twitter at @LangReads.

• There have been a few fast-food sandwich crazes in recent years that got a lot of people very excited. My story is an attempt to come to terms with all this. I spent a lot of time working out what kind of sandwich to use and finally decided on the potato sandwich, which in real life can be terrific, but in my story is just grease, salt, and emptiness. I sent it to the good people at *Rock and a Hard Place* magazine, and they helped shape it into something readable. It was a real thrill to have it selected for this anthology.

Aya de León teaches creative writing at UC Berkeley. Her award-winning feminist heist series, Justice Hustlers, includes *Side Chick Nation,* the first novel published about Hurricane Maria in Puerto Rico. Her first stand-alone novel, *A Spy in the Struggle,* is about FBI infiltration of an African American organization in the Bay Area that is fighting for climate justice and Black Lives. Her work has appeared in *Harper's Bazaar, Ebony, Essence,* and *Guernica,* and on *Def Poetry.* In 2022, *Undercover Latina* will appear—de León's first young adult novel, which will launch a spy girl series. Her latest adult book is *Queen of Urban Prophecy*—a novel that addresses misogyny in hip-hop, police violence, and climate justice.

• I was working on other heist fiction and attempting to enroll my kid in Berkeley schools when the editors of *Berkeley Noir* approached me to write a story. Despite having lived in Berkeley most of my life, I found it very difficult to prove my residence to the district's satisfaction. I was ambivalent about the district anyway, because Berkeley's gentrification has led to declining numbers of students of African heritage. These factors all conspired to create "Frederick Douglass Elementary."

Kristen Lepionka, author of the Roxane Weary mystery series, has won the Shamus Award and the Goldie Award and has been nominated for the Anthony and the Macavity. She grew up mostly in her local public library, where she could be found with a big stack of adult mysteries before she was out of middle school. She is a cofounder of the feminist podcast *Unlikeable Female Characters,* and she lives in Columbus, Ohio, with her partner and two cats.

• The idea for "Infinity Sky" came to me when I stayed at a hotel where a huge wedding was taking place. There seemed to be several million people involved with the event, and they were constantly having arguments and public meltdowns in the hallways, bar, lobby, rooftop pool, and so on. I don't want to say that they were annoying, but they were very annoying. They got me thinking about how guests show up at a black-tie wedding bringing their real selves with them—maybe some are better at hiding their personal messes during the event, but some people just can't help being who they are, even when trying to behave. Add an open bar to that dynamic, and look out. I thought it would be fun to set two such badly behaved people on a collision course, with a caper-ish feel. The character Jeramey—a has-been musician with a bad attitude—was one I'd been playing around with in another (now abandoned) story, and she just seemed to fit in as a foil to the hapless Midwesterner Doug Beavers. Once I introduced these two to each other, the story basically wrote itself.

Laura Lippman is the *New York Times* best-selling writer of more than twenty novels, most recently *Dream Girl.* She also has published a book of essays and a children's book; her second short-story anthology, *Seasonal Work,* is forthcoming in 2022. Winners of multiple awards, her works have been translated into twenty-five languages. She lives in Baltimore and New Orleans.

• Almost all my short stories start with what we call "writing prompts" —an editor, usually a friend, emails and tells me that there is an anthology in the works, then asks if the theme appeals to me. The theme can be as broad as true love or as narrow as golf. If I'm in the mood, I say yes. The collection for which "Slow Burner" was commissioned centered on lying, a wonderfully broad subject. And it began not with a burner phone, but with someone's observation that it's always a little suspicious when a long-married person goes on a diet without a pressing health reason.

Joanna Pearson's second collection of stories, *Now You Know It All,* was chosen by Edward P. Jones for the 2021 Drue Heinz Literature Prize and has just been published. (It includes "Mr. Forble.") Her first story collection, *Every Human Love,* was a finalist for the Shirley Jackson Award, the Foreword INDIES Book Awards, and the Janet Heidinger Kafka Prize. She lives with her husband and daughters in North Carolina, where she works as a psychiatrist.

• "Mr. Forble" started with the name itself—a gift from my genius husband, Matthew Buckley Smith, who is also a writer. We were talking about the sinister power of names, and how the scariest names are often not, on the face of it, the most overt in their menace . . . yet there's just something deliciously off-kilter about them. He brought up the beginning of *The Exorcist*, when Regan refers to her demon as "Captain Howdy," as well as the strangely alluring "Arnold Friend" from Joyce Carol Oates's wonderful short story "Where Are You Going, Where Have You Been?" This sent us down a road of concocting other Captain Howdy–esque names. Matthew was the one who came up with "Mr. Forble." He offered it to me as a challenge: Mr. Forble, write a story about him. While writing, I was thinking about the weirdness of Internet virality, and how so many of our urban legends have now moved online, swirling around with Internet hoaxes and conspiracy theories in this gross, fascinating stew. There'd been a viral Internet hoax around that time, called the Momo Challenge, and I found it unsettling. (If you don't remember it, look it up! The image is striking.) I was considering all of this—along with the chasm that can exist between parents and their children, the unknowability of our very own flesh and blood—and voilà. There was Mr. Forble.

Delia C. Pitts is the author of the Ross Agency Mysteries, a contemporary noir series including *Pauper and Prince in Harlem* and *Murder My Past*. She is a former university administrator and served as a US diplomat in Nigeria, Mauritania, and Mexico. After working as a journalist, she earned a PhD in history from the University of Chicago. Her short stories have been published in the *Chicago Quarterly Review* and in the crime fiction anthologies *Festive Mayhem* and *Midnight Hour*. Pitts is active in Sisters in Crime and Crime Writers of Color. She and her husband live in central New Jersey, too far from their twin sons in Texas.

• In the final scene of my mystery *Pauper and Prince in Harlem*, the Black private eye SJ Rook is thrust into a fresh assignment: drive a gun-toting mob muse and her baby from New York to Florida with hit men hot on their tail. The novel had wrapped in satisfying fashion, but this daunting new job cried out for a sequel. I wrote the story "The Killer" as a coda to the novel, offering readers a snapshot of the peril Rook and his charges face on their road trip south. The events captured in "The Killer" form an inflection point in that journey: we witness the moment when Rook feels the danger posed by a volatile assassin shift from abstract to urgent. To serve my purpose, I twisted the tense setup of strangers convened by fate in a rundown diner used by Hemingway in his classic story "The Killers." I wanted my new story to look beyond the violence of organized crime to comment on the racial and regional dynamics of contemporary America.

So I forced Rook to bet his life on an uncertain alliance of white and Black working-class Southerners as the frame of my story and the driver of its suspense.

Eliot Schrefer is a *New York Times* best-selling author and has twice been a finalist for the National Book Award in Young People's Literature. In naming his novel *Endangered* an "Editor's Choice," the *New York Times* called his work "dazzling" and "big-hearted." He is on the faculty of the Fairleigh Dickinson and Hamline MFAs in creative writing and lives with his husband in New York City.

• I was at lunch with a writer friend, enjoying my sandwich, when out of the blue he asked me where all the dads were in my books. "Of course I have dads in my books!" I said, then went really quiet and ordered more french fries. Before dessert was over, we'd challenged each other to write from a straight dad's point of view. His result was the novel *Lone Stars;* my result was "Wings Beating." In it I'm trying to capture the love and furious protectiveness a straight dad might feel for his gay son, a fury intensified by all the ways his own masculinity has been policed by other men. We men have to work if we want to reclaim our right to express soft feelings, and sometimes that work feels like combat. "Ecofeminism" sounds like a word that Rush Limbaugh made up to make fun of liberals, but it names a worldview that resonates with me and informs this story; the very same ways of thinking that marginalize some people also exploit the environment.

I'm grateful to Colette Bancroft and Johnny Temple of Akashic Books for inviting me to return home to write a story for *Tampa Bay Noir.* (Safety Harbor is actually lovely, if you ever want to visit!)

Alex Segura is an acclaimed writer of novels, comic books, and podcasts. He is the author of *Star Wars Poe Dameron: Free Fall,* the Pete Fernandez Mystery series (including the Anthony Award–nominated crime novels *Dangerous Ends, Blackout,* and *Miami Midnight*), and the upcoming *Secret Identity.* His short story "The Red Zone" won the Anthony Award for Best Short Story in 2020. He has also written a number of comic books, most notably the superhero noir *The Black Ghost,* the YA music series The Archies, and the "Archie Meets" collection of crossovers, featuring real-life cameos from the Ramones, the B-52s, and more. He is also the co-creator/co-writer of the *Lethal Lit* crime/YA podcast from iHeart Radio, which was named one of the best podcasts of 2018 by the *New York Times.* By day Segura is the co-president of Archie Comics. A Miami native, he lives in New York with his wife and children.

• When I was asked to craft a story about the border crisis, I knew immediately that I had to write about the ninety miles of water between the southernmost point in the continental United States, Key West, and Cuba itself. It's a stretch fraught with danger, double-crosses, and misplaced hopes. I wanted to try as best I could to show one possible story —one of millions, over the decades—and try to reflect how much people were willing to risk for one shot at freedom. I'm a Cuban American, and the story served as an amalgamation of tales I'd heard growing up. What some might see as a dark ending also provides a glimmer of hope to those looking for a better tomorrow.

Brian Silverman's writing career has spanned more than thirty years. He has written about travel, food, and sports for publications including the *New York Times, Saveur, Caribbean Travel and Life, Islands, New York,* and *The New Yorker.* From 2004 through 2013 he was the author of the annual *Frommer's New York City* guidebook. He co-authored, with his father, Al Silverman, the acclaimed *Twentieth Century Treasury of Sports.* His short fiction has appeared in numerous publications including *Mystery Tribune, Down and Out Magazine,* and *Mystery Weekly.* His stories were selected for *The Best American Mystery Stories* in 2018 and 2019. His first novel, *Freedom Drop,* was published in 2021. He lives in Harlem, New York, with his wife, Heather, and his sons, Louis and Russell.

• The genesis of "Land of Promise" began with a series of stories featuring a character, an ex–New Yorker, who leaves his family and the city for a fictional Caribbean island. I wrote the stories with the intention of writing a novel. I wanted to familiarize myself with the characters and setting before I moved on to a longer work. Why my main character, Len Buonfiglio, leaves the city for the island of St. Pierre, I purposely kept as a mystery to the reader in the stories but considered revealing his past in that potential novel. As I began to outline the novel, I decided to weave pieces of the main character's backstory into certain parts of the novel —to break up the action with snippets of Buonfiglio's New York past— ultimately revealing what drove him from New York. I did this in an early draft, creating a third-person account of what happened in New York and inserting pieces of that story within the novel, written otherwise in the first person. After finishing that draft, I found that the insertions were distracting to the flow of the story and took them out. I abandoned the idea completely and in the novel, *Freedom Drop,* like in the stories, kept the character's past as somewhat of a mystery. Instead, I used the material I took out of the novel, Len's backstory, and framed it as a short story. The result became "Land of Promise."

Faye Snowden is the author of noir mysteries, poems, and short stories. Her novels include *Spiral of Guilt, The Savior, Fatal Justice,* and *A Killing Fire,* a dark, Southern gothic tale featuring the homicide detective Raven Burns. *A Killing Fire* is the first in a four-part series; the sequel, *A Killing Rain,* is underway. Snowden has a master's in English literature. She has been awarded writing fellowships from Djerassi and the Virginia Center for the Creative Arts. Today, Snowden works and writes from her home in Northern California. Learn more about her at www.fayesnowden.com.

• My parents had always been active in the civil rights struggle, and my dad—purportedly affiliated with the Black Panthers in the late sixties—more militantly so. My mom, who left him and moved us kids to Louisiana, took a less confrontational approach. When the Louisiana schools refused to teach us anything about Black history, she did. I'd hazard to say that I knew more about the movement, Frederick Douglass, Marcus Garvey, and Malcolm X than most of my teachers. One thing my mom always impressed upon us was our duty to vote. She would tell us that it was the debt we owed to those who paid for that right with blood. Today my family and I vote to change the future and out of a deep gratitude for people who fought to give us that right. For people like Lionel. This story was written as tribute to my ancestors and all those who helped pave the way to the ballot box for the next generation.

Lisa Unger is a *New York Times* and internationally best-selling author. With books published in twenty-six languages and millions of copies sold worldwide, she is widely regarded as a master of suspense. Her latest release is *Confessions on the 7:45*. Unger's critically acclaimed books have been named on "Best Book" lists from the *Today* show, *Good Morning America, Entertainment Weekly, People,* Amazon, *Goodreads,* and many others. She has been nominated for, or won, numerous awards, including the Hammett Prize, the Macavity Award, the Thriller Award, and the Goodreads Choice Award. In 2019, Unger received two Edgar Award nominations. Her writing has appeared on NPR and in the *New York Times,* the *Wall Street Journal,* and *Travel + Leisure*. She lives on the west coast of Florida with her family.

• In 2018, I wrote a story for Amazon Original Shorts, the Edgar-nominated "The Sleep Tight Motel." So when AOS's editor Kjersti Egerdahl approached me to write for a new anthology, I was thrilled. I immediately connected with the original title of the collection, *The End of Truth,* which ultimately became *Hush*. In my novels, I often explore the subjects of identity, altered states of perception, and the twisting, unreliable nature of memory. Those themes loom in the shadows of most of my work. So in this new story, I was excited to explore how technology, social media, and self-delusion warp and subvert the truth in all kinds of ways, even in how we perceive ourselves. This is the central theme of "Let Her Be," about a lovesick and disturbed young writer who is struggling to distinguish between the fiction of social media, reality, and his buried past.

Other Distinguished Mystery and Suspense of 2020

TOM BARLOW
Honor Guard. *Columbus Noir,* ed. Andrew Welsh-Huggins, Akashic
LAUREN BICKLE
The Dead and the Quiet. *Columbus Noir*
MICHAEL BRACKEN
Blest Be the Ties That Bind. *Black Cat Mystery Magazine,* no. 6
LUIS CASTILLO
Local Waters. *Tampa Bay Noir,* ed. Colette Bancroft, Akashic
SARAH COTTER
Good Morning, Green Leaf Class. *Chesapeake Crimes: Invitation to Murder,* ed. Donna Andrews, Barb Goffman, and Marcia Talley, Wildside Press
GREGORY FALLIS
Terrible Ideas. *Ellery Queen Mystery Magazine,* September/October
RICKEY FAYNE
Spare the Rod. *American Short Fiction,* no. 72
CALLY FIEDOREK
Fright Night. *The Sewanee Review,* Winter
FRANCISCO GONZALEZ
Annulment. *Southern Review,* Summer
ANTHONY GROOMS
Come Like a Thief. *Alabama Noir,* ed. Don Noble, Akashic
GREG HERREN
The Dreadful Scott Decision. *The Faking of a President,* ed. Peter Carlaftes, Three Rooms Press
EDWIN HILL
Good Decisions. *Ellery Queen Mystery Magazine,* November/December
SANDRA JACKSON-OPOKU
She Loved Trouble. *Both Sides,* ed. Gabino Iglesias, Agora Books
LATOYA JOVENA
The Winner. *Ellery Queen Mystery Magazine,* November/December

PAUL D. MARKS
Nowhere Man. *Coast to Coast Noir,* ed. Andrew McAleer and Paul D. Marks, Down and Out Books

TYLER MCANDREW
The Storyteller. *The Baffler, Latest Posts,* August 7, 2020

CAILLE MILLNER
Whatcha See Is Whatcha Get. *Southern Review,* Summer

JOHN MUMMERT
Who We Were Then. *Wild: Uncivilized Tales by Rocky Mountain Fiction Writers,* ed. Natasha Watts and Rachel Delaney Craft, RMFW Press

DAVID NAIMON
The Blind Experiment. *The Adroit Journal,* no. 34

THOMAS PLUCK
Good People. *Vautrin,* vol. 2, no. 2

ELIZABETH REICHERT
Before and After. *Zyzzyva,* Spring

ERIC RUTTER
Raven Takes the Sun. *Alfred Hitchcock Mystery Magazine,* November/December 2020

STEPHANIE SOILEAU
The Whiskey Business. *Last One Out Shut Off the Lights,* Little, Brown

JEFF SOLOWAY
The Substitute Dealer. *Alfred Hitchcock Mystery Magazine,* July/August

MARY SOUTH
You Will Never Be Forgotten. *The New Yorker,* January 27

ART TAYLOR/TARA LASKOWSKI
Both Sides, Now. *Beat of Black Wings,* ed. Josh Pachter, Untreed Books

STEVEN TORRES
The Care of Widows and Orphans. *Alfred Hitchcock Mystery Magazine,* March/April

LINDA TOWNSDIN
Re-Entry. *California Schemin',* ed. Art Taylor, Wildside Press

SARAH WEINMAN
Limited Liability. *Alfred Hitchcock Mystery Magazine,* May/June

MATTHEW WILSON
The Wretched Strangers. *Ellery Queen Mystery Magazine,* January/February

THE BEST AMERICAN SERIES®

FIRST, BEST, AND BEST-SELLING

The Best American Essays

The Best American Food Writing

The Best American Mystery and Suspense

The Best American Science and Nature Writing

The Best American Science Fiction and Fantasy

The Best American Short Stories

The Best American Travel Writing

Available in print and e-book wherever books are sold.

Visit our website: MarinerBooks.com/BestAmerican